THE
JOURNEY
SOUTH

THE
JOURNEY SOUTH

A Cap Whitlatch Western

REAVIS Z. WORTHAM

PINNACLE BOOKS
Kensington Publishing Corp.
www.kensingtonbooks.com.

AUTHOR'S NOTE

The characters portrayed in this novel are not based on actual persons, though the names might seem familiar to some. They are simply names I wanted to keep alive in the pages of this work. The events are also fiction, while many historical locations and items are real. Any resemblance to actual persons or events other than those portrayed and depicted herein is purely coincidental.

CHAPTER 1

It was a damp spring afternoon and I was but a couple of miles outside of Panther Junction when I came over a windy little ridge that gave me a good, wide look at the wagon road winding down into the Indian Territories. It was late in the afternoon on that humid day and the thick shade of tall red oaks provided little relief from the sun.

The steeldust I was riding thought the same, for she paused and blew for a moment. I'd given the mare her head most of the day, letting her set the pace, for I was in no hurry to get back to my daddy's old place, where I'd been living.

The northeastern Indian Territories, where nearby Tahlequah and Stumptown were located, were a fairly safe place for criminals who robbed and killed in the surrounding states, then hid out on the tribal lands. Of course, they didn't slow down their habits much at all in the territories, and a man's life hung in the balance of an outlaw's wants at any moment in time.

Half the towns and communities had their share of dodgers, and most families had one or two wanderers who'd run afoul of the law and decided to disappear into the fabric of societies that resided under Cherokee law. Shoot, I had kinfolk down in Texas who'd run an iron or two on somebody else's cattle, or maybe took possession of a horse that belonged to someone else and went up there until things cooled down back home.

The towns themselves were safe, but traffic between them was down to a trickle that year. Even farmers didn't go anywhere unless they were armed. Pistols usually stuck inside a belt or waistband weren't as common as rifles or shotguns, but there were still plenty of them.

Men usually traveled in groups of half dozen or more. Ten or twelve together almost guaranteed safety, but not out toward Comancheria, far to the west. The plains were controlled by the Comanches, who refused to recognize those marks on maps they didn't understand. They traveled and raided whenever and wherever they wanted, controlling with an iron fist everything out beyond the tree line, even though the Treaty of 1883 gave them a specific territory of their own.

You could get your hair lifted in half a second riding alone out there. They hated everyone who wasn't born one of them, and that included most of the other tribes, whites, and Mexicans. I imagine even if you painted someone blue and sent them riding out toward Santa Fe or such, they'd have 'em staked out on an anthill before you could say "thunder."

Only the cavalry rode there in relative safety, and even that wasn't guaranteed.

You never knew where a war party was going to pop up. They might raid out near the Llano Estacado one morning and only a week later be back east of Kickapoo Town to the Deep Fork of the Canadian River, burning out a farmer's cabin or two just for fun.

Texas, west of Fort Worth, was in their area of destruction, too. There wasn't a county out there that hadn't seen raiders come through every few months, killing whoever they wanted and gathering up herds of horses along the way. It was the horses that gave them their freedom and the ability to roam at will.

I was bucking the odds on the way back to where I was raised down in Texas with the intention to build a little cabin by some clear-water stream not far from my daddy's place and raise a few head of cattle. There was Springfield money in my pocket from selling a string of saddle-broke ponies to a rich Missouri lawyer, and it wasn't the first time I'd made a killing on horses with him. I understood colts, and they broke gentle enough for a four-year-old to ride all alone. After six such trips, I was feeling pretty flush.

That last little herd came at a dear price to the lawyer. I usually put together a string and took them up there, but this time he specified what he wanted, and it took quite a while to round up a herd of ponies with the qualifications he required. By telegraph, we agreed on a price that was way more than I'd ever heard of anyone paying for horseflesh, but he was adamant about them and I never was one to argue with a man who was working hard to get rid of his money.

Like I said, the Indian Territories were dangerous for any man at any time, so I always took a different route up there, and then again back home to make sure no one put two and two together and was waiting to knock me in the head for the money on some trail. I'd learned long ago not to be predictable, and that notion served me well through the years.

This time, since there were so many horses, I paid an old cowboy named Chet Jenkins to go with me and take the herd up through the Kiamichi and Winding Stair Mountains into Springfield. It was rough country, up and down most of the time, and Chet told me it was the hardest job he'd ever had, but we managed without incident. Once we delivered the horses, I paid Chet off and he drifted on to St. Louis to find some lost family members.

I came back alone, and preferred it that way.

Unseen blue jays squawked from the post oak trees and a cardinal flickered into view, bright against the indigo sky. A squirrel on a black walnut limb took umbrage to my presence and set up a chatter, alerting his kinfolk I was around. I watched the irritating little rodent, thinking that if I'd been hungry enough, he'd be roasting over a bed of coals in about thirty minutes.

Fresh spring leaves rustled all around me, a soft, steady noise that covered most everything I should be hearing. Sitting there in the shade and thinking about the future was a good feeling that lasted until I saw a wagon down below, driven by what appeared to be a farmer with his wife. They were coming my way, uphill, and the team of mules pulled hard with their heads low. A tarp covered the wagon bed and I couldn't tell if it was because it was loaded with something heavy, or he was driving slow and easy on the way home from town.

I didn't want the couple to think I was any kind of a threat. Figuring I'd just wait there until they drew close, I'd wave and go my own way. Here in the shade, they could see me once they approached the crest and have time to think about what to do, instead of me riding down the winding road and coming out suddenly from around a thick growth of trees.

As I watched the wagon and its occupants, two men emerged from under a wide tree and stopped their horses in the road. They were all small in the distance, but I saw the driver rein up. The woman beside him sat straighter, and the word "stiffened" came to mind.

Reaching into my saddlebag opposite the one with the money, I dug around and came out with a pair of cavalry field glasses my dad brought home from the war. Tilting my hat back to get the wide brim out of the way, I brought them to my eyes and the situation jumped into clear focus.

Bearded and lean as a starving wolf, one of the riders had

a pistol pointed at the driver, who wore long black hair down to his shoulders, held into place by an old slouch hat. They were Indian and the young, slender woman I took to be his wife sat stock-still at the sight of the revolver.

The stocky, clean-shaven man dismounted and drew his own weapon. He gestured at the driver, who reached down by his feet and picked up a double-barreled shotgun and pitched it to the ground. The outlaw on foot glanced around them, then up toward my ridge. Knowing I was hidden by distance, shadows, and the trees around and behind me, I remained still for the moment. There was nothing I could do from that distance, so I kept the glasses to my eyes and watched, hoping the couple wouldn't do anything to turn a simple robbery into something much worse.

I was hoping those two highwaymen would ride away after getting what they wanted. It couldn't have been much, because the young couple appeared to be farmers who had little more than the sustenance they needed to survive.

Unfortunately, what those two gunmen wanted wasn't just those folks' possessions, and things were about to turn ugly. While the bearded man in the saddle held them at gunpoint, the other went through the wagon, throwing items out of the bed.

Jars shattered, the flying glass flickering in the sunlight. A sack of flour burst open in an explosion of white dust, and he cut two other sacks open and poured the contents over the side. Finished with his destruction, he carried a valise over to his horse, where he hung the long handles over the saddle horn. That done, he went back and motioned for the couple to get down.

They complied, and the rider waved an arm, issuing another order. When the wagon driver shook his head, the outlaw on the ground laid him out with the butt of his pistol. The husband went down like a felled tree and the woman

started for him, but now both outlaws were on the ground
and they grabbed her.

I knew what was coming next. Tucking the glasses back
into my saddlebags, I nudged the steeldust into a lope and
headed down. The ground was soft from recent rains and I
hoped the wind would cover the sound of the mare's hooves
until I was almost on them.

I needn't have worried, they were intent on the woman
and having a big old time as she screamed and fought back
with everything she had. It didn't take long to get down
there, and most of her clothes were ripped off by the time I
slowed the mare and reined up a few feet to the side of the
mule team.

Their horses were standing ground tied, and I would
have admired their training if there'd been time. I appreci-
ated something else, too. I had to hand it to the black-haired
woman who was fighting for all she was worth and screaming at the top of her lungs, but there were two of them.

One at her head held her arms down and there was a
good reason why. She'd already clawed his face with her
nails and it looked like a Mexican lion had gotten ahold of
him. The other guy had his back to me and was sitting on
her legs, yanking at her blouse.

They were laughing and concentrating on what they
were doing as I drew my Spencer pump shotgun from the
scabbard. There was no need to jack a shell into the chamber, because I carried it fully loaded.

Still mounted, I felt the blood start to pound in my ears,
accompanied by a high keening that always sparked violence. "It always takes more than one, don't it? Gentlemen,
y'all might want to stop what you're doing and leave that
woman alone."

The bearded man sitting on her legs stiffened and the
rangy one raised his head to look up at me from under the
brim of his hat. He stood, resting his hand on the butt of a

revolver stuck in his belt. "Mister, it's stupid to risk your life for an Indian woman. You better get on out of here if you know what's good for you."

"I don't."

His hand dropped to the pistol in his belt. Now that he was standing up, and the spread of buckshot didn't endanger the woman, I shot him in the chest. The report seemed soft to me, but the load of double-aught shot put holes in his dirty shirt from shoulder to shoulder. His knees folded and his full weight collapsed right on top of the woman.

The steeldust under me hadn't moved a muscle, for I'd trained her well. I pumped another shell into the chamber as the bearded outlaw came up with a cocked pistol coming to bear on my chest.

The shorter distance worked in my favor when I pulled the trigger again. The load didn't have time to spread out. The full charge took him in the midsection and the impact of all eight double-aught pellets looked like I'd hit him with a howitzer.

His pistol went off, the bullet plowing a hole in the ground. He fell sideways, trying to hold himself together with one hand. Even though I didn't need a second shell, I pumped another round into the chamber and kept it pointed at him.

The woman kicked the lean man's body off and rolled sideways to get out from under him. Hair untied and wild, her face was twisted in fury. Holding her torn dress together with one hand, she picked up the Beard's dropped pistol, cocked it with both hands, and shot him in the head.

She cocked it again and shot the other man the same way before raising the barrel in my direction. I kept the shotgun's muzzle pointed away from her. "Lady, don't you pull that trigger."

Realizing what she was doing, she pitched it on the ground and hurried to her husband, either unconcerned about how much skin was showing, or unaware that very little protected her modesty. Close now, I took them both to either be Cherokee or Choctaw from their features.

Kneeling beside him, she turned him over. "He's still breathing."

I dismounted and joined her. His scalp was split, but the wound was already clotting, which was a surprise to me because scalp wounds tend to bleed a lot. "Looky here at the size of that lump on his head. When it swells outward, he's fine. You have any water on that wagon?"

"There's a quart fruit jar under the seat."

I found it and returned. She'd moved around to hold his head in her lap and I had to look away as I flipped the wire holding the glass lid in place. It popped up off the gasket, and instead of smelling corn liquor, as I imagined, it really was water.

"Ma'am, is there another dress in the wagon?"

She saw her dilemma and angled her shoulders to turn away from me. "No, but there's material and a new shirt for my brother in a basket back there. Got it back in town."

I set the jar nearby and went to the back. The shirt was lying on the ground beside everything the lean highwayman threw out. They couldn't have been doing too badly as farmers, if they could afford to buy a shirt instead of making it herself, as most folks did.

Keeping watch all around us, I returned. She'd torn a piece of her dress off and wet it to wipe her husband's face. I handed her the shirt without looking. "Put this on."

She was a tough old hide and didn't make much more effort to hide herself. I turned my back and she put the shirt on and went over to check the outlaws' horses for a moment. They were both of good quality, though the saddles were worn and one was rat-chewed. "You decent?"

"Yes."

I took notice of her then. One eye was turning black and

the left side of her jaw was swollen, but at least I'd gotten there in time. "Y'all live close?"

She pointed back the way I came. "A couple of miles."

"You said something about a brother?"

"Yes. He lives with us." Her husband stirred and his eyes fluttered open. She cupped his cheek with one dry hand. "Hokta. Wake up." He jerked and tried to rise, but she held him down. "It is all right. They are dead and this man killed them."

He groaned and lay back. "Who are you?"

"Cap Whitlatch."

She raised her eyes to me. "I am Naach. Thank you for your help."

"I did what any decent man would have done."

Not wanting to talk, I used one of the outlaws' ropes and his horse to drag the bodies off into the trees, while Hokta shook out the cobwebs, but that was all the energy I would expend on such men. They didn't deserve a proper burial. Curious about the robbery, I kicked around until I found where they'd waited.

By the number of hoofprints and boot tracks, they'd been there a good long while. I puzzled out that Hokta and Naach weren't specific targets, merely a couple of unfortunate farmers in the wrong place at the wrong time. Had I been along a little sooner, they might have tried to brace me, instead, but the result would have been the same.

I came back and tied the outlaws' horses to the back of the wagon, throwing their saddles and bedrolls in the back. While Naach tended to her husband, I picked up with everything the couple'd purchased in town that wasn't broken, even scooping up dry beans with my hat and tying what was left in the cut tow sack.

The shadows were long by the time Hokta regained his senses enough to handle the team and take them back home. I helped him up into the seat and then held out a hand for

Naach. Placing hers gently in mine, she made eye contact with a look of hope mixed with fear, and gave me a crooked grin before climbing up.

Once seated, she adjusted the shirt, which was too big for her, and paid me with a small smile. "Come with us. We will feed you and you can sleep in the barn tonight."

"No thanks. I'm not one to backtrack, but I appreciate your offer."

"Let us pay you, then."

I shook my head. "No, ma'am. Hokta, there are two pistols in there that belonged to those guys, and a considerable amount of ammunition. I suggest you and your wife practice with them, and the next time somebody stops you like that, y'all shoot as quick as you see what they're up to."

He nodded and gestured back over his shoulder. "The horses are yours. You won them in battle. It is the way of our Old People."

"They're good stock. Well trained, but I don't need them. They don't have brands, so keep 'em or sell 'em to make up the supplies you lost here."

"You are a good white man." Naach made a sign in the air. "We will give one to my brother. He doesn't have a horse." She made another sign and spoke in Choctaw. "That is a blessing that will keep you safe."

"I'm just a traveler on this road, like you, but much obliged."

"Wait." She lifted her long hair with both hands and reached back to untie a braided cord. She lifted a small leather pouch from between her breasts and held it out to me. "You must take this, if nothing else."

Thinking it was coins or even paper money, I shook my head. "Ma'am, I don't need payment."

"This is my medicine. My father gave it to me as protection. It is yours now."

Hokta nodded. "You must take it. This is a special gift that cannot be denied."

I saw the beadwork and thought it looked like the Sioux had made it, though I couldn't understand why a Chocktaw woman wore it. "Your medicine didn't protect you with those men."

"Yes, it did. You came along." She had me there.

"Well, you might need it next time."

"No. I see something over you. Your eyes open into the spirit world, and sometimes that is good and other times bad. You will require this protection, and I will get another."

More than one person, male and female alike, have said my eyes are piercing green. They're a light shade that's as rare as hen's teeth and they startle people at first before they get used to them.

I took the bag, tied it around my neck, and nodded. Hokta clucked the mules and popped the reins and they drove away, while I turned my horse south and went to find a good place to make camp for the night.

CHAPTER 2

When I rode down the dirt main street in Blackwater, Oklahoma, the air was almost chewy and thick with humidity and woodsmoke. It worried me some that the rest of my trip down to Kerrville in the Texas Hill Country was going to be mildewy at best.

I'd already passed the Grand Hotel sitting out by itself on the outskirts of town, a wooden two-story box with an unpainted false front and a stable out back. It even had a two-story outhouse, something I'd heard of, but never seen. Accessible from the second floor, I wondered about the guy who had to clean out the top section, or the folks doing their business down below at the same time another patron was suddenly struck with a pain.

Such a luxury surprised me and I was tempted to stop and look at it a little closer, and would have if I could find a drink nearby. But I had no intention of riding farther into town, drinking for an hour or so, if I could scare up something to eat.

I got that from my old daddy who fought in the Union's Iron Brigade during the War Between the States. I once asked him how he and the rest of his infantry division could walk into hundreds, if not thousands, of Confederate guns firing at him at the same time and he said, "Getting started was the hardest part, but going back the other direction before I finished what I was doing never entered my mind."

It always felt like he was riding beside me after that, and because of that presence, I never wanted to disappoint him by turning back, though he'd likely never know of it.

The rest of Blackwater was about what I expected to find out there in Cherokee Territory, seventy-some-odd miles northwest from Fort Smith, Arkansas, and Judge Isaac Parker, also known as the Hanging Judge. Wooden false-front buildings in the bustling town lined a wide lane full of horses, mules, and wagons.

At one point during a wet spell, the dirt street had been churned to muddy ruts by the passing of heavily laden wagons. Dry now for the moment, those ruts were some-what worn down by hooves and steel rims, but they still made unsteady travel underfoot, and that included my own mount.

There were more men on the boardwalks than I expected to see, and a couple of women carrying covered baskets or waiting on buckboards for husbands to finish their business in the stores. Soiled doves sat on a second-floor balcony, watching people go by, but they minded their manners and didn't holler or wave at potential customers. Guess that's why the housewives didn't mind going about their business, but I 'magine they kept their eyes down as they passed a colorful sign for the Honey Hole.

Most of the folks were Indian, but there were more than a few whites on the streets of Blackwater, and I couldn't help but compare it to Tahlequah, the capital of the Chero-kee Nation. I'd passed through there once on my way to Springfield, and that place was growing like a weed, with brick streets and buildings.

This place had a long way to go, and by the number of drinking establishments under innocent names, I figured it didn't have much time before the laws rode in and either shut it all down, or burned the place to the ground. Alcohol was illegal in the Indian Territories, and most towns kept all that hidden from sight.

The reins slack in my hands, my steeldust mare snorted and stepped around a bloated hog covered in a swarm of flies. I'd seen vultures circling high in the air long before I reached town, but I didn't expect to come across a sow's putrid carcass right in front of the general-goods store.

Dead animals in a town weren't an uncommon sight. Hell, horses and mules fell out all the time, and usually when they were in harness. The laziest owners tended to just unhitch everything and walk off, leaving the town fathers or an aggravated store owner to foot the bill for dragging the remains out a ways for the coyotes to finish it off, if they didn't take a notion to do it themselves. I heard back in the big cities, like Chicago and New York, they just walked away from it all in great numbers and every street had at least one rotting carcass to deal with a day.

It was hard to imagine anyone so slovenly, but then again, they weren't raised by my daddy, neither.

Part of what must've been two hundred pounds of pork I had to rein around had been gnawed on, and I suspected it was by an old mammy dog lying under the board sidewalk on my right. Instead of being drawn down by the four pups sleeping in a pile a couple of feet away, her stomach was tight as a tick and I figured she'd stay close by the porker until somebody finally got tired of the smell and drug it off.

It was a busy street with false-front buildings that extended above the roofline and sides to create a more impressive appearance, supposedly showing stability and a respectable town. More than a few customers and townies stopped what they were doing out front of the stores to watch me pass. Most of them were Indian, but I couldn't tell what tribe. They could have been Cherokee, Choctaw, Chickasaw, or Creek. Four of the five tribes the government settled there decades earlier. I knew they weren't Seminole, I can tell most of them right off, by their color, features, and dress.

There were plenty of white folks, and I must have caught their attention, being a stranger and all. Most of them looked at me suspicious-like, as if I owed 'em money, and I figured they took me for one of Judge Parker's Deputy U.S. Marshals scratching around for outlaws or miscreants hiding out from the law.

Laughter boiled out of a door under a sign reading CHINAMAN BAKERY as I passed. There wasn't much to see through the dark open door that leaked the odor of spilled beer instead of baked goods.

I noticed the interesting sight of telegraph wires strung up on peeled cedar poles and disappearing down the street. I hadn't expected such a little one-horse town to have such modern conveniences.

The place was a budding metropolis.

It must have been a Saturday, because there were people everywhere, dressed in everything from hand-tanned leather pants, to some made of wool, to those Levi Strauss denim overalls I'd been seeing here and there, to dandies in suits and ties.

Regular folks, but then there were the others I was talking about earlier, hard-looking men who seemed never to blink, like rattlesnakes.

An aggravating horsefly kept buzzing round in front of my eyes. I snatched the hat from my head and slapped at the insect, and when I did, a gentleman on the board sidewalk in front of the butcher shop misunderstood the gesture and took his hat off and doffed it in my direction.

We nodded howdy and I went on past another general store advertising dry goods, such as boots, hats, shoes, valises, trunks, and carpets. A surveyor's office boasting CLAIMS AND DEEDS listed the rest of their services in flowery script on the front and glass on both sides of the door.

A blacksmith's hammer rang like silver over the chaos of rattling trace chains. Loud voices accosted me from businesses lining both sides of the street. A chicken waiting her turn in the pot squawked and flapped out of the way, while another cackled her excitement at laying an egg in an unseen nest. The steeldust gray I was riding ignored the flutter of feathers and saw a hitching post she liked. She turned and stopped in front of the Applejack Dispensary and Meals. That suited me just fine.

We'd passed half-a-dozen other false-front establishments in the whiskey town, and they all boasted medicinal drinks guaranteed to cure a variety of ailments, particularly those with a thirst for choc beer from old Choctaw recipes. Selling or providing alcohol to Indians—and anyone else, for that matter, in the eastern territories—was illegal by federal law, but the most entrepreneurial businessmen were working around that little stumbling block, at least until Judge Parker or the marshals found out about it.

In my experience, real whiskey in bottles was available in the right establishments all over the territories, but none in Blackwater carried the name saloon, bar, or watering hole, for that matter. The other establishments I saw on that day, in 1883, operated under such names as Winks, Apothecary, and Spring Water Inside.

I swung down and tied the reins in a loose knot around a bois d'arc hitching post worn smooth enough from use to have been sanded. Adjusting the Russian .44 I carried butt-forward on my left hip, I walked around the mare to get the short Spencer twelve-gauge pump, which slid easily from the leather boot, and held it muzzle down as I pulled my saddlebags free and threw them over my shoulder. I stepped up on the shaded walk and pushed through the single door propped open between two glassless windows.

The interior smelling of stale beer and tobacco smoke was cool and pleasant. Even the sound seemed muffled inside, though I can't imagine why, since everything facing out front was wide open. Saddlebags still over my left shoulder, I found an empty space at the bar running the length of the left-hand side and propped the shotgun against it.

A heavy spread of food took up a good section of the far end. Boiled eggs, pickled eggs, crackers, cheese, thick slices of bread, cold fried bacon, thick slices of meat I couldn't identify, and a full water bucket, with a dipper, made me realize I hadn't eaten in a while.

A roach crawled from under one of the metal plates holding what looked like fried squirrel or rabbit and scurried toward the crackers. Flies buzzed over the whole layout. Movement on the floor caught my eye, and I saw a mouse, with a chunk of yellow cheese in its mouth, disappear into a crack in the wall. I wondered if someone dropped it, or if he'd made his way to the plate and took what he wanted.

A cat shot out of nowhere and took up an ambush point beside the crack, digging in his back feet to pounce. I figured he'd have to wait awhile, because that was a big hunk of cheese and it might take some time for the mouse to eat it. Then again, maybe the cat knew the mouse was storing up for the wintertime and would be right back for a second go-round.

I decided to hold off on eating, though the flies didn't bother me at all. I'd eaten more than my share on the trail, and once had one fly into my mouth and down my goozle while I yakked and gagged in front of a dozen cowboys, who whooped and hollered in glee.

The counterman, with oiled hair parted in the middle, met me with a solemn gaze.

"What'll you have?"

"Beer."

"You want it cold?"

That was a surprise. "You have ice?"

"Sure we do. This is the coldest beer you'll find on this side of Fort Smith." He laughed loud and long at his own joke, and I had to wait for him to regain control before answering.

"That'll do."

"Two bits." He laid down his bar rag and reached for a draw handle.

"Kinda steep for beer, ain't it?"

"Ice ain't cheap. Had to build an icehouse, cut it in the winter, wrap it in toe sacks, and cover the whole thing in sawdust, and that costs money, when you have to buy all that." He inclined his head toward the street. "Won't be long before the railroad comes through here. They expect the tracks to run just out of town, right beside the new Grand Hotel. That's why it's so far out. They're building a station not far from it, so with all that, we're gonna be a city before long."

"I didn't think you could get anything to drink around here."

He grinned, finished filling the mug, and set it on the sanded pine bar top, holding on to the handle until I slid a solid quarter in his direction. "A little money in the right places'll do wonders, even here. The Lighthorse Police usually handle these kinds of things, but since it's white man's money building all these places, the Indian Police can't do much about it."

"So what do they do?"

"There's Indian nations here in the territories, and they don't have jurisdictional rights over anyone who ain't citizens, but the Indian Lighthorse can. They stop them who break the law and hold 'em over for Judge Parker's Deputy U.S. Marshals."

He gave me a wink. "But lately they've been staying away, except for one owns the Grand, where the rail line's gonna run. Fifteen dollars a month don't buy much law. You see what I'm saying?"

He gave me another conspiratorial wink and took a swipe at the bar top as I took a slow sip that went down as cool and fresh as spring snowmelt. It wasn't like any beer I was used to, and I remembered choc beer wasn't filtered. He nodded as if I'd asked a question and turned to ring up the sale.

The mug was half empty when I finally turned to scan the rest of the long, narrow interior lit only by the sun coming through the flyspecked windows. Most of the dozen mismatched tables were occupied, a few by as many as three or four customers drinking, talking, and smoking. The two back tables were filled with card players who paid no attention to anything except the pasteboards in their hands. I watched the tranquil scene for a while, until the beer was gone.

"'Nother one?"

I was about to tell the counterman yes, even at those prices, when fast-paced wooden boot heels caught my attention. Up to then, everyone outside had been walking, but that pair ran like the Devil was after the wearer.

More men ran in the same direction, deeper into the direction I was headed when I first arrived in town, while others shouted in excitement. I shoved the empty mug away with a forefinger, picked up the scattergun, and went to the door to watch men flow like merging streams down the bright, sun-washed street. It must have been something exciting, because one rider loped his horse in that direction, nearly running down a couple of pedestrians.

Already interested in what might be happening, I joined the flow and found myself swept along to an angry crowd gathered in front of the county sheriff's office. The Cherokee, Choctaw, and Chickasaw Nations had country or district sheriffs who were appointed by the Indian political leadership. Some of the larger towns also had constables.

Most of the throng was in the street, giving me enough space on the boardwalk to slip between the onlookers and the unpainted board-and-batten wall of the adjoining building.

It took a few seconds to make out what was going on. The sheriff, with the biggest pair of handlebar mustaches I'd ever seen, stood with his back against the closed door. He held a nasty-looking sawed-off ten-gauge shotgun in his hands. Both hammers were cocked, and if he pulled the trigger on that double-barreled street howitzer, it'd cut down two dozen men like a scythe.

His eyes were glassy with either fear or fury. I've seen that look on men who were about to do violence with either intention or in self-defense. Sometimes a man fighting for his life is much more dangerous than the predator.

"I done told y'all he's staying in that cell until a Texas Ranger gets up here and gathers him up." The sheriff's voice was even, but he was breathing hard, another sure sign that something was fixin' to happen.

"Texas law don't mean a thing up in here." The speaker had a fire in *his* eye, like I hadn't seen since I was a kid and two drunk cowboys took to shooting at one another over some little old German gal who'd bedded them both in the same week.

He had a deep scar that ran from his forehead, across a shallow gully on the bridge of his big nose, and down his left cheek. It looked to me like somebody'd took a swipe at him with an ax at some point. "He done kilt my little brother and we intend to hang him!"

"Let me tell you something, Cloyce Gluck." The sheriff looked him right in the eye. "You and them brothers of yours are on the wrong side of the fence on this one. He ain't a citizen of any of our nations, so I'm just holding him for now."

I'd stopped several feet away, with my right shoulder against the wall, so I had a clear view of the hotheaded man, who had two others who favored him on each side. It was easy to tell they were brothers, with matching noses that made two of mine, undershot chins, and eyebrows that looked like skunk pelts.

All three were loaded for bear, though Cloyce and one other still had their weapons in the holsters. A third, the shortest and the one I took for the baby of the three, had his pistol stuck through the belt in his pants. Looking at the sheriff's set jaw from my three-quarter view told me if those boys' hands even came close to them hoglegs, all three would wake up in Hell the next morning.

The crowd was too big for one man to keep an eye on, all at once. He was focused on those three bracing him, and missing what was happening on both sides. "*You* say he kilt Possum, but just saying the words don't make it so."

"Possum was winning at cards against that Vanderburg feller, who said he was tapped out on that last hand. Now he's dead and there wasn't a cent on him." Cloyce spat a stream of brown tobacco juice onto a pile of horse muffins. "If Vanderburg didn't have no more money, how the hell you gonna explain that pocket full of cash on him when you picked him up yesterday?"

That name jolted me and changed my interest in the proceedings. I grew up down in Fredericksburg with a German kid named Gilbert Vanderburg. The two of us were bad for one another, and we stirred up more trouble than we should have, running those live oak–covered hills together and getting into something every time we turned around. We stayed partners and ran together until we grew out of such childishness and left to be on our own.

I remembered he was hell with cards. Cloyce said his name, the sheriff mentioned Texas, and that told me there was a good chance the prisoner was Gil, as we all called him, and there was no way I was gonna let him get strung up by a Blackwater lynch mob.

The sheriff sighed long and slow. "He *didn't* have a pock-etful of money. That's hearsay. I didn't find nothing but a nickel on him, and I have that on my desk to cover his fine."

"What fine?"

"Vagrancy."

Several of the men chuckled, and I realized the sheriff was trying his best to cool everything down. I admired him for that. He spoke with a Cherokee cadence and I wondered about his ancestors. Indians don't usually have much facial hair, but this guy had a brush pile growing under his nose.

He wasn't finished talking. "I don't know nothing about gambling, but if I's in a game and losing and wanted out, I might say I was broke before I lost my shirt. Hell, Cloyce, we can't try the man out here on the street nohow, he de-serves a fair trial and he's gonna get it down in Texas. I got a paper on him says he's wanted down there. Let *them* ruin a good rope on him and call it good for Possum!"

A voice floated over the crowd, coming from a feller I couldn't see. "This ain't Texas, Kanoska! The Cherokee court needs to try him for killing one of our own and rob-bing him."

I hadn't paid much attention to who was het up until that moment. Most of the mob was Indians, and it took a minute to figure that I was one of the few white folks there in the street. Uncomfortable with that sudden knowledge, I shifted the shotgun lying in the crook of my left elbow, just in case someone decided they wanted to hang a second white stranger for watching their business.

"He's white and that muddies things up a mite." Sheriff Kanoska seemed to ponder the dilemma he'd found him-self in.

"Then let one of Judge Parker's marshals come get him."

"What difference does it make if he's hung by a Texas judge or one from Arkansas?" I could hear the frustration in Sheriff Kanoska's voice, and the tension. "Y'all just want him strung up and it ain't-a-gonna happen without a fair *trial,* so get that through your thick Gluck heads."

He kind of pointed at Cloyce with the muzzle of the shotgun, swinging it slightly in that direction. Some might have taken it for an innocent gesture from an agitated man, but I saw he kept those twin barrels more inclined toward Cloyce and his brothers as he spoke. "I saw Gil at the stable when Possum was killed. I don't believe it was him who did it."

"Why do you have him in jail, then?"

"Y'all are drunk and not listening. I done told you it's to keep y'all from stretching his neck, Cloyce. He's wanted in *Texas.*" He turned his head left and right to make sure the rest of the mob heard his words. "I got to looking at wanted papers after I picked him up and y'all started looking for him. Saw his name and picture, Gil Vanderburg, and wired the Rangers."

There it was. My old buddy Gil was in a cell behind that closed wooden door.

Sheriff Kanoska was locked in on Cloyce. "You take Itchy and Cheese there and go home and sleep it off. When y'all wake up with bad heads in the morning, I should have word about when that Ranger might be here to pick Gil up and we can all be done with this business."

Cloyce took a half step forward and crossed his arms. That put his right hand only a couple of inches from the pistol hanging butt-forward, like mine, on his left hip. It'd be nothing to finish the cross draw, if he took a notion to pull iron.

Those thick eyebrows of his met in the middle to form a solid line. "That won't be happening. We're taking that murderer right *now.*"

Sheriff Kanoska's full attention was on Cloyce and his brothers, and that was all another feller needed. The Negro man of large proportions, with a beard and long, curly hair to his shoulders, was far to Kanoska's left, and slowly took a revolver from under his coat. From where I stood, the man's movements were sure and dangerous. At the same time, I saw two dark-complected men ease forward through the crowd. They were Indian, for sure.

His concentration on the men before him, Kanoska's voice was whip-crack flat. "I'll cut you in half if you touch that pistol, Cloyce, and the spray from this ten-gauge's liable to punch holes in Itchy and Cheese, too. Think about y'all's mama and her having to bury all three of y'all tomorrow."

Cloyce's eyes flicked toward those men I was watching, who moved in on the sheriff like wolves, and Kanoska's back stiffened. He must have seen what was happening from the corner of his eyes and realized he'd been flanked and now there was no way out.

Except for me.

Even then, Kanoska didn't break his gaze on the Gluck brothers. I guess he figured he might take them all out with one barrel from that cannon, then have time to swing on the Negro only a few feet from where I stood.

"Even if you men get past me, Deputy Cornsilk's sitting in the cell beside Gilbert's with a twelve-gauge." Sheriff Kanoska's voice cracked with tension. "He'll mow y'all down as you come through the door."

Several men chuckled, and I wondered if it was the deputy they were laughing at, or the fracture in the sheriff's voice when he said it. Men can smell fear, and that crack might have turned the tale.

"You only got two barrels, Sheriff, and there's three more guns here!" The Negro's voice was deep and smooth as honey. His bright white teeth were pure in the midst of his rich beard, which appeared to be oiled. "Put down that scattergun and go on home while you can still walk."

There came that high keening in my ears again as the

blood rose. It wasn't wanted, and I didn't do anything to cultivate such intense feelings, but like the sheriff, I'd been on the receiving end of trouble from several men at one time. Because of that, I hated to see people gang up on one another.

Kanoska started to wilt, knowing he was outflanked, and I couldn't have that. With full attention on that big Black guy, I made sure my voice was strong and sharp. "You men there!"

With my breath coming up short, and that familiar sound rising inside my head, a wicked eagerness took hold of my body. Still leaning against the wall, I raised the Spencer pump across the crook of my left arm and slid my finger around the back trigger.

There was another in front, but that one was for misfires. If a shell proved reluctant on the first pull, I could push the front trigger forward to cock the gun again, giving me a second go at the paper-cased shell.

It's funny what a man notices at certain times. Here I was, pointing a shotgun at three strangers, and the deep blue of the sky registered in the back of my mind. A crow cawed from somewhere and a horse tied to the rail beside me lifted its tail to drop a steaming pile on the street, a common, natural act that suddenly seemed strange in the midst of what was happening.

"He might only have two barrels, but this here repeater's loaded with eight twelve-gauge shells full of double-aught buck." My voice was steady, and I concentrated on the tone and cadence. I didn't want them to get even a sniff of fear, not that I was afraid, because I was ready for anything that might happen. "When I get to pumping this thing, I'll be able to see the other side of the street in about three seconds."

My words, and the sight of the thirty-inch barrel, parted

the mob behind them like Moses commanding the Red Sea. The crowd around those three gunmen evaporated, to leave them standing confused and alone. From the corner of my eye, I saw the Gluck brothers ease back a step or two and understood the caliber of men they were.

The corner of the Negro's mouth tilted up in an arrogant grin. He was tough as whang leather and wasn't used to people throwing guns on him and his associates. "That damned contraption won't work."

"It has so far."

It was that big muzzle, or maybe the tone of my voice, but his attitude vanished. "What's this to you?"

"Same as you. Like Cloyce and his brothers there, I might have a dog in this fight."

Cloyce forgot Sheriff Kanoska for a moment, eyeing me up and down. "I don't know you."

"Don't need to." I didn't take my eyes off the big guy.

"What's that German to you?" Cloyce was doing his best to keep my attention away from the three men who got tired of waiting.

I've often wondered why men do what they do. Were they finished talking? Did they sense some weakness in me that I didn't recognize? Or were they so cocksure of themselves because they'd won every gunfight they were ever in?

Maybe because of my size, about five-eleven and very little fat, he thought he could take me. I never was built up, but I was fast and fit from working horses and a ranch all my life. More'n one man misjudged my size and demeanor, and paid for it with their lives.

I'll never know about those three, because they opened the dance when they pulled their weapons despite my warning. I wasn't as worried about the other two as much as Black Beard, who I took as the most dangerous of them all. A .44 came up in his hand, but he fired too fast. The bullet splintered behind me and I took that as his last shot.

My old daddy taught me to move with deliberation, because, he said, most men in gunfights start shooting too fast. He was right. I didn't have to aim, because the Spencer was already lined up with the big man and I always aimed at the biggest part of whatever I intended to shoot. I'd read in some of those penny dreadfuls about men who could shoot the pistol from a man's hand from a distance, but that was all make believe. When it came to killin', you shot for the heart.

My first shell filled his chest with a full load of shot and he dropped like a puppet with cut strings. The distance was so short, the pattern didn't have time to spread and he soaked it all up. Smoke billowed across the street from both his gun and mine, and I guess the other two thought they could take me.

They slapped leather, but the next two rounds from the Spencer followed quick, as I noted there was no one behind them and pumped the forearm and swept the street, just like I told 'em I'd do.

I'd practiced that kind of shooting not long after getting the Spencer only a few months after it came out. Setting up pine cones, rocks, and pieces of firewood on a downed tree, I went through several boxes of shells shooting those targets off as fast as I could pump, aim, and fire.

Because I come to be so good with small targets, two growed men were hard to miss. The twelve-gauge roared as the muzzle spat flame and smoke and the two stationary figures went down hard, ending my part of the gun battle at the same time that two empty paper hulls clattered on the dusty sidewalk boards.

To my side, the sheriff cut down on a man I hadn't noticed. The guy with a pistol in his hand might have fired first, but my shotgun made too much noise to hear his report. No matter, Kanoska's ten-gauge did its work. That feller dropped his pistol and crumpled to the ground as shrieks of wounded onlookers behind him filled the air. Kanoska wasn't as careful about who was behind his target, but I reckon he figured anyone in that mob should have expected to catch a stray pellet or two if things went wild on the street and should have shown more sense than to stand there in the line of fire.

A couple of horses behind the mob tried to unseat their riders as I swung the barrel back toward the trio of brothers, who hadn't moved a muscle. Stunned into immobility, they stood rooted to the ground and stared with their mouths open.

I was right. They were bullies, the kind of men who started trouble, but would back down in the face of a determined man. The only problem was, they were also the kind who'd shoot you in the back and go brag about it later.

I was mad by then, over them other three forcing me to shoot. By then, I'd shouldered the shotgun and was looking down the barrel directly at the one called Cloyce. "Y'all can have the rest of these loads, if you want to keep on with this!"

White-faced and hands raised, he and his brothers backed away. "That was pure dee murder!" His scarred and disfigured face full of fury, Cloyce spat toward me. "We ain't done with this!"

Just as I expected, they faded back and walked away, looking back over their shoulders now and then. Keeping my shotgun level with the rest of the milling crowd, I moved the barrel back and forth, looking for more threats. While all eyes were on me, Sheriff Kanoska broke his twelve-gauge and reloaded his one spent barrel as the worried herd of men drifted apart. When the brothers disappeared into a tavern down the street, he turned to me with the familiar look I've seen all my life as he became aware of my eyes.

It took him a moment to pull his attention from them and soften his gaze. "Thanks, friend. What's your name?"

"Cap Whitlatch."

"Well, Cap, you're a sight for sore eyes. Come on in."

I wondered if that was a joke as I followed him into the jail.

CHAPTER 3

The bustling sounds of the growing city came through Springfield attorney Holland Penn's open windows, along with a generous helping of flies and more than a few hungry mosquitoes. Hundreds of horses' hooves and iron wagon rims echoing on brick streets filled the air, along with bells, jingling trace chains, and a constant cacophony of voices and whistles that almost blotted out the ticking of his mantel clock above the cold fireplace.

The thick, rich odors of manure, woodsmoke, burning coal, and the occasional whiff of sewage from thousands of outhouses mixed with the stale body odor of the two men sitting across his desk in the well-appointed office.

After checking the gold timepiece in his hand, as if dealing with the two scruffy men was costing him money, the portly Missouri lawyer returned it to the vest pocket of his three-piece suit and adjusted the matching chain to hang properly.

Noticing beard dandruff on his dark vest, he brushed it onto his pants and addressed the sweaty cowboys slumped in polished oak chairs provided for paying clients. He made a note to reposition and line up the books in the two huge barrister bookcases against the wall behind them. A successful man had to keep up appearances, and an unkempt office spoke of a slovenly owner.

"I have a proposition for the two of you."

The taller man, with scruffy facial hair, smoothed his blond starter mustache and leaned his wooden chair back on two legs, as if he were sitting on a ruffian's front porch rather than a high-class lawyer's office.

He didn't even have the decency to take off his dusty and stained broad-brimmed hat. "I figured, since you sent for us."

"Don't get smart with me, Bill Johns, there are plenty of others like yourselves I can pay to do my bidding." Lawyer Penn glared at the man he'd used several times to strong-arm witnesses into changing their stories, or in other business dealings that required an even rougher hand.

Johns's gaze slipped from Penn's face and the attorney continued. "I want you to get some money back that's owed me by a Texas feller named Cap Whitlatch."

The other cowboy, Ed Gentry, crossed one ankle over his knee and used a thumbnail to pick at a chunk of mud caught against the heel of his boot. At least *his* hat lay on the floor beside his chair that was still on all four legs, but the mud landed softly on a rich, round carpet.

"He crawfish on some deal?"

"You might say that. I paid him a lot of cash for good horses and he didn't uphold his part of the deal."

"Why don't you let the law handle it?"

"I could, but that would take weeks in the courts, if not months. I need that cash now and I am sometimes a vengeful kind of man." Penn's eyes sparkled with the lie. "The two of you can catch up to Whitlatch in the territories, where there ain't no law and . . . persuade that feller to give you the money he's carrying. He's on his way down toward somewhere out of Kerrville, down in Texas."

"Gold was the deal. I have a written binding here from Judge Garrett saying Whitlatch didn't hold up his end of the deal." Penn tapped at a folded document on his desk that was in reality a foreclosure on land in someone else's name outside of town. "It authorizes agents of this office to retrieve the funds that were essentially stolen by Whitlatch and return them to me."

Penn checked his watch again, knowing every wasted minute he spent with those two gave Cap Whitlatch time to get farther away. The first four times he did business with the Texan, both were satisfied with the deal. Penn bought the horses for a fair price, and then sold them for twice what they were worth, usually to customers who liked the idea of riding "wild Texas mustangs."

But the market fell out after he shook on the last delivery, which was much more specific in horseflesh and ability, and he was stuck with stock no one wanted. In addition, he'd overextended himself on land deals, which also failed. The gold coins in Whitlatch's saddlebags were enough to cover his losses on the land, and he was confident the horses would sell for what he paid in a couple of months when the market rebounded.

He wouldn't have accepted the horses in the first place, but when he hinted that he'd have to pay Whitlatch later, there was something in the Texas cowboy's strange eyes that told him not to argue with the man who'd driven the stock hundreds of miles through dangerous territory to make the delivery. On the spur of the moment, Penn decided to go ahead and give him the gold, which Whitlatch insisted on, instead of paper money, and get it back later. Then he'd have both the money *and* the horses.

The balding, portly attorney never liked to *lose* money, but he could always deal with breaking even, every now and then. One dead Texas waddie wouldn't make any difference to anyone outside his limited circle of friends, if he even had *those*. He shifted his considerable weight in the wooden desk chair and rested both elbows on the desktop. "I need this done with extreme prejudice."

Bill Johns scratched at the hair matted flat by his hat. "Cash money. You ain't afraid we'll just take that gold and disappear?"

Penn smoothed his gray-streaked beard. "Naw, I know where your mama lives, Bill."

The men on the other side of the desk exchanged glances and their faces went blank. Bill Johns once let it slip that his mother and sister lived in a small farmhouse twenty miles from Springfield. Johns used that house as his base, often ranging far and wide doing things that his mother didn't need to know about, but Penn knew the young man always swung back around to check on her and drop off a little money.

"Good, now that we understand each other, I'll pay you the usual, and put you up over at the Crystal Hotel tonight, and the night when you get back. How's that?"

"Grub . . . and horses?"

Despising Ed Gentry for haggling, Penn shrugged. "Sure. I have on hand more than a hundred Texas ponies." He chuckled. "Go pick one out for yourselves, but not the best ones, dammit, and get your grub from over at E.M. Hastings's store. Tell Emmett to put enough for two weeks on my bill, but not any more."

Johns reached across the desk for the bogus court order, but Penn pulled it away. "This one's mine. Opening the right-hand drawer of his desk, he took a folded piece of paper from under a Colt Lightning revolver, kept there for irate clients. "This paper will suffice as a legal document authorizing his return."

He glanced up at their raised eyebrows.

"Well, we want this all nice and legal, don't we? There's a price on that man's head, too, and that's extra for you." He slipped a bogus wanted poster, printed up for him by a friend at the newspaper office, into a plain envelope. He lit a red wax candle, melted its end, and dripped it onto the flap. Pressing a seal on the cooling dollop, he slid it across the desk.

"The information inside is a Texas wanted poster for one thousand dollars, dead or alive. However, this is for you to use if you run into some of those Indian lawmen who question why you might be there and asking around." He gave them a conspiratorial wink. "Though I doubt many of those savages can read. Don't show this around, or open it up unless you absolutely have to, it might put others on Whitlatch's trail and muddy things up for us all. Otherwise, handle everything the way you have in the past for me."

"Kill him, you mean, and bring back the gold."

Penn's eyes flicked to the closed door. "Some things shouldn't be spoken aloud. Now, get gone."

"The territories are a big place." Gentry scratched under his arm, and Penn fervently hoped it wasn't something that would emerge into the sunlight. "What's he look like? Let me have a look at the wanted poster."

"You don't need that. He's built like you, Gentry. Sandy hair and the most distinctive eyes I've ever seen in a man's head."

Johns raised an eyebrow. "How's that?"

"I guess you'd call them green . . . maybe ice-blue–green if that makes sense. You'll know him once you see him, and that's all you have to ask folks. They'll remember him as well as if they ran into one of them hairy men folks say they see up in the mountains."

"Fine, then." Johns shrugged. "You have any idea which route he took back to Texas?"

"He's well-armed. Carries a new Spencer shotgun that pulls a shell into the breach every time he pumps the fore-piece. You won't see many of those where you're going, and a pistol. He was headed southwest and made mention of some godforsaken place called Blackwater."

CHAPTER 4

It was Gil in that jail cell, all right, and he hadn't changed a bit in the last ten years, still a slim, good-looking cowboy, with just the right amount of dimple and curly hair to keep the girls interested.

"Good to see you, Cap!" His smile under a thick brown mustache was bright as the sun, even though he was behind bars and had been pretty damned close to swinging at the end of a rope only a few minutes before.

There were only two cells in the Blackwater Jail, and the other was occupied by Deputy Cornsilk sitting on a wooden bunk fastened to the plank wall. His bare right foot soaked in a bucket of coal oil. A scarecrow waif of an Indian girl, with long black hair, sat on the floor opposite the bunk, with her back against the bars separating her cell from the one occupied by Gil. Her overalls were once blue, but faded from time, wear, and washings on a scrubboard.

Sheriff Kanoska laid the short double-barrel on a desk full of papers, while his deputy, in the other cell, withdrew his foot from the bucket. He reached through the bars and released himself with a large key. Kanoska jerked a thumb toward Gil. "You two know each other?"

"Grew up together down in Texas." I positioned myself to keep an eye on the door, just in case someone outside

changed their minds and decided to try and force their way
inside.

Hatless, Deputy Cornsilk limped out of the cell. There
was a rag tied around his foot and he left wet prints all
the way to a cane-bottom chair, where he sat to pull on
what was left of a pair of boots. A thin headband matching
the pattern of the rag on Cornsilk's foot kept a thick gathering of black hair pulled back out of the deputy's face.

The girl rose and took his place on a folded patchwork
quilt bunched up on the hard wooden bed. Cornsilk pitched
the keys on the desk full of papers and old dishes, which
needed washing, and two open boxes of ten-gauge shotgun
shells.

I watched him wince as he stood. "What happened to
your foot?"

Cornsilk looked sad. "Stepped on a nail and it went
plumb through the sole. Came out the top." He pointed an
accusing finger at the girl. "Bad medicine, likely because of
her."

"It's your own damn fault for not watching where you
were going. You shouldn't-a been dragging me down the
alley like that." The girl rose and grabbed two handfuls of
bars. "Kanoska, you afraid I'm gonna escape, or get out of
here and cut your throat?"

"Shut up, Gracie." Cornsilk went to the window to peer
outside. The hair that fell down the middle of his back was
thick and black. "I heard a lot of shootin'. Who'd y'all have
to kill? I hope it was those damned Glucks. I despise Itchy
and Cheese, though Cloyce's not bad if he ain't drinkin'."

"They're all still alive, but a few other old boys ain't
sucking air no more." The sheriff absently smoothed his
handlebars. "Didn't know 'em. They were on the dodge, I
figure. Three of 'em said they were standing up for Possum
Little Hawk. I figure they was likely friends of the Glucks
and riding the owl hoot trail."

I knew more than one man who had left the law-abiding world to become outlaws were said to be owl hoots, or those who rode the owl hoot trail. I adjusted the big Arkansas toothpick in the sheath held down by the gun belt near the middle of my back and leaned against the wall.

"Possum was the card player they were talking about?"

Cornsilk turned his back to the window and I felt my skin crawl. It wouldn't be nothin' for somebody to shoot through the glass. Only a year earlier, somebody shot Deputy Morgan Earp in just such a way while he was playing pool out in Tombstone, Arizona.

The sheriff nodded. "Found him dead out behind the livery. Ever'body took Gil there for the murder."

"It wasn't me. I done told you."

I'd heard that kind of thing before. "And Itchy and Cheese? Where'd they get those names?"

Hanging by two hands from the bars, Gracie took it upon herself to answer the question. "They call him Itchy 'cause he had lice when he was a kid and scratched himself bloody more'n once. Cheese just smells bad, like old cheese gone over in the bottom of a privy. Them names ain't much better than Thermopylae and China they was christened with."

I shook my head at the barefoot little gal with hair so black it looked blue, and wore-out overalls held up by one strap over her skinny shoulders. Her thin shirt with a light blue stripe was homemade and threadbare. I liked that kid a lot. "And please tell me Possum was a nickname, too."

"Nope." Deputy Cornsilk remained where he was at the window. Outside, the undertaker and two assistants collected the bodies lying in the street. A circle of onlookers watched them work, but didn't help. "Old Chet Gluck took up with a Choctaw woman named Sara Little Hawk and had a woods baby that killed her when she was born. Chet said the boy had possum eyes and that's what they stuck the poor guy with. Possum Little Hawk and them Glucks grew up together after their mama took in that baby and raised it like it was one of her own. Effie's a strong woman. Had to be in order to put up with Chet and them scatterbrained get of their'n."

Gil hung his forearms through the bars. "Thanks for keeping them out, Sheriff."

"It was a good thing, too!" Gracie's high voice was full of disdain. "This dumb Kronk didn't even have shells in his gun. You forgot 'em, didn't you, Cornsilk?"

"My foot was hurtin' when all this started." He looked down at his scuffed boots in embarrassment. "I got so het up when that lynch mob showed up, I didn't think to grab any shells, but I did have my knife and pistol."

Ignoring their argument, Sheriff Kanoska studied me for a long moment. "I didn't do it for you, Vanderburg. It's my job, and speaking of names, Cap, what was it again?"

"Whitlatch. Cap Whitlatch."

"Thanks for your help out there." Holding a Bible in his left, he held up the other. "Raise up your right hand."

I did. "Why?"

"You're now a sworn deputy."

"How come? You didn't say no words."

"To keep things lawful, and I don't need to say words. Things are different here in the territories. You killed some people out there, and I don't want to deal with anyone thinking you're some kind of gunhand. There's enough of them coming through here, as it is, and I don't want no more shootin' in the street. They might notice a badge on your shirt and think twice about shooting at you."

"The law's the law, as far as I can see. I was just helping you, that's all, and I don't have no badge and wouldn't wear one, anyway."

one coming after you later. So, what're you doing here in Blackwater?"

"Passing through on my way back home."

"Where's that?"

"Little town down in Texas called Kerrville."

"Never heard of it, and you just happen to know Gil there."

I studied my old boyhood friend. I'd noticed that it grew dark outside. Quick showers tended to pop up in the Winding Stair Mountains during springtime. Sometimes weather will come through and squeeze out a young flood. Sure enough, thunder rumbled and it rained for a minute, then quit. "I've run into other old friends before in strange places."

Gil shrugged. "Bad luck, me being here."

"It is for you." I picked up my shotgun. "I'm not wearing no badge, Sheriff. As soon as I collect my horse over there in front of the Applejack, I'm gone."

The sheriff shook his head. "That's not a good idea. Some of those folks in that mob are likely getting even *more* drunk in there than they were a few minutes ago."

"If it's them damned big-nosed Glucks, they was born drunk." Gracie dropped off the bars and paced the cell like a caged lion. "I swanny, they're all ugly enough to gag a buzzard off a tub of guts, and mean as snakes, drinking or not. One of 'em tried to have his way with my mama 'fore she died of the fever, and she damn near gutted him with a butcher knife.

"Wait, that was Possum, so it don't make no difference now, but if you want to see if I'm tellin' the truth, if you'd-a got Webb Fitzgerald the undertaker, to show you Possum's stomach before he planted him, you'd know I'm telling the truth. She cut him from navel down to his worm, and that scar'd prove it, if you'd ask old Webb over there."

long and hard. "You are an evil child that should have been drowned in a toe sack when you were a baby. You're probably a mean old spirit that caused misery to my ancestors. Just how old are you, anyway?"

Her smooth brow creased. "I don't rightly know. Old enough to start my cycle, if that means anything."

"Good Goshamighty! Women ain't supposed to speak of such things." Cornsilk shuddered. "Karankawa women know enough to go out somewhere alone when the moon pulls, but no respectable person *talks* about such."

"Never said I was much of anything, much less respectable, and I'm not Karankawa. I'm Chocktaw *Aniyunwiya,* one of the Original People." She pronounced it as *ah-nee-yun-wee-yaw.* "And you can bet my ancestors had things figured out a long time ago. Women owned the house and the fields, and you men worked for *us.*" She turned her attention to me. "Hey, mister."

I raised an eyebrow in answer.

"How come you to be wearing a Sioux medicine bag?"

Glancing down, I saw that the uppermost button of my shirt had come undone and the top of the beaded bag was showing. "Got it from a Cherokee woman outside of town." I buttoned back up.

"You kill her for it?"

"Nope." I shook my head, wishing Gracie'd find something else to talk about.

I didn't really want to get into the shooting out on that wagon trail that might fall under Kanoska's jurisdiction. Killing outlaws and rapists weren't much of a crime, in my opinion, but I didn't need the questions.

"I helped her and her husband out, and she gave it to me in thanks."

Kanoska tilted his head. "Naach Culstee wore that."

"She did, and Hokta watched her give it to me for my troubles."

Nodding his head at Hokta's name showed Kanoska that I was telling the truth. He studied me for a minute, and I figured he was considering my eyes, as most folks do. "Well, I'll ask her the next time I see them."

"Go right ahead."

Satisfied with my answer, he looked through the window, considering the street. "Cornsilk, go get Cap's horse and bring it down here so we don't have to shoot nobody else."

He held his foot up like a horse getting shoed. "You know my foot hurts, don't you?"

"It'll hurt whether you're setting there or going to get that horse, like I told you. At least getting the horse will accomplish something."

The deputy nodded and plucked a shapeless hat from a nail beside the door. He put the empty shotgun in a rack and adjusted the revolver sticking in his belt. "How'll I know which one's yours?"

"Steeldust mare. Two long scars down her left hip and a scarred left hock."

Cornsilk raised an eyebrow.

"Panther tried to kill her a couple of years ago. She kicked it to death."

"Sounds like Gracie and that mare have the same disposition." Cornsilk unlatched the door.

He limped out and I watched raindrops run down the window. Still jittery from the confrontation, Sheriff Kanoska paced the room. "You can put them bags down and stay awhile."

"Feel better with them on my shoulder. My Bible's in there."

Gracie snorted. "Bible, my ass."

"Watch your language, Gracie." Kanoska absently smoothed his mustaches and met my gaze, likely knowing there was more in there than the Good Book and a fresh shirt. "I wish that Ranger would hurry up and get here. I sent a telegram a week ago."

"They waited that long to try and string Gil up?"

"It's been building like that thunderstorm out there, and it happened just as quick, once it struck. I held them off for about four days, saying we were waiting for a traveling circuit judge, but I got word that Judge Sipes was laid up over in Boggy Depot. Somebody shot a hole in his stomach at the end of a trial they disagreed with, so my next hope was the Rangers. They'd already be here if that rail line they've been talking about was in, but I 'magine they'll ride as far as the tracks go and then come in on horseback."

"What about a marshal from Fort Smith? They're in charge of this territory, aren't they?"

"They are, but if they pick Gil up, he'll go straight to Judge Parker, who'll hang him, for sure." Noticing a puddle beside his desk, Kanoska sat a brass spittoon under the wet spot on the ceiling and water dripped in, slow and steady. "I'm not in the belief that he killed Possum, and I figured that warrant out of Texas is your friend's best chance."

I liked the way Kanoska thought. "They said they're on the way?"

"Telegram said they were sending someone, but not when to expect them." Kanoska stiffened and I followed his gaze. Despite the sudden shower, which had wet everything down and made the air smell like dust, men were gathering outside again, and voices were raised enough to be heard inside. "This ain't over."

"Whiskey and angry people don't mix." I hoped Cornsilk would hurry up with my horse.

The sheriff lit a kerosene lamp to chase away the gloom and turned back toward Gil. "I have an idea to keep them from stretching your neck."

Gracie interrupted. "It wasn't real."

"You're right about that." I finally had to know. "What's a kid doing in jail, anyway?"

"For no damned reason at all . . ."

"Shut up, Gracie, before I take this belt to you." Kanoska put one hand on the buckle and she sulled up. "Stole two eggs from Mrs. Henry's chicken house."

"Just two and you put her in jail?"

"Two was all I was hungry for." Gracie's voice was sharp at the indictment. "It don't take much to fill me up."

"Dammit, shut *up,* Gracie! She steals all the time, because she don't have no family and lives in a little box of a shack out behind the blacksmith shop." Rain fell again, rapping on the roof's cedar shakes. Kanoska saw another leak and placed his water bucket under that one.

I saw the men outside fade back under the cover over the boardwalks, but they continued to talk in little clots that formed, shifted, and reformed.

Kanoska saw where I was looking and went to the window to watch. "Folks finally got tired of losing potatoes and corn and eggs and meat out of their smokehouses, so I put her in there for a while so they can cool off."

"She's a lot like me." Gil grinned and winked at the girl. "She's more outlaw than I am, though."

"So he intends to let me rot in here for a couple more weeks, I think." Gracie stuck her tongue out at Gil. "You don't know what an outlaw is. There's a dozen lazy fools hangin' around this town's worse than you'll ever think you are. Shoot, there was a gang rode through here, about a month ago, scared the bejesus out of the whole town, and they never even slowed their horses. And, by the way, Kanoska, I was eatin' better out there than in this cell, and that's the truth. Cheese and crackers ain't fit for no innocent girl."

"Don't matter, Cap. I deputized you, and the two of us can take your friend out of here after dark. The odds are better with us traveling together, and I know you'll stand firm when it gets hard."

"I just don't like mobs, that's all."

Gil wagged a finger toward the door. "It don't do to get Cap all spun up. He's like sticking your hand in a bee tree. Once he gets started, he'll keep stinging and won't quit until a job's done. That boy right there'll fight a buzz saw if he thinks it's in the wrong and he's right."

I wished Gil would shut up.

He stood and gripped the bars with both hands. "Thing about Cap there that most folks don't know is . . ."

"Gil. That's *enough.*"

He continued like he hadn't heard me. "He's not capable of doing anything wrong, it just ain't in him, but others might say different . . . 'cause he don't mind killing a man who needs it. We all knew down in our county that he don't hesitate to shoot, and he's done it a fair amount of times, that I know of. I reckon since I last saw him, he's planted more than a few men who underestimated him."

Kanoska absently wrapped a hand around the revolver's butt hanging off his hip and lifted it half an inch, as if making sure it was loose in the holster. His action almost caused me to do the same with the Russian .44 on my left side. I didn't, though, because he was listening hard to Gil and I was afraid he'd take something wrong and jerk that piece on his hip. I never shot a lawman, and didn't intend to start on accident.

Kanoska watched me like a hawk. "He dropped three of that mob out there, all right."

"See, I told you." Gil looked pleased, as if I shot those men to confirm his thoughts.

After a minute, Kanoska relaxed. "Sounds like a man to ride the trail with."

I guess he worked it out in his head and figured I wasn't much of a threat to him, since we stood against that mob out there and were on the same side. I decided right then and there to have a talk with Gil about running his mouth when he should be quiet.

Back home, I already had a reputation for not putting up with another man's guff, and Gil was right. I've put flying shoes on more than my share of horse thieves, outlaws, and robbers who made the mistake of tangling with me. I've never looked for trouble, but I sure never backed down from it, either.

They say Billy the Kid killed twenty-one men before Sheriff Pat Garrett put him down like a mad dog one night. I hoped nobody ever counted them up for *me,* and there was no way they could, because I wasn't fool enough to notch the handles of my guns. I did my best to bury 'em in my mind so's I wouldn't have to think about what I'd done.

"I'll leave Cornsilk here to mind the jail and we can light out as soon as it gets dark." Kanoska noticed a badge on the desk and picked it up with a disgusted look on his face. "I believe it's liable to rain all night. I can feel it in the air. With a twelve-hour head start, we can get gone before they start looking." He studied the badge and seemed to realize he still had it in his hand. "Dammit."

"What?"

"This is Cornsilk's."

In spite of his situation, Gil grinned again and turned his head to look at the tiny, barred window high in his cell. "Sounds like a good plan." The sky was dark with the thunderstorm and a long, deep rumble seemed to confirm Kanoska's prediction. It'd be too dark in the jailhouse if not for that single lamp flickering on the sheriff's desk. "It's better than trying to get out through that little window up there."

There was enough light when Gil turned his head, I

noticed his brown hair was longer than I'd ever seen it, but not long enough to cover the fact that the top half of his left ear was gone. It was a fairly fresh wound, and blood crusted the clean cut. "What happened to your ear?"

"Part of it got cut off when the sheriff here arrested me."

Kanoska shrugged at my frown. "It wasn't my doing. He scuffled with us when we was placing him under arrest, and Cornsilk thought we were losing the fight. You know how it is, carrying that big pigsticker like the one you got there, Cap. Some people lean more toward edged weapons, and he carved off a piece of Gil's ear to get his attention."

"He cut it off and wouldn't go back to get it. I'd hoped there was someone who could sew it back on, so I wouldn't look lopsided every time I got a haircut."

The sheriff flicked a finger toward Gil. "You're lucky he didn't cut your throat for biting him the way you did. It wasn't till your ear hit the ground that I knew you were quit fighting." He turned to me. "That boy was latched on like a snapping turtle and I reckon he'd still have his teeth buried in Cornsilk's chest until it thundered, if my deputy hadn't drawed his knife and cut off that ear."

"It was just a fight. He didn't have no call to drag out a butcher knife and go to work on my ear. Besides, he bit me first." He pulled up his left sleeve to show me a half-moon bruise.

"Speaking of ears." Gracie pulled her black hair back. "That Cornsilk bit my ear too when I was trying to get away, look. Damned Karankawas."

It was bruised at the lobe.

"That's how Indians settle rank ponies when they want to break 'em." Kanoska shrugged and dug around on his cluttered desk until he found a tin of mustache wax, which he dabbed out and worked into the ends of his handlebars, which had started to fray in the dampness. "He just forgot he was rassslin' a little ol' gal, and besides, he was still all worked up about Gil chewing on *him*. Takes Cornsilk a while to get over being mad, and you shouldn't have been fighting with him, anyhow."

"Kronks've been known to eat a feller or two, when they're hungry." Gracie punctuated her comment with a nod.

Gil leaned into the bars. "Do I get my gun back when we leave?"

"You'll be in shackles, so no." The sheriff placed a war bag on his desk and loaded in cartridges and shotgun shells. "I'll pay you a day's wage for every one we're out, Cap. How 'bout that?"

I didn't want the job, but I couldn't leave Gil to be strung up in Blackwater, or cut up on the road south, if Kanoska tried to take him alone. Outside, Cornsilk caught my attention when he appeared at the hitching post and I watched him tie my mare with a quick release knot. Instead of coming inside, he glanced over his shoulder back the way he came and limped on down the street to disappear in the rain.

"Sheriff, I believe you just lost your deputy."

"That's what I figured when I saw this badge lying here." Brow furrowed, Kanoska joined me at the window. "He's Keetoowah, not Karankawa. Their tribe was already moving away from y'all before white people really got here and messed things up. I guess he decided he's had enough, and I don't blame him, but now I gotta go out and find me a new deputy."

He sighed. "And, Gracie, you better get our people straight when you're talking to white folks. All that inaccurate talk's what got a lot of us killed through the years when they can't tell one of us from another'n."

Gracie stuck her tongue out at him and I had to turn and stifle a laugh.

Gil pointed at me. "I thought *Cap* was your new hand."

"He is, and he's taking you on to Texas now by his own

self while I stay here and train a new man. Sorry, Cap, but that's all I can do. I can't leave this town with no law while I'm gone. You'll still get your money, though. Give me the name of a bank in Texas and send word on how many days it takes you to get where you're going. I'll wire the money then."

I studied the gang of blank-faced men staring at the jail-house from under the cover over the boardwalk across the street. Thunder rumbled again, and I decided getting gone from that dangerous whiskey town was the best thing for both Gil *and* me.

CHAPTER 5

The Gluck brothers gathered around a scarred wooden table in the Honey Hole, taking turns filling their shot glasses from the half-empty bottle of Thistle Dew they bought from the owner, who kept his whores away from the three who'd caused trouble in there before.

The Honey Hole served a lot of liquor, in addition to other things, but it came from a bootlegger who slipped across from Kansas every now and then with a load of commercial whiskey. Most of what others sold in town was cooked up in the woods not far away and poured into labeled bottles kept hidden under floors, chicken houses, or even buried in a corral or under a tree.

The room was dark from the storm and the owner was busy lighting oil lamps and candles. Itchy bumped the shaky table with one boot and the bottle jumped. Everyone grabbed their glasses as the container rocked for a moment and then steadied. He adjusted his seat and accidentally kicked the leg again, shaking the plank table a second time.

Cloyce punched him in the shoulder hard enough to make his brother wince. "You hit this table again and spill that whiskey, I'll whip your ass until you can't walk. That's the real stuff, you idiot."

Customers in the whiskey joint waiting their turn with

the girls, who were occupied upstairs, listened without comment. Some of them were part of the rabble in the street calling for the prisoner, but none of them wanted to engage the Glucks right then. Their family was known for quick violence, especially when they were drinking whiskey, and none of them had ever been brought to trial for several mysterious killings they seemed to be involved in, nor were they even picked up by the law.

Though he carried two oiled revolvers butt-forward, and had used them half-a-dozen times on those who weren't kinfolk, Itchy considered the idea of shooting his brother to be rude behavior. Instead, he scowled and leaned back. "You're just mad because that feller backed us all down."

"He killed them boys fast as swatting flies." Cheese rubbed the side of his nose, releasing more of the sour milk smell that led to his nickname. "I never figured on somebody like that coming out of nowhere."

"Neither did Black Jim." Cloyce threw back the shot of whiskey in his hand and reached for the bottle and another refill. "I never saw anybody shoot so fast without talking first. I never thought anybody could kill that big bastard, not so quick, anyway. It was them eyes of his that froze Black Jim. Never saw eyes like that, except in a nightmare."

"That's a lot of nevers." Itchy started to scratch the back of his neck from habit, but caught himself.

"It was a lot of killin' and strangeness." Cloyce intended to press Sheriff Kanoska with threats and the gathering mob until he folded in fear of his life and let the brothers have the man who killed their young stepbrother.

He was glad the old man was dead, because he'd have already taken a horse whip to his three surviving sons for not immediately hanging the man who killed a family member, even though he was a woods colt.

Chet Gluck always lived by a "vengeance is mine" code, at the same time he thought everyone was against him. It

served them well until the day he got crossways with Bill
Moon, who cut his throat with a bowie knife in the middle
of Chet's own pea patch over a shoat that was rooting up
the man's crop.

"What're we gonna do?" Itchy threw back his drink and
reached for the bottle, keeping an eye on the others, who
tended to be stingy with whiskey and always wanted to
fight when the level in the bottle got low and they felt
shorted.

They fought over the smallest things. Not a one of them
was without a scar inflicted by one or both of the others.
Cheese had a slightly cloudy left eye, which was the result of
a thrown rock when they were fighting over the last piece
of bacon on the table one drizzly and cold winter morning
when they were teenagers.

Cloyce took out the makings and rolled a cigarette in
silence. Snapping a lucifer alight with one split thumbnail,
he lit it and pinched the match out with two fingers. He
dropped it on the floor. Smoke rose and seemed to settle
into the chasm cut into the bridge of his nose by a raging
Comanche's war ax ten years earlier. "That German ain't
gonna get away with killing Possum."

"What're we gonna do?"

Cloyce drew deep on the cigarette. "We're gonna wait
right now."

"But he's sitting in jail, breathing air and eating crackers,
while Possum's in his grave."

"You boys remember how we was taught to hunt deer?"

"Which way, driving them or waiting?" Cheese tossed
his drink back and refilled the glass. Itchy quickly reached
for the bottle and filled his own, then Cloyce's, just in case
he was feeling slighted.

"Waiting. I recall the time he took us all and scattered us
along that little meadow down on Panther Creek."

"He set us about every fifty yards." Cheese watched one

of the girls follow a customer downstairs and escort him to the door. He left and she immediately took the hand of a young cowboy and they headed right back up to the second floor. The others waiting their turn at the bar shifted down to mark their place in line.

"Yep, and then he told us to wait, and I did." Cloyce let out a lungful of smoke through his nose. "Y'all wiggled around like screw worms in hot ashes for the better part of the morning and he found all three of you sitting under a tree, talking like you had good sense."

"Possum cried when Daddy took off his belt. I 'member. He beat the hell out of us, likely from him crying like a little tiny baby."

"You bet he did, but I stayed right where he put me and that big old doe stepped out half an hour later and I shot her where she stood. I got the backstrap and all y'all got was some stew you had to eat standing up."

"It was good stew, though. Had taters in it for once. I remember that." Itchy sipped at his whiskey. "What does all this have to do with Possum?"

"We're going hunting, but not for no deer. Itchy, you go back somewhere close to the jail and sit there and wait. Keep an eye on it, and on Kanoska and Cornsilk. Let me know what they're doing, and if they take a notion to move the German. One of us'll spell you after a while, and we're gonna watch and wait until we get a shot at that doe."

CHAPTER 6

The storm went around us, but the cloudy sky hung low and heavy, promising more rain. It was enough to pull cool air out of the north, which was more breathable. Dusk came early and the dispirited mob outside finally melted away. Sheriff Kanoska closed the wooden shutters over the window and dropped a heavy bar into place.

"I had these built two years ago after some yahoo threw a rock through the window at me. All of a sudden, I realized how easy it'd be for anyone to just look inside after dark and know what was going on and maybe draw a bead."

I didn't bother to tell him he'd been pacing back and forth in front of the windows since we got inside, backlit by the coal oil lamp on his desk. Gil and I were playing checkers through the bars, and he'd won four games already.

"You were thinking, that's for sure. Now we don't have to worry about anybody taking a shot through the window." The lamp was too far away from the board to see good and we were about to quit, anyway. I slid my chair back, walked across to a water bucket sitting on a washstand, and drank long and deep from the dipper.

Gracie was sitting on her folded quilt, watching and being quiet for once.

A light slap on the roof was followed by another, and a minute later, rain roared on the cedar shakes again. The sheriff picked up his ring of keys lying on his desk. "That's your signal."

I dreaded the thought of swinging into a wet saddle and riding away in the middle of a driving storm. A nice dry room in a hotel or boardinghouse sounded better, but I was trapped in a situation with no control over what might happen.

Gil picked up his hat lying on the bunk. "I'm ready."

"Not so fast." Kanoska held up a pair of shackles. "Turn around and back up to the bars."

"Aw, hell, Kano. I'll be good."

"You're damn right you will. You're not getting out of there unless your hands are shackled. I had enough fighting with you to last me a long time. Put 'em together."

Sighing, Gil turned his back to us and laced his fingers. The sheriff reached through the bars and slipped the shackles over my old friend's wrists. They were the kind that looked like horseshoes with an iron bar across the opening.

Locking them into place, he handed me the key. "Keep this in your pocket. If you lose it, you'll have to find a blacksmith to cut 'em off."

Gil spun around. "Then don't you lose them!"

I tucked it deep into my left front pocket. "I won't."

"You might want to get that knife out of his sock before y'all leave." Gracie gave Gil a sweet smile.

"You little shit!" Gil glared at her through the bars between their cells.

"You have a knife?" Sheriff Kanoska looked as if he'd swallowed a dose of castor oil.

Gil deflated.

"It's in his right sock. I saw it when he was laying on the bed." Her brow knitted as she watched Gil squirm. "You should have give me that piece of cheese I asked for you to share instead of wolfing it down just so's I couldn't have it."

Kanoska snapped his fingers to get Gil's attention. "Stay with your back to me and stick that leg through the bars."

Knowing he was defeated, Gil did as he was told. Kanoska knelt and pushed his pant leg up. Sure enough, there was a slim little dagger in his dingy, stretched-out sock, though I wondered how it could stay there. Kanoska pitched it onto the desk. "Other'n."

"There ain't nothing there."

"Do it, anyway."

Gil shifted position and stuck the other foot through. The sheriff raised that pant leg, too, and found an oval strap of wide iron in the other sock, which I recognized what some people called brass knuckles.

"Looks like Cornsilk wasn't too good at his job." I watched Gil steady himself against the cell door as Kanoska held on to his leg. "You better check his drawers. He might have a cannon or something hid in there."

The sheriff kept hold of that leg and reached up and grabbed Gil's bollocks. His shoulders tensed, then settled lower than before in defeat. "Easy there, Kano."

Finding no other weapons, Kanoska unlocked the cell and stepped back. "Okay, Deputy Whitlatch. He's all yours."

"I ain't no deputy, but I'll get him back to Texas." It suddenly occurred to me I had no idea which town had the warrant out for him. "Where'm I taking him?"

"Fredericksburg. You can drop him off with the Rangers in Austin, if you want to."

"That's only two days shorter and I'm going to Kerrville, anyway."

"I couldn't say. Never been to Texas, but I hear there's a post in a little burg called Duck Creek, if you want to stop there and hand him over and consider your duties discharged, that's all right with me."

"Where's that?"

"Northeast of someplace called Dallas, I hear."

"Not much difference there, neither."

"Well, you can do it and be on your way." Kanoska shrugged. "Up to you."

It wasn't like I wasn't going there already, but the idea of having a prisoner all the way, and he being a friend I'd grown up with, didn't set well. I wanted to argue some more, but it was useless. The rain picked up and pounded on the roof. Water splashed in the street and I knew it'd be a quagmire in an hour or so.

"We'd best get going. What's he gonna ride?"

"His horse is in a pen around back."

"All right, I'll mount up and ride around."

"Hit the door a couple of times when you get there and I'll open up and let him out." There was a bolted back door beside the cell, blocked by a thick two-by-six board.

I pulled an oiled slicker from one side of my saddlebags and put it on.

Gil watched me set my hat. "Hey, what'm I gonna use to keep the rain off?"

I raised an eyebrow at Kanoska, who shrugged. "He didn't have anything but what was on his shoulders when we brought him in."

"He at least have a saddle?"

"It's on the top rail of that pen."

"Then I'm gonna have to saddle up for him."

"We couldn't let that poor old horse stand around all day under a saddle. Wouldn't be right."

Gil nodded. "There's a bag hanging on the horn, but there's not much more'n some clothes and a knife. Hey, I had a pistol, too."

"That's right." Sheriff Kanoska opened his desk drawer

and took out an old .36-caliber cap and ball revolver. He handed it to me and I saw five loads were sealed with what looked like beeswax, leaving the hammer on an empty chamber. I stuck it into my belt opposite my revolver. "Gil, you at least have a blanket out here, right?"

"Yeah, I reckon it's soaked by now, though."

"Probably. Wrap it over your shoulders and it'll still turn water." Sheriff Kanoska stuck out his hand to me. "I'll keep up appearances that he's still in there as long as I can. It might be a day or two before they find out he's gone, and with this rain, that'll give you a good head start. Thanks for your help."

We shook and I threw the saddlebags over my left shoulder. I picked up the Spencer and held the shotgun with the muzzle pointed at the roof. It'd be quick to drop it down to go to work if there was trouble outside.

Kanoska opened the nearest shutter a crack and peered outside. Lightning crackled and lit the town and the trees farther away. Thunder rolled over the jail, rattling the window glass. "Street's clear, but I see Itchy Gluck over there, across yonder under that store's overhang. He'll see you leave, but there's nothing we can do about it."

"I won't be leaving with Gil, so he'll think I just cleared out and run. I can live with that." I opened the door and stepped out, keeping an eye out across the street. Lightning flickered again and I saw the man leaning back against the wall and out of the rain.

Pulling the reins loose from the hitching rack, I turned the mare so she was between me and Gluck and threw the saddlebags up behind the saddle, sliding it underneath the back housing enough to hold until I could take the time to tie it on with the strings. The gold coins inside jingled soft and heavy, and I wondered what I was thinking, escorting a prisoner while carrying so much money.

Rain thundered on my hat. Driving rain like that drenches a feller in a minute or two. My pants were soaked below the hem of the slicker that came down to the tops of my boots. I knew Gil would be miserable before we got out of town, protected by nothing more than his hat and a wool blanket.

Itchy Gluck hadn't moved when I mounted and reined away from the jail, shotgun resting horizontal to the seat rise just behind the horn. I expected to put it into the boot once we were out of town and away from trouble, but right then it would just have to get wet, for I have yet to find a way to keep long weapons dry in a rain. Rain funneled off my hat front and back as I resisted the urge to turn and look back at that feller I knew was watching me ride away.

I kneed the mare into a steady walk until I was out of sight of the hardware store, then turned between two buildings and circled around behind the jail. Sure enough, there was a wet saddle hanging over the top rail and a weary-looking roan standing with his head low and sad. He almost looked relieved as I saddled him and led both horses over to the back door.

Two knuckle raps on the door, and it opened and yellow light flowed out into the rain. Sheriff Kanoska stuck his head out and looked around before he pushed Gil outside. I kept an eye out as the sheriff slapped a hat on Gil's head and, along with several grunts and muffled curses, helped him up into his saddle.

Gil adjusted himself in the seat after his feet found the stirrups. "This is dumb, Kano. Let me loose so I can at least run if folks start after us."

"Letting you loose is the last thing I want to do." He handed me the reins when I was back in the saddle myself. "Good luck, Cap." He tucked a deputy's badge into my shirt pocket. It hung solid beside the medicine bag resting on my chest. "Just in case."

He went inside without another look. I led Gil's horse in the opposite direction Gluck saw me leave. One more twist for them to work out, if they took a notion to follow.

CHAPTER 7

Bill Johns and Ed Gentry watched the rain from inside an abandoned log cabin, not far from Yellow Horse in the Oklahoma Territory. The roof leaked, but it was drier than squatting under a leaky old shebang in the woods.

They came across the leaning building not long after the rains started. Kicking out a surly coon and several mice didn't take long. Two broken chairs, a rough plank table, and two rope beds were more than they had hoped for. There was even kindling and several dry pieces of split wood stacked beside the fireplace by previous travelers.

Johns pulled a small bone comb from his vest pocket and carefully drew it through the thin blond mustache he often told Gentry that he hoped to cultivate into something more impressive. "We'd already have him on the ground if it wasn't for this rain."

"I doubt it." Gentry oiled his revolver by the light of a candle. The pistol and his Henry rifle took a pretty good soaking before they found the cabin. He'd built a fire in the mud and log fireplace that was surprisingly intact enough to draw off most of the moisture from the single-room structure that saw its better days three decades earlier.

"What makes you say that?"

"Because one man alone rides faster, and we didn't get

on the road until two days after he's gone." Gentry squeezed a tiny bit of oil onto a ragged piece of gingham cloth and carefully capped the little can. Using a trimmed stick, he ran the swab down the barrel. He once had a gun misfire due to poor maintenance and vowed it would never happen again. "He might hole up in this rain, and that's what I'm counting on."

"You act as if you're in charge, by thunder. *You're* counting on, and all that." With any other man, the way Johns said that would have pissed Gentry off, but he gave his younger partner much more leeway than anyone he'd ever known. He often wondered why he tolerated such behavior in a vain young man, but could never put his finger on it. He simply liked Bill's company, and the fact that he was a good man to ride the trail with.

"I just voiced my opinion is all."

Johns stared into the fire without answering.

"Well, I guess it don't matter none. I hope we catch up to him pretty quick. I'm looking forward to getting my hands on that money." Using the oily rag, he ran it over the barrel and cylinder, taking care not to get any on the wooden grip.

"Me too. How much you think he's carrying?"

"I have no idea. Penn never said, but a big herd of horses ought to come to a couple of thousand dollars, at least."

Johns rubbed the back of his neck. "I've never seen that much money in one place."

"It's enough to start our own ranch. I've been thinking about going out west to raise cows. You know I have some experience with cattle."

Johns barked a laugh. "Did you see the look on that damned lawyer's face when he opened that door?"

Gentry chuckled. "I bet that son of a bitch didn't expect to see us at his house."

"He was probably still wearing that expression when he shook hands with the Devil."

Springfield attorney Holland Penn might have been a good businessman, and an exceptional double-crosser, but he had made a serious mistake when he threatened Bill Johns's mama. He was a dead man the moment those words had come out of his mouth back in that hot Springfield office. Nobody messed with Johns's family, and especially not his mama.

That afternoon, they left Penn's office and the two outlaws loafed in a loud saloon across the busy street, until Penn left at the end of the day. They followed him on foot all the way to his house, and then waited outside until dark. The attorney lived alone, having outlasted two wives, and the only other person in the house was the elderly former slave, who cooked and cleaned for him.

They had no truck with the bent old woman, so the two waited until she left for the evening. His grandiose house was well landscaped, and they waited in the darkness beside a tall bridal lace bush overhanging the brick street. Through a window, they saw Penn go into his office and pour a glass of bourbon. They watched as he lit a cigar and settled in for the night beside the fireplace.

Johns and Gentry climbed the steps to his front porch and rapped on the door.

An unlit cigar clamped in his teeth, and the glass of whiskey in one hand, the attorney opened the door and glared. He plucked out the smoke. "What'n hell y'all want! How do you know where I live?"

"Lived," Johns said, and stuck the muzzle of a derringer in the attorney's chest.

Wide-eyed, with the cigar falling from his mouth, Penn backed up enough for the two of them to enter his foyer.

Gentry closed the door at the same instant Johns pulled the trigger. The soft pop, muffled by Penn's thick wool suit vest, was barely loud enough to be heard.

Johns pushed the barrel even harder against the falling man's chest and fired again. The glass of whiskey that shattered on the polished oak floor was much louder. "Wouldn't have shot a second time, but damn that was quiet."

"It was." Gentry glanced down at the man drowning in his own blood and a pool of bourbon, and turned around to close the little drapes on the front door.

"You shouldn't have threatened my mama." By the time Johns tucked the derringer back into his pocket, Gentry was closing the drapes in the living room. The last thing Penn saw before his eyes clouded was Johns straddling his body and plucking the gold watch from his vest pocket.

They spent the next hour, rifling the office, and going through every drawer they could find. Johns lit a piece of kindling from the small fire burning in the fireplace and touched it to the drapes before they left, hoping the evidence of their crime would burn to a cinder. The street was quiet and dark when they left two hundred dollars richer, but there was still one thing to do:

Get that money from Cap Whitlatch while he was in the territories, and they were hard on the trail.

Gentry reloaded his pistol not far from Blackwater as rain drummed on the roof and lightning lit the surrounding woods; he returned it to his holster. The rain increased in intensity. "You want me to clean that derringer of yours?"

"Naw, only shot it twice." Johns drew it from his pocket. "Ain't this some punkin? Never thought a bitty gun could kill a man so fast."

"It'll do the job when you put it up against someone's heart."

"Ain't that a fact." Johns frowned. "Damn. I forgot to reload it."

Breaking it open by pushing the thumb release and pushing down on the barrel assembly, he extracted the two spent shells with his short fingernails and patted his pockets for a full minute in search of more ammunition. He found a cigar butt first, lit it with a splinter from the firewood stacked beside the crumbling hearth, and puffed it to life. Exhaling a cloud of smoke, he located two rounds in his vest pocket. The brass was turning green, but damn near half of his shells were that color, anyway.

CHAPTER 8

"You oughta let me out of here." Gracie's voice was accusatory.

Coming back inside after seeing Cap Whitlatch and his prisoner off, Sheriff Kanoska shook water off his hat and onto the plank floor. He cut his eyes at the girl. "I could, but where you gonna go? It's raining cats and dogs out there."

"I can't say, but at least let me out of this damned cell."

"Stay in there. I'm afraid of you."

She barked a laugh. "You should be. Cornsilk was right. Maybe I *am* a witch. My grandmother was a witch and she put spells on people who annoyed her."

"You must have been one of them who irritated her. She made you a mean little snake in a girl's body."

"You might be right about that, too." Gracie had to think on that one. "I've had a pretty hard time since my mama died. But you still oughta let me out. I ain't no outlaw, and stealing a couple of eggs from a mean old woman who keeps her mouth pursed up as tight as a dog's butt ain't enough of a crime to put somebody in jail. If it was, I reckon you'd have to arrest half of the people in this county—and most of your own kinfolk."

"Shut up, Gracie. I'm tired and I'd like to go to sleep." Kanoska wanted nothing more than to lie down in the empty cell and close his eyes while rain beat on the roof. "It's been a hard day. If I let you out here with me, you might accuse me of trying to have my way with you. It ain't proper for a grown man to be alone with a female of any age. Then I'd be the one to hang."

"I could say that, anyway. Who knows whether you kept me in here alone, or unlocked that cell door and came in to use this bunk for your dirty deeds? I bet you've done it before with some old hide you picked up for no reason."

The sheriff bristled at the accusation. "There ain't never been no woman in that cell, and you don't have any call to say such a thing. I swear, the mouth on you, gal."

"You have to let me go sometime. You can't keep me here forever."

Kanoska knew that for the truth; ever since Whitlatch and Vanderburg left, he'd been pondering that problem without coming up with a satisfactory solution. "It's already seemed like forever."

They listened to the rain beat on the roof for a while before she spoke up again. "Well, we have a problem, anyway."

"What's that?"

"I need to pee."

"Good gosh." He refused to look at her. "Can't you say it any better'n that? Use the chamber pot under the bunk to go outdoors. That sounds better. Say 'I need to go outdoors,' or 'I need to relieve myself,' or something that isn't rude to my ears."

"I'm not squatting over a pot while you're in here watching and listening."

"I'll turn my back."

"You'll still hear. It's different with girls, and it don't sound like rain or splashing, it's more of a hissing—"

"Hush that kind of talk, gal! Said I'll turn my back, and I'll put my fingers in my ears if that suits you."

Kanoska realized he'd unconsciously squeezed into the farthest corner from her cell. She grinned at him, and he felt as if she could see inside his head at those thoughts no man should consider.

"Just unlock the door and I'll run to the outhouse and be back in less than a minute." She paused to let that sink in. "And besides, I'll be doing you a favor. You won't have to empty out a smelly chamber pot later."

The sheriff's ear reddened even more than when she first started in. The only thing he knew to do was let her out so he could get some peace. Maybe she'd come back and go to sleep. "Fine, then." He picked up the keys from the desk and unlocked the cell, watching her as close as a rattlesnake. "You can use my hat if you want. But hurry up and get back."

"Use your hat for what?"

He flushed even more. "Quit it! You know what I mean. Use that hat to keep the rain off your head so you won't catch your death of cold."

Gracie grinned. "I will, sure 'nough." She plucked his dripping black Stetson off the rack and pointed to an old canvas coat hanging on a nail beside the back door. "Can I wear that to keep from getting soaked?"

"That ain't much more'n rags you're wearing. You ought not worry about getting them old duckins wet, unless you're afraid the rain'll wash off some of the dirt."

She slipped her arms through the coat's stiff sleeves as her bare feet padded across the boards to the door. "My mama gave me these duckins and it's all I got left of her, so don't be making fun of it. Oh, by the way, Cornsilk missed the knife under *my* clothes, too." She opened the door and flashed him a grin. "Don't need to pee, anyway. Bye!"

Gracie disappeared into the darkness like a spirit. He started after her and stopped. The cost of a worn-out old hat and a ratty coat Cornsilk found out behind the livery last winter was a small price to pay for getting rid of such an annoying child.

He opened the back door and emptied the buckets of rainwater and put them back under the leaks. Kanoska put wooden bars across both the front and back doors, and went into Gracie's cell. He folded the patchwork blanket into something similar to a pallet and lay down on the bunk for a little nap. He felt the feather pillow on that bunk was also more comfortable under his neck, and the ticking wasn't as stained. That's why he'd put Gracie in there. It had been a long, trying day and he needed his rest.

At least she hadn't done her business in the chamber pot underneath the bunk like that German did in his cell. Kanoska sighed and smoothed his mustache. With Cornsilk gone, he'd have to empty it himself.

He sure needed a new deputy.

CHAPTER 9

Gil and I were both so tired by dawn, it was all we could do to stay upright in the saddle. Riding had to be harder with his hands shackled behind him, and it takes a natural horseman's balance to ride that way for as long as he did. I could have unlocked them and let him have both hands in front to hold the horn at least, but there was no way I was gonna let such a good horseman have that much control over his riding. As it was, I couldn't put it past him to guide his mount with both knees and spur off into the night. Riding away would be an easy thing for him. I had his horse on a long lead rope wrapped around my saddle horn, just in case.

Even though he was my friend, I hadn't seen Gil in a few years and wasn't sure which way he'd turned in that time. We once cowboyed together and I watched him buck, rope, tie, and cut calves out of a herd with little or no effort.

The girls all wanted to partner up with him at barn dances, and he had his choice to go with any who took his fancy. He was a gentleman with the farm and ranch girls, as far as I knew, but when it came to the gals working the sally joints, or the whores over in Austin or San Antonio, that was a different thing. Back then, he had a sense of what the girls wanted, while I was mostly someone to hold up the wall by myself.

That was fine by me. Unlike Gil, I had only one girl I was interested in, and that was Angie Hamilton, who lived on a ranch out west of Kerrville. Her old daddy was a tough son of a bitch who wasn't afraid of anything, not even Comanches, though he walked soft around his wife and Angie.

She'd give me the eye at those dances, and we cut a rug together from time to time, but I was too busy raising horses to think of much else. Even then, Gil steered clear of her, and I suspected it was on my account.

The rain finally stopped as the eastern sky glowed yellow and orange, and by full daylight, nothing fell besides the drops on the leaves. The air was fragrant with fresh-washed leaves, both on and off the trees. A redbird flickered from one cedar to the next, and our passage kicked up a rabbit that shot away into the underbrush.

I always like soft mornings like that. Though the woods weren't silent, and they never are because of the wind, birds, and animals, it was quiet enough to lull us to sleep and my eyes grew heavy with the rhythmic thuds of our horses' hooves on the saturated ground.

Gil's voice came from behind me and I jerked upright. "How'd you know which way we were going all night in the dark and rain? I been turned around since we left town, 'cause I was never good at riding in the dark. I'd-a got lost and took us to the ocean, if our roles were reversed."

I had to shake the cobwebs out of my mind before I could answer. "I'd use the stars if it'd been clear, but I knew which way we were going when we left town, and then I caught this trail, so I figured it was the direction we wanted to go. It didn't make much difference at the time. I just wanted to get shed of anybody following us."

"I bet them Glucks are on us by now."

"I doubt they know you're out yet. One of 'em saw me leave, and they probably think I'm long gone and you're still in the cell. Besides that, they don't have any idea which way I went. The rain surely washed out our tracks."

"They're part Cherokee. One of 'em might be a tracker. I wouldn't put it past one of 'em to stand on the back of a horse to peek in that little cell window to see if I was there. If one did, then they'd know I was gone."

"You might be getting mixed up. I believe that stepbrother, Possum, was part Indian, but I think *their* mama's white."

"What difference does it make?"

"Well, you brought it up. Most white folks don't track as good as Indians, unless they're mountain men, and they tend to stay back up in the hills." We rode in silence for a while. "So they think you killed their baby brother." It was more of a statement than a question.

"That's what they say. It wasn't me, though. And saying it that way makes it sound like Possum was ten or so. He was full growed and covered with hair, and that rascal knew his way around a deck of cards, and a bottle, too. He was alive and kicking when I left the dispensary."

"They didn't say you killed him there."

"Well, I don't know where he went to get himself killed after we left. Like I said, I wasn't there."

"You were out of money when you left the game?"

"Nope. That's what I told 'em to get out. I believe somebody was cheating, but it sure wasn't me . . . that time." He was quiet for nearly a minute. A hummingbird buzzed past his nose, startling him back into the conversation. "I have some money here in my boot."

His statement caught me by surprise. "Bet it's crowded in there."

"Cut a slot on the inside of this right one, low down on the shaft, near my ankle. There's a twenty-dollar gold piece in there. I didn't have a room that night, so I slept in the stable so I wouldn't have to use it, and that cheap son of a bitch who owns the livery still charged me two bits to sleep under my own horse. I paid him when I got to town, before the game, so's I wouldn't have to worry about losing everything I had. I've done that before.

"Then they cleaned me out in their rigged game and that's why I only had a nickel left in my pocket when that damned Cornsilk jumped on me in the stable while I was asleep. I thought this roan had stepped on me at first, but then I realized it was somebody trying to get a pigging string around my wrists, and I had to defend myself." He thought for a second. "I wish we were back in town. I'd buy us some breakfast."

The mention of food reminded me that I hadn't eaten in town, and that glass of whiskey I'd been looking forward to was still inside a bottle that belonged to someone else. I had a side of bacon and some flour in my bag. Flapjacks and coffee sure sounded good right then.

"Let's find us some water up here and we'll build a fire. I have two cups, so we can cook up some coffee."

"Hey, Cap."

"Huh?"

"How about you take these chains off. You know I won't run, and it'll be sight easier to ride with you. It'll be like old times, and when we get wherever you want, you can lock 'em back up."

"Nope."

"That ain't much of an answer. I thought we were having a discussion."

"You're talking, but it takes two to discuss any one subject, and I gave my word to Sheriff Kanoska that I'd take you back to Texas. I intend to do just that."

"I knew you'd be that way. You haven't changed a bit." He fell silent for a few minutes before trying another angle.

"Well, *riding* with you there is as good as being *took* to Texas. Take these shackles off and I'll tell everybody you took me."

"Nope. That's going together. I'm taking you back in those chains, like I promised."

"You're as hardheaded as you were when we were kids."

"Thanks."

"It's not a compliment. I never saw anything like you. Remember that night we stole those watermelons from Old Man Crawford when we were kids? Man, those were the best-tasting melons I ever put in my mouth."

"I'll allow you had the best thumping ear in the dark of anybody in the county."

"That's right, because they didn't cost us a penny, and the next day, you went to his house and confessed to the whole thing."

"I couldn't stand it. Those melons weren't ours, and they tasted like ashes to me."

"Those were the sweetest I ever ate. Stole melons are always the best. I think it's because we bust 'em open and eat the heart out there in the dark." He sighed. "If we came across a melon patch tonight, I'd thump us a good one for old times' sake and be as happy as a clam."

"You ain't never seen a clam in your life."

"Well, I've seen oysters down on the gulf, and I like to eat 'em, too. So I reckon I can be as happy as an oyster. How about that?"

"Well, getting back to that watermelon, it sure was ripe. My mama said the one I brought home was good, but I couldn't stand it."

"What'd Old Man Crawford say when you went back and fessed up to stealing it?"

"'Thanks.'"

"What?"

"He told me thanks for being honest, even though we

stole from him, and I worked his patch for a week to help him out."

I didn't tell Gil how Mr. Crawford paid me for working, because he was glad to finally find out who was snitching his melons. He thought it was me coming in at night and threatened to turn me in to the sheriff for the thefts. But I led him on, thinking it was just me, and never told him otherwise. It wasn't much of a crime, but I couldn't live with myself and never took anything else without paying for it.

"You didn't say it was me with you?"

"No. I didn't lie, but I didn't tell him the whole truth. Sometimes it's easier to give someone a little information and let them make their own decisions."

A covey of quail exploded only yards away and I watched them sail across an open patch before settling into the edge of the woods. Something big crashed away in the distance and I figured it was a bear, because deer are quiet for the most part.

The morning sun stretched long shadows whenever there was an open meadow or glade full of grass. It showed us we were going in the general direction I wanted, though I wasn't exactly sure where we were.

To cap it all off, I was tired of being damp, and wanted to get on some dry clothes. The bottoms of my britches were wet, and despite the slicker that covered me, neck to hands to below my knees, some water had seeped through my hat and down my neck, wetting my shirt.

Gil had to've been miserable, since there wasn't a dry thread on him. A wet trade blanket over his shoulders wasn't much use in turning water.

My stomach growled. "The problem is that I don't have enough grub to last both of us very long. We're gonna have to stop in the next town for supplies."

"How far do you think it is?"

"I don't have any idea. I rode up to Springfield, farther to the east, mostly following the Mountain Fork through the Winding Stairs. Went pretty close to Fort Smith. I've come back this way, a few ridges over, but never along *this* trail." I considered the route in my mind. "I believe we're gonna come out somewhere north of Gainesville, in Texas."

"Well, I'd like a can of peaches when we get to the next store. I sure would like some coffee, too. You have Arbuckles' Coffee, or beans?"

"Beans."

"That'll take a while to roast. I like Arbuckles' that's already ground."

I did, too, but the beans were cheaper, though I didn't have a grinder. I just roasted them in an iron skillet and crushed them up with a rock most times.

Redbirds and blue jays fluttered through the trees. We rode through a hatch of tiny insects hanging in a sunbeam above the trail. One flew up Gil's nose and he yakked and gagged for a minute before a sneezing fit took over.

I couldn't help but laugh and he joined in between sneezes, and for a moment, it felt like when we were kids, running the Texas hill country. The trail rounded a grove of the same kind of red cedars we have down there and we came up on a big old tree that blew over in the storm. It blocked our way, so we rode around it and we picked up a game trail leading to a winding gully cutting through hackberry trees and brambles.

Our horse's hooves landed soft on the wet ground. Had it been dry, the leaves and twigs underfoot would have popped and crackled, but the whole world was soaked and their hooves sounded spongy and easy.

Gil's horse stumbled and he swore. "Damned gophers."

Seconds later, I saw a break in the underbrush that led back onto our original path; at the same time, a sound came to me that I couldn't identify. I reined up.

"What's that?" Gil sat straight in his saddle, head cocked like a puppy hearing a new sound.

"It's a buzzing . . ." Before I could finish my thought, we were in the middle of a mess of mad yellowjackets. His horse hadn't stepped into a gopher hole, but a swarm of those stinging insects that made their nests in the ground.

They enveloped us like a cloud and the steeldust mare snorted and went sideways. Gil yelped and I caught sight of him from the corner of my eye. Half a dozen of the stinging insects had already latched onto his face. He ducked his head and tried to wipe them off on his shoulder. "Cap! Get us outta here!"

My mare crow-hopped and a yellowjacket stung my hand. Another hit my cheek, and half a dozen my face. Each sting began as a hot pinch, then fire ran through the skin and burned like Hell must. The only thing that saved me was the oiled slicker that covered me, neck to my boots. Gil wasn't as lucky, and the wet blanket over his shoulders slipped off and was lost, taking away a thick layer of protection.

Left fist full of saddle horn, I kept a tight grip on Gil's lead rope with the other. If his mount jerked loose, he'd run from the stinging insects until my old friend scraped off on a tree or low-hanging branch like mud from the sole of a boot.

"Hang on!"

Gil's voice cracked when the roan came down hard. "Oh, hell!"

Able to only grip with his knees, Gil leaned forward over the horn as the roan ducked his head to buck. He showed his horsemanship by staying on, but no one was that good for any length of time.

We were covered in dry, buzzing, stinging insects angry at being disturbed. Unlike bees, yellowjackets have the ability to get a good grip on clothes or skin, and sting over and over. Hot needles sent jolts of pain through my neck, hands, and face, but Gil got the worst of the initial attack.

The only thing to do was ignore the stings and get us out of there. My mare went sideways and bumped into his gelding and, instead of losing his mind from the yellowjackets, the roan simply followed us when I kicked the steeldust into a run, likely saving Gil from serious injury at the very least.

The mare had the bit in her teeth, and instead of fighting her and the roan, I let her run for a minute. That yanked all the bucking out of Gil's horse, and my old friend leaned forward to maintain his balance.

Most of the yellowjackets turned back after we took off, but those that had a good hold wouldn't quit. I slapped at the ones on my face and slowed the mare down as the trail narrowed into a grove of hardwoods. We busted into the open, but half a dozen were still buzzing around the mare's head. Once we were in the clear, they were still all over us, holding on and looking for bare skin to torture us some more.

I reined up and smacked them off Gil and his roan with my hat. He winced. "Good Goddlemighty. That hurts as bad as these damned yellowjackets!"

"You ain't a woofin'. These things take a whack to kill them." The nearby chuckle of water caught my attention. I had an idea that cold mud packed on our stings would help relieve the pain. "Think you'll live?"

"Some parts are numb."

"So is my nose."

"I'm kinda swimmy-headed, too."

My eyes were watering from the pain and I couldn't decide whether to cry or holler right out loud. "Too many stings are dangerous. I remember a boy died from being stung by a swarm of bees outside of Dripping Springs."

"Wouldn't surprise me none. My skin's on fire in two dozen places."

"I hear water ahead and there's a clearing, too. Let's stop."

Gil rubbed one cheek against his shoulder. "That's the smartest thing you've said since we left."

The mare slowed, though she was still tossing her head, and I figured the horses had as many or more stings as we did. We stepped through a hole in the woods made by another big oak that had fallen long enough ago for all the leaves to be off and came out into a clearing. It was a perfect place to camp, with enough grass for two dozen horses and shade in the evening, if we decided to stay that long.

Other folks thought so, too.

A barefoot woman in a torn and ragged dress lay on the dirt beside a smoky fire, and then, all of a sudden, there were six rough men rising to their feet and drawing guns. I pulled up and we were looking down the barrels of five revolvers, and one rifle in the hands of the meanest-looking Indian I'd ever seen.

CHAPTER 10

Bill Johns and Ed Gentry stepped down from their saddles and tied the horses to the bodark hitching post in front of the Blackwater office that housed the Lighthorse Police. The Indian Police and Lighthorse Police were often deputized by U.S. Marshals to pursue and arrest non-Indian citizens, when necessary.

More inclined to barge right into the office, Johns settled his gun belt and started up the steps.

"Hold on." Gentry remained where he was, studying the muddy street churned up by hooves, wagons, and feet. It looked like every other small town in the territories, full of Indians who thought they were free to do whatever they wanted.

He heard stories from his old man how the Cherokees once lived in cities back east, owned land and banks and real houses, wore suits and beaver hats, and thought themselves the equal of every white man in the country. "Let's ask around here before we get the Lighthorse involved."

"You afraid of him?" Johns hooked both thumbs into the pockets of his trousers.

"I'm not afraid of anything, with this pistol on my hip, but I like to keep a card back when I'm playing poker. We don't need them to know we're looking for anyone. I'd just as soon keep them out of it. Maybe we can find out what we need from some of the locals. That way, we can get in and out without dealing with the law."

"We have the letter and poster that lawyer gave you."

"We do, but we ought to keep that ace in the hole until we really need it."

"Fine, then." Johns shrugged. "Where to?"

"Man like the one we're following needs two things on the trail. Three, really."

"What's that?"

Gentry watched a wagon loaded with supplies pass by, its wheels cutting three-quarters of the way to the hub in the muddy street. The driver hollered and snapped the reins on the mules doing their best to fight the thick mud. It was followed by an Indian in pants and a linen shirt toting a half-filled gunnysack over his shoulder. "Whiskey, food, and women."

"If he's that kind of man who likes a little pop skull and company."

"That too."

They surveyed the line of wooden buildings and false fronts. The Plummer Kelly general store was across the street. Farther down was the Honey Hole, Fashion Livery, Hart's Medicinal Drinks, City Bakery, Bush's Shoe Shop, Welborn and Son saddle and harness, a dry goods and cigar store.

"I don't see a saloon one. The folks in this little burg seem to follow the law." Johns set his hat. "Where do you want to start?"

"I want to get the least amount of mud on my boots and pants." Though Gentry lived much of his life on the trail and punching cattle, he preferred to stay as clean as possible in his new profession. He pointed down the street. "Most of that's boardwalk. Let's get some smokes. I'd like a cigar after a good drink of whiskey."

He drew the Henry from its scabbard and then stepped onto the boardwalk. Two men standing near the cigar shop's door took one look at the chiseled, heavily armed strangers and moved away, stepping over a gap of several missing boards.

The hand-painted sign outside read W.B. HARRISON, FINE CIGARS AND TOBACCO. The door was open, admitting fresh air and anything else that wanted to walk or fly in, not excluding chickens.

A nervous, wormy little proprietor, one assumed was Harrison himself, waited on them, seeming to already wish they were gone. "May I help you, gentlemen?"

Johns pushed close over the wooden counter as the owner backed out of arm's reach. He pointed at cigars in one of several glass cases lining one side of the long, thin room. "Two of them smokes and some information."

The proprietor passed the cigars across as gently as possible, trying not to make contact with Johns's hand. "That'll be ten cents each." Obviously afraid of Johns, he addressed Gentry. "What kind of information are you looking for?"

"We're working for a lawyer who sent us to find a man named Cap Whitlatch." Instead of letting Gentry speak, Johns broke in. "His last remaining relative died recently and he has some money coming."

"How much?"

Gentry took one of the cigars and slipped it into his vest pocket. Johns was making this way more complicated than it needed to be. He needed to stop the conversation that might get too detailed and slip them up. "Didn't say. Just hired us to find him."

"Don't know the name." The owner stepped back, as if to put as much distance between himself and Johns. It didn't get him very far away, because there wasn't much room behind the counter, as it was. "What's he look like?"

"Around thirty. Rides a gray mare. Dimple on one side

of his face. Strange eyes. People say they've never seen eyes
like his."

"Don't ring a bell. Can I do anything else for y'all?
Matches? I can light those for you."

Gentry saw the fear in the man's face and knew they
weren't getting anything else. Johns had somehow intimi-
dated him to the point that he didn't want to talk. "Naw.
Come on, Bill."

Johns held the cigar man's gaze. "Keep trying to remember. I might be back in a little bit for another'n. Go ahead
and light this one."

The smaller man's face turned ashen at the thought.
"Haven't seen anybody else. Most of my customers are
local." He used a wooden pick to punch a hole in one end
of the cigar before picking up a coal oil lamp. He held it out
and Johns leaned in.

The heat at the top of the glass chimney lit Johns's cigar
and he puffed it to life. "Thanks."

Back on the street, Ed Gentry shook his head when
Johns sauntered out as if he owned the whole world.
"Why'd you want to go and scare that little man for?"

"Because it was easy." Johns barked a laugh and smoothed
his mustache, an action that was by then completely uncon-
scious, as well as unnecessary, and starting to irritate Gentry.
"Where to now?"

"Any one of these places where we can get a bite to eat
and a drink."

"How can they sell whiskey in the territories? The marshals run through here pretty regular."

"Looks like they sell *medicines* you don't see anywhere
else. These'll stay open until Judge Parker sends in the
marshals and they'll shut it all down, and from the way
they're open free and easy, it won't be long. Besides that, I
don't know nothing about these territories other than it's
best to get through here as fast as we can. You might think

we're tough, but there's some old boys who kill for a living here."

"So do we, sometimes."

"Not the same way." Another team of mules pulling a wagon splashed by, sprinkling their pants with fat droplets of mud. Gentry frowned at his soiled britches. They were standing beside a barbershop. He rubbed the week's stubble on his cheeks. "I'm gonna get me a shave."

"We don't have that kind of time."

"Sure we do." Gentry flicked the latch on the door and they stepped inside.

The barber with hair that stood up every which way was reading a Bible under a sign that offered shaves and dentistry. He marked his place with a piece of faded red ribbon and stood. "Which'll it be?"

Johns hesitated. "Which'll what be?"

"You need a haircut, or a tooth pulled. Your face don't look swelled, so I reckon you ain't here about your teeth."

"I don't have any problems with my teeth." Johns tapped one for emphasis.

The barber flashed a smile and displayed several missing pearlies of his own. "A haircut it is. Which one of you wants to go first?"

Before Johns could answer, Gentry slapped his hat on a hook above two wooden chairs and took a seat in front of the barber. "I'll have a shave, too."

With an expert flip of the wrist, the barber settled a cape around Gentry's neck. "You can have a seat there. I'll be with you directly. Can I have my girl draw a bath for either of you?"

"Don't have time." Johns dropped into one of the chairs. "You ever hear of a feller by the name of Cap Whitlatch? Came through here within the last couple of days."

"Nossir. He might have been a customer, but nobody ever offers up a name."

"He has funny eyes. You'd know them if you ever saw 'em."

"Nope. Have a feller with a cloudy eye who lives around here. Name's Gluck. He has brothers, but none of 'em take to barberin'."

"That ain't him." Obviously irritated, Johns pulled at his little mustache and watched the barber work on his partner.

Preferring to stay quiet, Gentry closed his eyes and tried to enjoy the process, while the barber talked about the Glucks to excess. Half an hour later, he flipped off the cape with a grand sweep of his arms. "Next patient, uh, customer. I'll clean that upper lip for you in no time, sir."

"He's not in the market for a shave today." Before Johns could work up a mad and reply, Gentry paid the man and opened the door for his partner. "Come on and let's get a drink."

"Sounds like a good idea to me. I've heard all I can take about them damned Glucks." Johns glared at the barber as they left. "And nobody touches this mustache but me."

Gentry chuckled to himself, rubbing his smooth chin as they walked down the street. "I swear. I think you're aiming to make everybody in town mad, or afraid of you."

"Whichever it is, I'll deal with it."

They came to the Applejack Dispensary and Meals. Gentry stopped in front, looking inside before he went in.

A fly lit on Johns's ear and he waved it off. "I believe they have beer in here. Smells like it, anyway. I could have been in here having a good time while you got all prettied up. By the way, you smell like roses, with that water he sprinkled on you."

Gentry ignored him and led the way. They stepped inside and walked up to a long counter. The man behind, with hair parted in the middle, met them at the end. "Gentlemen. Food's thirty-five cents each, a nickel extra and you can have a glass of choc beer."

Reavis Z. Wortham

Gentry took over before Johns could alienate the man. "That sounds fine to me. Set 'em up."

Two glasses of cloudy beer appeared before them. Gentry nodded toward a table nearby. "They drinking whiskey?"

Half-a-dozen men were playing cards. One, a mean-looking individual with pistols on each hip, which was holstered for a cross draw, was paying more attention to the newcomers than the game.

"They're drinking some home brew from down on the Salt Fork." The counterman watched the card players a little longer than necessary. "It's good, though the color's not from aging. That feller who cooks it down there uses tobacco to brown it up some."

"Never mind." Gentry sipped his beer.

The counterman leaned forward. "You look like men of distinguished tastes. There's real whiskey down at the Honey Hole, if you've a mind."

"Honey Hole?" Gentry raised an eyebrow.

"Whorehouse, but a clean one. Most of the girls are Indians, if your tastes run that way, but there's a couple of white girls who ain't bad. I'd stay away from Molly. She's wormy."

Johns turned cold eyes on him. "And you get a cut of everyone who goes down there and says you sent them."

"You bet." The counterman was tough and he didn't bat an eye at Johns's attempt to cow him into providing information. He straightened, eyes suddenly glassy. "I intend to make money while this town's in business, and I don't figure it'll be that long. There was a U.S. Marshal through here last week, looking for somebody. I figured he'll be back with some other marshals as soon as he drops that prisoner off with Judge Parker in Fort Smith. I'll be out that door the day they show up."

Gentry angled himself so he could see both the card

players and the door. "Well, we're looking for something different."

"What's that? If it's soda sinkers, they have all you can eat over at the bakery."

He didn't like the fried bread some had come to call doughnuts. "Sweets ain't for me . . ."

"Let's get to it." Johns interrupted, irritating Gentry once again. "We're looking for a guy named Cap Whitlatch. Wanted in Springfield. Strange eyes."

The counterman frowned and almost reached for their beers to pull them back. "Y'all marshals? I don't see no badges."

Gentry shot Johns a disgusted look. "My partner's a little brief sometimes. We're working for a very wealthy man who got taken by this Whitlatch feller who has distinctive-colored eyes. Sold our boss some bad horses."

"You don't look like Pinkerton agents."

Knowing the bartender cum counterman was doing his best trying to pull information from *them,* Gentry decided to let him think what he wanted. "Cap Whitlatch. Rides a gray mare and carries one of them new pump shotguns. There's a wanted paper out for him with a reward."

"He was here. Yesterday. Got tangled up with something down at the jail and I hear he lit out last night with an escaped prisoner."

Johns and Gentry exchanged glances. "Which way did he go?" Ed didn't want Johns to push the man any harder than necessary. Information was coming free and easy without trouble.

The man with two guns who'd been watching them from the table folded his cards, then tossed back a drink. Paying no attention to those at the bar, he set his hat against the bright sun and left.

The counterman waved a hand at the departing customer's back. "See you later, Itchy." He wiped at the bar and returned to their conversation. "Well, no one rightly knows. He disappeared in the middle of that storm last night and could have gone any direction. That's all I know about that." He moved down the bar to wave flies away from the food drying out on the other end.

Johns drew deep on his cigar to maintain the fire, and the two outlaws considered their next move.

CHAPTER 11

"We got competition."

Cloyce studied Itchy, who was standing over him at the Honey Hole. Itchy was talking as soon as he walked into the room, and that irritated Cloyce. Everybody within hearing distance was suddenly listening.

Instead of standing there in the sally and talking with them, either Itchy or Cheese was supposed to be taking his turn watching the jail from across the street, waiting for Kanoska to come outside for his morning constitution. From there, whoever was watching could see the jail's outhouse down the alley and the front door at the same time.

Once the county sheriff closed the outhouse door, one of them was supposed to come get him, and their plan was to hurry down to the jail and shoot Vanderburg in his cell. Cloyce figured that by the time Kanoska got his britches back up and his belt buckled, they could be walking down the street as pretty as you please, minding their own business and innocent as all get-out.

But here was Itchy, with distressing news. "What kind of competition? Where?"

"There's two fellers drinking in the Applejack Dispensary and asking about that feller who shot Black Jim and his boys."

"How do you know that?"

Itchy looked uncomfortable. "Well, Cheese was on post, so I decided to go in and have a game. It don't take two people to watch one outhouse."

Irritated that he hadn't followed orders, Cloyce ground his teeth. "I still don't know what kind of competition you're talking about."

Itchy toed the boards, thinking and frowning at the same time. He'd never been fast on his feet when it came to thinking. He rubbed his virtually nonexistent chin. "Well, one of 'em says his name's Whitlatch, and since he knows that German over there in the jail, maybe they're after him, too. I think they're lawmen or such, or maybe they want the reward."

Cloyce's face started turning red, a sure sign he was getting mad or frustrated. "Him? Slow the hell down and tell me what you mean."

"What I'm saying is that a couple of gunhands are in town asking about Whitlatch, that feller with them scary eyes that killed Black Jim and his boys. Kanoska said yesterday there's a paper out on that German, and maybe those two I heard asking about Whitlatch in the Honey Hole want the reward, too. That's liable to cut us out of killing him ourselves. If we can do this right, we can shoot the German and pocket the reward money for Whitlatch, too, if there's really a price on his head."

"I'll be damned." Cloyce's face cleared and his eyes lit up. "How much is on his head?"

"Didn't say. They're just looking for him, for some rich feller in Missouri."

"I have to think about that." Cloyce absently rubbed the chasm across the bridge of his nose. "I wasn't planning on having any truck with Whitlatch, though."

The truth was, Cloyce realized how close he had come to dying with his brothers in the street the day before. Whitlatch shot Black Jim with that twelve-gauge faster than you can say "boo." Not many men shot so fast, and now it made sense that Whitlatch was on the run himself, maybe for killing the wrong person.

Cheese came busting through the door, out of breath and excited. "Kanoska's gone to do his business!"

Cloyce came up out of his chair like a scorpion had stung him. "Let's go."

They pushed through the door and headed down the street as fast as they could walk without attracting too much attention. Frustrated with how long it was taking to get to the jail, Cloyce almost slapped Cheese into the street, just to make himself feel better.

His brother was right, though. The outhouse door was closed as they passed by the alley. Itchy got to the jailhouse first and found the front door was locked from the inside. "Won't budge."

"Dammit!" Cloyce looked up and down the street. "Back door has to be open."

"We're gonna pass right by the privy."

"Can't be helped." Cloyce led the way around to the back. His frustration grew when he realized all three wore spurs with jingle bobs that rang like Christmas bells. He'd never noticed how loud they were before that moment, trying to sneak past the outhouse.

"Somebody out there?" Kanoska's voice came through the wide gaps in the planks.

Holding one finger against his lips, Cloyce drew his revolver and waved for his brothers to follow him into the jail. He was right, the back door was unlocked.

"Said anybody out there?" Kanoska's voice rose a notch. "I'll be out in a minute."

Cloyce yanked the door open and the Gluck brothers rushed inside with their pistols ready, only to freeze in shock at the sight of two empty cells.

"Son of a bitch!" Cloyce resisted the urge to look under the desk. He knew they'd been outfoxed.

"He's *gone*." A confused Itchy stood there with his pistol cocked and ready.

"What now?" Cheese always deferred to his older brother.

"For one thing"—Cloyce waved for them to follow— "we're gonna kill that damned Kanoska."

The outhouse door creaked at the same time the Glucks poured out the back door and spread out in front of the tiny structure. Guns already drawn, they fired on Sheriff Kanoska as soon as he opened the door. Itchy had a revolver in each hand and shot as fast as he could cock the hammers and pull the triggers.

The others followed suit and ventilated the surprised lawman in a roll of thunder as a hailstorm of lead let all the air out of him. It happened so fast, he never touched the revolver in the gun belt hanging over one shoulder. Kanoska dropped to the muddy ground, dead before he even knew what hit him.

"Let's go." Cloyce holstered his pistol and strolled down the wide-open space behind the line of stores, as if he didn't have a care in the world.

Itchy settled his revolvers and followed. "Where to?"

"We're gonna find Whitlatch and that German. They pulled a good one on us, I bet, but they're not getting away with making *me* look like a fool."

"But where to?" Cheese's baffled look made Cloyce even madder.

"He's a Texan. He's headed south, and that's all we need to know."

CHAPTER 12

"Look what the wind blew in." The speaker standing closest to the smoking campfire in the clearing was a tough-looking hombre pointing a big Walker Colt at me. He was no different than any other hard case in the territories, ragged clothes, slouch hat, and a week's worth of beard, except this one looked like he was about to cut down on me.

What brown teeth he still possessed appeared in what he might have thought was a smile, but there was nothing pleasant about it. That big Colt raised my ire quick as you please. I never did like people pointing guns at me, and wasn't going to take it for long.

A half-breed in a sleeveless brocade vest built a big white grin. Loose hair flowing down past his shoulders, he was the one with a Winchester, and I had no intention of being on the receiving end of that big bore, either.

Both his arms were a patchwork of scars. It looked like a Mexican lion had been clawing on him. "What got hold of *you* two?"

The others watched and waited as I settled the mare down and glanced over to make sure Gil was still upright in the saddle. He was, but a branch during our wild ride through the woods sliced across his cheek, which was pouring blood. One of his eyes was swelled almost shut, but it was hardly noticeable amid all the other yellowjacket stings puffing up red and angry all over his face, hands, and neck.

It annoyed me to no end to realize my shotgun was still in the scabbard, and because I had reins in one hand and a lead rope in the other, I was in no position to protect myself. The pistol on my left hip was too far from my hand to do any good, so I figured talking was my best weapon at the moment.

"Gentlemen, you can lower those weapons. We're not the laws, and I'm sorry to say we're here in your camp without a holler because we ran into a nest of yellowjackets and they've eaten us plumb up."

"I can see that." The guy with the big Colt held it steady on my chest. "Why you have that feller all chained up? You some kind of law or something?"

The others glared holes in us. It might have been that we startled everyone when we suddenly charged into their peaceful camp, but I doubted that. Men like those facing us earned a living by robbing others, and here, all of a sudden, they had two fat peaches to pick.

I thanked my lucky stars Sheriff Kanoska's deputy badge was in my shirt pocket, instead of being pinned on my chest. That's all it would have taken for those boys to throw down on us. All those guns on us meant we were a muscle twitch away from waking up in the morning looking at the wrong side of the grass.

The next words out of my mouth were likely the most important I'd ever speak. "Nope. This here guy tried to rob my mama back in Texas, so I'm taking him back to let my old man stretch his neck if he wants to."

Even outlaws had some sort of code, and I thought the mention of family might buy us a little goodwill. We all had mamas, and I hoped they at least had some respect for them. It seemed to work for the moment. They relaxed and so did

I, though Gil tightened up so much his roan started forward, but I held him back.

Hair covering half of her face and tangled as if she'd been in a cyclone, the woman on the ground moaned into the wet ground. Once of good quality, her skirt looked as if it had been dragged through the brush. What was left of her clothing barely provided enough decency for a good woman. Even if her hair was brushed out, and the filthy rags were replaced, the bruises up and down her arms spoke of torture and humiliation.

"Sorry we came in like this." Hoping to gain a few moments, I motioned toward her, hoping to get the bulge on them, if I could. "The missus all right?"

To a man, they all laughed. They were outlaws, thieves, and murderers, who had no fear of anyone else in the territories, and had likely left a string of innocent bodies along their back trail. My chest tightened with the knowledge that there was no way out of the situation we found ourselves in.

The half-breed licked his lips and took a step toward her, as if he couldn't decide between enjoying her again, or cutting our throats. "Got her from the Comanches. Cost us a pretty penny, but she's worth a fortune down in Austin. We're gonna take her down and sell 'er back to her family."

"What's left of her," another of the gang members popped off, and they laughed again.

I didn't believe a word they were saying. These men were no-good liars who existed below the level of animals, and none of them would ever rise above it.

I figured they burned out some poor dirt farmer and took the woman, or maybe she and someone else had been travelers, such as myself, but unprepared for such harsh and lawless country. It was a miracle she was still alive, and I doubted she'd last much longer, especially with that band of cutthroats.

She must have been playing dead, or pretending to be

asleep before we rode in, but she raised her head and I saw a face that had suffered much abuse. Bruises, cuts, and tangled and dirty black hair told a story that sent a red rage through my whole body.

She finally spoke, but the words came out soft and disjointed. "Help me, please. They didn't buy . . ."

"Good-looking horses." Walker Colt's smile disappeared. "Get off."

"Can't do it by myself," Gil said. I felt some relief, he'd already read the scene, too, and likely came to the same conclusion. "Somebody's gonna have to help me down."

Walker Colt pointed at me. "I don't like your eyes."

"It's something I can't help." There was that keening sound in my head again and I wanted to ride away and be done with everything, but I couldn't.

No, I wouldn't.

"You don't move, bub." Walker Colt held the pistol steady as a rock.

"Wasn't planning on it."

He pointed at Gil. "Kangee, get him down."

The half-breed stepped between us and reached up for Gil, at the instant a panther screamed from the trees only a few feet away. At first, I thought it was the dark-haired woman lying on the ground and she'd lost her mind, but it came again and it wasn't her. I'd heard all my life mountain lions sounded like a woman screaming in pain. They were right, and it sent a jolt up my spine.

The shrill sound froze the gang in their tracks. Walker Colt must have thought it was coming right at us from the woods, and he swung the muzzle of that big .44 off me, and that half a second was all I needed.

I kicked the mare sideways and she shoved the half-breed Kangee into Gil's roan, trapping him between them. Bless his heart, Gil kneed the roan into him at the same time and the man grunted as a ton of horseflesh knocked the breath out of him. He jerked up in agony on one foot as a hoof came down on his moccasin.

I snatched the twelve-gauge from the scabbard and threw down on Walker Colt.

There was no time for aiming, and the talking was done. He fired first, and the bullet whistled past my ear. Another round from a different gun tugged the slicker between my arm and side. Once again, my old daddy's experience and advice served me well. They were shooting way too fast, thinking it was best to get in the first shot, and then banging away until they hit something.

Taking your time to steady and aim usually made all the difference.

One other advantage I had was the Spencer's pattern. Careful aim wasn't necessary. I only had to point it in the general direction of my target and squeeze the trigger, cutting down on Walker Colt as soon as I lined up on him. The shotgun thundered and the load of buckshot dropped him like a buck deer. He went down, firing a second time into the ground, before landing face first in the mud.

The rest of the gang was still grouped together and some of that pattern punched through a man standing to his left. Holding one arm, he staggered sideways, cursing.

Shucking in another round, I hoped taking him out first might work the same as shooting a Comanche war party's leader. It sometimes takes the spirit out of the rest, or leaves them confused without someone to make decisions for the group.

It didn't work *that* time.

Their quick reaction to shoot came up faster than I expected, proof those men made a living preying on others. Pistols barked and smoke filled the air. The Spencer thundered again and the wounded outlaw fell.

Lead buzzed past us like angry insects and Gil grunted. I wasn't sure he was hit or not, but he did me a favor and fell with a thud on top of Kangee, who thrashed below me, either trying to catch his breath or attempting to regain his feet.

The roan on the other end of my lead bucked and sunfished his way into the outlaws' line of fire, yanking the rope out of my hand, but giving me some respite and time to make every shot count. The steeldust mare, on the other hand, remained rooted to the ground, because I'd trained her from a colt and shot quail from her back almost as soon as she was broke.

The shotgun arced from left to right. Bodies soaked up double-aught buck and wilted like flowers in the summertime, shredded by the heavy shot that swept them to the ground like a scythe.

A shorter outlaw couldn't decide to keep shooting or run. He fired, backed up, and fired again, before saying to hell with it and whirling to skin out of there. Maybe if he hadn't shot while he was running, I wouldn't have paid as much attention to him, but he was still a threat and throwing lead at me.

Pumping another round into the chamber, I shot him in the side and he cut a flip when he fell. Shifting my aim, I shot again as the terrified roan busted through the middle of them, dodging the fire and almost stepping on one of the bodies.

I sprayed the next outlaw, who fancied himself a gunhand, fanning the hammer with the palm of his hand. Another squeeze of the shotgun's rear trigger and he fell in a heap.

They were all down, but the fight below continued. Lying on the ground, Kangee was separated from his Winchester and rolled from under Gil and kicked him in the side, dodging the horse's hooves. Gil twisted in the long grass and kicked Kangee in the face with a boot heel as the outlaw tugged a pistol from his belt. I heard the crack of his jaw and switched the shotgun to my left hand to snatch the Russian revolver from its holster, throwing three shots into Kangee at point-blank range.

He writhed like the dying snake he was and stilled.

"Son of a bitch! I'm hit." Gil rolled around, trying to get up, as I bailed off the steeldust, thinking I'd shot my old partner in the melee. "They shot me as I fell off my horse."

Swinging down from the saddle, I knelt and checked his shirt. No blood. "Where at?"

"My ear!" He turned his head so I could see. "It stings like hell."

Blood poured from his missing earlobe. "They shot you in your good ear."

"Dammit!" He struggled to sit up. "I'm bleeding like a stuck hog. Unlock these damned things so I can make it stop bleeding."

I had greater concerns, keeping the .44 on the others, in case one of them was playing possum. It wouldn't do to be shot by a dead man. I moved from body to body, making sure they were all through drawing air, and almost shot a figure that suddenly stepped from the thick undergrowth only yards away.

It was Gracie in a black hat and oversize coat. She held both hands up as if to ward off a blow. "Don't! That was me screaming."

"You?" It took a minute to clear my head. "What're *you* doing here?"

"I got away from that half-wit Kanoska and followed you last night."

"How'd you do that in the dark?"

"Wasn't much of a chore, if you ask me. I don't believe I even had to trot to keep up with y'all." She saw the woman, who was resting on one elbow; her head was hanging so low, her hair was in the grass. "You shoot her, too?"

"I don't believe so." Thumbing fresh loads from my gun belt, I reloaded the Russian. Holstering it, I stuffed fresh shells into the shotgun from the pocket of my slicker. My old man taught me that you never holster a weapon without reloading first.

Gracie knelt beside the woman and turned her over. "Good Goddlemighty. Poor thing's beat so bad, her own mama wouldn't know her. Had to have been Comanches got at her at some point—they notched her nose, poor thing."

The gunsmoke had cleared and I looked around the clearing at Gil still struggling to stand, Gracie leaning over a half-dead woman, and the bodies lying around the camp-fire like abandoned dolls. The coppery smell of blood filled the air and I wondered what I'd gotten myself into.

CHAPTER 13

A chiseled man with a well-groomed gray beard and wearing a flat-brimmed gray Stetson stepped down from a fine-looking strawberry roan in front of the Blackwater Jail to find a crowd gathered outside. He adjusted his tooled gun belt, pulled a Winchester from the scabbard, and pushed through a knot of men peeking inside the open door.

"Texas Ranger. Give way."

His deep, authoritative voice worked magic and the men moved to allow him access. He paused inside the door at the sight of a bloody body lying in one of the cells. A man in a dark suit with his shirt buttoned to the neck was sitting at Kanoska's desk and writing on a sheet of paper, while half-a-dozen other men appeared to loaf in chairs or leaned against the bars or a wall.

"What's going on here?"

The man at the desk looked up over a set of spectacles perched on his nose. "You a U.S. Marshal? I swanny, I don't know how you could get here so fast for this killing when it takes y'all a month of Sundays anytime a regular person needs you."

"Name's Curtis Braziel, and I'm a Texas Ranger. I'm looking for the sheriff or, in his absence, a deputy marshal, and who're you?"

"I'm Webb Fitzgerald, the undertaker in this fair town." He pointed with the pen in his hand. "That there corpse is what used to be Sheriff Kanoska, at least he was a couple of hours ago before he went to relieve his bowels and found himself shot to death. What's a Texas Ranger doing way up here?"

"Came to pick up a prisoner he wired me about. Wanted back in Texas. Did my man kill him and escape?"

"We don't rightly know. Some of those old boys out there say that's what happened, but I counted the holes in the late sheriff and heard the shots, so unless that German had four hands all filled with pistols, I'd say that's not the case. Kanoska was hit by fourteen bullets, and any one of 'em could have killed him all by itself, I reckon."

"So, where's the prisoner that's supposed to be in here? Man name of Gilbert Vanderburg. I came all this way to pick him up, and this is damned aggravating."

"That's who I was talking about, and your guess is as good as mine. Kanoska and a stranger with spooky eyes turned away a lynch mob last night that wanted to see Vanderburg swing. That was close to dark, but the county sheriff came in here and closed up for the night."

"Forgive me, but I am somewhat confused. Was Kanoska a local or a county sheriff?"

"It is somewhat confusing up here in the territories." Fitzgerald laced his fingers on the desk like a school-marm lecturing her students. "It varies depending on where you are. The oldest law enforcement organization is the Lighthorse Company, under the purview of a captain and over twenty men, mostly tribal police.

"Here in the Choctaw Nation, we have county sheriffs and one Lighthorseman, or deputy, if you want to call him that. Now we have the United States Indian Police, in addition to county and district sheriffs who're appointed by our Indian leadership. Are you confused yet?"

"I got the gist of it. Now, tell me what happened to that man lying in there."

"This morning, we heard shooting out back. Apparently, he went to do his morning business and somebody killed him."

"They string Vanderburg up for it?"

"Not that anybody can find."

"Where's this man with the strange eyes?"

The undertaker shrugged. "Your guess is as good as mine."

"He have a name?"

"Somebody said it was Whitlatch. Heard two men asking about him down at the Honey Hole, but that's all I know, and I'm not a newspaper editor, so that's all the information I have."

Braziel tilted his hat back and studied Kanoska's body. "So Vanderburg is gone, this stranger is nowhere to be found, and nobody knows who did the shooting."

"That's about the size of it."

"He have a deputy, uh, a Lighthorse?"

"Yessir. Nate Cornsilk. He ain't nowhere to be found, but somebody said they saw him walking down the street last night about the time it started to rain. We ain't seen hide ner hair of him since."

"Would he have done this?"

One of the men leaning against the cell chuckled. "That's the furthest thing from anyone's mind."

The Ranger's gaze bored a hole through the man in a shapeless hat. "What's your name?"

"Israel Catawnee."

"What kind of name is that?"

"Cherokee."

"All right, then, Israel. You go find this Cornsilk and bring him here."

"Who're you to tell me what to do?"

"I'm the law here right now until y'all bring one forward, or until a U.S. Marshal shows up, so it's *me* telling you what to do."

"You don't have any authority in the territories. Only Cherokee and federal law goes here."

The room went silent as the Ranger's eyes drilled into Israel's face. The man finally looked at the floor and straightened. "Fine, then. I'll go find him."

"Thanks." The Ranger studied Kanoska's body. "Never saw a Cherokee with a mustache like that."

"We never were sure he *was* Cherokee." Undertaker Fitzgerald went back to writing, using Kanoska's pen and paper. "Said he was, from his mama. Only time he ever mentioned it to me was when we were doing a little drinking and he said his daddy was from Italy."

"That explains the mustache." The Texas lawman drew himself up, as if gaining that little dab of information was an accomplishment worthy of a Ranger.

Half an hour later, Cornsilk came limping at gunpoint into the sheriff's office, followed by Israel Catawnee, who had blood running down one arm. "Here he is, and to hell with both of you."

Ranger Braziel studied the pair. Cornsilk's face was bruised and he looked madder'n a hornet. Israel's swollen lip seeped a little blood, and a rag tied around his upper arm was red and wet. "What happened?"

"You told me to bring him to you, but he didn't want to come." Catawnee raised his arm as evidence. "Pulled a butcher knife and damned near gutted me before I knocked it out of his hand. Had to use an iron skillet to settle his ass down. Broke the handle on it, too."

"Good job, and thanks." Braziel waved Israel away. "You can go now."

Israel set his mouth to respond, then sighed.

The Ranger turned to the sullen Cherokee. "Cornsilk,

you're a deputy. Why weren't you here with the sheriff when he got killed, and why'd you fight the man I sent after you?"

"Not no more, I ain't no Lighthorse. Dropped my badge off yesterday and left."

"How come?"

"'Cause that little witch girl put a curse on me, and it looks like it's working."

Ranger Braziel raised an eyebrow. "What witch girl?"

"The kid who was in that cell there, while I was guarding the German."

"Kanoska in the habit of arresting kids?"

"That one. Gracie's her name. I believe she is *ka'lanu ahkyeli'ski,* the raven mocker who is an evil spirit and the most feared of our people's witches. She probably smoked some *tsolagayvli* and put spells on all of us."

"This is all confusing as hell." Ranger Braziel pulled at his mustache, which swept over his shorter beard. "Israel, what's *tsolagayvli*?"

"Special tobacco we use in our religion, but Cornsilk's wrong, if you ask me. Raven mockers are old and curled people who walk looking straight down on the ground."

Cornsilk shook his head, radiating sadness. "She was old, but turned herself into a young girl to fool everyone."

"Where is she now?" The Ranger was finished with such superstitious talk. He didn't believe in spirits, but only the evil that men do to each other.

Cornsilk glanced out the door, as if looking for her in the crowd outside. "I don't know. Hell, maybe she's dead. Did you look down in the outhouse? Maybe Kanoska killed her and left her body in the stink."

Ranger Braziel turned to the undertaker. "Can you explain all this?"

"Well, I can try. Yesterday the lynch mob tried to take the German out and string him up. Cornsilk was guarding him, and I heard Gracie was in for stealing eggs. She's a corker, for sure. Then some cowboy with strange eyes shot three of the mob, out there, with a shotgun . . ."

"A stranger meaning Whitlatch?"

"If that's his name. Anyway, I had to clean up that mess. After that, it came up a cloud and rained all night. I don't know nothing else."

The Ranger pursed his lips, thinking. "So it sounds like Vanderburg and this Whitlatch feller took off together. Could have been the two of them shot the sheriff and escaped? That'd account for the number of wounds in his body, if he used a shotgun on him."

"That makes sense to me." Israel Catawnee looked around for confirmation.

"It don't to me." The undertaker frowned. "I done told you, I heard the shots this morning and I don't believe it was them killed him. There was more than one gun, and that's a fact."

Cornsilk sat on the floor to examine his foot wrapped in a rag. "Them two knew each other since they was boys down in a Texas town like Fred something."

Braziel shook his head. Dealing with Indians was always vexing, and this bunch was worse than the rest. "Fredericksburg?"

"That's it."

"Did they come in together?"

"Naw. Gil'd been here for a couple of weeks. Pretty good feller, but he fought me when we arrested him." He paused in examining his foot. "Should have cut his throat then."

"So you're telling me a drifter came in and accidentally ran into his friend who was in jail for murder . . . and nobody thought anything about it?"

"Didn't study on it that long." Cornsilk looked around the office. "Is that bucket of coal oil still in here?"

One of the onlookers picked it up by the bail from where it still sat in the empty cell and brought it to Cornsilk. He bent his knee and settled his bad foot ankle deep and sighed. "Hope they took that witch with them, if she's not under the seat in the outhouse."

Ranger Braziel came to a decision. "Where's the telegraph office?"

"Over in the Applejack Hotel."

"Which way is it?"

The undertaker pointed.

"Much obliged." Ranger Braziel walked outside and through the crowd of men who parted to make way. He was done with discussing murders with people who couldn't tell a straight story.

The Ranger forked the strawberry roan and kicked it into a lope. He intended to dash off a quick telegram to his captain, and then turn south to see if he could pick up the trail of two murderers headed for Texas.

CHAPTER 14

Our group was a sorry-looking lot. Though the swelling was down on our stings, Gil's missing earlobe was still seeping. His horse followed behind Gracie, who was in the lead on one of the outlaws' horses. Still in cuffs, Gil complained to high heaven. "I swear, Cap. You've about killed me already and I'm liable to starve to death if we don't get to a town soon."

We still hadn't come across a trading post or little store to resupply, and I was down to a couple of pieces of jerky, and that's all. Coffee sounded really good right then, but there wasn't enough for all of us. I hadn't planned on feeding three adults, and whatever Gracie was; at this point, even the outlaws' food was scant.

And to make things worse, Gracie kept jumping off her horse and wandering into the woods, returning with roots and berries she said we could eat. Some of them didn't look bad, but a few looked like toadstools and I figured I'd swell up like a toad frog and wake up dead the next morning if I ate some of them. She also picked a mess of greens she stuffed into a sack and said they'd be good eating.

She had Gil's lead rope wrapped around her saddle horn, and acted like she'd led prisoners on horseback all her life. The woman who still hadn't spoken to me or to Gil followed them on a little bay. She stared at her hands holding on to the horn for dear life.

She kept her head down all that day, rarely making eye contact, and I didn't know if she was naturally quiet, or if she'd turned inward after what had happened to her before we rescued her. When she rode that way, I couldn't see much of her face, only enough to know she was more attractive than most other women, despite her notched nose.

The poor thing wouldn't look at neither me nor Gil after all the shooting, though she did grab Gracie and held her for dear life back there beside those dead bodies until I gathered the horses and got us ready to leave.

I cut a look at her, but she turned her head away, refusing to look at me. We didn't have bandages, but Gracie took over back at the outlaws' camp and attended her face and the fresh wound in her nose. I didn't know much more to do after that and left the girl to deal with such things.

She dismounted that first night and sat staring into the campfire until it burned down to coals; then she covered herself with Gil's blanket and slept as close to Gracie as possible. I was concerned, afraid she'd rise and wander off after we all went to sleep, but she stuck with us without issue.

I was last in line so as to keep an eye on both Gil and the woman, and because I was leading the other three ponies that trailed behind. There was no reason to leave those horses back there, and they were good mounts, likely stolen from some poor cowboys who had the misfortune to run into that band of murderers.

Each of the horses was still saddled, and I'd collected their gun belts and put them in the most decent of their war bags, along with anything else of value. That included Kangee's Winchester, which rode in a boot on Gracie's horse. Their bedrolls, clothes, and anything else that would burn went into the campfire before we left that bloody battlefield.

Like the two would-be rapists who would have also killed Naach, as soon as they were finished with her, I had no intention of taking the time to bury the bodies, neither. I didn't have a shovel, anyway. Using paper and pencil from my own possibles bag, I wrote five different notes and stuffed them in their pockets, describing what had happened and why they were dead.

There was no need to do that, either, but it seemed like the most Christian thing I could think of, in case someone came across them and wondered what had happened, though animals would take care of the corpses before anyone could read them.

Now, miles away on the second day, shadows stretched long in front of us, and my belly was growling. "It's getting late. I'm thinking we need to find someplace to camp for the night."

Gracie twisted in her saddle. "Cap, I see a good-size house up there. Maybe we can stay in their barn tonight, if they have one."

Rising in the stirrups, I saw what she was pointing at. It was the first house we'd come across since we found that good road. "Fine idea. Ma'am, how about we stop there for the night?"

She didn't answer, but I didn't expect it. I just wanted her to know we were considering her.

What I thought was a farm turned out to be a way station, of sorts, on our right. I knew it was a place built to take in travelers, because of a crooked hand-painted sign that read INN. Nothing like I'd ever seen before, it was a large plank-sided house resting high on bodark posts, with a decent front porch overlooking the trail. A brush barn on our near side and a sturdy corral, with two horses, were perfect for the new remuda we'd acquired.

A horse nickered from somewhere behind the house, and I figured they might have a picket back there, or another horse staked out. Maybe a mare in season, or a stud that didn't take to being in a corral with strange horses or mules? It didn't matter much, the thought of food drove most other thoughts away.

A thick, bald man was watching from the porch when Gracie and Gil reined up. He took his hands off the suspenders holding up a pair of baggy pants and opened the door and spoke to someone inside before turning back to address us.

"Saw you coming. Get down and rest. Welcome to our *gasthaus*." His German accent was thick and he spoke without expression.

Gracie didn't answer. For once, she looked back over her shoulder so I could do the talking. Right behind her, Gil tilted his head at the man and for once was quiet, too.

"Evening, sir." I urged the steeldust forward to talk without anyone between us. "Can you accommodate all of us tonight?"

"Can you pay?"

"Yes."

"Then ve vill make room. You and your wife can stay on a pallet in the front room. The girl too."

I had to concentrate on his accent, though I'd grown up with Germans and was used to working out what they said. But this guy was tough. Likely, a new immigrant who had wandered up from the Texas Gulf Coast. Lots of Germans came in through Galveston and then spread out into Fredericksburg and New Braunfels, while some drifted north. Though they usually settled together back home, most assimilated quickly into the Texas way of life.

"Much obliged." I made to get down. "She isn't my wife, though. She was taken by bad men and we rescued her."

"Ah. An odd band, indeed." He'd noticed Gil's hands

behind him. "Zees man seems to be your prisoner *mit* his hands tied behind him."

"Shackled, but not a prisoner in the strict sense of the word. I'm not the law. Just escorting him back to Texas."

"Escorting, in chains?"

"Seemed like a good idea."

"He can sleep in the shed with the horses. The roof posts are sunk deep and you can run the chain around them and *anfügen* . . . attach him that way." He paused to survey the horses. "You have many fine horses, sir."

"They're good ponies, all right." I swung down. Lightning bugs were already blinking in the damp air at the edge of the woods and the whistle of wind over the wings of a passing flock of ducks told me there was water nearby. A whippoorwill was already calling from the shadows. "We can eat a bite, too. Of course, I'll pay extra."

"*Natürlich,* you will."

"I'm Cap Whitlatch. This is Gracie here, and he's Gil, up there on the horse. Now the lady—"

"I sure would like to step down." Gil cut me off, speaking louder than usual, and nodded to the man on the porch. "Your name, sir?"

"I am Jonas. My wife inside is Susanne."

"Can you help me down, Jonas, while my friend attends to the ladies and horses?"

"*Jah.*"

Gil didn't meet my eyes, and I wondered why he was suddenly taking the lead on our discussion and asking for help from a stranger. Shrugging, I swung to the ground and reached up a hand to help the woman down. Looking up at her, I got the first really good view of the captive's bruised face since we rescued her, because all that long, ratted dark hair kept me from getting a good look at her features.

Though her eye and lip were still swollen from beatings, and the notch in her nose was raw and seeping, there was a rare beauty hidden by dirt and scratches that would make most men stop for a second look. For the first time since I helped the woman to her feet back at the camp, her eyes met mine and she looked deep into my soul.

Her voice came soft and low. "Thank you, sir."

My breath caught as something passed between us. We were making progress. "My pleasure." I really wanted to ask her name right then, but was afraid it would be too forward after such silence, and now that she was talking on her own.

Gracie was suddenly at my side. As soon as the lady was on the ground, she took over. "I'll help her."

"Good."

She addressed the lady. "Esther, lean on me if you need to."

I was relieved to have a name. Thinking of her as "that woman" didn't seem right at all. She was finally coming out of her daze, and I noticed a light was coming back into the slender woman's face.

I glanced over to see the innkeeper help Gil to the ground by taking most of his weight on his shoulders, and then setting him down. Gil crossed the few feet to the porch and sat with his back against a peeled cedar post holding up the overhang, taking in all that was around us. A stout blond woman I took to be Jonas's wife came outside with a stained cloth over one shoulder.

I removed my hat in greeting, but she ignored me for the most part, so I put it back on.

Her dress was wet at thigh level, where she'd wiped her hands more than once in the course of a day working in the kitchen. "Papa, let's get these ladies inside, while the men tend the horses."

It wasn't a question, or even a soft suggestion. She told him what to do and he did it in a heartbeat. *"Jah."* He took

Gil's reins and led the way to a cedar post corral. "They will be fine in here tonight. You can put the tack in the shed."

Susanne held a plank door open and ushered Gracie and Esther up the steps and inside. Keeping an eye on Gil, who seemed content to just sit and watch the proceedings, Jonas and I unsaddled the horses and put the gear in a little shed knocked together with warped boards.

"What do I do with all these heavy saddlebags?" Jonas waited for an answer as I slung my own set over one shoulder and picked up the Spencer. I hid the Winchester under the saddles. A man can carry just so many long guns at any one time.

I saw Jonas was watching my every move. Probably a good idea with strangers in that part of the territories. "I'll keep this one. We can leave the rest with the saddles."

"Nothing important that needs to come inside the house?"

"Nah. Just clothes and such."

He toed one of the bags. "Some *heavy* clothes in this one."

It contained the outlaws' guns and gun belts. "That one's full of books. I like to read."

He laughed and slapped his thigh, but I noticed there was no humor in his eyes. "Books. Books are useless to most people. They are good for kindling and not much else."

I've known men like that, who didn't see much mirth in the world and only went through the motions of laughing because people expect such things. Instead of answering, I checked to make sure there was plenty of water in the trough for the stock. "Do you have any feed?"

"*Jah.* That barrel there has oats, but that will cost you extra." He studied the horses. "Seven mounts. That will be five dollars."

"Kinda steep."

"Maybe you can find oats out there in the woods for them."

There it was, that matter-of-fact German attitude we'd

grown up with. The more I talked to the guy, the more I was convinced he was fairly new to our country, but that wasn't unusual. Out in our part of the world and on the plains, you heard German, French, Greek, Czech, and Spanish, of course, Italian, and dozens more languages that sometimes sounded melodious, and other times harsh and sharp.

That was this guy. Harsh and sharp. I should have been used to the tone after all those years of growing up with Germans, but his was so guttural, it almost raised the hair on the back of my neck.

We fed the horses and I followed him back to the house. Gil sat unusually still and quiet, still leaning against the same cedar post, with one leg dangling above the ground. I stopped at the puncheon steps, expecting him to say something, but he appeared to be studying the boards beneath him with some strange intensity.

"Ve vill eat soon." Jonas went up onto the porch and slipped both hands into the pockets of his wool trousers.

I didn't particularly like having the man standing above me so that I'd have to look up. There was too much of my daddy in me. We both despise talking to a man in the saddle when we're on the ground. I climbed the steps to his level. "I have a feeling this night is gonna cost me a pretty penny."

Gracie was probably inside, already working through her first plate. I hoped she'd save some for us.

"It vill be worth it. My wife made a stew today. We traded for some vegetables from a red traveler and ve always hef meat in the pot. I am a good shot *mit* a rifle."

Gil finally spoke up. "Y'all have a pretty nice place there. Did you build it as an inn for travelers?"

"No, I intended to farm, but it turned out that ve are on a fairly busy wagon road and often have travelers stop by for zee evening. It brings in a little more money for the family, so I added on a couple more rooms for paying customers."

I got his emphasis. This guy was all about money.

Gil adjusted his seat on the hard, splintered boards, which could have used a few more handshakes with a drawknife, or an adze at least. "How long y'all been here?"

Jonas scanned the trees surrounding us. "We bought it from a family who wanted to go west to the gold fields, about two years ago."

"Y'all raise crops out back?"

I wondered what he was after. Gil was always a talker and usually digging for information, but he still wouldn't look at me, though, and I had a nagging feeling he knew something I didn't.

Jonas nodded as if considering a serious subject. "A little corn and some potatoes in the *garten*. We have a milk cow behind the house."

"I was hoping for some fresh eggs in the morning. Of course, we can pay you for breakfast, too."

Now I was *really* wondering what was going on. We hadn't said anything about eating there the next morning, and even though I had money, I wasn't too excited about Gil arranging to spend it for me. I intended to be up and gone by daylight, not hanging around while Susanne built a fire and cooked breakfast.

"We don't have chickens. I'm sorry." Jonas held both hands out to the side and explained. "Possums got them all sometime back. That's the problem with country. Too many . . . *raubtiere,* how do you say . . ."

"You mean predators?" Like I said, I didn't speak a lot of German, but I could usually pick out what they were trying to say.

"Ah! You speak *Deutsch*?"

Gil shook his head quick. "Naw. He can barely speak English, but even I could figure out what got your chickens. Bobcats, hawks, eagles, coons. Predators." He laughed.

"Cap killed a possum just last night for our supper, and I guess it was on his mind."

Stunned at his speech, and such an outright lie, for we didn't eat possum at all the night before, I withdrew into myself, wondering.

"Come in. Come in." Jonas turned to hold the door for us and I finally caught Gil's eye.

All he did was raise an eyebrow.

Something was up.

CHAPTER 15

The sky was clear and blue when Cloyce, Itchy, and Cheese pulled up not far from five bodies lying neatly lined up at the edge of the grassy clearing. Uncomfortable with the smell of death, the horses shuffled and pulled against the reins.

Cloyce adjusted his seat in the saddle and studied the corpses as a swarm of flies rose and fell. "Lots of killing was done here."

Itchy dismounted and walked to the campfire. He knelt and held the back of his hand over the gray ashes. "No heat."

"The flies and the way them bodies are swole, it's been a while. Maybe a day?"

"You think it was Gil and that feller with him done this?" Cheese rubbed at his oily nose. "Could have at least buried these poor boys."

They'd come upon two sets of tracks a while back and decided to follow them, hoping it was the German and someone else, likely that man with the scary eyes.

Cloyce walked his horse around the campsite, while Itchy studied the bodies, taking in all the hoof tracks and so much crushed grass. He was already tired of trying to find the man who killed Possum, and would have already called a halt to it and gone to find some whiskey if his brothers hadn't been along.

Inherently lazy, Cloyce preferred his fights or events to happen quick and then be over. He wasn't one to worry at a problem for any length of time, though he held a grudge forever. Easily distracted by whiskey and women, Cloyce thought about getting himself lost from them and going back to Blackwater. They'd find their way back home, and by that time, he could shrug and admit that he wasn't good at tracking fugitives, confident they knew better than to push him on it.

He felt like they'd already wandered for over half of the territory, hoping to pick up their trail, but it was difficult, not knowing which way the pair went or what road or little game trail they followed. He knew the German and that gunhand were headed south or southwest, but that's all. In his opinion, they might just as well give up and go home, despite all this big talk back in town.

"They was shotgunned. All of 'em." Itchy waved the flies away with his hat and used a stick someone collected for firewood to poke at the bodies. "These are all shotgun wounds, except for the Indian. Somebody filled *him* full of holes with a pistol."

Cheese kept glancing around as if a war party was hiding nearby. His cloudy eye seemed to blink more than the other. "Likely, he was hard to kill."

Itchy rose and gave one of the bodies a light kick. "This old boy here took a whole charge. I swanny, his chest looks like a big bloody washtub."

Their luck changed when Cloyce stepped down and kicked through the grass. "Well, looky here. We found 'em." He picked up a spent paper shotgun shell and held it up. "That gunhand from back in town *has* to be riding with the German. You were right. Somebody must've said something them two didn't like said."

Itchy followed his older brother's lead and wandered around the camp, eyes downcast. Cheese remained in the saddle, scanning the trees around them, lest someone pop up, friend or foe. "You boys ought to be paying more attention to what's around us, at least part of the time."

Cloyce sniffed the empty shotgun hull. "That's what *you're* up there for." He expected everyone to know their job.

"You never told me to keep watch."

"Shouldn't have to." Cloyce counted the empties all lying within feet of each other. "Look at all the hulls. I saw that newfangled shotgun the other feller carried. I 'spect it was him, all right. That damned thing must shoot fast."

A shiver ran up his spine as he remembered how big the muzzle of that scattergun looked. He was glad he hadn't seen it in use against *him,* though Black Jim and his boys certainly felt the results.

"Gil must've shot the Indian, then, with his pistol." Itchy moved upwind from the bodies. "I always figured him for a back shooter, but every one of these shots were straight in his chest. Pretty good shootin', if you ask me."

"That German's a gunhand, all right." Cloyce preferred to keep them thinking that Gil was a gunslinger, and not Whitlatch, because that's the story he told after the accident between him and Possum, who'd refused to share his poker winnings with his older brother. Both of them had been drinking heavily most of the day he died, and Cloyce was on the prod because Itchy and Cheese were passed out in the livery stable.

"Look at this." Itchy picked up a piece of ribbon. "You think these boys had a *woman* with them?"

"Hard to tell." Cloyce took the bright red cloth from him, gave it a sniff, and wrapped it through his fingers. He worked the tracks he found that disappeared into the trees and returned a moment later. "Two horses, so no, they weren't no woman with them when they rode in."

"It's gotta be them two." Cheese rode in a wide circle. "Lots of horse tracks over here. I 'magine she rode in with this gang, if there was one with them. Maybe a captive? That one's an Indian, or half-breed. They like ribbons and geegaws and such. Might've had it in his hair."

Itchy paid no attention to his brother. "Whoever did this probably took her with them. Likely some slut riding with this little band and she took up with them to get through the territories, or maybe some Indian gal they bought. Either way, a woman alone out here's pretty much a target for every man she runs into."

"They did." Cloyce dropped the spent shell and swung back into the saddle. "Took her with them, I mean. No guns or saddlebags." He pointed at a piece of charred cloth outside of the fire ring. "Burned everything else."

"Good thing we had that rain." Itchy climbed back onto his mount. "Might have burned the whole country down if it'd been dry."

Cloyce shook his head at the brother who always worried about things that made no difference to the conversation, or even had anything to do with what they were talking about. "These tracks were made when it was still wet. We ain't a day or so behind them, so we need to step it up."

"Their bad luck." Cheese chewed the inside of his cheek. "Wonder why they killed 'em. Robbery?"

"No telling, but it takes a quick man to shoot this fast and accurate." Cloyce felt a shiver go down his spine a second time.

He didn't expect to find himself squaring off with two gunhands. All he wanted to do was hang the German for Possum's killing before Cheese and Itchy found out that Cloyce had murdered their little brother in a blind rage. He'd already convinced them Vanderburg murdered Possum, and once they lynched him, or shot him, for that matter, he wouldn't have to worry about watching over his shoulder for the rest of his days. There needed to be an end to this.

He didn't mean to kill Possum, but accidents happen.

CHAPTER 16

We stepped into an open barn of a house that smelled of raw and curing meat, onions, coffee, and unfamiliar spices. It wasn't a foreign odor, since Gil and I both grew up on scratch farms, where we killed our own beef. Since these folks didn't have a smokehouse, they must have done all their cutting inside. Houses often smelled of fresh meat when someone killed a deer, or a few squirrels or rabbits.

City people had no idea how bad quail stunk when you opened them up to draw out the entrails. Ducks and geese, too, so we always cleaned birds outside.

Hand-hewn beams and rafters stretched high overhead. Ropes over the beams supported homemade patchwork curtains that divided the area into several "rooms." Their idea of an inn looked as if they changed the layout whenever necessary, probably due to the number of guests at any one time, because short pieces of frayed rope dangled from a number of the beams.

Young voices came from behind one of the curtains and Susanne rolled her eyes. "My children are old enough to be married and out of the house, but, no, they still live with us, with no intention of leaving." Her accent was strong, but not as much as Jonas, so she was easier to understand.

"Kids these days, and them coming on to eighteen years. Sir, you can lean your shotgun there beside the door."

I propped it against a handmade cedar bench and thought about taking off my revolver, but I always felt naked without it, and she hadn't made mention of me disarming myself. I did remove my hat, and Gil's, too, for him, and hung them on pegs above the bench and shotgun. We were both raised to take our hats off inside someone's home.

"Otto! Olinda!" Jonas walked around a large table in the center of the kitchen. He removed his slouch hat and pitched it onto the floor beside a large stone fireplace taking up one end of the room divided by a curtain hanging close to the far side of the table. "Come and meet our guests."

Blond haired and blue eyed, they were built exactly alike and must have been twins. Otto was muscular, while his sister was a stout young woman. They nodded in unison. Olinda gave me a shy little smile, but Otto seemed to take my measure.

"Good to meet you."

They disappeared back behind the curtains before any of the others could offer their pleasantries.

Susanne set a cast-iron Dutch oven full of steaming stew in the middle of a scattering of china plates and bowls and gestured with a wide smile full of bright teeth. "You with the shackles, sit here." She indicated a seat to her husband's right. "And you, sir, can sit across the table and next to Jonas."

I didn't mind being told where to sit. She'd indicated an empty chair catty-corner across from the one she held for Gil. Even though my cane-bottom chair backed up to the curtain on Jonas's left, I could see both Gil and the door, and that suited me just fine. "Gil, turn around."

His eyes brightened when I dug the key from my vest pocket. I knew he was right-handed, so I unlocked that shackle and immediately slid the cuff through his belt and clicked it shut. It hobbled him some, but that way he could eat with one hand without someone feeding him.

Gracie had taken that duty on the trail and fed him pieces of jerky every now and then. We'd worked out his privacy when he relieved himself when Gracie and Esther showed up, and that was one thing I had no intention of helping him with.

The solution was simple. Each time he needed to go, I had him lay on his stomach and, with knee in his back, unlocked one hand and secured the loose end of the cuff around a stirrup. Whether it was on a horse, or lying on the ground, there was no way he could mount up and ride away. It sure kept him from running off, and no one could cause trouble toting around a McClellan saddle.

"Cap, can you set me free, just this once?" He spoke soft and low, like a chastised child. I almost felt sorry enough for him to do it, but that door was only a couple of steps away and it wouldn't take much for him to skedaddle out while I was trying to get around the table after him.

"Sorry. I thought this would satisfy you."

"Well, it don't. Not completely."

Gracie finally spoke up. "He's gonna be left-handed for sure one of these days if you keep that right one all tied up like that. Personally, I'm tickled to death right now that I can eat my supper in peace and not have to spoon-feed him like a baby."

Jonas's eyebrows met in the middle. "In my country, children are silent until addressed."

"Well, this ain't your country," Gracie fired back, quick as a striking snake. "It's mine, or I reckon it belonged to my people until all these white folks swallered everything up."

Ignoring her comment, Esther sat next to me with our backs to the curtain. Gracie took the last empty seat directly across from her and beside Gil. I looked for Otto and his sister, but they'd disappeared. "Your kids gonna eat with us?"

"No." Jonas settled himself at the head of the table beside Gil and immediately reached for the ladle sticking in the stew. "They are children. They eat after the adults. The only reason that sassy child with the busy mouth is allowed here with us is because she's a guest and with you. Susanne, light the lamp for our visitors."

Susanne nodded. "It is our way. Eat." She lit a splinter from the fire. When she had the oil lamp going, she brought it around and set it in the middle of the table.

Apparently, that wasn't enough for Jonas. "Another. It is still too dark."

I found that odd, because it seemed there was enough late-evening light coming from the window directly across from me.

Apparently not liking the speed in which Susanne was following orders, Jonas rose and lit another, setting it on the table and closer to his plate. "There. That's better. Does that help you back there, Otto?"

"Yes." His voice came from over my shoulder. "It was a little dim back here."

The hair prickled on the back of my neck. He hadn't spoken to Otto or his sister up to that point, so I wondered why he was suddenly concerned with them. I didn't have much space between myself and the curtain behind me, so I had to use the back of my chair to push it back and get some breathing space.

"I don't see how that little bit of light could help back behind that curtain." Gracie filled Gil's shallow bowl with steaming stew, then dipped out some for herself and Esther. Finally situated, I ladled a portion into my own bowl. A current of air must have pushed through the room, because the thin curtain behind me waved and undulated like a flag.

Gil picked up a fork and speared a piece of meat. Popping it into his mouth, he chewed and studied me across the table. I stuck a chunk of potato and blew away the steam to cool it down.

There was too much silence for Gracie. "Thanks for letting me sit at y'all's table. I sure do appreciate you for that."

Susanne looked surprised. "Why?"

"Well, I'm Cherokee, and lots of white folks wouldn't even like to have me in the house. And I know I'm kinda mouthy and can see Mr. Jonas would prefer me to be silent, so I guess what I'm saying is—"

Jonas broke in. "Vell, everyone offers something. Gil, push back a little if you need more room."

That curtain was still against my chair and arced over my head enough that it was irritating, for sure. It rubbed against the back of my head every time we moved.

Gil stared straight at *me* instead of looking at our host he addressed. His eyes flicked from my face to the curtain behind my shoulder. "You know, Jonas, your daughter sure is a cute little thing."

Jonas paused, looking from Gil to me, then back, but Gil didn't stop talking, though it seemed as if he were talking to me. "Back when me and Cap were kids, we knew a family who had a good-looking daughter with yellow hair, just like Olinda."

He looked past me and then Esther, seeming to study the thin cotton curtain.

"Her name was Helga, and they were so poor, her mama made her dresses out of anything she could find. That one summer before we left home, me and Cap went over to visit her late one evening. She come out of the house and stopped in the yard, with the sun behind her, and that dress she wore was so thin and backlit with such a bright sun, we could see right through the material at her legs that were as sharp and clear as if she wasn't wearing nothing."

Susanne's mouth fell open at such talk at the table, and Esther sat stock-still, staring at Gil as if he'd suddenly grown another head. My mind whirled at the lie, and right then, I knew something was up. I watched Gil's eyes skim back over the curtain to our host.

Suddenly grown another head . . . That damned curtain kept rubbing the back of my head . . .

"Jonas." Gil finally turned his attention to the stout German beside him. "I don't believe we're chickens."

I glanced over to see the man's eyes widen at the same time Gil flipped the fork in his fist and stabbed the man in the throat with those three long, sharp tines. "Behind you, Cap!"

Blood spurted across the table in a red gush as Jonas's arteries pumped blood through the puncture wounds at an astounding rate. In shock, I stood and something hit me in the back, hard enough to knock me forward. The loose curtain took some of the blow, and had I not stood, it would have caved in my skull.

As it was, I grunted with the pain of the blow and shoved the chair back. Esther rose with a shriek of horror at what was going on and got tangled in the curtain that pulled loose from its moorings on the rafter. She fell, taking it with her in a waterfall of dingy white cloth.

All of that happened in a blink as Gil rose, planted his feet, and stabbed Jonas again in the throat before dropping the fork. I was still trying to get my breath back from the blow when he picked up his bowl of stew, hot off the fire, and flung it directly into Susanne's face as she pushed up from the table with an astonished look. She shrieked and fell back from the table as the steaming contents coated everything not covered with cloth.

By that time, I had my wits about me and drew the Russian .44.

Esther was on her knees, trying to free herself from the tangled curtain that half covered her up. "Cap!" Struggling with that dusty old material, she lunged at Otto's legs; he had been standing behind me with a short-handled sledge-hammer cocked for another swing at my head. Had I not stood when I did, that first blow from behind would have crushed my skull.

Adding to the horror of what had exploded in that inn, Olinda's smooth, pretty face was frozen in a terrible expression of bloodlust. Seemingly unsure what to do, she took in the scene, while at the same time holding a butcher knife ready to cut and slash. Someone taught her about edged weapons and how to use them.

Behind them were several Number 5 washtubs filled with an assortment of clothing—belts, boots, and hats—and cut-up meat that wouldn't have been unusual if we'd been in a smokehouse. However, one tub contained easily recognizable human body parts.

It was too much. I twisted, thumb cocked the Russian, and shot Otto in the chest. He staggered, dropped the sledgehammer, and I shot him a second time before swinging the barrel to cover Olinda, who was as still as a statue, as if trying to decide what to do.

A beat.

Another beat.

Susanne shrieked and struggled to her feet. Olinda's eyes changed and I saw it coming. "Don't."

Silent as a striking water moccasin, Olinda launched herself at me and I shot the beautiful young woman dead from only five feet away. A bullet in her heart, Olinda landed face down on the hard floor with a thud. Through all that, I was aware of a fight going on around me, but in dealing with those two immediate threats, it wouldn't have been prudent to turn around.

By the time I did, I found Jonas pumping blood all over the table and Gil strangling Susanne to death with one hand.

The lamp nearest me had tipped, spilling coal oil across Jonas and the floor. Esther had divested herself of the curtain and pushed Gracie behind her against the nearest wall, a fork in hand as her only weapon.

"Good God Almighty, Gil. Shooting someone is one thing, but strangling a woman is another."

"Not this bitch!" He looked up, eyes glassy in fury and the skin around them white around the edges. "These people are *animals*."

Before I could answer, Jonas's limp weight took him backward. His chair fell into the fire, knocking coals onto the stone hearth and into the stream of coal oil that flowed across the puncheon boards to soak into the downed curtain. It burst into flame.

I whirled. "Go!"

Gracie and Esther yanked the door open and were out in a heartbeat. Gil was still squeezing Susanne's neck, but it was unnecessary. The light had already gone out in her eyes. I holstered the Russian and stepped around the table and picked up my Spencer. "You know she's gone, don't you?"

He finally came back to the world and his face calmed. "I know it. Just wanted to make sure." He stood and surveyed the house. Curtains still hid some portions from our view. "You better check back there. Might be folks like us still alive."

He remained where he was, despite the flames racing along the curtains and already licking up the wall beside the fireplace. Without thinking, I handed him the Spencer, which he took with his free, bloody hand. I drew the .44 again and yanked the curtains down . . . to find even more horrors.

CHAPTER 17

Texas Ranger Curtis Braziel was standing beside a small spring surrounded by hardwoods, watering his pony, when another horse snorted on the trail behind him. He spun, the pistol in his hand appearing in a flash.

Two mounted cowboys held up their hands. "Don't shoot, Marshal!" The older of the pair gave him a grin. "Sorry we snuck up on you. Didn't intend to. The horses smelled that spring and we let 'em have their heads. That's why we came up all of a sudden–like."

The younger man with a scraggly mustache remained still, both hands on his saddle horn, lest he get shot.

Angry with himself for not hearing them earlier, Braziel lowered the pistol, but kept it pointing somewhat in their direction. "I'm not a marshal. Texas Ranger."

"Up here in the territories?" The younger mustached cowboy raised his eyebrows and slowly lifted one hand to tilt his hat back. "You lost?"

Irritated by the accusation, Braziel holstered his pistol. "No, I ain't lost, and I find it offensive that you would suggest such a thing. I'm on the trail of a wanted man, escaped outlaw name of Gil Vanderburg. I intend to take him back to Texas to hang, if I don't have to shoot him first. You ever hear of him?"

"Nope. But that's funny, because we're looking for someone, too." The older cowboy rested a fist on his thigh. "My name's Gentry. Ed Gentry. This here's my partner, Bill Johns. We're trailing a swindler headed back to Texas. Stole from Lawyer Holland Penn back in Springfield."

Ranger Braziel drew a deep breath. "Well, this country's full of criminals, I hear. One more won't make much more difference to the total, I reckon."

"They'll make a difference to Lawyer Penn. He was madder'n an old wet hen about losing that money."

"I bet. Y'all U.S. Marshals?" They exchanged glances and the back of Braziel's neck prickled. His hand drifted toward his Colt.

Gentry raised up in his stirrups, as if that action might give him a moment to think. "Well, sir, we're *agents* of the law, you might say. Got a paper here from Lawyer Penn authorizing us to act on his behalf."

Though it sounded suspicious, such things happened down in Texas, too. Law was sometimes thin in places, and nonexistent in others. Whether you happened to wear a badge, or acted under the auspices of some branch of government, it was generally agreed upon that those on the right side of the law were accepted when they, as Braziel once put it, behaved theirselves.

He was intrigued by the pair. "You intend to shoot him, or hang him, when you find this man?"

"Nossir." Gentry and Johns exchanged glances again. "We're neither judge nor jury. Our intention is to take him back to Springfield and the law there."

"Old Judge Parker might not like to hear two men are acting without benefit of a badge, and with the weight of the law behind them. I suspect you should take him to Fort Smith and Judge Isaac Parker. He'll likely pay you for bringing him in."

"Well, sir." This time, the younger man with the mustache

wanted to have his say. "We hate criminals, and them who abide such men. We just considered ourselves good, honest Americans who do the right thing out here on the frontier. I figure if everybody has the same ideas and feelings, this would be a better place to live."

"I don't have such feelings, nor ideas." Ranger Braziel pulled the strawberry roan between them and swung onto his mount. "But I am the law, even in this godforsaken territory, and I came all the way up here from Austin, Texas, to take this man into custody."

Gentry nodded as if listening to a judge on the bench. Johns drew a serious face and concentrated on his saddle horn as if an answer to their dilemma was written there. "A man after my own heart."

Once settled, Braziel rested his fist just above the Colt's handle. "You have any idea where your outlaw might be heading?"

"South, or southeast, as he's been traveling, to this date. Would you mind, sir, if we rode with you?"

Ranger Braziel considered the offer. Any other time, he would have declined it, but just that morning, he'd come across five swollen corpses laid out in a row, with crows picking at their eyes and flies filling the air. Keeping his distance, he studied the tracks of numerous shod horses and deducted that it wasn't Indians who killed them—though in his opinion, they likely deserved it, for such bands of men in the territories were likely desperados.

Two extra guns might come in handy if he came across such a violent and well-armed group that took out those five in one gunfight, though they should have taken the time to bury the dead instead of leaving them out to feed the crows and buzzards.

"How about we join up to the next town? I've noticed a lot of tracks in the past day or two that might indicate three guns together might be more prudent than just those in the hand of one man."

"Fine, then." Gentry waved a hand. "Lead on."

"I'd rather the two of you take the lead." Ranger Braziel kept his horse still as a sculpture. "Y'all are liable to know the country better than me."

Gentry and Johns nodded at the same time and rode two abreast, followed by the Texas Ranger, who loosened the pistol in his holster, just in case of trouble.

CHAPTER 18

Stanton Sparks, a tall and slender Cherokee, pulled his horse up and turned to his partner, Chito Dawes, who was born of a Black dad and Seminole mother. Rubbing his extra-wide jaw with one hand, Sparks pulled back long, stringy black hair that reached past his shoulders and was so thin his scalp showed white, if not for the hat that covered everything from his ears up.

"Would you look at that horse coming yonder?"

Almost the same age, but shorter and stocky, Dawes tilted his hat to shade his face from the sun. Thick hair curled over his collar, more than enough to make up for Sparks's lack of natural adornment. "Even from this far away, I can tell that be the best-looking horse I've ever seen."

The two drifters watched a lone rider coming their way down a two-track wagon trace. Tall hills rose on either side of them and the spring air was filled with damp humus and the scent of pines warm in the late-evening sun.

The rider's horse shied for a moment when a flock of turkeys broke from cover and crossed the road at a run. More than a few flushed, great wings rustling and their huge bodies looking incongruous as they flew over small red cedars. Others scattered and ran in all directions to get away from a perceived threat.

Recovering quickly, the young man drew a pistol and threw a shot at the fleeing birds. More flushed, yelping in alarm and sailing in all directions. Laughing at the sheer joy of shooting, he emptied his revolver without hitting anything but dirt.

"Come on." Sparks squeezed his legs to walk his horse. Dawes did the same and fell in beside him. They were almost onto the fruitless hunter by the time he saw them.

The cheerful, smooth-faced man riding a slick black stud, standing nearly sixteen hands high, holstered his pistol, smiled, and waved a greeting. He wore a tall crease common out in West Texas. "Well, howdy!"

Riding boot to boot with Dawes, until they reined up and split to either side. Sparks returned the wave and smiled along with the cheerful man. He'd never seen anyone so out of tune with their surroundings, and that made his fresh idea all the better.

He took in the stud, the white drip between his eyes and two socks on his back legs. It was an animal that could be the foundation of a good horse ranch, or he could run, an ace in the hole at small-town races, no matter where they went.

Sparks breathed deep of fresh, new leather heated by the morning sun, knowing the man's new saddle hadn't been out of the shop for more than a few days. He used two fingers to slip a stray strand behind one ear. "Good morning. You from around here?"

"I am not. I fear I'm somewhat lost in this country." The traveler adjusted his seat with a creak of leather and folded both hands on the saddle horn. "I just left a town back there and tried to get my bearings. I was lost as a goose before I got to Margarite, over yonder. Heading for Tahlequah." His friendly smile widened. "I'm Theodore Olsen and I'm going up there to get married."

"How much farther is it?" Sparks glanced past the man,

but the trail curved out of sight. Now that they were still, he noticed the wind was at their backs and could have pushed the gunshots back to town, if it was close enough. That could kink his plans some, but then again, there were ways around what he had in mind.

Sparks was from Tahlequah and hadn't been down to that part of the territories in quite a while. He'd heard Dawes say he'd stayed close to his folks over in the Winding Stairs until he was almost grown before getting sideways with the local law over the theft of a heifer. He left one night under the cover of darkness after hearing that the marshal would be out to their farm the next morning. Since most of that cow had already been eaten, he told Sparks, he didn't figure they'd be too hard on the folks, but with him there, things might have gotten to the point of gunfire, and he loved his mama too much to have the laws shooting at her or the house.

"Couple of miles, I reckon. Maybe a little more. I'm not too good at distances."

Dawes tilted his hat back. "How come you to be headed up there to marry in some place you ain't been? Most fellers I know marry in their own towns, or contract for the women to come to them." He turned to Sparks and laughed big. "I heard of a feller who bought himself a bride all the way across the water in England. She showed up and was ugly as sin and that old boy lit out of the shipyard like the Devil was hangin' on to his collar."

Olsen laughed along with him. "Well, sir, Maizie's what you call a pen pal. You ever hear that term?"

Sparks shook his head. "Can't say I have. Didn't get much schooling myself, and Dawes here can barely read."

"You're not alone, I understand. Most of those old boys I grew up with barely made it through the third grade, if they went that far at all. Well, sir, I saw an ad in a newspaper back home two years ago and it was a woman looking for someone out west to correspond with. I answered her request and sent a letter and we have been writing back and forth ever since. Oh, I have a likeness here on a paper card."

He plucked the thick paper photograph from his coat pocket and passed it over to Dawes, who whistled in appreciation. "I'd have a go at that one."

For the first time, the young man's grin faltered. "She's some punkin, that's for sure. Anyway, last week, I'd had enough being alone. I sent her a telegram after I got this picture and asked for her hand in marriage and she answered right back and said yes! Ain't that something? So I told her I was on my way and I sold my farm, bought this fine stud and saddle, and now I'm going to get married."

"That right there's a happy man," Sparks said, making direct eye contact with Dawes.

"You're right about that." Olsen stood up in his stirrups and spread his arms. "This is what I've always wanted."

"You know, Mr. Olsen, something I've always wanted was a horse like that one." Sparks pointed between his horse's ears. "This pony under me is all right, but that stud you're on is splendid."

"He is, that."

"A man traveling alone in this country shouldn't be riding such a horse all alone. You're bound to attract the attention of someone who'll try and take it from you. Bad men are thick as fleas on a hound dog around here."

"I've been fine so far." Olsen's attention flicked back and forth between them, as if looking for assurance. "And I wear this iron." He patted the grip of the pistol on his belt.

"You're lucky, so far." Sparks reached down and fingered the rope strap hanging on his saddle. "Look, name your price and I'll trade horses with you and throw in, say, a hundred dollars to boot. You can keep the saddle."

Surprised by the offer, Olsen twisted his head back and forth like an owl between Dawes and Sparks. "Well, sir, that's a generous offer, but I bought this horse for my bride. See, we're going into the horse business in Missouri, after we get hitched. This stud here's gonna make us rich."

Dawes spoke up. "Mr. Olsen, I'll add fifty dollars to my friend's offer. We're doing you a favor. Getting through the territories is hard enough for man alone, but that horse is like waving a flag to robbers, asking them to come get you. Someone'll shoot you, for sure, for that animal."

Olsen's gleeful expression fractured. "Thanks, gentlemen, but I can't." He gripped the reins and heeled the black forward.

"Sure you can."

Dawes reached for Olsen's reins and Olsen jerked them away. "Stand off, sir!"

Sparks urged his mount forward to cut him off. "Take it easy, we're making you a fair offer."

Face twisted in fear, Olsen snatched his revolver free of its holster and aimed it at Sparks, thumb-cocking it at the same time. "Stand off, I said!"

Both Sparks and Dawes burst out in laughter. Looking as if they were playing a game, Dawes pulled the knot to release his lariat rope and fingered the coils. "Easy, hoss. We were just funnin'. And now it looks like you're funnin' us. That pistol's empty, mister. You just shot it dry."

It took a moment before Olsen properly understood the situation. He looked down at the revolver as if it had somehow betrayed its owner.

"So there you go." Dawes drew his own pistol, drawing a horrified expression from Olsen. "This one's loaded, though."

At that same instant, Sparks dropped a loop over Olsen's head and snatched the rope tight around his neck. Taking a dally around his saddle horn and backing his horse, he yanked Olsen out of the saddle. The man hit the ground with a thud, clawing at the constriction around his neck.

Kicking his horse into a lope, Sparks dragged him through the brush toward a wide live oak some distance away. Eyes bulging as he was dragged across the rough ground, Olsen groaned and struggled with the noose.

Dawes followed, leading the black by the reins.

They were soon at the live oak and Sparks pitched the rope over a low-hanging limb, again taking a dally. Expressionless, he backed his horse, dragging Olsen aloft. Without a word between the two of them, Sparks and Dawes watched the dying man thrash at the end of the rope, feet barely three feet off the ground.

Dawes hooked a leg over his saddle horn and rolled a smoke from the makings in his shirt pocket as the young man strangled to death. One of the scattered turkeys gobbled nearby, a peaceful, natural sound defying the situation. "Damn, you sure wanted that horse."

"The son of a bitch should have sold it to me when I asked." Sparks tied the rope off around the trunk and swung down to rummage through the man's possessions tied into a bedroll. He straightened, shaking a muslin poke full of coins. "We just made money."

He pitched the little bag up to Dawes, who caught it with one hand and squinted at the still body swinging gently in the breeze. He avoided the man's face. "What's in his pocket?" Squinting from the smoke rising from the cigarette stuck between his lips, he urged his horse forward and plucked out a folded piece of paper from Olsen's coat pocket. "It's a letter from his gal."

Sparks shrugged, more interested in what he was doing on the ground.

"Damn."

"What?"

"I just saw people coming down the road. I wish you'd 've drug him farther in the woods."

"This was the first limb that caught my eye."

Dawes glanced back. "I see four riders. We have a minute before they see us."

"We better come up with a story."

"I have an idea." Dawes dug into Olsen's coat pocket and grinned. "I knew that kind of a man would carry a writing instrument." He licked the nub of the pencil. "By the way, why'd you tell him I couldn't read or write?"

"Just talking until I decided what to do." Sparks watched as Dawes quickly scrawled on the back of the letter.

"Hand me that little stick right there."

"This is a fine new saddle, too." Sparks picked up a twig from the ground and passed it to Dawes who reached over to the corpse.

Rubbing a hand over Olsen's saddle, Sparks stuck one boot into the stirrup and swung up onto the black. The stirrups were almost perfectly adjusted to his height. "What are you doing?"

"Tidying things up." Dawes pushed the thin twig through the paper and then through a button hole on the dead man's shirt. "There. That ought to do it."

Rustler and horse thief.

The sounds of loping horses made them turn to see four horsemen riding in. When they drew close, it was obvious they were well-armed Cherokees headed for town. The oldest, with graying hair and dressed in a farmer's clothes, spoke first.

"What happened here?"

Dawes jerked a thumb. "We just found our friend a few minutes ago."

The old man took off his hat, as if that would help him better examine the hanged man. His face was a road map of wrinkles burned deep by the sun. "Your friend? You two ride with a white man? What happened?"

"Don't know." Sparks picked up the narrative. "We all got separated when Theodore went out to shoot us a turkey.

Fancied himself a crack shot with a pistol and we heard him banging away over here. When me and Dawes here rode in, we found him like this."

"Just now?"

"Only a minute ago." Sparks knew they'd seen them, and needed to explain their actions. "I was looking for tracks, but there's not much to go on."

One of the Indians started to dismount, but Sparks held up a hand. "Nothing to find. I figure we'd better not muddy up the water here until a marshal can take a look."

The old one nodded and spoke to the others in Choctaw. They backed their horses away. He made a hand signal. "I am sorry about your friend."

"He was a good guy. We were riding with him to Tahlequah, where he was gonna get married. You can look in his pocket there if you want. He has a likeness of his girl."

"So he *wasn't* a horse thief, then?"

"Not by a long shot."

The old man shook his head as the others milled around, keeping an eye on their surroundings. "Come on, boys, we'll ride in with our brothers and find the marshal. There's murderers loose in this damned hard country, for sure."

CHAPTER 19

Gil was standing in near darkness beside the corral and holding my Spencer shotgun with the butt on one foot when I came outside of the burning inn and into fresh air. Esther and Gracie were behind him, watching the house as smoke boiled through the cedar shake roof and rolled out the top of the door.

Resting my hand on the butt of the Russian, I stepped off the porch and pointed at the shotgun. "I'll be having that back."

His shoulders slumped. "I figured as much. And I reckon you'll want my hands behind me again."

The light from the burning house lit the area. His left hand was a bloody mess from jabbing the fork into Jonas's throat. I had to think for a minute. "You moved quick back there. How'd you know what they were?"

He held out the shotgun and I took it, noting the rusty color drying on the barrel from where he was holding it. "You weren't close enough to hear when we rode up, but he told Susanne over his shoulder to get ready, because there were more chickens riding up."

"And he said it in German."

"Yep. Big mistake on his part."

"And they were using the lamplight to skyline me in

order to knock me in the head. That's what you were telling me with that made-up story of yours."

He grinned, the dimples digging deep. "It was a good'un, too, wasn't it?"

"Sounded like a man who lies from experience."

"Now, there ain't no call for that."

"We need to get out of here." The house was going up like a torch and the heat already reached where we stood. "Gracie, run around back there and see if a cow's really staked out close to the house. Turn her loose, and anything else you see."

"Sure thing." She took off like a shot, her bare feet silent on the ground.

Without asking, Gil turned and opened the corral's pole gate and went inside. I followed while he stuck his free hand into the water trough to wash off the blood. Still silent, but looking immensely sad, Esther followed. She stopped beside him and helped him wash by taking his hand in her own.

He winced at one point and jerked away. She bent and looked closely. "What's wrong? You hurt?"

His eyes and mine met over her head. It was the first time she'd shown any indication of living in our world. "I think there's a piece of glass from that lamp in the heel of my hand."

She gave it a close examination. "I don't see any, but it's too dark to tell." She squeezed the meat between her thumbs. "Nothing's coming out except for a little spot of blood."

While she worked on him, I saddled the horses. Four horses trotted from around back and scattered into the darkness.

Gracie came back into view, followed by a Guernsey cow. "Didn't think you wanted to fool with more horses."

"You're right about that. Those ponies must've belonged to other folks those people killed."

She jerked a thumb over one shoulder. "They're all back there."

"Ponies?"

"No. It's too dark to see much, but I saw a garden of graves back there. They've been at this for a while." For all the horrors she'd seen, the kid was much calmer than I would have been at that age. She rubbed the Guernsey's bony hip. "What do we do with her? She needs milking."

"Turn her loose."

Gracie thew up her hands. "I did, and she followed me around here."

"We have enough on our hands without taking a cow with us."

She slapped her hand on one bony hip. "Go find somebody else to milk you." She picked up a bridle and slipped it onto Gil's roan, like she was expected to do it. "I sure hate to see a cow needs milking. Hope somebody comes along soon."

"This road's busy enough that they opened a slaughterhouse on it. Somebody'll be here directly, and likely pretty soon if anybody's nearby and smells all this smoke."

"Cap." Esther's voice was strong. "Do you have any bacon left?"

Surprised, I turned to see her reaching for one of the saddlebags. There was spirit in her face for the first time we came upon her. "Gal, you may be hungry and I'm glad to see that, but we don't have time to fry bacon, and right now I don't think my stomach could take it. We've gotta get gone."

"Not for me. I just need a piece of the fat to wrap around Gil's hand while it's still light enough to see. It'll draw that glass out in a day or two, for if we don't, it's liable to get infected."

My old granny did that once with my mama when she got glass in her finger, but it took nearly a week. "There's a little piece wrapped in that old rag, but make it quick. We got to go."

It took longer than I wanted, but saddling four horses by myself wasn't no quick chore. The heat from the burning house felt like the gates of Hell were open before we were all mounted up again. I considered taking the outlaws' spare horses with us, but seeing as how we needed to move fast, I turned them all loose.

Gil sighed. "Nobody should ever leave good riding stock behind." His right hand was still attached to his belt. The left had a piece of rag tied around his thumb. "Thanks for not hog-tying me up again."

It would be nothing for him to unbuckle the leather belt with his free hand and slip it off to get loose, but I owed him some freedom, at least temporarily, for his actions in there. I wasn't about to let him completely loose, though.

I picked up the lead rope and led his horse. "You bet."

The house was so hot, we had to swing out to the far edge of the trace, and I still wondered if our clothes would catch fire as we passed. A couple of trees closest to the burning structure were already smoking, and it wouldn't be long before they, too, burst into flame.

The horses didn't need any encouragement and we passed quick with me in the lead, followed by Gil, then Gracie, and finally Esther, who rode with her head up and seemed more interested in her surroundings than she had been.

She'd impressed me with her actions inside, and I hoped she would continue to find her way back into our world. She didn't look as pitiful as she did only a couple of hours earlier, and I swear, I think more of the swelling was already down on her face.

Anxious to put as much distance as possible between us

and the burning house, it was all I could do not to kick the horses into a lope, but we moved fast in the silver light of a full moon, so fast that we were a mile down the road before I remembered we left all the outlaws' guns and saddlebags behind us.

An hour later, we still hadn't met anyone coming our way. I slowed the mare down and we rode in silence through the moonlight. The north breeze had cooled considerably and I knew we'd all be chilled before morning.

After a while, Gracie rode up beside me. "I have a question for you."

"Look, I know you're still hungry, and I didn't even get one bite."

"It's a good thing, too. That meat didn't look right. I believe they were about to serve us up some long pig."

"What's that?" I'd never heard the term before.

"People."

I didn't tell her she was probably right. She hadn't seen all of what was behind those curtains, and I figured I wouldn't be hungry for a month.

"Never mind that."

"It wasn't my question, anyway." She twisted in her saddle to check on Esther riding drag back there. "My question is, how can you kill so quick? And Gil, too. I know some of my own people, and especially them Comanches'll cut a man down before you can say 'spit,' but I've never heard of no white man shooting so fast, unless they're murderers, and I don't believe that fits you."

I thought about telling her that it was none of her business. It was something I kept locked and buried in a strapped trunk down deep in my mind, and I had no intention of relating to a kid that my mama was murdered by Comancheros when I was little.

A dozen cutthroats busted down the door of our little cabin one afternoon while Dad was off rounding up strays.

Mama tried to defend us with an old percussion pistol she kept on the cupboard near the wood stove. The single load did for one, but the next murderer through the door knocked it out of her hand, and as one held me down and laughed, the rest raped and murdered her.

The bearded and stinking Comanchero who was last in line knocked me in the head with a piece of stove wood when they were finished and left me for dead. One set fire to our log house on the way out, but it was made too well to catch. Another fired the barn, too, and the hay we'd stacked inside went up in a *whoosh* and burned up two horses and a mule.

Dad saw the smoke and came a-running in time to save the house and me, but the war party was gone. He and a posse chased them from Fredericksburg all the way north to what became Doan's Crossing on the Red River before the band separated as they were wont to do, and they lost the trail.

Never one to run, he rebuilt the house and barn, with the help of neighbors, and raised me by himself. Most say I grew up to be the mirror image of him, both in looks and actions.

I cut the story short. "Well, something happened when I was a kid, and right then and there, I figured that I was never gonna let bad people get away with anything as long as I lived, if I could help it. My dad taught me to shoot first and ask questions later, and I reckon that's how I am."

She rode in silence for a few minutes. "I don't know what to say to that."

"You don't have to say anything. Sometimes it's best to just be quiet."

"I don't know how to do that, either."

CHAPTER 20

Ranger Braziel drew his strawberry roan up beside Ed Gentry and Bill Johns, who stopped a distance from the remains of a smoking house. Johns glanced around, nervous. "You think it was a war party?"

Ranger Braziel knew better. "Comanches tend to raid farther west and south of here. I'd suspect outlaws."

"Maybe it just burned." Gentry dismounted and searched the ground.

The fire left little standing, just the stone fireplace and part of a back wall. The cedar rail corral caught from the intense heat from the nearby inferno and burned all the way around, leaving a near-perfect circle of sweet-smelling coals. Two tree stumps nearest the house smoldered and smoked. However, when the wind shifted, they caught the horrific odor of burned meat.

Ranger Braziel nudged his mount closer to the house, though the stud rolled his eyes and showed he was uncomfortable with the scene. "I believe I see human skulls in there."

Johns split away from Gentry and dismounted beside the thatch shed, which was far away from the house. Though the corral fire came close, it hadn't caught, preserving the gear stacked up inside.

"Look here." He picked up a saddlebag and shook it out. "All this stuff was left, and it hasn't been here long. Wonder what this is all about." When he found nothing of interest in the first one, he moved to the second. "There's all kinds of things in here, but no bedding or anything like that. Wonder what that means."

Gentry considered the scene. While the Ranger and Johns concentrated on what caught their interest, he rode past the house and followed four sets of tracks.

"There were a lot of horses in here." Johns picked up something from the dirt. "Well, looky here what I found." He held up an unfired shotgun round. "Looks like somebody dropped this while they were gathering up their gear. I bet they were in a hurry."

Ranger Braziel deliberated the significance of the red shell. He rode back and joined Bill Johns on foot. The tracks of four horses heading southwest were clear in the dirt road, but he found something else, too. "Look at those footprints over yonder. These are bare feet and small. I'd figure them for a woman and child, and I doubt the child's ever had shoes on for more than a few hours at a time, and them were probably moccasins. Looky there at how wide them toes are splayed."

"Folks who lived here?" Johns continued digging through the gear that was left behind.

"Could be, but they're mixed in and on top of all these hoofprints heading that way," Braziel said. "I saw similar splayed tracks back at that camp full of dead highwaymen."

"I still don't know what that means." Johns pitched the shell onto the pile of abandoned gear.

"It means the men we're tracking killed those others we found, burned what they didn't want, and stole the rest."

Gentry returned and joined them and pointed back the way he'd ridden.

His account was intended to build a fire under the Ranger and keep him on edge. He had a hunch this was Whitlatch's work and he based it on that shell. Of course, there were lots of single-shot and two-shot shotguns, but this was the first real clue that they were on Whitlatch's trail.

Gentry flicked a finger. "Four horses going that way. They must have turned all the others out, like that cow over there."

A Guernsey cow stepped out of the nearby woods and lowed loud and miserable, her bag full and in need of milking. Ranger Braziel watched her bellow in pain. "Somebody fired the house and turned out all the stock."

Gentry agreed with the Ranger. "That's gotta be Whitlatch. He's picked up some stragglers along the way, looks like."

Braziel's expression told him he shouldn't have mentioned the man's name when the Ranger frowned. "Whitlatch?"

"That's who we're after. Man with strange eyes."

"You haven't mentioned a name."

"Well, it didn't come up."

"It's up now." The Ranger smoothed his beard. "Kinda funny, us running into each other out here, and all of us are after the same person." His hand dropped and lingered near the butt of his pistol.

"Ain't it?" Gentry watched the man's eyes, waiting for a signal that he might draw his weapon. Johns was fast, and he hoped his partner was paying attention.

The air thickened with tension as the Ranger rolled over this new discovery. "You hear the name Vanderburg mixed in with Whitlatch?"

"Naw." Gentry made sure his eyes didn't slip off the Ranger's face to see if Johns was on point.

Thinking, the Ranger glanced up at the smoke rising

straight into the air. "Why would a man on the run allow a woman and child to join him? That don't make sense." He stopped. "Wait a minute. Didn't Deputy Cornsilk say there was a girl in the jail with Vanderburg?"

Neither Johns nor Gentry answered, knowing the Ranger was talking to himself as the tension that had been building evaporated like the wisps of smoke.

"That's it. This is that kid that was in jail. I see boot tracks here and over there." He walked away from the corral, seeming to forget the other two men. "Here there are shoes. I bet this is Whitlatch and Vanderburg, and the barefoot girl they're probably misusing along the way. I suspect the woman was with those brigands they killed back there, too, for I'm sure it was them that done it."

Gentry broke his thoughts. "What brigands?"

"Found several bodies laid out a ways back."

"They killing people across the territories?" With a worried look on his face, Johns considered the smoking pile of coals that was once a house. "I didn't agree to track down murderers. We're supposed to be after a common thief. Ed?"

Gentry used one hand to pat the air between them. "It's all right, Bill. There's three of us."

"Yeah, well, I'd prefer not to tangle with someone of such caliber."

Gentry was seeing a side of Bill Johns that was new to him, and he felt his confidence in the man slip a little.

Johns shook his head, looking at the carnage. "Why would they murder the people who lived here and burn down their place? It don't make no sense."

Johns and Gentry exchanged glances. Thinking quick, Gentry put a bug in Ranger Braziel's ear. He needed Johns to settle down. "Covering their tracks. I bet they robbed those folks who burned up in there and lit out."

"We can loaf around here all day and talk about it, but we'll likely find the answers when we catch up to them two outlaws." Ranger Braziel sat straighter. "Let's get after them murderers. I doubt I'll take either of 'em back. I intend to hang them both when we catch them, by God."

CHAPTER 21

It was late in the day and the air was clean and cool when we came upon a two-track wagon road, not much wider than the pig trail we'd been following. Grasshoppers buzzed away with the dry sound of rustling paper. Gnats had been a problem in the woods, hanging in our faces and getting into our eyes and ears, but, thankfully, out in the open, there was enough breeze to blow them away.

Wagon tracks, along with the prints of mules, horses, and oxen, churned up the ground, evidence we were close to a town of some size. I pulled up and the rest stopped beside me. We were all worn out and needed the rest.

I pointed off toward a grove of blackjack and pin oaks. "Let's make camp over there and I'll go into town for supplies. We can rest up here a day or two, and, Esther, you can go in with me and we'll see if they have a sheriff and a telegram office, if it's big enough. Maybe he can telegraph your family."

"My people won't want me around anymore, not after those men . . ." She went silent, but I knew what she meant. Some high-and-mighty people shunned their kinfolk when they'd been misused by Indians or captors. It happened time and again on the frontier and sometimes their behavior toward rescued or released captives led those unfortunates to disappear forever, or even take their lives or die from grief.

She shrugged and settled in on herself as if someone had pulled out her backbone.

Afraid that she'd withdraw into herself once again, I tried to keep the conversation going. "What's your last name, ma'am?"

"McKinney."

"We'll get you home, Esther McKinney."

"I don't know if I have a home."

"Well, if that's the case, and your family proves to be sorry enough to turn their backs on you, I know some folks near my dad's place that'll surely make you welcome."

She built a wan smile and nodded.

We hadn't been there but a minute when a wagon, pulled by a team of mules, came by, heading toward town. Chickens riding in crates on top of several wooden boxes complained about the ride. The mustached driver slowed his team when he caught up to us and rolled to stop. He removed his hat at the sight of Esther, revealing a thick mop of gray hair. "Afternoon, folks."

His eyes went to Gil and his restraint, then Gracie.

I raised a hand in greeting. "Howdy. I'm Cap Whitlatch. Can you tell me the name of this town we're coming up to?"

"Why, I can and will. I'm Albert Simms." He pulled at a stray mustache hair at the corner of his mouth. "This new railroad town is called Margarite. It'll be a big city someday."

"I'm sure it will."

The elderly man held up a hand behind his ear. "Heh?"

"Said I'm sure it will."

"You'll have to speak up. Lost most of my hearing on this side at Chickamauga. Feller shot right beside my ear before a Yankee drilled him through the eye. You and the family passing through?"

I raised my voice so I wouldn't have to repeat myself. "Yessir. On our way back to Texas."

"Well, they have a fine hotel and half-a-dozen places to get a good meal. They'll likely even make accommodations for your prisoner there."

Gil frowned at the observation and I glanced over into Albert's wagon to see what he was carrying. "We'll likely camp out here. Save our money."

"A man after my own heart."

"I'd be willing to pay cash money for two or three of those chickens you're hauling."

"Dammit." Gracie muttered under her breath. "I don't know if I can eat chicken after what happened back there with them Germans."

Mr. Simms put a hand behind one ear. "What was that?"

"She said three or four, if you'll sell 'em. We're pretty hungry. Down to some cured hog scraps and a few beans for all of us."

His eyes shined and I knew we were in the presence of a haggler. "Well, I'll get six bits apiece in town for these laying hens."

"Those might have been laying hens some time ago, but they're stewing hens now, and I bet they're as stringy as rawhide." Every one of us shot Esther a surprised look. She seemed taller, straighter. "He'll give you thirty cents each, and I doubt you'll get that in town."

Old Albert frowned. "Why, these hens are my best layers."

"They were." Esther stepped down and peered into the back of his wagon. "But they're long out of their prime. Are those dandelion greens?"

"Yes, ma'am." Albert drew a long, sighing breath and I figured he'd met his match. "I get fifty cents a mess because they're so hard to pick."

"Cap. Would you please give this man two and a quarter? That's for four hens, enough greens for all of us, and I see a bucket of dewberries in there, too. They'll add up to less than that, but it'll pay you for your troubles."

I noticed he heard her just fine. Albert gave her a slight nod. "I suppose you want to pick out your own broilers."

"They're broilers now, huh?" Esther opened the tiny door in the top of the crate and reached in. Bypassing a number of startled hens, she grabbed one by the neck. It came out flapping and she wrung its neck. Pitching the body onto the ground to flop around, she reached in for them, one at a time.

"Wish I had an apron." Even her voice sounded better, and it was probably because she was on familiar ground.

The headless chickens flapped and jumped on the ground as she used the front of her ripped and tattered dress to gather up enough greens and dewberries for all of us. Holding the bundle with both hands, she stepped back to her horse and waited.

Feeling bad about the sad old man, I handed Albert the money and he dropped the coins into a pocket. "I hope y'all don't open no store in town. I don't believe I'd make a cent haggling with her."

"Don't worry." I grinned. "Like I said, we're just passing through."

"Good day to you, then, sir." Slapping the reins, Albert continued on his way and I swung down to collect the chickens that had mostly bled out by then. I had a muslin sack in amongst my things and we put the greens and berries in it so Esther could properly ride.

A clear-water stream led us away from the road and against a line of trees, where we found a good, level place to camp. There was a nice cool breeze to blow away the mosquitoes, and for once, we were free of flies. Esther and Gracie plucked the chickens, while I built a fire, and Gil sat on a log and watched.

"My nose is itching off." Gracie used the back of her

hand to scratch. "Happens every time I pick a dry chicken. Wish you'd've thought to buy us a pot from that deaf old man. We could scald these damned birds and be finished with it already."

Gil sighed. "Good Lord, girl. You'd gripe if you's to be hung with a new rope."

"Of course, I would. I'd druther they used an old rope that'd be more likely to break, though I'm damned near starved to death on this trip and I doubt I'd weigh enough to even snap a string, let alone my neck."

I wasn't listening, because I'd taken notice of something we'd all missed when we found the campsite. A wide live oak, 150 yards or so from where I stood, bore a fruit I wish I hadn't seen.

A man swung from just such a rope as we were talking about.

Gil followed my gaze and grew solemn. "We're in a damned harsh territory."

"It is that."

He sighed. "This is what happened in the first place to get me here. A dead man and no witnesses of his demise to speak for me."

CHAPTER 22

"I'm not going anywhere until I eat." Esther's voice came steady and strong.

I'd suggested we go on down the road and leave that trouble swinging behind us, but she dug her heels in, showing a recovering spirit, likely rooted in hunger. I couldn't blame her. My spine was rubbing a blister on the back of my stomach.

She held the last plucked and gutted chicken and reached out a hand for the long, peeled cedar stick to use as a spit. I handed it to her and she pushed it through the carcass to join the other three.

Gil cleared his throat. "You want to cook and eat those hens, with that poor feller swinging just over there? I don't know that I can abide looking at him during dinner."

"We do." Gracie took the chickens from Esther. The fire had burned down to a good bed of coals and she laid the spit across two small stacks of downed wood on either end, positioning it to keep the birds high above the heat. "I was wrong about eating. I'm starving."

Without being told, Gracie raked the coals to even up the cooking surface. "And besides, he's gone on to his reward, and if we don't eat soon, we'll all be just as dead as him."

She waited for an argument from me. When I didn't

answer, she gave a quick nod of satisfaction. "Besides, he'll keep the flies over there, so they won't bother us."

Spoken in a chilly and matter-of-fact way, her statement made me consider her spunk all over again.

For once, I didn't know what to do about our traveling party. Gil and I were even more shocked when Esther reached out a hand to Gracie. "Come on, girl. We're going over there to wash up in that stream, and I don't know what it'll take to get this stink off me. We might have to skin all the way down to nothing. Cap, do you have any soap?"

Shocked that they were determined to bathe at such a time, I looked for something to say, but came up empty. Instead, I dug around in my possibles and found a sliver of lye soap wrapped in a rag.

Esther accepted it with a nod. "Thanks. You two stay here and turn these chickens every now and then. Don't you dare let 'em burn."

"You need to take a pistol with you."

"Nope, we won't be far. Just barely out of sight over there, and if we see anything, I'll holler and you can come a-runnin'."

"Nope." I dug Gil's cap and ball revolver from my bedroll. "Take and keep this with you all the time."

The way she handled it when I passed it over told me she was confident with guns, and I felt a little better for it. They walked off and Gil surveyed the area around us. "*We're* cooking, and *they're* bathing, and there's a man swinging from a short rope across a tall limb over yonder. My Lord."

"Ain't this something?" I kept an eye out in the direction they went.

"It's something, all right, but I can't say what it is. What're we gonna do?"

I came to a decision that I felt was the right thing to do. "I'm riding over there to cut that man down, for one thing.

I can't abide what I keep seeing. You watch our supper and don't let it burn."

I kinda forgot Gil was my prisoner, with one hand loose, but the events of the past few days had me rattled, so without another thought, I rode the steeldust mare over to the body.

There was a scrawled note held on with a twig through a buttonhole that told the tale.

Rustler and horse thief.

He wasn't the first man I'd seen lynched, and especially not for such accusations as those flapping on his shirt. People swinging from ropes are a terrible thing to see, and the man didn't look any different from others I'd seen, both properly executed or lynched. He hadn't been there long, for he hadn't swelled and there was no odor.

The much-used rope around his neck that ran over a limb and down to the trunk was old, and it was a wonder it hadn't snapped. I almost grinned thinking about our earlier discussion with Gracie.

Using the pigsticker on my belt, I cut him down, wincing when he landed first on stiff legs and then falling sideways with an awkward thud. As I said earlier, he wasn't the first person I'd ever seen like that, but it was the first time I'd seen someone hanged without their hands tied behind his back.

His clothes were dirty and torn, as were his hands. Somebody'd drug him over to the tree, and that was a tale I couldn't explain. I sat there on my mount, looking at the body and wondering what to do. *I* hadn't strung him up, we still didn't have a shovel, and I had no intention of using the big knife at the back of my belt to scrape out a grave.

Instead, I rolled him onto his back, for that seemed a little less barbaric than leaving him on his side with his face in the dirt and leaves, and left him there as tidied up as the outlaws way back behind us.

When I got back, Gil had undone the shackle from his belt, leaving the end dangling from his right wrist. He almost looked as if he needed to apologize. "I had to get loose to turn the chickens. The balance was all wrong and I was afraid I'd drop them into the coals with just my left hand." He held it up. "That piece of glass in there's giving me fits, too."

"It's fine." Weary as all get out, I squatted by the fire. He'd also dug out the skillet and had some coffee beans on to roast. A pot full of water sat nearby, ready to put on when the beans were ground.

"Where'd you get them beans? We ran out back there the other morning."

He looked sheepish. "Well, I had a handful squirreled away in my spare shirt."

Gaping like a fish out of water, I realized I hadn't gone through his bedroll and the little bundle tied onto the back of his saddle. If he had coffee beans in his war bag, what else was in there? I knew right then I wasn't cut out to be no lawman. There might have been a Gatling gun in there, for all I knew, besides his pistol that Sheriff Kanoska took when he locked him up.

Esther and Gracie came back with clean faces and hair. I was shocked to see Esther in nothing but a pair of fluffy drawers that were ripped and stained with blood in more than one place, proof that she'd suffered at the hands of the Comanches and those cutthroats we'd killed.

She carried her wet dress and Gracie's dripping shirt. Gracie's overalls were soaked, too, but modesty prevailed and she likely didn't have anything on underneath, besides a strip of material cut from Esther's ragged dress and tied across her bosom.

I turned so I wouldn't have to look at her.

"Don't say a word." Esther spread the clothes on a nearby bush to dry.

Her wet hair framed her face, which looked much better now that she'd washed off the dirt and blood. Even the notch in her nose didn't look as bad, and had quit seeping. Most of the scratches were scabbed over and healing just fine, and much of the swelling had gone down, as had the yellowjacket stings on me and Gil.

"I didn't intend to." I realized she was a handsome woman.

"We did the best we could with what we had to work with."

Gracie toiled around the fire as if she wasn't half clothed. "I swear. If this woman'd scrubbed me harder with those handfuls of wet sand and all that stinkin' lye soap, I wouldn't have any skin left at all. She rubbed me plumb raw."

Her long black hair was also wet, and for the first time since I met her, she looked like a young lady, even in her overalls.

Esther picked up the coffeepot, peered at the water inside, and grunted. The next thing I knew, she stuck those dandelion greens inside and put the pot near the coals.

Gil raised a hand. "Hey! We were gonna make coffee."

"Well, you might have been planning on that, but we need them greens more'n some black water. We'll all get sick if we don't get something else inside of us besides meat, dried or fresh, either one. Coffee can wait till we're done eating."

"We have those dewberries." His face was one of pure anguish. "I dearly wanted some coffee."

"We do, and we'll eat them, too. I'll make coffee after we finish." She turned to me. "Mr. Whitlatch, when you go into town, you'll need to get us a pot to cook in."

Since there were only two metal plates and two forks in

my bags, I was wondering how we'd all eat those greens when she addressed me. Startled by her declaration, I paused. "Well, ma'am, I was intending to drop you and Gracie off there so you wouldn't have to travel no more."

"Nossir." She turned the spit, and chicken grease sizzled in the coals. "I'm not from here. You said y'all were heading down to Fredericksburg or Kerrville, or somewhere like that, and I'll ride with y'all down that way until I get to my house in Young County, if it's still there. That's where those Comanches took me."

My mouth opened and closed like a bluegill out of water. I knew the county well. "Young County?"

"West of Jacksboro."

"The Butterfield Stage goes through there."

"When it can. The Comanches've been raiding out that way a lot in the past year."

I'd gotten hold of a *Dallas Herald* paper that talked about how dangerous it was anywhere west of Fort Worth. "Y'all should've gotten out of there when the going was good."

"That's what I told my husband, God rest his soul, but he said no savages were going to run him off the land he'd worked so hard to claim."

"He wasn't trying to farm out there, was he?"

"No. He had a mind to raise cattle."

"The Chisholm Trail came through there. I doubt people would buy cattle when so many drove straight through town."

"Those were longhorns. He was trying to breed a heavier, fatter cow." She stared at the ground and wiped a tear. "They killed all his stock, too." She set her jaw. "I expected never to see it or my family again."

A whole list of questions popped into my mind and she must have been ready for them. "I was just married, only a couple of months before those savages came. They killed my husband and his brother, and knocked me on the head. I woke up tied across a horse, and that's all I know."

"When was this?"

"Three months ago. That sorry excuse for a human being you shot there on the ground between y'all's horses knew the Comanches and traded for me. Kangee'd come hunting for me, but not for my family."

"That half-breed was in charge? I thought it was the white man with the Walker Colt."

"That was Charley. He thought he was the boss of that outfit, but only because Kangee let him think that. Both of 'em were mean as snakes, though. There wasn't an ounce of difference between the two of 'em.

"Kangee'd heard they had a white woman and he wanted one he didn't have to steal himself. He tied up with those men after he traded five horses for me, but then they all took what they wanted after we got shed of them Indians, and I never expected to live much past that day you found me."

I felt my face flush in anger and noticed Gracie was watching me with intent. I believe she was waiting on me to get mad, to see what I'd do, but I wasn't going to give her that satisfaction. I'd done for the men who abused Esther and was finished with it.

"Ma'am, it's a long and dangerous journey down through Texas. For all I know, we'll run into more Comanches on the warpath, or Comancheros riding with them, or robbers or murderers or—"

"They'll still be there if you drop me off in this little one-horse town and I have to go later."

"I'm hoping to come across a railroad at some point, if there's not one here."

She turned the chickens again over the pecan wood fire, and they were smelling wonderful. "Then I'll ride with you until we find a town with a station."

She had me trapped. I couldn't leave her anywhere that

wasn't safe, and a town with a railroad was likely the safest place I could find. They'd have a hotel, restaurants, and the law, which was the most important thing.

Looking into the coals, I considered my options. "Fine, then, but you keep Gracie close by with you when we find just such a place."

"Hey!" Her forehead wrinkled in anger. "You can't make decisions for me. I been making my own since Mama died."

"And look where it took you." Gil couldn't stay quiet. "Right smack into a jail cell beside my own."

I ignored his point, for I was in charge of our little troupe and intended to continue making all the decisions. "I can, and will, young lady. You're not full growed yet, so you do what I say, and besides, it ain't right for a girl your age to go riding alone with men who ain't kinfolk."

"Esther's with us."

"She ain't you."

Instead of answering, she put both hands over her chest and frowned. That action spoke volumes and I couldn't help but grin. Esther saw my face and laughed, while Gil just sat there and picked at his hand with the glass in it.

The chickens were reduced to bones not long after, and the greens were gone, as well as the sweet, tart dewberries. I was on my second cup of coffee as the sun rested on the hardwoods when Gracie stood. "I have to go outdoors. I think them greens are working on me."

Esther rose. "I'll go with you, and, Gracie, you shouldn't say such things around men. It isn't polite."

"I've never been polite, nor much of anything. We all have the same pains, so I don't see the harm in saying what I need to do." She pointed. "We went through some thick brush coming back from bathing back over yonder."

Esther threw me a slightly embarrassed grin and they disappeared into the understory brush beyond the horses, which were still saddled and picketed in the green grass nearby.

I'd meant to relieve them of their gear after we finished eating, but being full for the first time in days kinda slowed me down. It wasn't like me, because I always took care of the horses first, but a little bug in my ear kept telling me to wait.

They hadn't been gone but a couple of minutes and I was about to take the horses down for water in the opposite direction when men on horseback suddenly appeared around us from all angles and every one of them was pointing guns.

Kicking myself for being so full and drowsy, I stood. One man with his shirt buttoned to the neck and a star on his coat lapel pointed a revolver at my belly. When he saw I wasn't going to fight or run, he nudged his horse a little closer. "You there in the camp. Don't move. The two of you're under arrest."

"Dammit!" Gil hung his head.

Instead of doing what he said, I stepped forward, keeping both hands free. "Under arrest for what?"

"Why, for lynching that man over there, Theodore Olsen. I'm the county sheriff of Margarite and this is my posse."

"I didn't lynch nobody, and how do you know somebody was hung?" You couldn't see the body from where we stood.

He pointed at an Indian with the scraggliest long hair and widest chin I'd ever seen. He scowled and looked up to no good, in my opinion. Another half-breed rested close to him, looking to be a mix of Black and white. I took him for a Seminole, for there were a few of them in the territories. "Sparks there saw him earlier and come to get me. Said Olsen was hung."

"We've been here a spell. Took you a while to get here."

"Rounding up a posse takes time." The sheriff looked sad. "Few men'll load up to go after a killer."

Another man in a suit and wearing a badge pointed. "Sheriff Bronson, that other'n there's in manacles."

The sheriff took notice. "Looks like you might have broken a prisoner free, sir. What's your name?"

"Cap Whitlatch, and it's just the opposite. I'm taking him back to Fredericksburg, Texas, to stand trial. Took the chains off of him so he could eat and do his business later."

"What's his name?"

Gil spoke up. "Gil Vanderburg, and, technically, I'm not a prisoner, but like Cap said, he's escorting me back to Texas to sort all this out."

The sheriff nodded as he absorbed that bit of information. "You the law?"

"Nope." I had that badge in my pocket, but didn't want to take it out right then. "Said I'd do it for Sheriff Kanoska up in Blackwater, some miles northeast of here."

The entire posse stiffened and I wondered what I'd said. "What?"

"Got a telegram that Kanoska was murdered and his prisoner was gone. Looks like you boys stumbled right back into jail."

CHAPTER 23

The Gluck brothers rode almost three abreast on the well-traveled wagon road, hoping to arrive at a town before nightfall. It was Cloyce who was slightly in the lead and saw the flicker of a campfire in the gathering gloom.

"Y'all stay here out of sight. I'm gonna ease up on that camp and see if it might be that German." He grinned. "If not, I bet it's someone I can *borrow* something from. Who knows, they might be rich travelers or folks with plenty of bacon to share."

They laughed as he dismounted and took a wide route from the road to swing in from the side. More than once in the course of any trip together, the brothers borrowed food or money from travelers too weak of spirit to protect themselves. Cloyce remembered his dad once said the strong always preyed on the weak, and he was proven right, over and over again.

Water gurgled in a small stream to his left, covering any noise he might make as he carefully worked his way through the underbrush. He heard voices first, and eventually closed in on the camp to see Gil Vanderburg sitting on a log beside the fire.

Cloyce grinned, exposing yellow teeth. It was the German, and another man was also there, sitting with his back to Cloyce. He saw a pump shotgun leaning nearby. Whitlatch really was with him, just as they'd suspected.

Excited, but still afraid of Whitlatch, he backed away to get his brothers. The three of them would have better odds if Whitlatch came up firing. They'd surround him and, with surprise on their side, could empty their guns into both of them and be done with it.

Once he was away from the camp, Cloyce hurried back. "We almost rode past them. It's the German, all right, and that Whitlatch feller, I believe. Itchy, picket these horses and we'll ease up on them when it gets full dark."

The youngest brother took Cheese's mount and led them back into a patch of woods. He'd barely returned when the sounds of approaching hooves sent them hiding in the brush. "That's a bunch of horses."

Cloyce held up a finger. "Hush, until they pass."

The horsemen weren't in any hurry, simply letting the mounts walk down the wagon road at their own speed. When the scattered line of mounted men grew near, the Gluck brothers drew back together to crouch beneath a huge thicket of spreading buckeye trees.

"That's a posse, if I ever saw one." Cloyce kept his voice low, lest they missed a straggling lawman.

"They're gonna get those two before we can." Cheese scanned the area around him.

"That's good, ain't it?" Itchy asked.

"Yes and no." Cloyce chewed his lip in thought and absently rubbed the deep scar cut across the bridge of his nose. "They might take them in and then let 'em go, but I doubt it. If they've heard about that German's escape and that Kanoska's dead, they're liable to hang 'em, but then again, they might get away a second time, if they try to take them alive, or something could happen in a courtroom."

He rubbed his head in indecision. "I never did trust these Indian courts."

The only thing Cloyce wanted was to see those two cold and dead on the ground. Riding away and letting the posse have them might work, but then again, they might someday come to Blackwater, all free and clear from a court, and bring Possum's death back up. He needed to have that issue settled, once and for all, and the only thing that would finish the job was lead.

"What do you want to do?" Itchy adjusted his knee on the ground.

"I don't know. Let me think."

"We don't have much thinking time." Cheese held out a hand. "Shh. I hear more horses." They peered into the long shadows of evening. "There. Three men, but they're riding fast. Making time."

Hat in hand, Cloyce rubbed his oily hair and wondered why there were so many people in such a little space. "Don't move. Let's just sit here and find out what's going on."

CHAPTER 24

Sheriff Bronson kept that big .44 pointed right at my chest. "Mr. Whitlatch, use just the fingertips of your left hand and unholster that pistol and pitch it back this way."

"Nossir."

"What?" He was clearly taken aback, and his mouth hung open.

"I said no, sir. I won't pitch this weapon anywhere. I'll lay it on the ground slow, but I won't throw it."

"Dammit, man, I'm holding a six-shooter in my hand, and there's half-a-dozen men with me who'll blow holes through you big enough to pitch a dog through." He swallowed and waved the pistol for emphasis. "You're supposed to do what I say."

Those men with him weren't gunfighters, not by any measure. One was definitely a storekeeper with a double-barreled fowling piece, and two other cowboys with pistols stuck in their belts were likely looking for some entertainment. The rest were a mix of townspeople, with cheap revolvers, who likely felt it was their duty to join at the sheriff's request. Not a one of them carried a rifle.

"Cap never was one to take orders." Gil's tone was matter-of-fact from his seat on the ground. "He'll be more likely to listen if you was to ask him."

"I'll be damned if I'll request anything of a murderer, sir."

I was starting to steam. "Well, I haven't murdered any-body, though I've shot my share of those in self-defense who intended to harm myself or friends. Now, that man you're talking about was hanging there when we pulled in and set up camp. Didn't notice him till after we built a fire and settled down for the night. For the life of me, I can't figure out why anyone with any sense at all would think we'd hang someone, a feller we never laid eyes on, and then set down so close by and have supper. It don't make any sense."

The others looked uncomfortable, and I hoped they saw the wisdom in my words. Common sense is sometimes slow to take hold, when men are fired up for justice. Talk-ing calm as if we were gathered around the dinner table might help.

I once saw two cowboys fistfighting one another in front of a saloon one night, and it was between just the two of them. However, one of those boys didn't get back up. His neck might have broke, or he had a heart attack, or just decided to give up the ghost right then and there, for reasons known only to him, but the next thing I knew, someone watching from the crowd hollered "murder."

Another voice picked up the cry, and there was no rea-soning with them after that. Fair fight, accident or not, they had a rope around that poor man's neck in the blink of an eye and were about to throw the loose end over a sign beam in front of the stable when I had to step in. It wasn't my fight, but there was no reason to hang an innocent man, in my opinion.

Once again, it was a similar crowd like those old boys around our camp, and they backed down pretty quick when I made it clear, by shooting one or two of them, that I wouldn't let them string that feller up. That's how you stop a mob, and it works every time.

I was hoping it would happen now.

"He's right, Sheriff." The shopkeeper with the shotgun was sharper than the rest, and I could tell he didn't want to use that bird gun. He'd already worked it out and was ready to go home for supper. "Nobody in their right mind would kill a man and have dinner this close. It just don't make no sense."

The long-haired Indian named Sparks, who I didn't like the looks of, was losing his patience. The half-breed I took to be his partner'd ridden over to the dead man to look him over. His name was Dawes and he loped back, trying to make out like he was upset, but I thought it was all an act.

"That's my buddy over there dead," the scraggly-haired man said. The black stud under him looked to be at least sixteen hands high and I could tell he was much of a horse. "They cut him down since we found him and just left him a-laying there with a paper on his chest that says he was a horse thief. You need to do your job, Sheriff."

"What would you want me to do, Mr. Dawes?"

"Well, I got a rope here and that limb's already proven solid enough for the job. I say we hang these two."

"Not without a trial, we won't, and besides, this man's a fugitive." Sheriff Bronson glared at Dawes and Sparks. "He's murdered a sheriff up north of here and got us all arguing about Olsen." He flicked the barrel of the pistol in his hand toward me. "We're taking you in, sir, for that murder and we'll let the courts figure out what happened here."

"We haven't murdered anyone. What *you* need to do is ask those two right there if we were here when he found the body."

Sparks frowned. You could tell he didn't like his charge to be questioned.

"What do you mean?" Bronson looked perplexed. "He's done told us enough to round up a posse."

"He didn't make any mention of us when he came to town, did he? And he would have if we'd been here. He read that note pinned to Olsen's chest and didn't bring us up when he came to you?"

I had 'em there, and was feeling pretty good about myself, when a loud voice full of authority cut through the evening.

"You men in the camp. Lower your arms. Texas Ranger, and I'm coming in."

We looked over at three new men riding from the underbrush. That gray-bearded man looked about as tough as boot leather and I could tell he wasn't someone to take lightly. He looked to me like one of those fire-and-brimstone preachers who travel from brush arbor to outdoor revival and beat the Devil with a Bible. The badge on the lapel of his coat briefly flickered when it caught a bit of light from the setting sun and shot a beam through the leaves, so I knew for sure he wasn't no preacher.

"Well, hell." Gil seemed to shrink in on himself. "That just about does it for me. Cap, just shoot me and let's get this over with."

The three riders came forward at a slow walk. The Ranger rode with a Colt, held muzzle up in his right hand. Two others followed behind, on both sides, hats pulled low and hiding their faces.

"Who'n hell are you to tell me what to do?" Sheriff Bronson was working up a mad. He turned his horse to better see the trio coming up from the side. "This ain't Texas, not by a long shot, it's fifty miles to the Red River, and you're in no position to be issuing orders to me."

They say I have strange eyes, but those the Ranger was looking through were darker and broodier than any I'd ever seen in my life. I raised a hand in greeting. "Glad you made it, sir. I'm Cap Whitlatch and this man here in the shackles is Gil Vanderburg. I'm taking him down to Texas for Sheriff Kanoska, and I'd sure like your help a-doin' it. You can have him, right here and now, and I'll go my own way."

"You won't get any help from me, murderer." The Ranger's eyes blazed and my spirits sank. "I've seen your work across half of these territories. Now, you take that pistol off and throw it on the ground."

Gil barked a laugh. "We done chewed that fat. Bronson, why don't you tell him what I told you."

The Ranger's eyebrows rose, tilting his hat upward. "Why, what do you mean? I've issued a lawful order."

Bronson looked sad. "I told him the same thing and he's just standing there, arguing."

"Damn you, sir." The Ranger pointed his gun at me. "Remove that firearm from its holster or I'll shoot you where you stand."

"What I said was, I'd take it out slowly and put it on the ground." I knew I was sounding as stubborn as a toddler, but I didn't like the idea of pitching a fine pistol on the ground, and I was getting aggravated at so many people pointing pistols at me for whatever they thought I might have done.

"Do that, then, and place it on the ground."

Sheriff Bronson stepped down, his pistol still pointed at my middle. "Hold on. This man is my prisoner and you're not taking him. He's going to town and stand trial for murder."

Still not moving, because there were way too many guns pointed at me, and one nervous townie was all it could take to start a dance I didn't want to finish. "Would y'all put them guns down before something happens?"

"You're under arrest, and, I-God, you're going in with me." Bronson approached us as if he was done talking. "Boys, shoot this man if he moves. Sir, extend your arms. I'm going to cuff you."

"No, you're not!" The Ranger's voice rang sharp and clear. "Sheriff, you'll not arrest him. This man is my prisoner."

"You have no authority here. This is Indian Territory."

"Vanderburg is my prisoner, assigned to me by Kanoska back in Blackwater, so that means a territorial sheriff has exercised his authority and transferred custody of that man to *me*."

The muzzle of Bronson's pistol dropped just a hair, but I couldn't breathe any easier, because of all those *other* guns aimed at me. "Well, you're after Vanderburg, then. So, which one is that?"

Gil raised a hand. "That's me."

"All right." Bronson chewed his bottom lip. "You can have that one, and I'll hang the other'n."

"No." The Ranger glared. "I'll take them both. I feel that I'm a representative of Sheriff Kanoska, and if they killed him, I'll take them to Texas and hang 'em myself."

"That won't do. The murder of a lawman here in the territories falls under the purview of Judge Isaac Parker in Fort Smith, not a Texas Ranger." Bronson waved a hand toward his men. "I've already organized this posse, and that lynching occurred here. We'll have them both."

My Spencer was too far out of reach, and there was no way I could draw down on them without someone opening fire and filling me full of holes. Rangers had a reputation for harsh justice, and I was well outgunned by those surrounding us.

The air thickened with tension. The Ranger and Bronson were in a pissing match, and those kinds of things could get out of control in a heartbeat. Some of those old boys were looking nervous, and I was afraid one of them might shoot me or Gil just so they could get out of such a situation.

I didn't intend to go with either of them, but made sure my right hand was still high and clear. "All right. Let's all cool down and lower these guns before somebody's finger slips. I'll take it off, but like I said, I'm just going to lay it on the ground. Then y'all can work it out between your-selves."

It's funny how the mind works. It was dusk and light-ning bugs flickered against the dark woods. A bat darted in the filtered light above, chasing insects. Birds tittered in the limbs, settling in for the evening.

I tried not to consider all those muzzles pointing at me. "All right. I'm going to put it down, now."

"When he does, you don't put those cuffs on him." It might have been my imagination, but it seemed as if the Ranger shifted his position to concentrate on Bronson.

And that's when it happened. Red-faced, Bronson squared off at the Ranger and approached with his pistol in hand. "I'll tell you what . . ."

Guns in the hands of those two behind the Ranger rose, and at first, I thought they were aiming at Bronson, who raised his voice. "He's mine!"

I could see the Ranger had no idea those men with him drew their weapons. "Stay still, Sheriff . . ."

A bat darted between us.

Spooked, the Ranger's strawberry roan shied, side-stepping just a hair.

We were all shocked when a volley of shots came from a line of trees. Three men threw up their arms and pitched off their mounts at the same time. Half a second later, those two cowboys behind the Ranger put holes in both him and Bronson before you could say "scat."

Sheriff Bronson looked down at his chest and put one hand over the wound, which poured blood. His knees folded and he dropped at the same time that the Ranger pitched off his horse and fell on his head, landing as limp as a dishrag.

Shocked, the posse of townspeople froze when that now-familiar panther scream ripped through the air, once again adding to the panic and confusion. The rifles in the woods fired again. Horses jerked, guns blazed, and those with their senses fired back at the flashes thirty yards away, filling the world full of lead.

Voices shouted in fear and pain as men fell from their mounts.

The two Indians who'd started the whole thing put spurs to their mounts and rode past, low over their horses' necks, the big black ridden by the one with long, stringy hair led the way.

I threw myself at Gil, knocking him off the log, as angry bees buzzed past my head.

CHAPTER 25

I've read the word "chaos" in books, for I love to read when I can, but what was going on around us was the best example I've ever seen. Gil and I lay behind that big timber as guns fired and hot lead whistled all around us. The thud of falling bodies was sharp and clear, as were the cries of wounded men. Horses not used to gunfire bucked and snorted.

We cringed against the log as a horse bucked right over us, its hooves landing only inches away. The rider lost his seat and took air. He fell across the log with a grunt and lay still.

Those boys in the posse weren't really there to fight, it's the way of some men. They preferred to hide within numbers and string up a man with his hands behind his back. Honest confrontation is foreign to them, and that's what saved us at the outset.

The shopkeeper with the double-barrel wheeled his horse and lit out as if the Devil himself had his claws hooked in that man's back pocket. More unseen guns fired from the woods. Shots came and whanged off the log, throwing long splinters into the air, and all of a sudden, the rifle fire coming from the trees was directed at us, as well as the panicked posse. My Spencer was on the other side of the log, lying in the open. There was no way I could reach it without getting shot.

The two who'd arrived with the Texas Ranger whirled and lit out. They disappeared like ghosts down the road, followed by what was left of the posse as it evaporated back toward town.

But the Russian was an old friend, and I fired a string of bullets right back at the bright muzzle flashes and puffs of smoke coming from the trees. As far as I could tell, I was the only one who returned fire. Someone in there yelped and I had the satisfaction of knowing I'd hit flesh. A horse thundered by, its rider hanging on for dear life.

Dropping back down, I snapped open the top-break revolver, plucked out the spent shells, and thumbed fresh rounds from my belt loops into the cylinder. Now beyond that, I couldn't figure out who was shooting from the trees, or why those two riding with the Texas Ranger murdered him in front of us all, along with the sheriff from Margarite. I'd assumed those other two were Rangers, and that put a whole new light on the subject that I didn't have time to work out right then, with all that lead flying around.

"Gil, roll over this log and get that shotgun and Winchester while I cover you."

I didn't have to tell him twice. When I opened up again, he slithered over the top like a snake and then flung himself back over with me a second later, then came up and shot half-a-dozen times with the Winchester. Those guys in the woods opened up again, probably shooting at shadows, since it was nearly dark, but one of those chunks of lead found Gil. He grunted and writhed on the ground.

I glanced over to see blood running off the fingers of Gil's left hand. "Hurt bad?"

"Depends on what you think's bad." The pain in his voice was sharp. "Went plumb through my hand. The one with the glass in it."

"You can still squeeze a trigger, then."

"Some of these fingers don't work no more, but I can

still get enough of a grip to shoot." He cocked the lever as if to show me he was still in the fight. The shackle still on his wrist jangled and I was glad I'd left him loose. I reloaded the Russian, holstered it, and waited with the shotgun tucked close, expecting to be rushed at any moment.

Drifting gunsmoke hung low to the ground, barely moved by the air, so much so that it and the diminishing light covered our movements. Cooling bodies lay around us, and one poor old horse limped away, back toward town. My mare stood with her ears pricked forward and Gil's roan didn't like all the noise and was stamping his feet, but they hadn't pulled loose of their reins tied onto the stout limb of a nearby sapling. The other two horses had been doing their best to yank free of their pickets, but now that the gunfire'd settled down, they calmed.

The sound of rushing footsteps came from the creek and I spun around with the shotgun against my shoulder. Esther's voice came to my ear. "Don't shoot. It's us!"

Instead of running to where we lay, she angled off and yanked the mare's reins free. She untied the roan and led them to us at a trot, keeping herself between them. Pretty fast thinking, if you ask me. Gracie pulled the others free; then, quick as a wink, we were all mounted and lit out as fast as we could, heading west.

Why west when we were going south all that time?

It'd make it harder for someone to follow us, because no one in their right mind would intentionally go into Comanche Territory.

CHAPTER 26

"Well, that went to hell in a hurry." Ed Gentry drew his horse up at the edge of town. Despite the late hour, it was buzzing like a beehive. They'd taken off their scarves and left them on the trail, so the shouting men with torches wouldn't recognize them for the two behind the dead Ranger.

He watched a tall individual in front of the jail call for volunteers to join still another posse. "You want to tell me why you shot when you did?"

Johns took in the lively street of Margarite lit by the glow from every store in town that was open. He smoothed his little mustache as if the street had been filled with girls interested in his company. "We had to stop that sheriff from getting Whitlatch's gold. I couldn't stand the thought of losing all that money."

"Well, I believe you shot the Ranger, instead."

"His horse shied just when I pulled the trigger." Johns's expression said he was sorry, but the timbre in his voice meant the opposite. "I was aiming for the sheriff."

"Um-hum." Gentry shifted his attention to the activity in the dusty street. Since it had been so dark back at camp, there was little worry they'd be recognized by anyone who might have been with the posse. Just in case, he punched the crown of his hat into a new shape, and curled the brim more on the right side than the left. "I wonder who was shooting from the woods."

Johns used the edge of his hand to knock the crease lower in the front of his own hat, then punched the back higher into a Montana cowboy crease. "I couldn't even begin to guess, but they fouled things up for us all."

"There's a lot going on here."

Two men on horseback loped down the street and pulled up in front of J.D. Carpenter's Dry Goods. The owner was passing out rifles and pistols to anyone who wasn't armed. Any other time, Gentry and Johns might have attracted attention as strangers in town, but the chaos around them drew everyone toward the mob gathering in the street.

Features hidden by darkness, they passed the railroad depot without raising a glance. A yellow glow from inside lit up several men gathered around tables, gesturing in excitement. Farther into town, a land office was also still open, as was a building with COAL CLAIMS painted on the window.

Too old to join in the fervor, an elderly man, with long gray hair and a week's growth of whiskers, leaned back on the back legs of a cane-bottom chair against the front wall of a stable, watching the world go by. An oil lamp on a milking stool beside him provided just enough light to see.

Irritated at the events of the past hour, Johns waved at the unpainted building with the sign C.W. SAIN, STABLE, FEED, AND GRAIN. "I say we stop here for the night and think things through."

"I don't believe that's a good idea. We should put some distance between us and all these gun-toting storekeepers. Let's go on and find a place to camp, and then we can pick up Whitlatch's trail. The two of us can move faster than whatever new posse they put together. We can get that gold and be gone without ever being noticed."

Johns shrugged at the demand. "I'm tired of being on the trail. I want a bed and some whiskey."

"The next town'll have all that."

"When we finally find one." Johns sulled up like a little kid. They reached the stable and he swung down. An old man creaked out of a stall and Johns waved him over. "Hey, old-timer. You the owner?"

"I am. Name's Claude Sain."

"Well, Mr. Sain. How about a bait of corn?"

The stable owner rose and reached for their reins. "You bet. Y'all gonna bed down in here with 'em?"

"We got money for a hotel." Johns hung both thumbs into his vest pocket.

His comment annoyed Gentry, who preferred to pay to stable the horses for the night without letting on how much money they had. Now the old man would likely up the price, at the very least for the corn.

He was right. Mr. Sain named his price, which was likely twice what he required from others who boarded their mounts there, but Gentry handed it over. Mr. Sain tucked the coins away in a pocket. "They'll be in the corral out back when you're ready tomorrow morning. If I's y'all, I'd stay in the Rawhide Hotel, across the street there. Best place in town."

"I know of it." Leading the way, Gentry dodged both men and horses rushing toward the action down the street. A wagon rattled by as they clumped up the steps and under the false front and into the two-story hotel.

Lit by several oil lamps, the dark-stained interior was filled with fine furniture and even a round red settee. The desk manager glanced up from the ornate mahogany desk and put down his pen. "Welcome, gentlemen. How can I help you?"

"We'd like a room." Johns spoke before Gentry, which annoyed the older man even more.

The manager eyed them up and down. "The stableman didn't offer you accommodations there?"

Face flushing with anger, Gentry held out a hand to silence his younger, impulsive partner. "We have plenty of money." He dug into a pocket and withdrew a twenty-dollar gold piece. "Been on the road up from Texas. What's going on out there?"

"Sheriff's been murdered, along with several unnamed others at this time. Somebody shot up a posse north of town and they're forming up another one. Said a gang of Comancheros rode in and killed them and was heading toward McAlester."

"You don't say." Gentry resisted the urge to meet his partner's eyes. The rumor mill that served all small towns was in full force, meaning they were safe as babies in their mother's arms. "Two rooms, two baths, and some whiskey if you have it."

"This is Indian Territory, sir. Whiskey is illegal."

Gentry added another coin. "I bet you can kick around some, out by a corral or chicken house, and find a jar, but we'd prefer the real stuff. That should cover it, and some company."

The manager looked aghast. "If I understand what you're saying . . ."

"You don't remember me, do you, Chester?"

The man's mouth opened and closed. "I don't . . ."

Gentry tilted his hat back to remove the shadows.

"Why, Mr. Gentry. You don't look like yourself without the beard. You were here two years ago with that herd up from Texas. You were about to quit being a trail boss, as I recall. Said pushing horns wasn't for you."

Johns tilted his head in surprise.

"I was, and I haven't followed the back end of a cow since." They shared a chuckle. "I'd like the same thing I had last time."

The coins disappeared from the countertop and the manager gave them a wide grin. "I'll see what I can do." He handed them two keys and disappeared outside.

Johns weighed the key in one hand. "That's why you didn't want to come in here."

"That's right. I have a reason for everything I do. You shouldn't be as impulsive. Now he knows I'm in town, and he'll mention it to somebody else at some point, and I'd've preferred to slip in and out real quiet."

"They're not after you in this part of the world, are they?"

"Naw. The other way around. I was the marshal here for a couple of weeks after I quit the trail, while they found Bronson to take another sheriff's job."

"That old man at the stable didn't recognize you, and neither did Bronson."

"Kept my head low, but Bronson wasn't here when I left. Came in the day after, but a couple of old boys with that posse were."

"Which ones?"

"The ones who claimed they were friends of the hanged man. I knew 'em from the trail and I'd bet all I own they're still running iron on cattle out of Texas." Gentry took a deep breath. "We're in the clear, but we need to get gone before daylight in the morning, or we'll get yanked into whatever they were about and I don't intend to get tangled up in this place."

CHAPTER 27

"Well, that didn't happen like we expected." Itchy wrapped a bandage around a deep gouge where a bullet took a chunk out of Cheese's upper arm.

Lucky for them, a full moon provided enough light through the trees, so they traveled a good distance away from their ambush site. The silver glow from above allowed them to doctor Cheese without a fire.

Furious at the outcome, Cloyce stomped around their dry camp, listening for the thunder of a horse's hooves telling them someone was on their trail. It was quiet, though, and for the moment, Cloyce felt safe.

Cheese hissed with pain. "What'd you shoot for, Cloyce? We coulda just let 'em all kill one another and then rode off if that German was dead."

"Thought that if I got 'em shooting at one another, they'd kill Vanderburg and we'd be done with this."

He recalled the shiver of fear that went down his spine at the thought of either the posse or that extremely capable-looking Texas Ranger arresting Vanderburg. A jury trial would surely bring out the German's innocence in killing Possum, and there was a good chance a witness would come forth to say who did the shooting.

"I was aiming at Vanderburg and Whitlatch. Y'all are the ones trying to shoot everyone else."

The night Possum died, Cloyce stood over the body, horrified that he'd killed the man he'd grown up with. And over money. Some woman might have been a possibility, for there were few available women in that part of the territories who'd even take a second look at him.

But they'd argued over money, and the liquor took control. He shivered at the recollection of that night as Possum lay there, bleeding out. When the light went out of Possum's eyes, Cloyce felt there was someone hiding in the shadows, watching. Every instinct told him to search the area and root out whoever witnessed their argument, but shouting and alarms coming from the street out front told him he only had seconds to flee the scene and feign innocence when Possum's body was discovered.

Itchy sucked a tooth in thought. "I thought you were shooting at them others for some reason, so I did the same."

"So did I." Cheese dabbed at the blood on his hands. "You shoulda told us what you had in mind. We sure killed a lot of people to get that started."

"They weren't our people, though, except for that big-jawed son of a bitch riding that big black, and his friend. It's a good thing you didn't shoot them."

Cheese touched his fingers together and pulled them apart, watching the sticky blood hold them together for a moment. "I believe I missed everyone I shot at. I'm not near as good as Itchy with a handgun, and half that with a rifle."

When that Ranger declared who he was, Cloyce saw a way to get them all. "I hoped that shooting from cover would startle the townies and maybe they'd fire on Whitlatch and Vanderburg for us. I was as shocked as anyone when those two shot the *Ranger*. For all the world, it looked like they shot him in the back intentionally, and I can't figure out why they'd do such a thing."

"Now here we are, sitting in a cold camp and soon to be hunted if we don't get out of here before daylight." Cheese tested his arm and hissed at the pain as Itchy used his neckerchief to make a sling. "There were lawmen littering the ground back there like fall nuts under a pecan tree."

"Well, y'all beat all I've ever seen." Cloyce shook his head. "What difference does it make?"

"The difference is this hole in my shoulder." Cheese took a sip of clear corn liquor. "I think we shoulda just kept watch and waited to see who would will out. Then we could have just taken those two away when they all divided up."

Cloyce shook his head. "Or they would have gone into town together and we'd've lost our chance." He snatched the jar from Cheese and swallowed deep and long. The whiskey burned all the way down before igniting a pleasant glow that took away the sick feeling that had been there since the gunfight.

"That damned panther nearly caused me to wet myself." Itchy tied the sling, slipped it around Cheese's neck, and was done. "It ain't that bad a wound. I've had worse from a whooping from the old man."

"He whipped me to death once." Cheese flexed his fingers to see if the damage impacted his grip.

Cloyce shook his head. "Sometimes I wish he had. Where'd that woman and girl come from? Did y'all see them?"

"You sure it was a girl?" Cheese looked surprised.

"Took her for one." Cloyce heard a slight noise and thought it might be a deer. "Got a pretty fair look at her when they got close to the fire."

He stopped talking when a fat sow followed by a dozen piglets walked past as if they didn't have a care in the world. One of those young porkers would have been good roasted, but shooting one would have been a foolish thing to do at that time. "Hair was too long for a boy, even an Indian."

"Don't believe that's true." Itchy spoke with authority. "I've seen some of them bucks with hair braids that went damned near to their butts. That'n who skint out of there on that black stud had hair down between his shoulders."

The presence of an uninterested sow also meant there wasn't any mountain lions around, and with that fear off his mind, Cloyce spoke aloud. "Well, it was a girl, all right, and I believe one of them was what made that scream. It wasn't no panther, not with just one holler."

Itchy rose and watered a nearby tree. "We should have let 'em kill those two and be done with it."

Cloyce's spirits rose. Itchy was coming around to his way of thinking.

Cheese shook his head. "Well, I'm mad. I done been shot, and nobody shoots me, or shoots *at* me, and gets away with it."

"Boyd Cass did, once."

"We was kids, and he only shot at me 'cause I hit him in the head with a horse apple." Cheese held his wounded arm out to his side, as if Cloyce and Itchy might have already forgotten his wound. "He only shot over my head."

"Anyway," Itchy came back, buttoning his pants, "we don't know which way that German and them went."

The three brothers studied on that statement for several minutes. Cheese finally spoke up. "They went west."

"What makes you think that?"

"They've been going south, but all those men came from a town not too far from here, and I'd figure they'd go around it to avoid being seen by others."

Intrigued by Cheese's idea, Cloyce sat on a log to listen. "Why not east?"

"Because we'd have heard them coming this way, I

suspect. They're heading for Texas, where Vanderburg is from, so I say they're headed west."

He could have been right. Cloyce considered what he'd do. "If it was me, maybe I'd just go around the town and then on to the river."

Itchy considered the idea. "Could be, but there aren't many good crossings there, and I doubt a woman and a child would like to swim a horse across deep water, if they could avoid it. That river's dangerous as hell, full of whirlpools and quicksand. I think they intended to cross somewhere west."

Cloyce nodded in the silver moonlight. "Doan's Crossing."

"But them Comanches raid down there all the time." Itchy paced back and forth. "Why don't we just let 'em go down there and get scalped. Won't be no skin off our nose."

"I'm with you," Cheese said.

"Not me." Cloyce shook his head. "I intend to finish this thing. I thought we were together in this. You two, go on back if you want to, but I'm going on. Tell the old man y'all quit, but I won't. Not now."

Cloyce had a reputation as a hard case, and intended to prove it to his brothers. If not, no one would ever be afraid of him again. He leaned back on his saddle and pulled up an old blanket. "I have an idea."

Itchy quit his pacing. "What's that?"

"Well, I say we try this nice and legal. You saw that posse and heard what their sheriff said before we got to shootin'. Why don't we ride into whatever one-horse town they came from and find the new sheriff, 'cause somebody has to take over and I'm hoping he's kinda green.

"Then we tell him we've been tracking those two for murdering our brother and how we came across all those bodies over there. We'll join up with them and let the law lead us to Vanderburg and Whitlatch. We'll talk it up how dangerous they are, and when we come on 'em, they'll be as afraid of them as they are the Comanches.

"By then, they won't be in the frame of mind to take prisoners. They'll shoot 'em on sight. It don't make no difference who pulls the trigger, or holds the rope, and then we're done with it. It'll be a sight more productive than what we've been doing."

He closed his eyes and hoped such an elaborate plan might come together, but with their luck so far, it'd be about as guaranteed as bucking the tiger in a faro game.

CHAPTER 28

Ed Gentry and Bill Johns took their breakfast in a dining hall called the Red Rooster. The fare wasn't much, but it beat what they'd eaten on the trail. The frenzy on the street hadn't settled with the sunrise. More than a dozen horses were gathered in front of the livery as a second posse formed.

Two dusty, heavily armed cowboys came in and plopped down at a nearby table. One slapped his hat on the surface and called to the woman slinging hash in the back. "Hey, Annie! Whatever it is you got on the fire, bring us some."

"Mornin', Cecil. You want the same, Josh?"

Cecil answered for both of them. "Sure 'nough."

His partner, Josh, rested both elbows on the scarred table's edge and rubbed at a two-day beard. Their conversational level was as if they were the only two customers there. "Now that I looked at that bunch out there, I don't believe I want to join up with dirt farmers and city fellers."

"Me neither. Henry Arney's not much sheriff, in my opinion." Cecil tilted his sweat-stained hat back to reveal a catfish-belly white forehead, the trademark of a cowboy.

"Well, they had to give it to somebody. I doubt he made much of a deputy, neither."

"They'll never catch those two Texas boys who shot everybody up."

Josh scratched under his chin again. "Men who can come all this way from down south and through the territories—both times—are some to be reckoned with, that's for sure."

"How do you know all that?"

"I heard it this morning when I was saddling the horses. They said a telegram came through from Fort Smith. Judge Parker sent two more marshals down here, after that Texas Ranger got shot yesterday."

"It'll be more'n a week before they show up." Cecil watched the disorganized, freshly sworn-in lawmen mill around instead of forming up. "That posse out there'll run 'em off, and those two guys that killed Olsen will be out in Arizona by then."

"I still can't figure what a Ranger was doing up here."

"Don't matter none. With marshals coming from one way, and a company of Rangers riding up from Austin, Whitlatch and Vanderburg are done for."

"That their names?"

"Yep. Heard they killed the sheriff of Blackwater."

"You say a company of Rangers are headed here? I can't believe that. Judge Parker won't allow it."

"That's what I heard. Henry Arney got a telegram saying they were on a train and headed this direction."

Josh raised an eyebrow. "I thought the Rangers was disbanded."

"They were. The governor down there sent 'em packing and formed up the Texas State Police, but those melonheads weren't worth the powder it would take to blow them up, so the Rangers are back in business.

"But here's the thing I heard, though I don't believe it." Cecil leaned forward as if he knew a secret. "There was a Kiowa came to town this morning, name of Long Fox or something, I disremember, but anyway, he was drinking from the trough out behind the livery and Littlejohn said he heard that buck say he'd passed two men, a woman, and an Indian girl on their way west."

"Why would a liveryman mention something like that at all?"

"Said the Kiowa was kinda taken by the young girl's looks and wanted to buy her, but one of them fellers drew down on him with some new kind of shotgun and ran him off. She must've been some punkin for him to still be talking about her."

"Goddlemighty, there's a lot going on in this little burg."

"You ain't a-woofin'."

Ed Gentry's ears perked up. He'd been only half listening to the story until they reached the description. He twisted around in his chair. "Where can I find that Kiowa?"

Cecil shrugged. "Purt' near anywhere, I reckon."

"How long ago are you talking about?"

"Hour, maybe."

"Come on." Gentry rose and headed out the door in a rush.

Johns followed right behind and they paused on the boardwalk. "You think we can find that Indian and find out where he ran into Whitlatch?"

"All those men forming up over there, at least one of 'em should have seen him."

They hurried down the street and stopped short of the horses and men milling around. Gentry saw the liveryman come outside, leading a little bay. A man in a suit and bowler hat took the reins and handed the older gentleman a coin.

Gentry caught Old Man Littlejohn's eye and jerked his head to show he wanted to talk. They met up by the corral. "You boys ready to pick up your mounts? I have y'all ready to go with this bunch in two shakes."

"No. We're looking for a Kiowa name of Long Fox who took water out behind the livery early this morning."

"What about him? He steal something of yours?"

"No, but he might have some information we can use."

"What kind?"

Instead of answering, Gentry handed him a coin. "Just something about what he saw out west of here."

"There's nothing out there y'all want."

"That'll be for us to say." Gentry dug out another coin and held it up. "You know where he is?"

Littlejohn licked his lips. "Why, yes I do. He went down thataway, back of the Chinaman's laundry. Chao's been known to give out a bite or two for such strays."

"Much obliged."

"How about your horses?"

"Saddle 'em up. We'll be back to get 'em in a little bit."

The old man nodded and turned away as Gentry and Johns went to talk to an Indian afoot in such harsh country.

CHAPTER 29

Itchy and Cheese stayed at the edge of the milling party under a wide oak outside of Margarite. It was their tracks the posse followed back to town, instead of Whitlatch's band that had somehow disappeared like ghosts. Pretending not to know his brothers so they wouldn't attract any undue attention, Cloyce sat apart from them and did his best to tamp down his rising fury.

Just outside of town, newly sworn-in Sheriff H.E. Arney addressed the two Indians who'd been friends with the hanged man. "I thought you said there were four, Sparks. Two men and a woman and a kid. Ain't that what y'all said, Dawes."

Stanton Sparks rubbed his wide chin in thought, studying the hoofprints of three horses leading toward town. As baffled as everyone else about where Whitlatch and Vanderburg disappeared to, Sparks shrugged his shoulders. "Maybe that kid run off and that's why there's only three horses."

He and Dawes rode like hell out of the ambush and didn't slow until they reached the edge of town, where it was safe. They mixed in with the remnants of the shot-up posse as they drifted back into town. Intending to continue their act and avoid suspicion, they decided to join in the new posse the next day. Sparks figured they'd peel off at some point when the newly organized group grew dejected and gave up the chase.

"Nope. That don't make sense." Sheriff Arney was proving to be every bit the equal of his dead predecessor. "I think we're confused somehow."

The black stud under Sparks lowered his head to nibble at a tuft of green grass. "Why would they come around through the woods, circle around town, and come in to the very place where we have men looking under every rock for them?"

The three sets of tracks they'd followed eventually rode straight into town to disappear in thousands of horse and mule prints. One of the deputies found a couple of spots of blood on the trail, indicating that one of the trio was wounded.

Sheriff Arney pointed back down the road, and then turned to sweep the busy main street with one hand. "We're right back where we started. For all we know, they could be looking at us right now."

He and his uncertain posse sat their horses in confusion.

Cloyce caught the eye of a bearded rider, who shook his head in disgust. The man adjusted his seat on a mule and settled back down. "You know what I'd do in this situation?"

With no other option than to wait until the posse disbanded, Cloyce shrugged. "What?"

"I'd do what my old daddy told me about hunting quail."

"Birds?"

"Yep. When he wasn't skillet-shooting them on the ground, he was a fine wing shot and always took a bird with each barrel on the covey rise."

"I don't know what that means."

Beard waved an arm toward the sky. "He said when you shoot flying birds, you don't shoot where they are, because they're moving. You shoot where they're *going*."

Understanding began to dawn on Cloyce. "So you're saying, don't look here where they've been, but to look where they're headed. These people the sheriff's after."

"I heard before we left town that those men are headed down to Texas. There's only a handful of ferries across the river, and they'll have to cross there."

"Well, how in the world would you know which one to use?"

"Ah, that's where my experience comes in. See, I work in the land office and spend a lot of time analyzing all the information that comes in. The closest ferry is south of here, and I think they'd avoid being seen this close to everything. After that is Fulton's Ferry, Doan's Ferry, and Cranford's Ferry. That's the farthest, but I'd think it'd be too dangerous to cross that far away, especially with the Comanches raiding out there. It'd be a hard trip, so if I's in charge of chasing those murderers down, I'd cross here and work up-river through towns on the Texas side. Somebody'll have seen them."

The sheriff was talking to one of his deputies and the bearded man rode closer to hear what they were saying. Sensing an opportunity to distance themselves from the man who was a little too friendly, Cloyce split off from the party of inexperienced posse members. Itchy and Cheese saw their brother leave and followed a few minutes later.

They caught up with him on a wide trail south of town, but Cloyce's horse kept walking. They split and rode up on both sides. "What's your plan?" Itchy asked.

"We're going to Texas to find that German and kill him."

Cheese sighed. "And me with a fresh hole in my arm."

CHAPTER 30

Out front of P.E Pettigrew's general store, the tall and slender Stanton Sparks patted the black stud that once belonged to Theodore Olsen. His stocky partner, Chito Dawes, curled a leg over his saddle horn and watched the posse ride southwest, chasing ghosts.

Sparks waited until the street was clear and grinned at Chito. "Looks like we're free and clear."

"I never thought it would have worked."

"I told you it would. That fool shoulda knowed he couldn't push through this kind of country with a stud that looked that good. Anybody with any sense would have expected to run into men like us."

Rolling a smoke from a bag of Bull Durham, Chito licked the edge of the paper and stuck it between his lips. He returned the bag to his shirt pocket and lit the cigarette. "He should've sold you that black when you offered."

Sparks barked a laugh and checked around to be sure nobody was close enough to hear their conversation. Just to be on the safe side, he nudged the stud, with the white drip between his eyes, forward and headed out of town.

"You know, your idea seemed a little complicated." Chito absently patted his other shirt pocket, which held more cash than he'd seen in months, from splitting the money for Sparks's horse and tack, plus the cash from Olsen's pockets.

"But it worked out just fine." Feeling the other half of the money in his own shirt pocket made Sparks sit straighter in the saddle. He'd felt generous after considering the black stud, and shared his good fortune with Dawes.

Two men standing in front of a saddle shop watched them pass. One frowned at the pair and Sparks drew a frown at them. Unnerved by the long-haired man's glare, they turned and walked down the street.

"I think you're right. I never made money so easy."

"You think we can do that again?"

"Naw, it was just one of those things that worked out right. Running into those people camped right beside Olsen's body was a series of events that would likely never happen again."

"So, where are we going now?" Chito asked.

"I say we go down to Jeremiah, find a saloon, and spend most of this on whiskey and whores."

"That sounds good to me. I'd like to do a little gambling. Where's Jeremiah?"

"Out west a ways. It's a small town built in the middle of a huge upside-down horseshoe bend of the Red River. Sits on a bluff two miles south of the river and well above flood stage."

"You've been there before."

"I have. It's grown in the last twenty years." They rode boot to boot through town. "Started as a stop for travelers heading for California, but it was a rough town from the beginning. I hear the fine people of that town hung over thirty suspected Unionists during the War Between the States, not counting dozens of other outlaws, either convicted or suspected."

"You sure know a lot about that place."

"I do. When the stage line came though, the place really

took off, but when the railroad came through, it got as big as Gainesville, and the last I heard it's still growing." Sparks got a distant look in his eye. "I'm missing Texas, and I have an idea."

"What's that?"

"I used to work on a ranch out that way and knew a couple of old boys who're up for just about anything. What say we gather up a few of them, and maybe some more, and head down toward the Butterfield Stage Line out there and go into the stage-robbing business."

"I'd never have thought of something like that."

"Well, you didn't think about old Theodore Olsen, neither, but that worked out pretty well for the both of us."

They laughed and left Margarite behind them.

CHAPTER 31

Gil's wounded hand was giving him fits when we reached the north bank of the Red River days later. Twenty feet below, the thick muddy water swirled and gurgled around a tree washed down from somewhere upstream. Two big snapping turtles sunned on the wide trunk, heads raised into the sky as if they saw us coming.

The clear sky was a big blue bowl stretching from one horizon to the other—a cool, beautiful day, but such clear air would allow roving war parties to see us from a great distance across the plains. I did my best to lead us down to the river during our journey by staying below the horizon and following tree-lined streams, when they led the way we needed to go.

A doe leaped away, across the wide prairie, startling a covey of bobwhite quail that flushed with a whirr of wings before spreading out and settling down less than a hundred yards from where they came up. Doves called from the cottonwood trees behind us, but the quiet afternoon ended when Gracie took one look at the roiling water below.

"Well, we ain't crossing here. The river's up and I can't swim a lick."

"I doubt anybody could swim it, with the water this high." Branches, leaves, and other trash roiled, rose, and sank in the reddish water. I watched a crow swoop down to give us a look, then tilt its wings and drop below the steep twenty-foot bank to skim the surface of the river, before it turned toward Texas, so close I could identify the leaves on the trees. "I don't think we've gone far enough yet. Cranford's Ferry shouldn't be much farther."

"Well, I don't like being this deep into Comanche Territory." Gil was no longer shackled, since I figured he was in no shape to run. His face was flushed red with a fever and his swollen left hand, which gave him fits all night, rested on his thigh. "But I'd like to get to a town pretty soon. Do you think they'll have a doctor there? This hand's throbbing like thunder, and I'm burning up."

"Then what?" Gracie had been a bear all day, and I couldn't understand why.

I watched something rise in the water before going back down. "Then we find a doctor and hope they have a telegraph office in town."

"How long will it take to get there?"

"Another day to the ferry." I figured we've been averaging over thirty-five miles a day. "Once we get across, it's anybody's guess to a town. I don't think we're far from the Three Fork Ranch down in Texas. It's a big outfit, and I hear there's a town growed up just outside of there. They'll have everything we need."

We'd come across a trading post the day after the shoot-out at Margarite and I left everyone camped a mile or so away and laid in supplies and a pack mule. The owner, who operated out of a soddy store, near a similarly made house, said I'd been his best customer in a month. That proclamation worried me some, because we'd be easy to remember if he was lonesome for people and wanted conversation with the next travelers coming through. Folks with little to talk about were the worst at gossip.

It didn't help that I bought Esther a dress to replace the

rags she was still wearing, and clothes for Gracie, who refused to wear a dress or shoes. She insisted on a new pair of bib overalls and shirt if I came across such. Buying those things had raised the storekeeper's interest and he quizzed me pretty good on who they were for.

Those purchases would be fodder for discussion weeks after we'd passed through.

I didn't think anyone was following us after that shoot-out near Margarite, but a man could never be too careful. Not one to run from trouble, I'd have squared off with those after us, instead of leaving them behind us, but saddled with one wounded prisoner and two women, I had no choice but to avoid trouble as much as I could.

Esther drew up beside Gil and put the back of her hand against his forehead. "Let me see that hand." He unwrapped it and she shook her head after a quick look. "It's gone bad." She leaned forward and gave it a sniff. "That's *really* bad."

"Not much we can do about it right now." His face was feverish, eyes glassy and sharp.

She pulled his sleeve up and examined his arm as that crow swooped past again. "Cap. We have to fix this *now*."

Those words made my stomach sink and I could tell they terrified Gil. We all knew what she was suggesting.

"Here?" He paled.

Holding her abdomen, Gracie listened, eyes wide. I'll have to give it to that little gal, she didn't hesitate when action became necessary. "I can kick around and find some roots and leaves." She surveyed the area around us. "We can make a poultice. That should help."

"Yeah, a poultice sounds good." Gil clutched his bad hand with the other, as if extra support would help. "Let's do that. A poultice'll hold me till we get to a doctor. Even a dentist might know what to do and they can fix me right up."

"Gil, there's very little Gracie can find around here to help. We're too far out on the plains. I hate to do this here and now, but Esther's right. You've got the blood poisoning in that hand and it'll kill you if we don't do something about it right now. Remember Old Man Dollar? He'd have died if Dad and a few others hadn't done what was necessary after he cut himself with that ax."

Old Dollar refused to let anyone see his foot after an ax slipped while he was chopping wood. It was already rotten by the time he sent for a doctor a week later. Neighbors poured a quart of stump liquor in him; then four men held him down while the doctor, an old veteran of the Civil War—and a man seasoned by hundreds of amputations therein—sawed off his leg at the knee.

In answer, Gil leaned sideways and lost his dinner. Wiping his mouth, he straightened. "Feeling hot in this sun."

"It's not that hot," I said.

"Fine, then. Argue with me if you want, but I suspect you're right. Where'd you intend to do it?"

Esther pointed a little behind us, where a grove of cottonwoods indicated a branch running down toward the river. Cottonwoods and sycamores grew best when water is nearby. "There'll be water there, and wood for a fire."

Gil wiped cold sweat from his face. He retched again, but nothing came up. "Well, let's get to doing it then."

Though it wasn't that hot in the sun, the shade was a relief. While I hobbled the animals, Esther and Gracie gathered downed wood and set up camp. Gil slumped on the ground with his back against the slick trunk of a sycamore tree, talking quietly to himself, and pretty soon I realized he was in and out of his head.

Despite that, it took us a while to get up the nerve to do what needed to be done. The fire soon burned down and a good bed of coals glowed hot and bright. We couldn't wait any longer. I knelt beside my old friend, who'd puked twice more, whether from the infection or the nerves, I didn't know.

"Gil, we've wasted enough time on this. You ready?"

He squinted, trying to focus on me. "How much you gonna take?"

I looked at his hand, a dark red mess full of pus that would soon kill him if left alone. There was a fair red line running up his forearm. "To the elbow."

"I'd hoped you could take most of what's infected and leave my thumb. It'd be useful to have at least a thumb on what'll be left of that hand. I knew an old boy down in Mason who had just a thumb and he used it like a whole hand. Can you leave just that?"

I met Esther's sad eyes. She shook her head. Using my index finger, I followed the red streak going up his forearm. "It's gotta be at your elbow. I'm sorry."

Gil hissed in pain at even that light touch. He kept wanting to talk, putting off the inevitable. "How you gonna do it? Tell me so's I'll have my mind right."

He broke out in a hysteric giggle, which quickly turned into a short cry, until he got hold of himself. He thought of another story to stall what we had to do.

"I knew an old Confederate soldier who told me how they cut his leg off with a rusty saw, and I don't believe I could stand hearing and feeling them teeth cut through the bone. That'd be an awful sound."

"Well, you're in luck. We don't have a saw." Trying not to be frustrated at his reluctance to lose part of his body, I reached for the Arkansas toothpick in the sheath on my belt. I held it down low and out of sight. "She's sharp as sharp can be. I believe I can cut through hard and quick before you know it."

"Oh, I'll know it, all right." He barked another hysterical laugh and looked into the fire, where our recently purchased cast-iron skillet full of boiling water sat on the coals. Shimmering heat rose, looking like one of the hinges from Hell. "That to cauterize it?"

"If we have to. He's gonna try and sew it up right, if he can." Esther nodded and looked as if she wanted to cry. "He's gonna boil his knife for a minute to keep down infection. We'll do what we can do for you, hon."

"I sure wish we had some whiskey and that I'd-a stayed in Kanoska's jail cell. Maybe they wouldn't have hung me, after all."

Gil was talking it through as I held the big blade in the boiling water for a few moments. I knew if he had his druthers, we'd sit there until dark, but we had to get it over with, for all our sakes. I held the knife ready and behind my back to cool.

He was still leaning against the tree, but a huge, fairly straight fallen limb was running alongside, a perfect support for what we had to do. I stretched his left arm along its length and pushed up his shirtsleeve. Pulling his arm forced him to adjust to the odd angle, so he wriggled around until his armpit rested on the rough bark.

Instead of watching, he took Gracie's hand with his right and focused on her young face. "How *you* doing with all this?"

Her eyes welled with tears and glistened. "'Bout the same as you, I reckon."

We had strips from the hem of Esther's dress, and I wrapped one around Gil's upper arm and used a stick to twist it tight. Gil winced, but he knew why it was so tight. Using another strip, I tied it around the stick to hold it in place.

Esther knew we had to move fast after it was in place. "Gil, I'm going to sit on your arm to hold it steady, hon." She gathered her ragged skirts and straddled the log, her back to him and holding on to his upper arm with both hands. She lowered her weight down on him, ignoring modesty. "I've seen this done once, down in Seguin. A man got snakebit by a big rattler . . ."

She nodded at me and kept talking. "That thing pumped a whole load of poison into his hand, nearly a quart, I reckon, so much that clear fluid was leaking out of the holes."

"Yeah, what'd they do . . ."

I dropped my knee onto Gil's forearm, like I'd do to hold a calf down, between where Esther's hands held him tight enough to whiten the skin, and his elbow. "Gracie, do what I said."

He gasped at the pain from the weight on that sensitive arm and Gracie fell on him and wrapped herself around his upper body, pinning his free arm with her arms and legs. When her weight landed, I used the razor-sharp edge of that big knife to cut through his elbow. I hit it just right, between most of the bones and pulled the blade through the meat and tendons, like I was slicing through a deer's leg joint.

It was fast and I'd cleaned more than my share of deer and hogs. The hand clenched when the edge went through the joint and I bore down and cut completely around and through the skin. The infected arm came off clean, falling onto the sandy ground.

Gil squalled and yanked hard, but Esther held on like a snapping turtle, tightening her legs around that log as if she were clamped onto a bucking bronc. Gracie did the same, throwing her weight onto his arm and holding on for dear life as he thrashed and screamed before he went silent, passed out.

There were a couple of arteries that needed to be closed off. They were large enough to be obvious, so I used a needle and strong thread from my possibles bag to tie them off and sew the ends. Thinking ahead, I'd left a flap of skin loose. Large enough to cover the wound, I folded it over and went to sewing again. When I was finished, the whole thing looked more ragged than I liked, but it might have been enough to save his life.

Gracie kept looking back for that skillet and I shook my head. "I think we don't need that."

"Thank God." Gracie reached out and touched the Sioux medicine bag hanging around my neck. "I thought that bag was to keep you safe, but it looks like it works for everyone around you."

"I guess not. This happened."

"We're all still alive. It's good, strong medicine."

I tucked it back into my shirt and stood. We'd done our do and it was over. Relieved, I released the tourniquet and Esther bandaged the stump. Relief that Gil was quiet washed over me and I picked up the rotten hand and forearm to dispose of it.

That's when Gracie's voice told me something else was wrong. "Well, hell."

I looked up to see the inside of one leg of her overalls was wet with her own blood, but her attention was on the mounted and painted Comanche war party watching us from only a few feet away. Their leader was on the ground between us and the others, and he was a big son of a gun who must have been six feet tall, to look me straight on and square in the eye.

Standing there with my friend's amputated arm, the only thing I could think to do was hold it up and wave.

CHAPTER 32

Texas Ranger Curtis Braziel opened his eyes to find he was lying on his stomach in a doctor's office. Cool wind came through an open window and washed over him like a soft wave. An oak cabinet, with partially open glass doors, was full of medicine bottles containing dark and clear liquids, as well as an assortment of ominous-looking instruments and bandages.

"Am I alone?"

Rustling noises precluded a steady voice coming back from behind him. "No, sir. I'm right here."

"I don't see you."

"I'm surprised you see at all." A middle-aged man stripped down to his shirtsleeves and suspenders came into sight. He settled on a chair within Braziel's vision and rested both elbows on his knees. "You've been out for days, and, frankly, I wasn't sure you'd ever wake up again due to that split skull of yours. I'm Dr. Holley, Mr. Braziel."

"How do you know my name, and it's Ranger Braziel."

"I understand. Saw your badge right off. Found some papers in your coat pocket and read the name."

"What were you doing going through my pockets?"

"Why, emptying them out, of course. My wife took your clothes to wash out the blood and mend the bullet holes."

"What happened?" Braziel's mind whirled. He remembered holding his pistol on two men he was hunting, and a lot of people who were fuzzy, for some reason, then nothing.

"You hurting?"

"You're damned right I hurt, and I asked you a question. Shot?"

"You were. One bullet in the back. You're lucky, though. It was a defective round that broke a rib and skittered off under the skin and came out behind your left arm. If it'd been a good bullet with adequate velocity, I fear you'd be on the undertaker's table, instead of being cross with me."

Braziel turned his head to see the doctor better. The action sent a sharp jolt of pain down the left side of his back. "You're damned right I'm cross. Someone shot me from ambush? I intend to find out who it was. How long have I been here?"

"Couple of days."

"Were those two with me killed?"

"I'm told it was one or both of them that did it."

"Accident?"

"Can't say, but them that was there told that they were aiming right at you, so I assume you're right about an ambush."

"Damn them. I took them for desperados when I met those two, but they had a smooth talk that lulled me. I'm having a hard time thinking, too."

"You also hit your head when you fell from the mount you were riding. Again, you've been out for a few days, which likely accounts for your lapse in memory and, for sure, the bandage on your forehead. I'd lie still for a while, if I were you, or you'll get swimmy-headed when you get up."

The Ranger felt the bandage with his fingertips. "Where are they, those who shot me, and, damn it all, right now I can't recall their names. Did that sheriff leading the posse arrest them?"

Dr. Holley lifted the bandage on Ranger Braziel's back. "The bleeding has stopped. I think you'll be fine, if you stay calm with the news that no, there weren't any arrests, and we also have no names. Sheriff Bronson is dead, shot from a different direction, they say, as well as several men killed who were with them."

"I remember now. Gunfire coming from several directions as I passed out. Must have been part of a gang. I wonder if Johns and Gentry were in cahoots with them as well." He turned in excitement and groaned from the pain in his back. "That was their names."

"I have no idea, but maybe you're right and it was more members of their gang shooting from nearby woods. Anyway, the other pair of murderers the posse was after got away. It's a crying shame, too, after they hung that poor cowboy."

"You're confusing me with all this new information. Who'd they hang?"

"Some cowboy named Theodore Olsen. He was through here with a stud horse he was going to sell, and his Indian partners found him hanging right where you were shot and came to get help. That's the reason Sheriff Bronson gathered up some men and went out there."

Though his back hurt, Ranger Braziel's mind was clearing fast. "You say two Indians who found their friend strung up left him there and went into a strange town to get a sheriff? That don't sound right."

"Well, nobody saw it, 'cause of everything that happened."

"It's right confusing, that's for sure." Braziel's mind whirled with possibilities. He didn't believe the story for a minute, but being out of his range of authority, there was little that he could do. "Describe those Indians."

"I heard one had long, stringy hair. Rode a black stud. The other'n was stocky and was half Black. Anyway, you're lucky to be here, because a new posse that went back out the next morning brought you in. They say you were incoherent in the wagon with fever and threatened to shoot everyone there, unlike the rest of the bodies that lay there nice and quiet like they were supposed to."

"That's a likely thing I would have said." Ranger Braziel remained still while the doctor rummaged through the medicine cabinet. "When can I get up?"

"Well, I wouldn't rush it. Since you just woke up, I'd say in a day or so, until your mind clears. You've been here so long that your wound has scabbed over, so I'm not worried about you bleeding much anymore, though strenuous effort can cause it to open up again. Your rib is broken, I 'magine, so that'll take a while, too."

"Am I laid open across the back?"

"No." Dr. Holley used his index finger to show Braziel, with a light tap, where the entrance wound was. "I'll be gentle. It went in here." His fingertip traced the bullet's path. "The slug slipped off this rib, traveled under the skin to here, where it reemerged."

Ranger Braziel flexed his shoulders to see how badly the extra movement might hurt. The wound jolted for a moment, then settled into a dull ache. "I've stopped bleeding, yes?"

"You have."

"Bandage it tight. I'm getting up."

"Sir, I would recommend you stay here for at least another day. Even if you don't start bleeding again, infection might set in if these bandages aren't changed regularly, and you could die. I had a woman in here last year who popped a pimple on her nose and she was dead a month later from blood poisoning. It's a dangerous thing."

"I've been shot by arrows, knifed once down on the

border by a Mexican bandit, and shot half-a-dozen times by outlaws reluctant to be taken in. I'm sure you saw the scars. I've been hurt worse than this and was still capable of doing my job."

"I was afraid you were that kind of man."

The doctor disappeared from view and Ranger Braziel remained still when he came back with a handful of bandages and dressed the wound. He finished by wrapping it with several strips of white linen around the Ranger's chest to hold the new compress in place.

"There." He stepped back when he was finished. "That's the best I can do if you insist on getting up."

The Texas Ranger carefully rolled onto his right side, hissing with the pain. After a moment, he pushed upright and sat on the edge of the bed to catch his breath. His holstered pistol hung over a nearby chair, which held his washed and mended clothes. The hole in his shirt was patched by someone familiar with a needle and thread.

"Who did all that?"

"My wife, sir. I told you that. Is your mind unclear?"

"No, it's just fine, I'm trying to collect my thoughts is all."

"Well, your shirt was soaked in blood, and you'd been there so long, your pants were wet. My wife did the best she could, but it's lucky your shirt had a design, so the light stains don't show."

For the first time in years, Ranger Braziel's face flushed with embarrassment, when he realized that his crotch was likely wet when they brought him in. "There were some coins in my pocket."

"They're still there. She replaced them when your trousers were clean."

Grunting in pain, the Ranger stood and crossed to the chair. He took out two gold pieces and placed them on the bed. "That should cover your ministrations and the efforts of your wife. Please tell her I apologize for my embarrassing condition."

"She's seen worse."

It took a while, but Ranger Braziel pulled on his pants. The shirt was more difficult as he put both arms through and buttoned it. Tucking in his shirttail, he buckled on the gun belt, slipped on his vest, and with the help of Dr. Holley, he shrugged into his coat.

The doctor handed Braziel his hat, which wouldn't fit because of the bandage. He unwound it, felt the wound, and seeing it no longer bled, he gingerly set his hat well back from his forehead.

"I wish you'd stay here for another day at least. Such severe bumps on a person's head are dangerous."

"I have to go."

"Give me a few minutes. I'll have my wife wrap up some food. You haven't eaten in a while, and drink as much water as you can hold."

"My horse?"

"In the corral out back. I'll have my son saddle it for you."

"Much obliged."

"Where are you going, if I may ask?"

"To kill some people, and two of them are named Bill Johns and Ed Gentry. They're the ones who shot me in the back. I intend to hang them from the nearest tree to where they're found. Then I'm going to find those fugitives that started this whole mess, Whitlatch and Vanderburg.

"Once I finish with those four, I'm coming back here for new ropes and to pick up the trail of those two Indians. I smell a rat and suspect they hung that feller for his horse, and I doubt he was any friend of theirs. Do you have their names, by chance?"

The doctor frowned, thinking. "I remember their descriptions, but that's all. You'll recognize one by his stringy hair, lantern jaw, tall physique, and a black stud sixteen hands high. The other one is Indian and Negro mix. That's all I can tell you about him, but I heard one man mention that he's plain."

"Names will be helpful."

The doctor paused, thinking. "Sparks and Dawes. Sparks rides the black and has the wide chin structure. That's all I can recall being said."

"Sparks and Dawes. That's good to know."

CHAPTER 33

It would have been funny if I hadn't been through so much and was as afraid of that tall Comanche as I was of a bear. Shocked, the others backed their horses, not taking their eyes off the arm I was holding.

That tall Comanche jumped like a rabbit and vaulted onto his pony's back before you could say "scat, cat!" Terrified, the rest of them whirled their mounts and lit out at a dead run through that tall prairie grass, with not one whoop or holler. In fact, nary one of 'em made a sound, they were so scared, and I wondered if they thought I had a habit of carving up folks and waving their parts around.

It wasn't like war parties didn't do the same when they killed white folks. Or white folks didn't do for them the same way, neither. I'd seen and heard about horrifying atrocities on both sides. It might have been the expression of terror on my face they mistook for something else, but no matter what it was, they were gone.

When I glanced down at Gil's arm, I saw that Sioux medicine bag was hanging outside my shirt again. Could they have recognized something in the beadwork that added to their fear of the arm? I had no idea, but I thanked Naach for her gift that was working as hard as a hand pump.

Gil was still out, and that was a good thing for all of us.

Esther took their sudden appearance worse than I did, and I saw she was white as snow and shaking like a leaf. I wanted to go to her and wrap my arms around those thin shoulders, but held back.

"You okay?"

She swallowed and finished tending to Gil's stump. "I'll be all right in a little while. Those were the ones who . . ." She touched the notch in her nose and looked back over her shoulder as if they might have already come back. "The ones who killed my family and took me down in Texas."

Their ponies were long gone, but the trail of crushed grass behind them was clear as a fresh-cut road. "You think they recognized you?"

"I doubt it, in this new dress. I stayed bent over and my hair was in my eyes. All they saw was a woman at work and an Indian girl." She frowned and looked around. "Where'd Gracie go?"

Some of the brush was thick down by the water and I caught a glimpse of those bright blue duckins just as she stepped behind a bush. "Must have scared her worse than us."

"It wasn't that." Esther finished tying Gil's bandage and picked up some rags torn from her old dress. "You stay right here and we'll be back."

"I don't much like y'all being down there out of sight with these Indians around. They might get over being afraid and come sneaking back."

"The way they were riding, they'll go a couple of miles before they get hold of themselves. She has her knife and I have this pistol you gave me." She patted the folds of her dress and the big hidden pocket inside. "We have plenty of time to do what's necessary."

I realized I still held Gil's forearm and hand and shuddered. It wasn't right to simply stand around holding a human body part. The remains of Esther's torn dress lay draped over the log and I wrapped it around the arm and tied it all in a neat package.

Growing up, men talked about ghost body parts and said that someone who lost a part of themselves often felt that appendage, like it was still attached. Down in Mason, Texas, I heard about an old boy who lost his leg from a bad accident and someone inexperienced in such things simply kicked out a shallow trench with their boot heel and covered the leg with sand.

A day later, the man who was in bed recovering from the amputation started twisting and thrashing around so bad, they had to tie him down. One person attributed it to fever until the amputee regained consciousness and hollered that ants were stinging him.

There weren't any ants in his bed, and an old woman tending to him realized what was wrong. She ordered them to go fetch that leg, and when they did, it was covered with ants. They brought it back and she washed and wrapped it and gave them instructions on how to go out and dig a proper grave. That man healed up, made himself a peg leg, and never said another word about that piece of him now properly buried.

With that story in mind, I took my big knife and dug an arm-deep hole in the cool sand, not far from camp. Lowering it carefully down into the damp hole, I covered it up.

By that time, Esther and Gracie were back with Gil. Gracie's overalls were wet from scrubbing, but the bloodstain was gone. Not having been around women much, I didn't know a lot of things, but even *I* figured that one out. We didn't make eye contact for a good long while.

I didn't want to stay there that night, afraid the Comanches might come back, but Gil finally settled into a deep sleep as the sun went down. Even if we'd left, they were good enough trackers to find us, and running wasn't an option. At least we were in a pretty fair defensive position, with our backs to the stream, so we figured to take our chances there that night.

Taking my rifle, I found a good place to see the camp by moonlight and sat there until I figured it was about an hour before sunrise. Gil woke that morning, silent, but hungry. We ate without building a fire, broke camp before dawn, got him into the saddle, where he rode with his shoulders slumped.

Our party reached the river the next afternoon, because we rode so slow. Two hours later, we came to Cranford's Ferry. A husky man sitting on a stump across the river saw us and waved. "Hello! I'll be over shortly if you have money to pay!"

Never much for yelling, I waved back and he took that as a yes. Though the river was down, the current was still strong, and he had to work at it to pull the wide, flat ferry to our side. He was tying it up in preparation for us to load, when he saw Gil's wrapped stump.

"Indians shoot his arm off?" The ferryman was built like a barrel, with arms thick as those of a blacksmith. He tied the ferry off and removed a long cedar post that served as a rail to keep men, beasts, or wagons from going over the edge. "They've been raiding over here and all over North Texas."

I didn't want to lie to the man, so I told him just enough to answer. "Shot is right. Bullet wound and his hand went bad."

"That's a hard thing." He gave Gil the once-over, noting how ashen and weak he looked. He shook his head. "Y'all must've been in a helluva fight and it looks like this old boy got the worst end of it. Cut off ear on one side, the lobe gone on the other side, all them red marks on his face . . . What're them from, bees?"

"Yellowjackets."

"Yessir, and a missing arm, to boot. Y'all must've had a rough time of it." He looked at Esther way too long, and then turned his attention to Gracie. "I don't cotton to Indians."

I almost laughed when she swelled up like a mad coon. "Well, you can kiss my ass."

Shocked that a child would speak that way to him, the man made a fist and I stepped in. "Don't you raise that hand, mister. She's with me and I'll pay."

"She has a smart mouth for a kid."

"She has a smart mouth for an *adult,* but you tend to get used to it. I won't allow you to discipline her in my presence." Texas was just across the river and I wanted to get back on home soil. "What'll it take to get us all over there?"

"Well, I don't like her." He glanced over his shoulder at the house sitting only a few yards from the ferry's landing, then looked guilty for a moment.

"Most people don't, I believe. So, what'll it take?"

"Well, she's irritating, so I'll have to charge a little extra." He told us the cost for the four of us, the horses, and the mule. The way I was feeling, double the price would have been just fine. I paid him from my pocket and we led the horses onto the ferry. It was a good solid craft, with plenty of room for all of us. I let Gil stay in the saddle, but me and the girls remained close to the horses' heads.

"River's higher'n I like it, but it's gone down since last night." The ferryman untied the craft and grasped the rope stretching from bank to bank. Using both hands, he started us across. "I guess all that rain upriver's finally gone. I wouldn't have come over to get you yesterday. Too much floating downstream."

He threw a second glance over his shoulder at the shack where he lived. It must've been built with planks from some other building that fell down from neglect. The lower third was made from split logs, but the remainder was warped and split boards.

The tail of a horse flicked into view from the other side and disappeared. A gray backed up until one flank was visible, then shuffled in an indecisive dance before disappearing.

I've been around horses all my life and knew someone over there wanted it to follow them back out of sight.

I expected him to start pulling, but he hesitated, staring across the river as if waiting for something. "You folks been on the trail for long, you and the wife?"

The Texas bank was empty, except for the house sitting a few feet above the water, the landing, and a small garden to the left, which was growing tall and green. A flock of crows flew in from the west and set their wings to land in the garden. Their course took them out of sight behind the house for a moment, but instead of reappearing over the opposite side, they burst into view over the roof and scattered in all directions.

Trying to work out what I'd just seen, I checked back over my shoulder. The bank behind us was devoid of life. I turned back around and saw concern on Esther's face. "What's wrong?"

"I don't know."

"Hold up there, friend."

The ferryman stiffened and that's all I needed. Yanking the Winchester from its scabbard on Gil's horse, I swung the muzzle to cover the man. The Spencer was great for close-in work, but I needed the reach the rifle would give me across the river. "Hold this boat steady or I'll blow you into that river."

Gracie gasped, confused.

"Y'all get back off and take Gil with you. Gil!"

Partially tied into the saddle, he raised his head and focused on me as Gracie reached for his reins. "Huh?"

"Y'all get off, now!"

He straightened at the tone of my voice.

"Wait." The ferryman kept looking across at his house and his voice was way too loud, telling me my instincts were right. His expression was wild and desperate. "You've already paid and I don't give money back."

"You do what I say." The hammer was back on that Winchester and it wouldn't take but a twitch of my finger to shoot, then swing toward the house if necessary.

Esther yanked the rail from its mounts and dropped it into the river. Gracie led Gil's horse and the others followed. Slapping the steeldust on her hip, I kept the rifle on the ferryman and backed off as she trotted toward the others.

"Help!" the ferryman shouted toward the house, and I expected to see someone come a-running.

Instead, two men emerged from around the side to stand and watch.

Behind me, the others raced up the steep bank, throwing up dust and clods that rattled down to splash into the water.

One of the men on the other side took a knee and shouldered a rifle. A golden glint told me it was a Henry, and those were deadly in the hands of an experienced man. I swung the Winchester and hit the ferryman in the face with the barrel. He staggered back and I shouldered the rifle and threw three quick rounds toward the man with the Winchester as fast as I could jack the lever.

The first one struck the surface of the river and ricocheted off, whining up toward those two. The man on one knee jumped and I figured that bouncing bullet startled him. He fell sideways and caught himself with one hand. The next two rounds were higher and struck close by the pair who ducked around the house and out of sight.

It wasn't over, though. The ferryman threw himself at me, but I ducked a shoulder and bent at the waist. Committed to his jump, his arms reached for me and missed. I rose using his momentum and threw him off. He landed on the ferry's rough boards with a thud, and came back up for another shot at me. I butt-stroked him with the Winchester across the forehead and he went down like a felled tree.

Jumping onto the bank, I snatched the big knife from its

scabbard on the back of my belt and cut the rope across the river. The ferry drifted downstream at a walking pace before the current caught it. The ferryman sat up and held on to the rail, looking back at me. Blood ran from the split in his forehead, covering one eye.

"I'll kill you for this!" His shout was full of fury.

"This was your doing!" I watched the ferry spin, while keeping an eye on the house, in case those two reappeared to continue the fight. "Why?"

He hesitated, watching the river and banks spinning by. I didn't think he was going to answer, but just before he drifted out of shouting distance, he yelled something, but it was lost in the wind.

I read his lips, though, and it looked like he said "money."

CHAPTER 34

"Maybe you have another plan. That last one didn't work out at all." Ed Gentry stared straight ahead from under the brim of his hat as he and Bill Johns rode side by side down a stagecoach road. They stuck close to the wide Red River after Cap Whitlatch and his band escaped their ambush.

"It wasn't my fault." Johns shrugged and turned in the saddle to check their back trail. As had become his habit, he smoothed his silky mustache, which had refused to thicken up. "That fool ferryman gave us away."

"I suspect your horse backing into view at the wrong time had something to do with it."

"It was the fault of that man's stupid wife coming out and spooking him. Why couldn't she wait to throw out the dishwater at another time?"

"We didn't tell her she had to stay inside, and she fed us a pretty good meal, to boot. A woman has to do the dishes."

"Should have tied her up, like I wanted to."

"There was no need."

They rode in silence for several minutes before Gentry cleared his throat and chuckled. "Think that ferryman ever got off that spinning contraption?"

Johns laughed. "Well, it's a study, that's for sure."

"Whitlatch damned near got me with that rifle." Gentry

shook his head in wonder. "I figured I could hit him over there, it wasn't much of a shot, and I would have, but I swanny, he threw lead at us faster'n anybody I've ever seen. Got me to rushing."

The road bent around a thicket of shin oaks hiding five men sitting on horseback in the two-track road. Two had guns out, and the rest sat there, with grins on their faces.

"Whoa!" Gentry raised both hands and caught Johns from the corner of his eye doing the same. "Easy, boys. Lower them guns."

The leader was thin as a knife blade and the look on his face was ratlike. "You two keep them hands away from those pistols."

"Whatever you say." Johns did as he was told. "Can we help y'all?"

Rat showed his teeth in a nasty smile. "Those are some good-lookin' horses."

Those words told Gentry everything he needed to know. He tensed, knowing from experience what was coming next. "They oughta be. A man needs good horses to work cattle."

"You don't look like cowhands to me."

"Well, we are."

Gentry kept his focus on Rat, but took notice of the other four who seemed overconfident. He took a quick note of their positions. One of them had a battered Winchester rifle in his hands. Big and powerful, he looked to be the most dangerous of the gang—after Rat, that is.

They'd done this dozens of times, Gentry suspected, drawing down on innocent travelers and stages filled with passengers, who usually gave up their money and possessions without a fight in order to preserve their lives.

"You boys look like hands to me." Gentry adjusted himself with the creak of leather. "You ride for a brand nearby?"

Two of them chuckled, a nasty, caustic sound. They

favored and might have been cowhands at one time, but men like them often swung back and forth across the invisible line between right and wrong.

Johns's voice came soft and low, a sure sign he was about to strike. "Y'all find robbing stages too hard, or dangerous?"

"No." Gentry watched Rat and Big Guy like a hawk. "They likely lean more toward rustling cattle from some big outfit that's not likely to notice a few head missing from time to time."

Rat's expression went flat. "You're on dangerous territory there, bub."

"No, you are."

Big Guy grunted and took his hand off the rifle's forepiece. "This guy thinks he's tough."

Quick as a snake's strike, Gentry's Colt leaped from his holster, spewing streaks of flame and lead. Their reaction surprised the gang, who'd likely never had anyone fight back. The first slug caught Big Guy in the chest and he swayed backward like a tall tree in the wind. The rifle's muzzle flashed as the slug drilled a hole in the ground.

Johns snatched his pistol free of its holster and shot Rat, who went over backward, dropping the rifle. Landing hard, he scrabbled crablike toward a buckeye bush and away from the fight.

More flashes came from the other three, who tried to shoot and control their frightened mounts at the same time.

Johns's revolver belched flame again, which lanced toward the one sitting to their far left. A stocky half-breed doubled over and fired from an awkward position, missing whoever he was aiming at.

Gentry's horse lunged sideways and he heard the buzz of a bullet, which missed by mere inches. Yanking the buckskin back around, he swung a leg over the saddle on the offside, away from the highwaymen, and heard the solid thump of a ricochet off the cantle, which whined away.

Once on the ground, he sidestepped the horse and swung on the next bandit, who thumbed off two rounds. Firing as if he was shooting bottles on a log, Gentry shot the man in the chest. The outlaw staggered sideways from the impact. Gentry's next round caught him in the neck and the man went down, spraying blood.

He didn't know when Johns got off his horse, probably as soon as the shooting started, for shooting from horseback is a chancy thing. Johns dropped one revolver Gentry hadn't heard him empty and sidestepped into the shin oaks, drawing his backup. Bullets clipped limbs, which fell around him, and Gentry heard him hiss as a round sliced through his pants, cutting a gash in his outer thigh, which quickly welled with blood.

When his Colt ran dry, Gentry reached over his mount and slid the Henry from its scabbard. There were still two bandits left alive, and one of them was Rat. The other wheeled his horse and put the spurs to its flanks. Leaning over the saddle horn, he tried to make himself as small as possible as the horse thundered away, hooves kicking up dust and dirt clods.

Silence closed in on them, enough so they could hear Rat's feet pounding hard on a deer trail through the little oaks. Brush crackled, limbs snapped, and he was gone.

Dropping to one knee, Gentry shouldered the rifle and lined the sights up the fleeing rider's back. Pleased at the going-away shot, he rested the front bead high between the man's shoulders and squeezed the trigger.

The rifle bucked and half a second later the big .44 round slammed into the highwayman, knocking him forward before he fell to the side in a hard roll of limp arms and legs. His horse bucked once, empty stirrups flapping, and disappeared over a low rise.

"Johns, you hurt bad?"

"Naw."

"Good, then I'm going after that other one." Gentry reloaded his revolver, and though most of the bandit's mounts had disappeared, Rat's horse stood nearby, watching where its owner had disappeared into the woods. Speaking low and soft to the spooked animal, he raised a hand only inches at a time until he could grab the reins. Leading it to where the outlaw disappeared in the oak grove, he slapped it on the rear and watched as it darted through the woods.

He followed on foot, carrying the Henry casually over one shoulder.

The animal loped ahead, and furious that someone tried to rob and kill him, Gentry set a steady pace behind. Like most horsemen, he disliked walking any great distance. He'd ridden with men in the past who refused even to walk across a street in town.

His boots were killing him, making him madder the farther he went. The going got easier when the horse found a deer trail and slowed to walk. Gentry kept an eye out in the heavy shade, but the horse seemed to smell something that interested him.

Not but twenty yards behind, Gentry saw the animal's ears prick forward. As he'd hoped, a rustle in the understory told him the man he was after wanted that horse.

Holding his rifle as if quail hunting, Gentry slowed and listened. The horse blew and a shape appeared, reaching for the reins from the cover of a thick bush. Gentry aimed at the side of his upper chest as he leaned out farther and squeezed the trigger.

The rifle barked and the last of the gang fell at the horse's feet.

Gentry advanced with care, keeping the rifle on the man's body. He stopped at a soft groan from the form lying only feet away from the horse that had betrayed him. Though terribly wounded, the highwayman raised his head.

Gentry drew his Colt and shot him. "I can't stand thieving bastards like y'all."

CHAPTER 35

Nate Cornsilk, the former deputy, was resting on a stump out front of his little board-and-batten house, which sat high off the ground on cedar posts ten miles out of town, when a tall man stepped from the woods surrounding the clearing and held up a hand in greeting. Recognizing him, Cornsilk put down the harness he was repairing and turned his attention from two crows that had been watching him all morning.

He always thought crows were friends, and wondered if they were sitting on the branch of a nearby peach tree to try and tell him something. Maybe they were telling him his foot was well enough to go visit Miriam Gray Cloud, who lived about two miles down the creek. Cornsilk was craving some of her excellent biscuits, and her company.

He endured her company for the biscuits covered in butter and honey.

Cornsilk waved his old friend to come in. "Long Fox. It has been many months. Come sit."

Dressed in white man's pants and a shirt way too large for his frame, Long Fox stopped beside a bucket of water sitting on a split log in the house's shade, his moccasins only inches from a rat snake dozing nearby. A simple twist of leather held his long hair back. "I would take the water."

"It is fresh and cold from the spring."

"It will be good not to spit grit from my teeth for a while." Long Fox picked up a gourd dipper lying on the bench and drank loud and long. Taking a deep breath, he drank again and finished by pitching the remaining contents of the dipper onto the snake. Raising its head, it stuck out its tongue and slipped underneath the foundation resting on cedar posts, which were sunk into the sandy ground.

Cornsilk tried not to be irritated by the mistreatment of his pet snake. "My horse drinks quieter than you."

"I will drink quietly if you have any whiskey." He sat on the ground in the shade as Cornsilk put down his mending and limped inside. He came back out with a quart fruit jar full of clear liquid and handed it over. "Don't waste any of this on my rat snake."

True to his word, Long Fox swallowed silently, and followed the whiskey with another dipper of water. "That was good. Why are you limping?"

"I stepped on a nail in town that went plumb through. It doesn't hurt as bad because I have been soaking it in coal oil."

"That worked for a friend who cut his hand cleaning a deer."

Cornsilk sat back down. "You've been on a long trail."

"I have. I went to a magic spring, off to the west, to drink water guarded by an old white woman with powerful medicine."

"I have heard of her. They say the Comanches won't kill her or run her off."

"Her magic is too great. She killed two of them with one bullet. She is a witch."

Cornsilk absorbed that information. "I got rid of a little witch myself, here, a while back."

"Did you kill her? That's the best way I know. If you don't, they can come back as a spirit animal to infect someone else."

"No, but she disappeared in a storm."

"Did you see it?"

"I was on the way back here to the house when I heard about it. She was in jail with that white German who killed Possum Little Hawk. I bet she turned them both into birds and they flew out through the jail's window. It is something I expect."

He paused to consider that the crows were Whitlatch and Vanderburg, but decided that Gracie would be with them to watch, so the numbers didn't add up.

"I heard they both got away." Long Fox took another sip of corn liquor and smacked his lips in satisfaction. "Then somebody killed the sheriff the next morning."

"Kanoska?" The news was startling. Cornsilk turned to see the crows still sitting there. Maybe that's why they came, to tell him, or one could be Kanoska's spirit traveling with a companion.

"Yes."

"I've been here alone for many, many days. No one has come by to tell me."

"Well, he's dead and in the ground. Are you going back to town to take over?"

"No. I would rather stay here and speak with the wind."

"It speaks the truth, unlike what you just told me."

"I do not lie."

"You do not have the right story, then. You didn't have the right one about the German, either. He didn't kill Possum. It was Cloyce Gluck."

A great sadness washed over Cornsilk. "How can I know that's not a story you are telling me?"

"Because I saw him do it. The brothers were arguing about money behind one of the buildings in town. Cloyce wanted Possum to share what he had in his hat, and he did not want to, so an angry spirit took Cloyce's hand and made him draw his six-shooter and kill him. I watched Cloyce when he saw the light go out of his brother's eyes, and then he ran away."

"I wish I knew that when they were in jail."

"I left that night so that I was not taken for the killer. White men like to hang us when they can't find the right ones."

"A wise thing to do." Cornsilk drew a long breath, trying to decide what to do.

"I know something else."

"What is that?"

"I think I saw that German that Kanoska had in jail. He was with a white man with strange, cold eyes. They were with a woman and that little Cherokee girl who goes by Gracie. She carries poison in her words."

Cornsilk felt a shiver go down his spine. "That was the witch girl I was talking about."

"I made a mark in the air to block her words."

"I tried that."

"I think it worked. After she glared at me for trying to buy her, she didn't say anything else, but those two with her pointed their weapons at me, but couldn't pull the triggers, so I left."

"Which way were they going?"

"Southwest. And I know something more." Long Fox took another sip of whiskey. "There are many people after them."

Absently rubbing the place on his shirt where he'd worn the deputy's badge, Cornsilk wiggled the toes on his injured foot inside his shoes to see if he could put more pressure on the wound. "How do you know this?"

"Two men in town asked me about Cold Eyes. They say he killed a friend of theirs up in Missouri."

"He has killed before."

"That's what I hear. The Glucks left town right after Kanoska was murdered, too. I heard they want to kill the

German. I reckon because Cloyce does not want him to tell what he saw. I think they're after Cold Eyes as well. They say he pointed a shotgun at them and then killed others only a few minutes later."

Cornsilk stood. "Don't drink any more of that."

"Why not?"

"Because we need to go warn Cold Eyes and Vander-burg about who is following. I think a dark spirit is on Cold Eyes's shoulders to attract bad people. You are the best tracker I know. Take me to where you saw them."

"This is between white people."

"I am still a deputy, and that German is innocent. I also have an idea they might have killed Kanoska, for the timing is right. He was my friend and he needs to be avenged."

"Where is your badge?"

"We have to go to town and get it, but after that, I don't know for sure what to do."

"I will lead you to Cold Eyes and the German man."

"What about the others doing the same? By your count, there are several bands after them."

Long Fox stood and placed the jar of whiskey in the shade. "Once we find them, I think the spirits will bring the others to the witch girl to fight. We should be there."

"I have a mule you can ride."

"It will be faster."

CHAPTER 36

I was fast running out of patience in the territories. We made another camp that night on the north side of the river.

That was no posse waiting for us back at the ferry. I wondered if it had something to do with that Texas Ranger who was shot outside of Margarite, but they shouldn't have been hunting us over that. Everyone there saw what had happened. He was murdered by those two with him.

It was clear as day to me. We were simply standing there talking to him at gunpoint when someone opened on us from the woods at the same time those two men with him started shooting. One shot past me at the sheriff while I was looking, while the younger of them shot the Ranger in the back.

Could those two who shot the Ranger have been the same men waiting to ambush us back at the ferry? That part made sense, and if they hadn't been so quick to shoot, I'd've thought they were some of Judge Parker's marshals after us. Come to think of it, quite a few of those old boys were known to be quick on the trigger.

But I figured that before he was murdered, Kanoska would have sent a telegram down south to tell them I was bringing Gil in. Why would marshals be after us with deadly intent, unless, like Sheriff Bronson back there, they, too, thought it was us that committed that deed.

Lightning flickered to the northwest as the sun went down. Another late-season cooling was on the way. Gracie pointed to a nearby draw filled with sycamore trees. "I see a bee tree over there."

She shook me from my thoughts and I followed her finger. "Looks like one, but we don't need any sweetening."

"I think we do. My grandmother says honey is good for healing. I bet if I make a poultice from the medicines I picked and we apply some to Gil's stump, it'll help it heal up quicker."

For the first time since we took his arm, Gil perked up. "I'd like a taste, too."

"Y'all, we have people chasing us. We don't have time to rob bees."

It was Esther who took up for them. "Gil, it won't hurt to rest tonight, and she's right. The old folks who raised me used honey on wounds."

I was too tired to argue. Tired of being on the road for so long, for I'd have already been almost back home by then if it hadn't been for my responsibilities, so I gave in. "Fine, then."

I picketed the horses while Esther made pallets and built a small fire. I dropped my saddle and made to kick it out. "We don't need a fire tonight. Somebody might see it."

Esther was up and between me and the flames before I could say "spit." "We do. If I don't get something hot in Gil, he might just dry up and blow away. He already looks like Job's turkey, and I'm afraid he's gonna fade away from us."

Taken aback by her vigor, I had to stop and think. "Spunky" wasn't no word for it after she started coming back from an experience that would have killed most women, or driven them mad. I liked it.

"She's right. We need a fire for once." Gracie was busy tying a bundle of sticks and leaves she'd gathered. "And besides, I'll need it to light this and use it to smoke the bees out."

"That's the way we did it when I was a little kid." Gil lay propped with his back against his own saddle. He was still gray as ashes.

"Come go with me." Gracie rose and motioned for me to follow.

"Shouldn't we find the hive first?"

"I already did." Gracie picked up two other bundles she'd already made. "You were too busy unsaddling the horses."

I didn't like it one little bit that I'd been so busy with my work that I hadn't noticed she was gone. A little waif like her could disappear in that country like a puff of smoke.

She stepped away from the fire. "You ready?"

Picking up the Winchester, I made to follow her. "Lead on."

A game trail led in the direction she indicated. I walked along behind that little imp, enjoying the shady walk. "I wish you wouldn't go stringing off without me."

"You weren't around when I was little and strung off everywhere on my own." She slipped under a bush I had to push through. "I got along just fine."

"Until you wound up in jail. Kanoska and Cornsilk were nice guys, but it could have been men of low position. Out here, you could run into bandits, criminals, or any kind of fugitives, not counting stray fighters off looking to lift somebody's hair."

"They'll have to catch me first."

Shaking my head, I kept the Spencer ready in case we should run into a band of bad guys or a bear. I once knew a guy who tangled with a Mexican lion guarding a deer carcass in some thick brush down in South Texas. He was on it before he saw the big cat and it cut him to shreds before he shoved his revolver against its chest and killed it with six shots.

We heard them humming before we came up on a dead oak without limbs of any substance. Energetic bees buzzed in and out of a hole, twenty feet over our heads.

It seemed a long way up there to me. "How're we gonna get at that honey?"

"We can light a fire here at the base and burn it down."

"That'll draw every person twenty miles around."

"I figured you wouldn't like that idea." Gracie grinned. "I'll just shinny up there from one stob to another until I get there, and then I'll light this bundle and smoke 'em away from the hole. When I can, I'll reach in and grab a handful of comb and drop it down. You get ready to catch me, 'cause I'll be right behind it and we'll light out of here like turpentined cats."

Neither idea sounded good to me, but she'd already started up that tree like a little squirrel, digging in with her bare toes. The bees took little notice of her, even after she straddled the butt of a broken-off limb. Holding on with her legs, she struck one of my last lucifers on the metal button of her gallus and the friction match burst into flame. She lit the bundle and soon it was smoking like a locomotive.

She held it in front of the hole and there must've been another'n in the top, because that tree drew like a fireplace. In no time, she reached into the opening and withdrew a chunk of dripping honeycomb bigger than my hat. She dropped it and I caught the chunk with my left hand covered by the last clean piece of Esther's old cotton dress.

That smoke must've made them bees sick, because not a one of 'em stung her. In no time, she was back on the ground and we ran, laughing, back to camp, only to find that Texas Ranger and two Indians waiting for us.

CHAPTER 37

This time, the Ranger wasn't pointing any guns at me, which was a relief, and neither were the two Indians, standing behind him, wearing hats.

Stunned by what we'd found in our camp, I rooted myself to the ground, the shotgun's muzzle pointed toward the sky and the other hand well away from the Russian .44 on my hip. It was a good thing they were relaxed, for I was sticky from head to toe and not inclined to get into a shootout right then.

He nodded as we walked up and passed a cup of coffee to Gil, as if they were old friends. "Howdy, gentlemen. Sit down."

Still weak, Gil accepted the cup and raised a bemused eyebrow at me, signaling everything was all right and silently saying, *Wasn't this strange?*

Esther gave me a soft smile. "They rode in right after y'all left. We've been talking, and everything's fine. This here's Ranger Braziel, from Texas."

Taking note of the lawman's relaxed seat on a short log someone had pulled up after me and Gracie left to rob the bees, I handed the wrapped honeycomb to Esther. When I did, I realized one of the Indians was Deputy Cornsilk, and he was once again wearing his badge.

"She really is here." Cornsilk's eyes fixed on Gracie as if she were a poisonous serpent. He plucked a turkey wing fan from several items lying on a red piece of cloth on the ground in front of him and waved it as if shooing flies. "*Ishtahullo-chito,* protect me from this witch child." He picked up a handful of cornmeal and pitched it in her direction, then sprinkled a pinch on his head.

Gracie guffawed and licked honey off her fingertips. "It'll take more'n a prayer to the Great Spirit, a wing fan, and a little uncooked corn bread to save you from me if I take a notion to get you."

"See, Long Fox." Cornsilk seemed to settle in on himself. He dropped a pinch of cornmeal on the man's head beside him. "You need this for protection from her. This is the one I was telling you about. She has been with that German and you can see he's losing parts of his body as fast as leaves falling from a tree before winter."

"I've seen her before. I tried to buy her, but that one right there threw down on me and threatened to shoot." A tall, lanky Indian pointed at me. "Why do you think she put a curse on him?"

"Probably because she has demons who tell her what to do."

Another truth took me by surprise. I finally recognized Long Fox as the Indian I'd run off several days earlier when we were doing our best to put distance between ourselves and those who ambushed us outside of Margarite.

I kinda felt bad about the way we had treated him, but he had insisted on trying to buy Gracie—and I felt it was necessary at that time, and that was behind us.

The Ranger grunted and adjusted his position on the log, favoring his left side. "Relax, Mr. Whitlatch. I'm no longer looking for you and Mr. Vanderburg, though I've explained to him and Mrs. McKinney, we're in a slight pickle here. The facts that seemed to exonerate Mr. Vanderburg have come to light when Cornsilk here told me what happened back in town and Long Fox corroborated his story."

I gestured toward a canteen nearby. "I need to wash some of this stickiness off my hands."

"Fine with me. It's your camp. Y'all took a notion for some sweetening, I see."

Esther let water dribble onto my hands from a gourd she'd hollowed out the day before when we found them growing wild at the edge of a meadow. I washed the honey off as Gracie mixed up a poultice for Gil's stump. "The honey's for Gil, there, to help heal him up."

"I understand. I noted a distinct lack of balance on that poor man's body when we rode up. My old mama told me when I was a kid that the Romans used honey as a healing agent. You can relax, sir."

He was addressing me again, because I couldn't take my eyes off his hands, half expecting him to draw his firearm. "Well, that's kinda hard to do on such short notice. The last time I saw you, I believe you were about to trigger that six-gun there."

"I was indeed, and that's right before those two assassins shot me in the back. It would have been a miscarriage of justice, had I shot you that evening. However, you *were* vexing in your refusal to lay down your arms."

"I'd be the same way here, too." Getting back into my reasons why wouldn't make any difference at that point, and was liable to antagonize the lawman, who seemed to be friendly at the moment. "How'd you come to be alive and kicking so fast after being bushwhacked? One of 'em shot you at point-blank range."

"Faulty ammunition on the round that struck me, and a misfire, or a miss from the second weapon on their part, I suspect. Lucky for me on all counts."

"So, how is it that you believe these two about me and Gil?" I waved a hand toward Cornsilk and Long Fox.

"Nobody else within a thousand miles would take Indians at their word."

"Well, sir. I was on the trail of those two back shooters when I came across Cornsilk and Long Fox. I saw the badge on Deputy Cornsilk's coat, and he saw mine. I'm inclined to trust a badged lawman—"

"It's a good thing I put it on," Cornsilk interrupted. "He would have shot us, I believe, had we not been identified."

"You came on me suddenly in that wagon road cut." The Ranger held out his hands, palms up. "Didn't expect that trail I was on to intersect with a wider byway. I wouldn't have shot you, but I'd-a durn sure been ready to." He turned back to me. "We spoke on the trail and I discovered who they are. They separated themselves from a posse looking for you and those others, and went their own way to find Sheriff Kanoska's murderer, and they related to me what they knew."

"Assassins killed him while the poor man was taking his morning constitutional." Ranger Braziel tilted his hat back and shook his head, as if such a thought was embarrassing. He averted his eyes from the women. "Sorry for such an indelicate thought, ladies, but a man shouldn't have to worry about being shot at such a private time. I assumed it was you, until these two told me you were already gone."

When I raised an eyebrow for explanation, he continued. "A witness saw the sheriff step into the privy and heard the shots that came later, though they didn't see anyone running away. My summation is that y'all'd been gone too long. Anyway, we come together here, under interesting circumstances."

"So, why are you here, if you're not hunting us?"

"Why, purely by chance. I'm after those two who insinuated themselves into my trust, and then shot me in the back."

"Well," I said, drying my hands on my pants. "Why

don't you tell me what you know, because there's a couple of fellers who're doing their best to kill us. You were shot up close."

"My guardian angel saved me. The doctor back in town said the bullet that hit me was weak, almost a misfire." He added more details. "It hit a rib at an angle and missed all my vitals, but I hit my head when I fell and was out for some time."

"There were two."

"I've been thinking about that. I have no evidence, but the second man either missed, or shot at someone else rather than me. Neither matters, one attempted cold-blooded murder and, though it was poor marksmanship or an intentional miss, he knew the other shot me. They'll both swing for it, if I have my way."

Gil finally spoke up, more to be part of the conversation than for information, I surmised. "You reckon those 'others' you're after are friends of the back shooters you referred to?"

"Well, sir, if you recall, there were three factions back where that poor man named Olsen was lynched."

"I lost count of who was shooting that evening."

"I bet you did. I'll clarify it for you, at least as well as I know." He held up fingers as he counted. "There was myself, though I never fired a shot. Gentry and Johns, the posse, and a collection of rifles from the nearby trees, which I suspect they were desperados tied in with those two back shooters."

"That's a lot of hearsay and supposition."

"It's some hearsay, from reliable sources, such as the townspeople. Anyway, I was after only yourselves, until I learned the details of your predicament. Now I'm going to find those two, Ed Gentry and Bill Johns, and then those who ambushed us from the trees. I believe Gentry and Johns are the ones who shot at you on the ferry."

Gil adjusted the wrapping on his stump. "You base that on what?"

"The Henry rifle Mrs. McKinney mentioned, for one thing. Also, something tells me those two might have used me to get to you."

I looked at Gil, then the Ranger, and back. "Why're they after me? I haven't done anything to anyone to draw fire."

"Said you stole some money from a Springfield lawyer."

Baffled, I had to take a moment and consider the accusation. The deal between me and Penn was legal as all get-out. I delivered horses and he paid me what I asked. There were no hard feelings or words between us, from the time I arrived until I left his office.

"I've never stolen anything in my life. He paid me for a herd of horses I delivered."

"I believe you. They likely learned you are carrying money, then, and want to take it from you. Is it a significant amount?"

I sure didn't want to tell him what was in my saddlebags. "It's gold."

"Even the word can drive men to robbery and murder. Knowledge of that much from the sale of several horses is a guarantee of menace."

I scratched at the whiskers on my jaw. "Can you describe them?"

"One tall and slimmer than the other and cultivating a blond mustache that's a long way from filling in. The other is a run-of-the-mill waddie that looks like anybody else who ever forked a horse. Neither is stocky. Is that what you saw?"

"It was hard to gather any details at that distance, and while we were under fire." I told him what happened and he laughed at the part where we sent the ferryman spinning downriver.

"But one used a Henry, I'd bet."

I recalled the bronze glint. "I'd bet on it, too."

"So now you're looking for somewhere else to cross."

"We are. I don't like going so far into Comanche Territory in order to find a shallow place, but I want to get back into Texas."

"You crossed it to get up here."

"I did, but that was back a little northeast of Paris, where the Red widens and shallows over a sandstone bed." I explained my sale of the horses, but didn't mention why I'd taken a different route back.

Long Fox spoke up for the first time. "There are many places up and down this river."

"Well, we didn't know where." I had to admit one fear I've always struggled with. "I'm afraid to take someone in the water who might drown."

They all watched me like I was one of those play actors on a stage.

"My brother and I were fooling around beside a river that was up when we were kids and I talked him into swimming across. He wasn't good enough and went under. I never saw him again, and because of that, I carry the weight of his death on my shoulders and I'm afraid of wide rivers."

"That's fine with me." Gracie looked up from retying the healing package onto Gil's arm. She slapped his hand away. "Quit messing with that! Besides, you know I can't swim a lick, anyway."

Cornsilk perked up. "That's the way we can get rid of her. Long Fox, take us to deep water and this witch might drown."

The Ranger frowned. "That's enough, gentlemen. Mr. Whitlatch, maybe I can relieve some of that strain on your shoulders. I'll take your prisoner down to Texas and you can go about your business."

"My business *is* taking Gil down to Fredericksburg, like I promised Sheriff Kanoska."

"I understand that was your charge, but I have the

authority and the will to escort Mr. Vanderburg, as was my original orders, once I hang those two I'm after." He noted my raised eyebrows.

"But you said you weren't after us."

"I wasn't, but there's no animosity at hand here. I've run across the two of you, so I can take him and save you the trouble. Despite your troubles, I still have a warrant for Mr. Vanderburg. That's why I was in Blackwater in the first place, to pick him up after receiving a telegram from Kanoska."

Gil looked insulted. "You just said yourself I'm innocent."

"I said these men vouched for you in the murder of Possum Little Hawk, and told what they saw. However, I doubt Judge Isaac Parker, as well as no court of law or judge in Texas, will take the word of Indians. That means I will send a telegram to Judge Parker at the next opportunity to explain the circumstances. Then I will escort you back to Judge Leland Ivan, who issued your warrant in Texas, and explain what I've discovered. I'm sure he'll believe me and it will all be official."

"Well, hell." Gil laid his good forearm over his eyes.

Something in his voice made me ask, "What?"

"Leland's mad at me."

"Explain yourself." Ranger Braziel settled himself for a story.

Gil reddened and turned so he wouldn't have to look at Esther. "His daughter, Alice, wanted to marry me and I wouldn't do it and left."

"There's more to it." The Ranger heard the same unspoken thing I did.

"Well, she had to move to Austin to live with her aunt, because she was, well . . . She and I . . ."

"She was expecting." Esther's voice was as flat as a handclap.

"That's what they say." Gil licked his lips. "I'd already

left town, 'cause her daddy didn't like me nohow, but I never knew what state she was in until I'd been gone awhile and ran into someone in Fort Worth from our hometown. I haven't murdered anyone. Hell, I haven't ever even shot at a white man in my life. That old fart's just wanting to get me back to Fredericksburg because of Alice." He shook his head again, a habit that was beginning to annoy me. "It's my bad luck to mess with the daughter of a judge."

I tilted my hat back. "Gil, no offense, but Ranger Braziel's idea sounds like a good deal to me."

Gil wriggled around for a better position on the ground. "How's that?"

"I was going to take you down and drop you off at the jail. Going with Ranger Braziel'll give you a better chance, and, frankly, his word will carry a lot of weight and might help you with a jury. With you under his charge, I can go find out who's gunning for me. I can't abide people like that, and they won't be expecting me to come after 'em."

"Well, I can't afford to lose any more body parts on the way." Gil's voice was thick with sleep. Telling that story seemed to have worn him out. "Maybe my luck will change."

"Your luck will change when you shed yourself of this witch child." Cornsilk looked around, apparently expecting some comment, but we grew silent in thought.

The Ranger pondered his coffee. "However, I have a more pressing concern that might be beneficial to us all. I have an idea. Long Fox here gets us back to somewhere shallow, and then you continue on, as you've been doing with Vanderburg and Mrs. McKinney, until I find the men I'm looking for. Once I hang 'em, then I catch up with you and take Mr. Vanderburg off your hands, and then you can go after those who ambushed you."

"I planned to deliver Mrs. McKinney to her family first."

Gil roused up and frowned in concern. "Hey, you didn't say nothing to me about that."

"You were under the weather."

"If that's what you want to call it."

The Ranger shook his head. "You two knew each other at the outset, I assume."

"We did, but I made a promise to Kanoska that I plan to keep, one way or another."

He slapped his knee to punctuate our conversation. "Well, then. We have a plan. Long Fox, where is the nearest crossing?"

"Two days west."

Gracie looked in that direction. "Well, shit."

"Looks like we're traveling companions, then." Braziel held his empty cup out. "Ma'am, I'd take a little more coffee if it was offered."

Cornsilk rose. "I will sleep somewhere over there, away from the witch. My foot has healed and I wouldn't care for any more wounds." He looked down on Gil, who was drifting away. "Maybe I should take him with me over there, so he won't wake up with anything else gone off his body."

CHAPTER 38

Two days west put us right smack in the middle of Comancheria, and we found out real quick it wasn't somewhere we wanted to be. The rope ferry Long Fox told us about was gone, recently burned out on our side by a war party.

The look of horror on Esther's face broke my heart when she saw the charred, blackened timbers of the house and the heavy rope chopped to a frazzle and pulled in a tangle of blowdown limbs and stripped trees washed down from far upstream. You didn't have to be a mind reader to know she saw that as her last hope of getting home.

"Well, shit." Gracie jumped off her horse and stomped over to the hand-hewn timber that once anchored the rope. "I'm about done with all this."

Gil sat slumped in the saddle, looking half dead. "That tears it with me, too. Cap, I'm gonna go lie down there under that tree over yonder and just die."

"Nope." I shook my head, watching Cornsilk ride down the slope to the water. Most of the riverbank we'd been following was high and steep, with only game trails winding back and forth to the bottom, where animals drank.

This crossing was different. The wide bank sloped gently down to the river, as if the good Lord scooped it out with a giant shovel. Our side was a wide, shallow beach overlooking strips of sand bars out in the middle of the red, muddy water. The other side was the same as where we stood. There was essentially no bank, just a line where the water ended and the land began rising in a long slant.

Ranger Braziel studied the river for a moment, then turned his mount to look northward. "This is hostile territory, all right."

Cornsilk came back and stood beside Long Fox, who was squatting in the shade of his horse. "This man who ran the ferry was a charlatan."

His statement piqued my interest. "What do you mean?"

"He was a thief."

"I understand what a charlatan is, but why is . . . was he a thief?"

"Because there was no need for a ferry here. This is a ford used by the Old People, way back when our ancestors first rose from the ground. We can ride across, and the water will barely reach the horses' bellies. He was stealing money from people brave, or stupid, enough to try and pass through here."

Gracie and Esther walked to the edge of the swirling water. Esther shook her head. "It looks deep and mean to me. See that current?"

Long Fox pointed with his index finger. "He is right. The current looks strong because it is shallow." He laughed. "That dead man over there made money off something everyone could wade, but it cost him his life."

I hadn't seen the bloated body stretched out in the grass fifty yards from the house, proving I was about worn out and needed rest. Once he was pointed out, the arrows sticking out of his corpse were bright and clear in the sun.

For the first time since I'd met him, Cornsilk talked and used hand signs at the same time. I attributed that to an attack of the nerves at what he'd found. "It hasn't been that long since they were here. There are many fresh tracks here, coming and going.

"War parties are crossing here pretty regular, and the ground is all torn up by stolen horses. I think this is an old war trail that he had the misfortune to find and try to make money off of. It looks like a band came through, within the last day or so."

"I'm surprised that dumb ferryman lasted as long as he did." Long Fox squinted toward the north. "I bet them Comanches come through here all the time. He just caught them in a lull long enough to build this house and pull a line across. Probably built it during the winter—"

Cornsilk cut him off. "Riders coming. I believe they're Comanches."

The Ranger saw to his weapons and kept an eye on shapes heading our way. "I just hope he was out here alone and he doesn't have a family lying out there where we can't see them."

Gracie pointed across the river. "Are those horses over there?"

They were. I saw a flash in the trees and realized it was a herd of stolen horses. They milled for a moment and I caught a glimpse of a young Comanche, who ducked down when he saw me looking. They'd left them on that side under his care for some reason and we'd stumbled right into the middle of trouble.

Another youngster in leggings hid behind a tree. All I could see was a bare shoulder as he peeked around the trunk at us.

"I'd shoot them now, but I can't bring myself to kill a kid for just watching me." The Ranger squinted to the north. "I suspect I'll regret that decision in a few minutes. They'll fight hard to pick up that herd and those boys with them. Dismount and prepare to defend yourselves."

On the ground, Esther stifled a scream at the sight of a

band of warriors racing in our direction across the prairie, and drug her pistol from the deep pocket on her dress. She grabbed Gracie, as if holding her would help. Cover was scant around us, but a tangle of sun-bleached logs several feet above the waterline was our best chance in the face of what was bearing down on us.

I kicked the steeldust toward that tangle of driftwood and jumped off, dragging her a little farther away into a cane break growing thick and lush only feet away. The presence of the cane proved the water and slope were shallow. Another silver maple log, washed up from a distant flood, offered a place to tie her and the other horses as everyone rushed to join me.

An arrow arced over the river and buried itself in the mud. I threw a pistol shot in that direction to keep their heads down. They were kids, and like the Ranger, I felt it would be hard to deal with that threat, though they were more than capable of killing us, and were trained to do just that.

Having our backs to the river was the best we could do, even with the kids over there shooting arrows at us. While Esther tied the remaining ponies, I joined the others preparing to fight. Taking a knee behind the tangle, I watched the whooping band draw closer.

"I should have gone on." Long Fox opened a leather bag he carried on a strap over one shoulder and sat it on the ground. Dipping his hand inside, he pulled out a few shells and stuck them between his fingers like spikes, then drew an old .44 from inside his belt and cocked it.

Cornsilk knelt beside him, rifle ready. "I'll shoot far. You shoot close."

"If you hit what you're aiming at, I won't have to shoot close."

A puff of smoke from one of the Comanche's rifles was followed by the whine of a bullet that sailed over into Texas.

Ranger Braziel handed a revolver to Gil, who was leaning over a thick log. "I'll have that back when we're finished."

I knelt beside Esther. "Right now, your job is to keep those kids from shooting one of us."

The shock on her face spoke volumes.

"I didn't say kill them, but keep an eye on what they're doing and pitch a shot over there every now and then to keep them nervous."

"What if they try and cross to get a closer shot?"

"Then you do what you have to do to stay alive."

She shook her head. "What kind of world is this?"

"One that'll take your life in a heartbeat."

There were about fifteen warriors in the band, and when they drew close, four men on each side split off. "Uh-oh. They're gonna try and flank us on both sides." I lined the Winchester's sights up on the leader out in front, waiting for him to get closer.

I felt rather than saw Long Fox disappear into the cane break at the same time I squeezed the trigger and missed the Comanche bearing down on us. The bullet wasn't lost, though. A horse behind him stumbled and went down, throwing its rider, who landed on his head and lay still.

Braziel fired and I levered another round into the chamber. Their guns opened up, and for several seconds, there was lead flying in both directions. A twig snapped off a limb not far away from Gil's head and he returned fire.

Those on horseback came within fifty yards and then swerved, breaking off the attack, but I knew the others on foot were closing in around us. Shoving fresh shells into the Winchester, I twisted around and threw a shot at the trees hiding the horse guards. That one landed close enough that I saw the youngsters mount up and push the herd upstream.

I leaned the rifle against the log in front of Esther. "Use this if you have to."

Ranger Braziel fired, levered his rifle, and fired again as

I snatched up the Spencer. Breaking from cover, I ran toward the tall grass on the far side of the beach to meet those who'd split off and went to cover downstream.

Dust from the warriors' ponies rose as they reined up, mixing gunpowder smoke and making it hard to see individual targets. Mouth dry as cotton, I dashed across the open beach and worked my way close to the water, where several thick mesquites provided some cover, intending to surprise that little bunch that split off.

I hoped I'd get there before the Comanches and surprise 'em when they showed up to catch us in a pincher movement. Behind me, gunfire picked up again in a crescendo that rose and fell. Three individual shots came from a pistol in the cane breaks, and then silence.

Crouched in the shade of those bushes, I shouldered the Spencer and waited. This was exactly the kind of situation where I knew the twelve-gauge would do the most damage. A horse screamed behind our makeshift fort and the sounds of legs thrashing against brittle cane filled the air.

They were killing our horses.

Another screamed, followed by a shot, silence, then a rapid hammering of several rounds. Reprimanding myself, I worried that I should have gone to protect the horses and help Long Fox, but it was too late to change my mind. I was committed to ambushing those four who would soon be in position to shoot from a dangerously close range.

I sure hoped Cornsilk was adequate to his similar task as well. The Ranger was a man who'd defended himself in the past, and though Gil wasn't completely up to snuff, I remembered he was still a good hand with a pistol. They'd manage the direct charge that was intended to divide our attention and distract from those who would shoot us from behind.

Once he ran through the six cartridges in that cylinder, Gil had Gracie or Esther to reload for him, if they could.

In my mind, he'd then use Esther's pistol as she reloaded. It was his, to begin with, but here it was up to me alone, and where were those damned bucks who'd come this way? They should have been moving in by now, so I could deal with them and get back to the main bunch. It didn't feel right to be sitting and waiting while people were fighting nearby.

A flutter of movement, which shouldn't have been where it was, caught my eye. The tall grass in the open, twenty feet away, moved ever so slightly, and the still leaves on the brush around me proved there was no wind, not even a slight breeze.

One.

The gurgling water near the bank masked some sound, but I knew they were close. Being as still as a boulder, I moved only my eyes, for it's movement that gives you away. Gunfire from my friends rose and fell again. Whoops and cries from the Comanches filled the air as the Ranger's rifle fired steady, seven or eight times, and then quieted.

During that exchange, I saw even more movement in the grass.

Two.

I was sure they could see my chest pounding as my heartbeat accelerated. The warriors had left their horses hidden back behind them somewhere and were crawling on their bellies. They hadn't expected me to leave our band and move in their direction. I was out of pocket, and that worked in my favor as another crept past on their way to the fight.

Good. There were two, but where were the others?

A dove swooped in, looking to land, but something spooked the little bird and it darted back into the mesquites.

There! Three.

One had separated himself from the other two so they

wouldn't be bunched. Good thinking on his part, if I'd been waiting back there with the others behind the driftwood fortifications. Spread out that way, they'd have a better chance of charging, or throwing fire onto us from several different directions.

So, where was the fourth?

Dammit!

A twig snapped behind me and I realized he was right on the edge of the water with me, between him and the others. Like a rabbit in berry vines, I held completely still, feeling the hair rise on the back of my neck. Rabbits give themselves away when predators around them stop to sniff, look, and listen.

That tactic unnerves the rabbit so much, he can't stand it and finally panics, giving himself away. Well, I didn't have a hole to run to, so I waited as my skin crawled, expecting to feel the impact of a bullet or arrow at any moment.

Unlike that rabbit, I lay still as death while they inched past my position, attention fixed straight ahead and concentrating on those defending themselves behind the logjam. Gunfire rose and fell again, the thunder of the shots closer than I expected.

Was I waiting too long? Should I have been there, defending Esther and Gracie and waiting for these four to break into view? Naw, these boys grew up shooting from cover and I knew attacking them when they least expected it was going to pay off.

And it did.

Intent on what was in front of him, the painted warrior closest to me rose on one knee and looked left, giving me a clear view of his face blackened on one side and striped on the other. He then motioned with one hand, and a second rose between us, holding a bow with a notched arrow. Beyond him, still on his elbows, the third raised his head.

They'd found their targets.

I had to aim around a low-growing mesquite. A needle-sharp mesquite thorn lying on the ground sank deep into my knee. My mouth flew open in pain, but if I made a sound, the next pain I'd feel would be much worse.

Choking it down, I tucked the shotgun's butt tight into my shoulder and found the nearest warrior. Shotguns aren't made for exact aiming, but the front bead centered on the back of his neck and I gave him the load of aught-buck. Not waiting to see the impact, I pumped another round into the chamber, swung on the second man with the bow, and when the bead found the broad target of his side, I fired again.

That one yelped and convulsed, falling hard. Shucking in a fresh shell, I threw the third load into the one who had time to push up in an effort to gain his feet so he could swing around and shoot back. I'd waited until I was almost fully behind them, so it took him a moment to find me, and in that moment, I shot, pumped, and shot again.

Four shots in less than two seconds.

He dropped and a bullet splintered a limb right next to my face, filling one side of my head with fire. The mesquite tree that took the round was in my way when I spun, and the Spencer's barrel hit it like I was swinging an ax. It was too late to extract myself.

I saw the warrior throw a single-shot rifle to the ground and charge me from only yards away. He plucked a butcher knife from his belt and whooped, closing as fast as he could pump his legs. I snatched the Russian from its holster, but he slammed into me like a bull and we went down on the hard ground.

The back of my hand hit a dead limb and the pain was so intense that the pistol flew from my grip. There was no time to make an issue out of it, though. The man's knife flashed and I caught his wrist, preventing him from opening me up like a deer, and twisted my whole body back and sideways, throwing him off.

We hit the ground hard and I felt it in every bone. Turning loose with my left hand wasn't an option, because he kept trying to jab me with that knife. He grabbed a handful of my shirt, and stiffening the nearly numb fingers of my right hand, I jammed them into his eye, feeling the pop of his eyeball. Such a horrifying act was enough to make him scream and jerk his head away. Instinct took over and he tried to twist free, giving me the opportunity to reach back and snatch the Arkansas toothpick hanging over the back of my right hip.

The razor-sharp blade sank to the hilt in his belly and he recoiled. I pulled it free and stabbed him again and again, in rapid succession, until he quivered and went limp.

I was shaken and hurting all over, but there was no time to sit and catch my breath. Sticking the bloody blade back into the sheath, I picked up the Russian with my skinned hand and holstered it.

Grabbing up the shotgun, I stuffed fresh shells into the magazine and rushed down to the river's edge, and back to the rising sounds of gunfire.

CHAPTER 39

Cheese leaned back in his chair, which was pulled up to a poker table in the Rabbit Saloon. They'd been in Jeremiah long enough to finish half a bottle of whiskey each, and consider the girls who seemed disinterested in their suggestions. Maybe it was because they still had considerable trail dust on them and hadn't yet entertained the idea of baths.

"We missed 'em." Itchy hunched over their table, tired and irritated.

Rubbing his oversize nose, Cloyce Gluck wondered how he could be related to Itchy. In his experience, younger brothers usually seemed a little different, wilder than their older brothers and sisters, usually going off half-cocked over the least little thing, and not thinking their actions through. Itchy didn't take action, but he did always speak before considering all the facts, which often got him in trouble when they were growing up.

"We didn't *miss* anybody." Cloyce glowered at him, and then turned it on Cheese, just in case he pitched in on the wrong side.

"I guess what he means is that we expected to find that German and his buddy, once we got here."

Rubbing his forehead in frustration, Cloyce resisted the

urge to shout. "I doubt we'd find them here in the first saloon we stopped at."

"So you think they'll be here?" Cheese grinned at a whore, who turned up her nose and then ignored him, likely because of his bloody shirtsleeve and, of course, his ever-present odor, which seemed magnified in the humidity.

"I do. This is the first town of any size this far west, so I imagine they'll come across at Doan's Ferry and wind up here. Either way, it's going to be fine."

At least if they caught them before Whitlatch could deliver that German to the laws.

Cloyce grew up with a number of excellent Cherokee and Choctaw trackers, learning to read signs from an early age. By the time he was four, he learned to identify every wild animal track in the territories. When he turned six, he'd mastered the art of reading the difference between individual horse hooves. Some were trimmed, others un-attended developed distortion issues, abscesses always affected an animal's stride and weight distribution, while those that were properly shod carried distinctions left by the blacksmith's shoes.

One specific track left by Cap Whitlatch's horse was as original as dirt. Whoever had shod the horse neglected to smooth the animal's left rear hoof. It could have been an oversight, or the animal might give to that side because of an old injury, but the print was distinctive.

They'd seen it at the outset, following the pair out of Blackwater, and it had appeared more than once in damp places along the trail, when they took time to look. By the time they reached the Red, Cloyce knew exactly what to look for, and the tracks led west, but they lost them among dozens of others on the well-traveled wagon road.

More than once, they discussed the reason the men were

headed due west, when they could cross anywhere into Texas and take a more direct route. Hell, if it'd been Cloyce, he'd have crossed north of Paris and then taken the train to Dallas, and then Austin.

It was by sheer luck that Cloyce looked down on a wide sandstone ledge over the north bank of the Red River two days earlier. They'd come upon the tracks of four shod horses, two walking side by side. The tracks ended abruptly at the edge of a sheer descent. Whitlatch and Vanderburg had apparently been looking for a path or game trail leading down the sharp bank, when the one hoof he'd been looking for became printed in the damp crust of sand.

He puzzled the tracks out for most of that afternoon, but overthinking what he'd found, the Glucks wasted hours continuing on, thinking maybe he'd misread the tracks, or the horse might have turned around for some reason while they sat there and studied the river. Maybe the rider was watching their back trail, or they were avoiding a war party, something perfectly logical in that part of the plains.

Frustrated to the point of giving up, Cloyce led them to a little farm tucked into a grove of blackjack oaks, just off the wagon road. Their mounts needed grain. Grass wasn't quite enough for horses they'd pushed so hard, so they stopped to buy some feed and hopefully information from a mountain of a man, who, frankly, frightened all three brothers.

Any other time, they'd consider simply shooting the family and taking what they wanted, but that old boy was different. Standing six-six, with long brown hair nearly to his shoulders, and a thick mustache, he had a hard, mean look in his eye, which Cloyce took as a sign of an experienced killer. He also carried an oiled Walker Colt in a well-worn holster, which looked absolutely small against his massive frame.

Maybe the man had tired of taking lives for his own gain

and decided to marry and settle down. More than one outlaw had done the same, or it could be he was just one of those old boys nobody ever messed with. Whatever reason, his horse-faced, well-armed woman was also menacing.

Unnerved by how well they were prepared for trouble, Itchy and Cheese remained in their saddles, hands folded carefully on their saddle horns, while Cloyce dismounted and talked with them, hat in hand.

"Name's Cloyce. We'd like to water the horses there in your trough, and buy a little grain for them, if you have some to spare."

"Mack Smith." The big man nodded toward his wife and several half-grown sons that ringed them as if settling themselves for trouble. "Water away, and I reckon we can scratch up a little grain, if you have the money."

Cloyce ducked his head, concerned that direct eye contact and any attitude at all might spark the well-trained family into action. It was then that he noticed that odd left-hind hoofprint they'd been following in the dry dirt beside the trough. He realized they were back on Whitlatch and Vanderburg's trail.

While the woman fetched a bag of oats from the barn, the strapping teenage boys kept an eye on the strangers. All had a weapon of some sort nearby and Cloyce knew for a fact they'd all shoot in a heartbeat, if need be.

"Many thanks for the feed." He bobbed his head, doing his best not to look anywhere near dangerous. "We're trying to catch up with the rest of our group. We got separated back west of here when we saw Indian signs and split up to make less of a target. I'd hoped they came through here. A man with strange eyes, another feller likely in manacles, a woman, and an Indian girl."

Despite his preparedness, the farmer was open to conversation as they waited for his wife to head back from the barn.

The big man removed a shapeless hat and rubbed the tangle of hair. "They stopped by. Two days ago." His eyes drifted to Itchy and Cheese. "Can't say I'd split up with Comanches around. The more guns, the better, and the other feller wasn't shackled, not with that missing arm. How'd he come to lose it?"

Vanderburg had lost an arm? That information surprised him.

Cloyce chose his words carefully, making up a story as he went along. "Well, like my brother there, he took a wound when we tangled with them Comanches the first time. Shot us up pretty good."

"I can see that. I'm surprised they're making better time than y'all, him hurt so bad."

"Good to know they're ahead of us." Cloyce had no intention of weaving much more of a story, concerned by what Whitlatch might have told them. "We was afraid they'd try to cross the river somewhere behind us, and then it'd be hell to find them. The one with the eyes needs us to help with his prisoner."

"Like I said, I don't know if he was a prisoner or not, but that one feller you're talking about looked better than I'd expect, after what he went through."

"Uh, well, he's tough." Cloyce wondered what the man was talking about.

"You'd think a feller who lost his arm would need to lay up for a while, but Becky asked if they'd like to stay a day or two, but Mr. Whitlatch said no, they needed to move on with some haste after they spent the night in the barn, saying he needed to get to a telegraph office so they could get word to that lady's family that she'd been found."

Such an avalanche of information was almost too much for Cloyce, who needed time to puzzle it all out. And what did he mean by the woman being found?

"Well, they likely won't be moving too fast, so we can catch up."

Becky came out of the barn with a half-filled sack of oats, which she passed up to Itchy. Cloyce replaced his hat. "What do I owe you for the oats?"

The dad answered quick. "Four dollars should do it."

Cloyce's face flushed at the cost, but he knew better than to argue. Here was a family tougher than his own, and they were making a go of their little farm in a world full of Comanches, inhospitable frontier, and travelers who still carried the burden of the War Between the States on their shoulders.

Cloyce dug four silver dollars from the pocket of his dirty and stained pants. "Here you go. Thanks for the oats and information." Cloyce stuck his boot in the stirrup and swung into the saddle. "I don't suppose you know where my people might have crossed into Texas, do you?"

"Yessir." Mack pointed upriver. "Sent 'em a few miles down that way. Said they needed a ferry for your one-armed man. They have one there at Doan's, just north of Jeremiah, and then they intended to catch a train through to Fort Worth and then down to Austin, so y'all better hurry."

Doing his best not to smile, Cloyce simply nodded his head. "Much obliged."

All three brothers turned their mounts at the same time and lit out for the ferry. In two days, they were across the river and in Jeremiah, where they pitched off their horses in front of the first Texas saloon they found . . .

And that was the Rabbit Saloon.

CHAPTER 40

The firing stopped as I reached the open slope where the ferry once operated. From there, I saw Ranger Braziel partially hidden behind one of the logs, reloading his rifle. Arrows stuck from the sun-washed timber and several flash blazes showed where bullets struck.

Gil's arm emerged and fired once from an upended tangle of roots, then returned, but I couldn't see what he was aiming at. He was game, though, and you couldn't call the man a coward.

It must have been fifty yards to their position, and all of it in the open. I looked up the slope, but there weren't any live Comanches in evidence. Three lay in the open, one beside a dead horse. Two pops in the cane breaks told me Long Fox was still back there, and then silence.

"Braziel! Gil! It's me. Coming in."

The Ranger waved and I crossed the opening at a dead run, but no one shot at me. When I reached the tangle, I planted one foot on their barricade and leaped over, to find Esther reloading her pistol and Gracie plucking more rounds from a box in her lap.

"Everybody all right?"

Esther covered her mouth. "How bad are you hurt?"

"Why, I'm not hurt at all."

"There's blood all over your hand and shirt."

I felt my shirt to see what she was talking about. "None of that's mine."

She wrapped her arms around me. "Thank God."

"Glad you're all right." Ranger Braziel turned back toward the burned-out house. "They were back there for a while, but I don't see anyone now. We might have run 'em off. No one likes to take this kind of losses."

"Where's Cornsilk?"

Gracie jerked a thumb. "They were in there, killing the horses. Cornsilk went in to help Long Fox, and then we heard some shots."

The tall canes swayed and a voice called out, "Do not shoot us. They have gone."

Cornsilk and Long Fox stepped into view. Both held pistols in their hands. Long Fox smiled for the first time I'd known him. "We killed a couple, and your mare kicked one to death. She crushed his chest. You need to paint her. She is a warrior."

"She is that. Glad they didn't hurt her."

"I watched from the top of the bank up there." Cornsilk waved a hand. "They have gone because they lost too many men. This was a good position, and you killing those over there helped."

"Never was one to fort up."

"Some of their ponies are back there, grazing." Long Fox stuck his pistol in his belt and went back into the cane break. "We will need to catch them to ride, because they killed two of ours."

"Wait!" I held up a hand until they turned. "Are those kids gone that were over there?"

"Yes, they shot all their arrows, to no effect, and then they left." Cornsilk grinned. "They were good warriors, but inexperienced."

I saw a sense of pride in his eyes and wondered if it was

because the kids were brave and tried to fight, or because they were Indians and, though not part of Cornsilk's tribe, showed that some bands were still fighting us.

Either way, it was an interesting thought. I made a note to talk with him about it the next chance we got. "Bring back stolen horses if you can. They'll be easier to take the saddle than Comanche mounts."

Cornsilk nodded and they disappeared into the canes.

Ranger Braziel kept an eye out, but I could see he was no longer tense. "As soon as they bring those ponies back, we need to get across the river. This was a good place to defend, but I'll feel better on the Texas side, not that borders mean anything to the Comanches. Hell, them kids over there'll probably try to kill us the minute we step out of the water."

Smoothing his beard, as was his habit, Braziel kicked at the spent brass beside his knee-high boots. "Had we been in the open against these fighters, we might have lost our scalps."

"Came close as it was." I took off my hat and ran a hand over my matted hair.

Half an hour later, we rode into the river, which came up only to our horses' bellies. Though it was only a few yards to get across, I felt an immense sense of relief as the steel-dust mare stepped onto the Texas side of the Red.

The young Comanches and their stolen horse herd were gone. They'd be back, once we were down the trail, but we weren't after them. They'd have plenty to do with gathering their dead, and would be no threat to our band.

Instead of gathering to consider where we were, we rode up the long slope leading out of the bottoms and turned our faces south.

CHAPTER 41

The town of Jeremiah was hot and dusty when we arrived, and we must've been a sight, riding in the way we were, all beat up and plumb wore out. Ranger Curtis Braziel led the way, with me and Gil riding together so I could keep an eye on him. He wasn't as gray as he was two days earlier, but he was still weak. I glanced over when we reached the edge of town and was startled by the dark circles around his eyes.

If he didn't raise his head every now and then, I'd think I was keeping company with a corpse. Behind us came Esther and Gracie. It was funny to think about, but our guides, Cornsilk and Long Fox, brought up the rear. They'd drifted back, once we were in Texas, and I figured they didn't want to range out too far ahead, lest they come upon some old boys who didn't like Indians and tended to shoot first before they saw us.

Sitting straight as an arrow in his saddle, Ranger Braziel didn't turn his head, neither left nor right, but stared straight ahead as if someone was about to take his picture. I wondered if he wasn't too keen on being seen with all of us, but it didn't matter to me.

Unlike Blackwater, where I'd picked up Gil and Gracie, Jeremiah was everything I'd hoped it would be. It was almost a shock to come out of the territories, where outlaws would kill a man for his hat, to find a bustling town big enough to be a railroad stop.

We passed the wagon yard in the middle of town. The hard-packed ground was relatively dry and smooth, except around the town well, which sat in a wide, damp area.

I read the business signs: MCCLANAHAN'S DRUGS, ATKINSON AND BRO BOOTS AND SHOES, RUTHEY'S SHOE STORE, J.L. NORTH & CO. SADDLES AND HARNESS, and R.D. GILLENWATER GROCERIES AND PROVISIONS. All of this signage showed it was a thriving town.

We'd already passed a mill on the way in, two hotels I didn't like the looks of, and, of course, saloons lined California Street, north of the railroad station. As I'd feared, Cornsilk and Long Fox caught everyone's eye and they stopped to stare at our procession as we continued down the street.

Youthful voices came from behind and I turned to see several youngsters gathering behind us, running not far from our scouts. Letting the mare drift back, I moved in behind Cornsilk and gave the kids a warning shake of the head. The younger ones peeled off, but the older kids kept on right behind us. One carried a stick and I was afraid he'd swing at one of the horses. If he did, I hoped it'd be my steeldust mare. She'd teach him some quick manners.

The Grand Central Saloon caught my eye. A cold beer sure sounded good, but I couldn't stop there with Esther and Gracie in tow. Farther down was the two-story Hotel Benjamin, standing on a corner not far from the Katy and Santa Fe rail station. That's what I was looking for. Once past the wagon yard, I urged the steeldust forward and caught up with the Ranger.

"The Benjamin looks like where I want to stay with the ladies. You can do what you want."

The others must've read my mind, because we all reined up at a long hitching post in front of the hotel at the same time. Ranger Braziel seemed indecisive for a moment, but then gave a slight shrug and stopped as well.

I swung down and a young boy came running from where he'd been squatting in the porch's shade.

"Howdy, mister!" He looked to be about Gracie's age, and he took us all in with an astonished expression. His hair looked as if it'd been cut with sheep shears. "Holy hell! What'd y'all tangle with?" He studied Esther and Gracie, probably noting how they sat astraddle of the horses like men. Gracie looked down on him as if the youngster was a stray dog.

"The territories." I relaxed for the first time since I rode into Blackwater nearly two weeks earlier. Activity swirled around us. Freight wagons passed, filled with everything from kegs to wooden boxes to crates. One pulled by a team of six mules was loaded with brick. Men on horseback rode every which way, and the elevated boardwalks thumped with the hollow sounds of boot heels.

The kid finally noticed Ranger Braziel. "Wow, a Texas Ranger! You here to shoot somebody?"

"Likely, one of these kids back there pestering my scouts." He stepped down and pulled his coat back to show the revolver. "You boys get on out of here 'fore I take that stick from that one there and wear you all out with it."

Smarter than they looked, the boys heeded his warning and drifted across the street and out of his reach, where they could watch us.

I swung down. "We need to stable these horses for a few days. How about a livery?"

The boy nodded and adjusted a blue waxed cotton newsboy cap that covered his red hair. "Yessir. My daddy owns it. That's why I'm here. I keep an eye out for anyone who comes in, and I sell papers, too. You want today's edition of the *Jeremiah Hesperian*?"

"Yes, I will." Ranger Braziel stepped up on the boardwalk

and paused in front of the hotel doors. "You bring one up to my room. Mr. Whitlatch, I'll not take responsibility for your people at this time. The state doesn't provide funds for such. You can do what you wish. I will meet you back here at six this evening. Boy, stable my horse."

I wasn't sure what he wanted me there at six for, but I was too tired to ask questions. "Fine with me." He stepped inside and I turned to the boy. "You must make a pretty penny doing all that. What's your name, son?"

"Rogier." He pronounced it as *Rog-er* and spelled it for me. "It's an old Norse name, and has some German in it, too. My old man might run a livery, but he's a reader. Right now, he's got a place marked in Mr. Twain's book *Roughing It*. Dad laughs a lot when he's readin' it, 'cause he said Twain don't know nothing about it being rough, but he says it's a good book.

"Anyhow, the old man gets most of the money I make, but I'll tuck a few cents away between here and there."

He gave me a bright smile that showed a missing front tooth. I couldn't tell if it was a late permanent tooth coming in, or if someone knocked it out.

"You want me to take your horses down to the stable, too? I'd recommend it, 'cause it's coming up a cloud from the north and I reckon it'll be raining within the hour."

Standing on the street and talking about books and the weather was the furthest thing from my mind right then. I just wanted to get everyone settled in the hotel, soak in a hot bath for an hour or two, and then chew on a steak for a while.

I couldn't help but notice the look on Gracie's face. This kid talked more than her, and had just about as much vinegar and sass. "Here's five dollars." I handed him the last silver coins from my pocket. "Tuck one of 'em away and give the rest to your daddy for right now. Make sure they get plenty of grain and tell him I'll be down tomorrow to settle up."

Throwing the saddlebags full of money across my shoulder, I pulled the Spencer shotgun and the Winchester from their scabbards and leaned them against the rail. "Where's the livery?"

He pointed south. "Across the tracks there, past the depot. See where they're laying bricks for a new road down yonder by the station? Before long, every street in town'll be brick. I'll lead some of your horses down there and come back for the others."

"That'll be fine. You make sure all that tack's wiped down and put somewhere dry."

"Wouldn't take your money if I didn't intend to do it right. I ain't that kind."

Grinning, I went back and helped Gil down from the saddle. He had to steady himself for a minute until he could get his land legs again. Rogier's eyes widened at the makeshift sling holding Gil's stump. I gave him a pat and turned back to the kid. "Where's the doctor's office?"

He jerked a thumb back the way we came. "'Bout a block. Think he'll make it through the night?"

"He's made it this far. He's tougher than he looks."

"Well, he looks to be only about one shade above dead. How about I have old Doc Jenkins come over here, instead."

"That'll be fine. I expect you'll need another coin or two for that service?"

The boy laughed. "Man has to make a living." Rogier remembered his manners and started to help Esther down, but I stepped between them.

He offered a hand to Gracie, who gave him a look cold enough to freeze blood in his veins. "Don't you touch me. I've managed to climb up and down on horses all my life and I don't need some townie kid to help me down now."

He held out both arms and looked to me for advice. "What'd *I* do?"

"You're just breathing her air." I turned my head to hide a grin. "She's like that. Don't worry."

"That's what *he* says." Gracie didn't back down. "I don't need anything from a sawed-off little runt. You touch me and I'll bite you."

"She'll do it, too." Cornsilk removed his previously injured foot from the stirrup. He and Long Fox remained in their saddles. "She's done been working on me."

Ignoring Cornsilk's comment, the boy took my mare and Gil's horse first and threw Gracie an aggravated glance. "I'll allow I'm as old as you. I'll be back for the other two, and maybe her as well. I don't imagine old Nick in there'll let an Indian sleep under his roof. You two can come with me. Dad'll let y'all sleep in the shed out back."

Gracie bared her teeth and I thought she might actually bite the boy, but she turned her back on him to kick at a horse muffin for a minute. I saw we'd gathered a crowd of onlookers, in addition to the kids, and I didn't like that one little bit. Gil took Esther's arm and folks watching might think he was simply being a gentleman on the street, but in reality, he was holding on to her to steady himself.

Esther's eyes suddenly filled with tears and I hurried forward to help them both onto the tall sidewalk. "You all right, Esther?"

Water rolled down her cheeks. "We're in a town and we're safe." She took a deep, shuddering breath and wiped her eyes. "Three weeks ago, my family was murdered and I was taken by Comanches, and they . . . And now look at this town. How can we have raiders sweeping down from up there and killing folks only a few hours away? These people don't know what's going on up there."

Gracie appeared at her side and took Esther's hand. "We're fine now." Her soft voice helped Esther get ahold of herself. The crowd was even larger in those few moments, and knowing Gracie's disposition, I motioned for them all to go inside the hotel and out of everyone's sight.

As Rogier crossed the tracks with our horses, Cornsilk and Long Fox followed him, looking neither left nor right. I led everyone inside the lobby, which was cool and shady. It was much more than I expected, all dark, polished wood, heavy drapes, and even thick rugs under the round green settee in the middle of the floor. We hadn't been inside more than a few seconds when the clouds blocked out the sun and the interior became gloomy.

The lobby was empty and I assumed Ranger Braziel had already gone up to his room. The desk clerk glanced up and frowned. He looked at us as if we'd turned out the lights, and then he noticed Gracie.

Frowning, he hurried around the counter. "You can't bring that Indian in here. I just checked a Texas Ranger in and I doubt he'd like to have a savage under the same roof as him."

I held Esther's arm tighter with my free left hand, carrying the Winchester under my right arm so I could hold the Spencer. Despite his weakness, I felt Gil slip the rifle free, relieved that I wasn't responsible for it right then.

Already getting mad, I tried to swallow it down. "Are you referring to the girl, or this lady?"

"Both."

"Um-hum. Well, we just rode into town with that Ranger and he's been with us for a couple of days, along with two other *Indians,* so you can get off that subject right now. This lady happens to be white and her name is Esther, and she was taken by Comanches a few weeks ago and I am now responsible for her. She needs a bath and a bed."

I stepped closer, crowding the pompous ass. "As for Gracie here, you're right. She's Cherokee and has the dis-position of an old sore-tail tomcat, but she's a kid and she needs the same as Esther." I pushed in harder and the man backed up a step. "You don't have problems with one-armed men, either, do you?"

His nervous eyes skittered from Gil, and his blood-stained sling, to me, and finally to Esther. The desk clerk came to a decision and scurried back around behind the counter. "This is a respectable place."

"It still will be, if I don't burn it to the ground in a few minutes."

"Why, you can't threaten me! I'll get the marshal . . ."

"Please do." I reached into my shirt pocket and retrieved the tin star Kanoska gave me. I pinned it on my shirt. "He'd be glad to speak with you after we're finished, and I imagine Ranger Braziel'll have something to say to him as well. Now, as for my prisoner here—"

The clerk straightened. "Why, that man has a rifle. How can a prisoner have a gun?"

"He took it to free me up with you, and right now, I'm getting damned tired of arguing with a man who shaves his mustache down thin as pencil lead and oils his hair. Now, we're gonna need a room, and you don't have to worry about him one little bit. You can put the ladies in together."

"This place isn't cheap."

Taking a deep breath to control my anger, I laid the shotgun on his counter, nearly knocking over an inkwell. He grabbed for it and started to make another comment, but thought better of it.

I reached into one pouch on the saddlebags. Placing a twenty-dollar gold piece beside his hand, I plucked the quill pen from its holder, dipped into the inkwell he still held steady between two fingers, and signed the register upside down, next to that of Ranger Braziel, so the desk clerk'd have one signature that stood out from the others.

"Keys, sir. And make sure those rooms are close to the Ranger's as well."

"I've never seen such a thing." He plucked two keys from their cubbyholes behind the desk and slid them across the polished mahogany. "I'll have a boy take your horses."

"Rogier?"

"Why, yes." He scanned the window and door behind us, looking for the kid.

"Already settled up with him." I saw the irritated look on the man's face when he realized that he'd get no cut from the enterprising youngster.

As I helped Gil up the stairs, the desk clerk's mouth was pursed so tight, it looked like the old boy had been sucking on green persimmons.

CHAPTER 42

Ed Gentry and Bill Johns rode two abreast into Jeremiah, ahead of a dark line of storm clouds, forcing a number of riders to move out of their way, much to the annoyance of a young cowboy who looked as if he wanted to say something. He might have, any other time, but the oiled revolvers carried by the two men spoke of danger. His eyes skipped off them, to the ground ahead, and he rode on to live a little longer.

Thunder rumbled as cool air swept down behind them, promising moisture in the coming hours. The sun winked out and Gentry turned in his saddle to judge the distance. "It's gonna rain pretty soon. How about we get us a room somewhere and then find a saloon?"

"That suits me to a T." Johns smoothed his dusty mustache and frowned at all the bustle around them. "How're we gonna find Whitlatch in all this, though? Especially if it starts raining. He'll hole up somewhere to stay dry."

"We know they were headed this way, so it should be easy." Gentry smiled at a woman on the boardwalk, who ignored him and passed, staring straight ahead. "We're gonna hit every sally joint in town before we're through, asking about a man with strange eyes. Then we're gonna do the same in the hotels, and down at the livery. Someone'll remember them if he's come through."

"You think that feller back at that store told us the truth?"

Gentry grunted, thinking about the struggling soddy store in the middle of nowhere and the man who was starved for company. He told them about an unusual sale he'd made, saying it wasn't every day he sold a dress and overalls, along with so many provisions, to a single traveler.

"If I find out he lied to us, I'll go back and kill him. Liars bring on their own retribution. Anyway, I suspect he told us the truth. Whitlatch didn't want any more of the territories."

"Then what?"

"We're gonna kill him, as quick as we can, and get back across the river. This place is way too civilized for me."

"We've been to Springfield—what makes *this* a civilization?"

"It's Texas, and look around us. I see farmers and businesspeople. There's wagons and buildings everywhere. I'd rather be in a town where we're with people like us. You know, I've been thinking about Dodge City. I hear it's still fun there."

"Well, we, for sure, can't go back to Springfield for a good long while."

"I don't intend to go there at all. From Dodge, we can go on to Colorado. I have a notion to scare up a little gold there, too."

"I'm not mining, and I sure don't intend to do any panning in that cold water."

"Did I say anything about work at all?"

"Well, no."

They passed the town well as a man worked the handle of a protesting pump. Water gurgled in the pipe and gushed into a wooden bucket. He glanced at the line of black clouds, poured the water into a nearby trough, and went back to drawing another bucket.

The jail was across the open town square full of wagons from Ruthey's Shoe Store and J.L. North & Co. Saddles and Harness. The marshal sporting a thick brown mustache under a black Stetson stepped outside and lit a cigar. He drew smoke deep into his lungs and leaned on a porch post to watch them pass.

Noting the revolver partially hidden by the man's suit coat, Gentry nodded and kept talking, hoping not to attract too much of the man's consideration. "You're damned right about that. You don't pay any attention to what's going on around you. I bet you missed that lawman standing over there, and don't turn and look."

His admonishment was too late, and Johns's head swiveled to survey the jail. "Well, I ain't never seen a Texas marshal in a suit before. Looky there, standing around with one thumb in his vest pocket like he's something."

"Here's what I'm thinking." Shaking his head in disgust, Gentry kept his mount going straight toward the railroad station in the distance. "The Butterfield Stage Line runs through this burg. We'll spend a little time here, looking for Whitlatch, but I'm about done with chasing that gold.

"Anyway, we hang around here for a while, asking around, and if he don't show up, we watch how the stage runs and when it's loaded. Then follow that stage road west until we find a good place to set up an ambush.

"We rob the stage and then light a shuck for the mountains. This town is full of city people, and I doubt that marshal back there can rustle up half-a-dozen men who know how to use a gun. We ride hard for Mobeetie and meet up with a few old boys who're headed for the gold fields. The smart thing will be to travel with them for safety, until we get through Indian country to the mountains—then we make our fortunes by letting some other fools work to dig that gold out, and we just take what we want."

Fat raindrops landed with hard splats on the packed street. Gentry pointed. "How 'bout we get us a real bed tonight?"

"It beats sleeping under a horse in a stable somewhere."

CHAPTER 43

It rained hard after we got settled into the hotel, hammering on the shake roof, and I wanted to take advantage of the first hot bath I'd had in weeks. The bathhouse was on the ground floor, out back, and something like I hadn't seen since the last time I was in Austin.

Each one of six small rooms held a zinc tub filled by lugging hot water in buckets from the fire sizzling in the rain outside. I took one look at the setup and went back to the lobby and found the desk clerk busy issuing orders to the water boy.

A look of irritation crossed the man's face, but I didn't care. I leaned the Spencer shotgun against the front desk and drummed my fingers, waiting for him to finish. I might have been wrong, but it seemed to me that he took his time laying out what he wanted of the boy, before moseying around the counter and laying both hands on the surface.

"What can I do for you, Mr. Whitlatch? Are your *ladies* finding everything satisfactory?"

"I'd like a bath, and I'm sure my friend would also, but I'd appreciate it if you'd have a tub brought up to Miss Esther's room. I doubt they'd want to come down and be in such close proximity to men doing the same thing."

"That'll cost you extra."

The satisfied look on the lout's face made me want to wipe it off on the floor, but I was almost too tired to argue. "Put it on my bill."

"I suppose you'd like a female attendant as well. Why don't you have that Indian girl fetch the tub and the water."

Thunder rumbled outside, mimicking my own feelings. "Mister, I don't like you, but right now, we're stuck with one another. Gracie is your guest, the same way I am, and if I was you, I'd be careful. More'n one person I know thinks she might be a little Cherokee witch. You wouldn't want her to put an Indian spell on you."

He looked uncomfortable and ran a finger around the inside of his collar. I believe the storm outside emphasized my words as a thunderclap rattled the hotel's windowpanes, because he finally nodded. "Fine, then. Are you ready for my boy to draw your bath as well?"

"Nope. I'll be back in a little while and let you know."

"The doctor is in with your one-armed *prisoner* now."

"Oh?"

"I saw you step into the bath area, and he went up behind you." Hooking both thumbs into his vest pockets, he almost rocked back on his heels in satisfaction. "I sent him to your room."

I considered going up, but figured Gil could deal with the doctor on his own. "Thanks for that."

Outside, water poured off the roof over the boardwalk, splashing into a stream flowing down toward the train station, where it merged with several other streams that grew into an even larger current winding past the tracks and out past the livery.

The Spencer was under my slicker, and mostly out of the rain. No one could ever tell, but I carried it with my right hand through the cutaway pocket in the slicker, and holding it by the comb, which most people would call the pistol grip.

I wanted to settle into the room, but there were things I had to do first. The hotel sat on the corner of an intersection, which meant I'd have to cross the muddy road to the other side, where I'd be in the shelter of another boardwalk for a bit before it ran out altogether.

The rain showed no sign of slacking off, so I set my hat against the downpour and stepped into the deluge. The felt was soaked by the time I reached the other side and a drier, sheltered walk for a minute until the boardwalk ended.

Water was funneling off my hat when I reached the train station and the shelter of their porch and lightning ripped the clouds overhead. Affixed to the outside wall of the station was the schedule board written in chalk. Like I'd hoped, there was a train headed for Fort Worth the next day. Noon was a good time to get underway.

Even luckier, there was a telegraph office there, too. The skies darkened even more as I stepped inside to find the telegrapher busy tapping the key so fast, it sounded like a steady stream of ticks. Two flickering oil lamps pushed back the gloom, and a bucket on the counter caught a steady drip of water from the ceiling. I waited until he looked up and lifted the unnecessary green shade over his eyes.

"Help you?"

"Yessir. I'd like to send a telegram down to Fredericksburg."

He nodded and picked up a printed form. "Fredericksburg, Texas, I presume."

I hadn't considered there were other towns with the same name, but it made sense. I remember my dad talking about the Battle of Fredericksburg, in Virginia, being one of the bloodiest engagements of the Civil War.

"That's right."

He gave me a smile and handed me a pencil and a telegram form. "That'll be six bits for a dozen words."

"Kinda steep, ain't it?"

"Faster'n the mail, though."

Lightning flashed outside and a sudden wind blew drops against the window. I licked the end of the pencil and leaned over the counter lit by an oil lamp. "This'll go to John B. Whitlatch down there."

"You have to write it there on top."

"I did, just thinking out loud. Do I have to say who I am?"

"Nossir. That's included."

"Good to know. You charge as much for little words as big ones?"

The telegrapher chuckled. "It's all key taps. Most folks don't get wordy."

I thought for a second and then wrote the telegram.

I slid the form across and he read the message. Meeting my eyes, he threw a look out the window. "Trouble following you?"

"It was, but I'm gonna meet it head-on now."

CHAPTER 44

Drinking Dripping Springs whiskey, Stanton Sparks sat at a scarred table in the Grand Central Saloon in Jeremiah with his stocky buddy Chito Dawes, watching curtains of rain turn the inside of the building dark and gloomy. From Sparks's position, he could see little in the street other than horses standing at the hitching post with their heads low.

Several men had frowned at the two Indians when they first came in, but the look in their eyes backed them off to concentrate on their whiskey and cards. One man muttered "half-breed" under his breath, but Sparks was surprised to see Dawes ignored the comment . . . for the moment.

It was their money that made them welcome in the two-story saloon with a staircase leading to the second floor that opened all the way around the bar area. Wooden rails separated the wide-open walkway overlooking the tables below. Soiled doves maintained a steady business in those upstairs rooms, leading customers, trapped inside by the rain, up and down with remarkable speed, for time was money.

Sparks took a tiny sip of whiskey and turned his attention from a poker game going on in the back corner. He watched the main street turn to mud. "I do love the rain."

"Since when?"

"Since we're sittin' in here high and dry."

Chito laughed and stopped. "Those poor bastards look like drowned rats."

The saloon's shades were raised in the cool air and Sparks saw a pair of wet cowboys. They rode straight for the saloon, but seemed to be in no particular hurry. Reining up at the hitching post, they tied their horses, stepped onto the walk, and removed their hats to shake off the water.

Chito squinted in the dim light. "Hey, do you see who just rode into town?"

Putting down his glass, Sparks leaned on the table to peer outside. His stringy hair fell forward to hide half his face. "Those two?"

"Yep. You recognize them?"

"Hard to tell through all that falling weather." Both men had their chins down as they shook water that streamed off their clothes. As if choreographed, they raised their heads at the same time, revealing their features in the gloomy light. "Why, I believe I do. It's those two cowboys who shot that Ranger from behind outside of Margarite. I never saw such."

"Neither did I."

"What do you expect they're here for?"

Chito shrugged. "I couldn't venture a guess, other than they're probably on the run for killing that Ranger, but it don't make no sense to kill him in the territories and then come back down here to this side of the border where he was from."

"Well, they got sand, that's for sure. I doubt anybody in Texas knew they were riding with him, 'cause they sure weren't Rangers themselves." Sparks lowered his voice as those at the poker table grew silent in concentration. "Maybe they'd like to join up with us. They look like men who'd be interested in making some quick money. It'll be easier'n just the two of us."

"What makes you think they'd have anything to do with me and you? We ain't the same color."

"Well, I reckon they would if we put it to 'em the right way."

"Maybe they'd remember who was in the posse that day." Chito threw back his drink. "They're liable to shoot both of us 'cause we saw 'em kill that Ranger."

"I wouldn't put it past 'em to think that, if they recognized us, but there was a bunch of riders there that evening, and the light was going. It was as hard to see out there as it is right now. There's no way they could place us there." Sparks poured them both another drink. "Well, I'll be damned. They're coming right to us."

The two back shooters stepped through the open door at the same time the skies opened up, dumping torrents of water. Rain hammered the roof and fell so hard, it was difficult to see the marshal's office on the opposite side of the open square.

"Looks like it's quittin' time out there." Sparks held up two fingers. "Bartender, bring us a couple more glasses. Those boys look thirsty."

The bartender scowled at the order, but turned and picked up two glasses.

Sparks used one foot to shove a chair away from the table and in their direction. "Have a seat, gentlemen."

They paused, studying the room and the two Indians drinking whiskey and offering to share their table closest to the door. The younger one, with a mangy mustache, spoke first. "Thanks, but there's plenty of tables. Wouldn't want to crowd y'all or take advantage."

"You look like men to ride the range with." Sparks slid the bottle toward them as the bartender deposited two glasses on the table. "Grab one and have a drink on us. We have a business proposition for you."

After exchanging questioning glances, the older of the

pair pulled out a chair and moved it so he could see the door, as well as the interior. "Much obliged. I've never been dumb enough to turn down free whiskey."

Smoothing his frog's-hair mustache, the younger man took a seat without judging his position in the room. His expression was almost a glare, but Sparks had seen that look before on young gunmen. The Indian knew it was usually put on, or used for intimidation from those who thought they were shootists, but instead measured up to far less.

Chito shared their whiskey, pouring four fresh shots. He held his aloft. "Good health, gentlemen."

The four tossed them off and Chito refilled their glasses again as rain blew under the boardwalk's overhang to run down the glass. Sparks rested his elbows on the table and laced his fingers. "I'm Stanton Sparks, and this here's Chito Dawes. We have a business proposition for y'all, if you're interested."

The gunslinger with the wispy mustache smirked. "You look Cherokee, but what's that sitting beside you?"

Sparks set his wide jaw, expecting Chito to come up shooting, but he instead placed both hands flat on the table. "I'm Seminole. Mama was Cherokee and my dad was black as the ace of spades. That explanation enough for you?"

The older of the two cowboys cut his partner off before the younger man with the mousy mustache could speak again. "Sorry 'bout that. Bill's just tired and edgy, that's all. No offense. I'm Ed Gentry, this younger feller with me's last name is Johns, Bill Johns. What do you boys have in mind?"

"Is this job legal, or illegal?" Johns couldn't stand to be silent. "Neither of us wants a wife with a picket fence and biscuits every morning, so you can tell we're choosy."

"So are we." Sparks knew what it was like to deal with an impetuous, younger associate. He'd have to keep an eye on him if the back shooters threw in with them. "Well,

Mr. Johns, Mr. Gentry, y'all look like men who've walked a gray line with law and order at one time or another."

"You two sure speak good English." Johns let one hand drift near the butt of his revolver. "Not much of that Indian accent, neither."

Sparks's eyes went flat. "Mister, if you're on the prod, we can have it out right here, but I seen y'all work and might have some use for you, if you're still alive in five minutes or so. Chito here's about to shoot you, and then gut you with that knife on his hip if you don't simmer down and listen."

The impetuous cowboy's face went white. "Just want to know who I ride with, if we take a notion to ride on your side of the picket line."

"It don't make no difference." Gentry adjusted his seat and leaned the chair back on two legs. "We could be a couple of cow punchers and nothing else."

"Most of those old boys I've known in cow camps have a spirit of adventure, and a need for money. Y'all remind me of us, and what's more"—Sparks casually rested his hand on the butt of his pistol—"we were outside of Margarite the night y'all tangled with that Ranger."

Johns slid his chair back to stand, and Gentry dropped his chair back on four legs, but Sparks held out a hand. "Hold on, now. Hear us out."

"Hang on, Bill." Gentry's eyes sparkled with interest, and though he'd tightened, he seemed as relaxed as a little old lady in church, but he could act quick as a rattlesnake strike. "I'd like to hear what Mr. Sparks has in mind."

Casting a glance around the room, the tall, whipcord-thin Cherokee outlaw leaned in, expecting the others to do the same. Sparks spoke soft, lest the bartender hear, for he was the only one in the saloon close enough to overhear. At that moment, one of the poker players laughed and conversation at that end of the room increased.

"We were there that night on our own business that had the interest of that posse. Your reaction with the Ranger was surprising, but I liked it. I never had any use for lawmen."

"You were with the posse, right?" Gentry picked up the glass of whiskey in front of him and took a sip.

"We were, but it was an idea we were working on. Y'all helped more than you know, so we'd like to return the favor."

"Go on." Gentry took another sip. "You interest me."

"Good. I don't know if you boys are so informed, but the Butterfield Stage runs through here. Goes all the way to Springfield to the northeast, and west out to California."

Johns downed a shot of whiskey. "We were just talking about that."

"I see. Well, maybe you'd be interested to know the stage line's working hard to get out from under some financial difficulties. They're hauling a lot more freight than usual, and carrying more passengers at a greatly reduced rate. In fact, I heard one guy paid only a dollar to ride from Springfield all the way to San Francisco. All because of those rail lines they're laying all over the country."

Sparks could tell Gentry was interested. He paused for a moment, staring into his shot glass, letting the two outlaws who shot the Ranger soak in the idea.

It was like fishing when he was a boy. He'd throw a worm out into the creek back home that was so clear he could see the fish. The plop alerted the catfish that there was something new in the water, and they'd ease up close and study the wriggling worm for a moment before taking the hook.

That was exactly what he was doing with Gentry and Johns.

"Because of that, and to make ends meet, the stage is now carrying a lot of gold to the banks back east."

Licking his lips, Johns tilted his head, listening hard, and Sparks knew he had him.

Gentry took another tiny sip and studied the pair across the table. "So you intend to relieve some of the weight off those stages."

"I saw one unload over there when a couple of passengers got off. The man riding shotgun stayed right where he was, on the seat, and he kept an eye out, like there were Indians in the area. When they lifted the tarp on the boot and took out some luggage, I saw two wooden boxes banded with steel. Those two things together spells only one thing in my mind, money."

Gentry nodded.

"We have a mind to make some money in Colorado," Sparks added. "To do that, we'd like to pick up some traveling cash, so I propose we go about a day's ride west, stop the next stage coming this direction, and relieve it of anything valuable."

"A day's ride? Now you're talking Comanche country."

"That's part of my idea. See here, we stop the stage, get the money and whatever's in the boot, cut two of their horses loose from the harness to haul whatever we get, if it's heavy, and turn them all loose. They'll have to ride slower with only four horses, and that gives us a two-day head start of any posse, but there won't be, 'cause townspeople don't have any stomach for being shot at, or Comanches.

"Then we go our own way, or ride together for safety for a while." The corners of Gentry's mouth curved down as he considered the offer.

"Exactly." Sparks leaned back and held his glass up.

Johns's voice went flint hard. "What makes you two think they won't shoot you out there just for being an Indian and a half-breed?"

Chito's face lost all expression. "Because we'll kill the first ones who call us that."

The table went silent. Johns locked eyes with the Seminole, then grinned. "That's the right answer."

They all relaxed, understanding where each man stood.

Gentry turned loose of his pistol's grip, relieved that his partner hadn't started a dance with those two they could use. "Well, me and Mr. Johns here have to meet someone here first, and that'll be a day or two, and then we're finished." He glanced over at Chito, who nodded back. "You see, we've been working on a job for the past couple of weeks that we intend to finish, and you boys might be interested."

Gentry hoped Johns would stay quiet and listen, until he had time to explain. They were both poker players, and maybe Johns wouldn't be so impatient for once. He'd almost gotten them shot twice in the last few minutes because he didn't like Indians.

Gentry put down his glass. "Me and Bill here have been on the trail of a feller for a good long while, to finish a job given to us by a Springfield attorney. See, we've been sent to get some gold back from this feller who stole it. I know this attorney pretty well, and he has some deep pockets. How about I guarantee you men two hundred dollars each to help us."

He shot a look over at Johns, hoping he'd stay quiet. Gentry had no intention of giving them money. The quick plan that crossed his mind would pit the four of them against Whitlatch, increasing the odds when they braced him, if back shooting wasn't an option.

Four guns against one would be excellent odds.

Then, in his mind, the minute Whitlatch drew his last breath, they'd shoot their new accomplices and leave with the gold, because, after all, they were just Indians, and one a half-breed at that.

Simple, brutal, and effective.

He watched the expressions on their faces. Just as he

expected, they perked up at the mention of gold. The mere idea of that soft yellow metal ate at men's brains and took all common sense away. "How'd the two of you like to help us when we find him?"

"And then?"

"We'll pay you right then and there. Y'all can go on separate from us, or we can pitch in with you to make more money with the stagecoach robbing. I could use a change of scenery."

Sparks and Dawes searched each other's faces, looking for doubt or excitement.

What Gentry saw there was neither. It was greed, and in a flash, he knew they would do the same as he planned, shoot him and Johns, and take the money.

The glint in Sparks's eyes was nothing but greed. There was no honor among thieves and murderers. "We'll be proud to ride with y'all."

CHAPTER 45

The rain slacked off as I finished composing my telegram, paid the man for the message. "Now, I need four tickets to Austin."

The stationmaster shook his head. "Nope."

"Why not?"

"'Cause this spur ain't finished." He jerked his head toward the side of the building. "There ain't no track out there yet, but they'll be here by next week. That's why they're laying the brick streets, getting ready for a celebration. I can sell you tickets on the train leaving next week."

"It'll be too late. I don't intend to be here that long."

"Well, sir, that's all I can offer, other than the telegram. You still want to send it?"

"I do, but that'll delay the results of my request."

It was just my luck to find a railroad town that didn't yet have a completed spur. That changed my plans in a dramatic fashion, but there was nothing I could do about it.

Disheartened, I stepped outside just as the storm increased with a vengeance.

The street was empty except for a few horses tied to hitching posts, or wagons waiting in the muddy yard back toward the middle of town. The men who'd been laying the brick street were somewhere high and dry, leaving stacks of bricks slowly settling into the mud pulverized and softened by a million hooves and narrow wagon wheels. It was easy to tell why they needed a harder surface in a town growing so fast.

Not worried about melting in the rain, I picked up my pace and hurried down to the peeling, red painted livery. Both front doors stood open, admitting light into the wide hall running from front to back and lined with stalls. Most held horses watching the storm from over the stable doors. The odor of dust, damp hay, and sweet manure filled my nose, reminding me that I missed my own horse ranch down south.

I was tired and ready to be done with all my require- ments, but a few more things had to happen first. I needed to drop off Esther and Gracie before getting Gil down to Fredericksburg; then I was going home to my little ranch house and would stay there until next spring.

Rogier came out of one stall with a pitchfork in one hand. He closed the gate behind him and latched it. "It got a little wet after I saw you."

I liked his grin. "Bottom fell out, for sure. I'm here to pay your daddy."

He pointed to an open door I'd passed without noticing. It led into a small, dirty office lit by an oil lamp. "He's in there asleep. You can wake him up if yont to, but I'd advise against it right now. He's soaked up most of a bottle of whiskey today and won't be in a mood to discuss business until tomorrow. My mama died three years ago on this date, and he does this each time. How about I take the money for him."

Looking into the office, I saw a man with his head on his desk. Face puffy and mouth slack, he snored softly into a puddle of drool on the desktop. "It'll probably be faster, that's for sure. I'm going to look in on my mare, while you make me out a receipt."

"You don't trust me?"

"I just want to make sure your old man knows the money came in when he wakes up."

"Well, suit yourself. Your mare and the rest of y'all's horses are down at the far end on the right." Rogier went in to write up the note, while I walked down the hall. Halfway there, I looked into a stall to see a black stud with a drop of white between his eyes, watching over the gate.

Something about the stud was familiar, and I paused to give him a good look. He stepped close and sniffed at me, maybe hoping for a piece of apple or a lump of sugar. I rubbed his nose and squinted down into the dim stall. I'd seen that little drip on his forehead and the two low white socks on his back legs before.

One of the Indians back outside of Margarite rode that stud. The hair on the back of my neck rose. Something was up, but I couldn't figure out what it was. I stood there rubbing his nose and thinking, when Rogier brought me the receipt.

"Here you go, Mr. Whitlatch." He held out one hand. "This is for the night, and remember I went and fetched the doctor for your friend. That's not on the receipt. I'd prefer cash, if you don't mind."

"You know who this black belongs to?"

Just like any kid, he switched conversations quick as a wink. "Yes. It belongs to a tall Indian with a big, square chin who got here not long after y'all. That's some horse, huh?"

"He have a name?"

He wrinkled up his face, thinking. "Well, let me think. Tall. Had a crooked grin and needed a bath, and that long hair of his needed to be stripped, like his friend."

"There were two? He riding with somebody?"

"That bay over in the stall beside this big guy. Half-breed, shorter." Rogier snapped his fingers. "Now I remember. Sparks is his last name, the one who owns the black."

I jumped as if somebody brushed against me with a hot branding iron. Sparks! For sure he was with the posse back at Margarite and was the one who found the man hanged beside our camp. I didn't like him then, and now he showed up here with his buddy.

They were following us. I felt my face squinch up like Rogier's when he was thinking. Recognizing the struggle going on in my head, the boy simply waited as rain hammered the split shake roof above and water dripped into the barn from a dozen places.

"You have any idea where they might be right now, Sparks and that other guy?"

"Nossir. They looked like drinkers to me, so I 'spect they're in a saloon somewhere that'll serve Indians. I'd say the best shot's the Grand Central. That's where most people go after they drop their horses here, 'cause it's the first one they come to after leaving."

Thunder rumbled through the washed air and every horse in the barn prickled their ears. Digging in my pocket, I produced a few coins for the boy. "That's for the errands. Make sure these animals are watered and grained. If this Sparks comes back before I find him, come a-running to the hotel."

CHAPTER 46

The rain still fell and lightning fractured the clouds, illuminating their ever-shifting forms from behind. I took the same route back to the hotel and saw two men, the only ones on the street, riding in my direction.

Rain soaked, I trotted across the muddy avenue and stepped onto the covered boardwalk and out of the weather. Tilting my hat back so the rain would drain off the back, and concentrating on getting inside and finally having a bath, I wasn't paying any attention to them until we grew near to each other. When they closed with me, I raised my head and nodded hello.

They passed only feet away, and I heard one of them say, "That's him." The excitement in his voice cut through the raindrops sharp and clear.

"Whitlatch!"

Surprised at hearing my name, I looked back over my shoulder to see the riders yank their horses around and claw for the pistols under their slickers.

"Kill him!"

Right then, all hell broke loose, along with a clap of thunder that rattled the windows up and down the street. There was no time for questions with strangers drawing iron.

Lucky for me, they didn't know I carried the Spencer

under my slicker. The barrel rose through the unbuttoned front. Instinct and experience led my left hand to grab the forearm and it came up level with the men who'd whirled their horses around.

Their pistols came into view as the man who sat shorter in the saddle fired first. The muzzle flashed, lighting his face and a mousy little mustache. The bullet disappeared into the rain that caught the smoke and drove it to the ground. Another muzzle flash froze the action for a second, like a photographer's black-powder flash.

The older man riding beside him reached for a rifle, half drawing it from under his leg and quickly changed his mind, snatching his own pistol and thumbing back the hammer. Uncertain which weapon to use, he was slower than the first, and therefore not an immediate danger, though everything was happening in seconds.

I squeezed the shotgun's trigger, but for the first time since I'd owned the Spencer, it failed to fire. There was no mystery there, because I was familiar with paper shotgun shells that can swell from water or dampness, bleeding down into the primers and causing misfires. But the designers of Spencer shotguns anticipated such a failure when they fabricated the weapon.

A waterfall of memories and information swept through my mind. Maybe in reality, or maybe through my mind's eye, I saw the man's eyes widen with fear and it seemed that he'd suddenly found himself in the middle of something that made him want to be gone. His horse stutter-stepped, throwing off his aim, and he missed again.

Another shot was only a blink away, and though he looked afraid, he was the immediate threat. It struck me that his wispy mustache would never grow in now, thick and lush, due to his actions.

Eyes blazing with both fear and anger, he pulled the trigger and the pistol snapped. Throwing a glare at the weapon, as if it had intentionally failed to fire just to vex him, he thumb-cocked it again, but by then, it was too late.

The other, older cowboy sitting taller in the saddle was faster than I expected and he shot. The bullet snapped my hat cockeyed, making me think at first that I was shot.

My pointer finger pushed forward to reset the shotgun and then found its seat once again on the back trigger. This time, the primer fired and the big twelve-gauge bucked in my hands at the same time another bullet whistled past and thunked into a porch post behind me.

The load of buckshot caught the young man full in the chest. His dying muscles constricted and he threw both hands into the air and fell backward over his horse's rump, landing with a muddy splash in the street.

I pumped still another shell into the chamber and swung around on the older mounted man to fire. He'd thumb-cocked the pistol and was about to shoot when his horse shied. The barrel of his pistol waved as he fought the reluctant animal.

Standing there in the open, I fully expected one of his rounds to strike me, but his shooting reminded me of once watching a man fire at a swimming snake with a pistol. Bullets struck the water all around the thin body the same way they plowed through the raindrops falling around me, without hitting a thing but water.

The rounds snapped past, sparking that keening sound of fury rising in my head, and I damn near saw red. Feeling invincible, I pumped the shotgun's forepiece and pulled the trigger. Again, it failed to fire and I shucked that shell from the magazine as the remaining horseman kicked out of the saddle and landed on his feet with the frightened animal between us.

Instead of advancing and firing, he yanked a Henry rifle from the boot, ran across the street, and ducked down behind a stack of bricks.

Again, my mind separated itself from the immediate action. One part concentrated on staying alive, but somewhere down deep inside, an itch arose that quickly bloomed into the realization I'd seen that Henry before.

A man with a rifle was another whole problem. Most men snap-shoot pistols, and that gave me an edge with the twelve-gauge. However, someone with a rifle, especially that big .44, wasn't about to shoot at random. A man taking careful aim at such a distance was as dangerous as the Spencer, and I wasn't about to get into a stand-up gunfight with him.

Thumbing fresh shells into the Spencer, I threw two loads of buckshot at the bricks that shattered and crumbled under the impact of the double-aught shot, hoping to drive him back or at least make him more cautious. Pumping the shotgun, I stepped back behind wooden boxes stacked near the telegraph office.

The sounds of men yelling cut through the noise of the rain and the ringing in my ears from all the shooting. Doors opened and people raised windows, craning their necks outside to see what all the ruckus was about.

The door to the Hotel Benjamin down behind me opened and I was glad to see Ranger Braziel step outside, a pistol in his hand. He saw me behind the boxes with the shotgun against my shoulder and immediately sized up the situation.

I was about to shoot when the man behind the bricks shot at me again and I flinched and crouched. That's when the Ranger raised his revolver and fired. Flame licked out and smoke hung in the still air. He thumb-cocked and fired again. I squeezed the trigger on the Spencer, but again the damp paper shell refused to fire.

Switching the shotgun to my left hand, I drew the Russian and did what I always do. While the Ranger and the man behind the bricks exchanged fire, I advanced.

One of my rounds barely missed him, flicking the collar

of his shirt. Cocking the revolver again, I held it straight out, planning to shoot at the next body part I saw, but the man behind the stack of bricks threw a shot at me and the Ranger stopped. Digging in his heels, he straight-armed his pistol and shot at the assassin. The bullet barely missed the gray shape, and striking a brick, it shot off into the distance with a nasty whickering sound.

He fired again, this time missing the bricks and the man with the Henry, though planks splintered behind the figure partially obstructed by the driving rain. The firing stopped and I kept going, the Russian cocked and pointed at his hiding place.

When I got there, the rain covered for the stranger, and he was gone. Blood pounding in my ears, I looked down the narrow alley and saw dark trees in the distance. It was no use following, for he had three directions in which to disappear, and though he was on foot, there were horses everywhere he could steal and ride away in the storm, leaving nothing but the sound of rain and a few last wisps of gunsmoke the droplets finally drove to the ground.

I'd've done the same in trying to get away.

Ignoring the weather, Ranger Braziel walked out into the middle of the empty street, pistol in hand, looking for more targets. Grateful for the help, I met him there.

"What'n hell was that all about?" Never taking his eyes off me, the Ranger scanned the buildings around us.

"Beats me. Somebody said my name and then all hell broke loose."

"You hit?"

"Naw, they shoot like my granny."

"You have any idea who they were?"

"Nary one."

We walked down the street to where the man I'd shotgunned lay sprawled out like an Apache'd staked him out.

His eyes were partially open, but he was looking at the Devil in Hell.

There were dozens of people in the street now, and the shooting was over. Ranger Braziel holstered his pistol and studied the man at our feet as rain pelted the corpse's face. "Well, I'll be damned."

I'd already put the Russian away and out of the wet. "What?"

"This is one of them sonsabitches who shot me in the back. Name's Bill Johns. He was with Gentry."

"The ones who shot you in the back."

"Yep, and the pair that was on your trail from Springfield. I'll allow that was Gentry with him."

Nerves still jangling from the shoot-out, I kept turning to check out the buildings around us.

The Ranger grunted. "Well, you saved me the trouble of hanging him. I need to get Cornsilk and Long Fox and go after him."

Water funneled off our hat brims and joined hundreds of rivulets cutting small courses in the street. "He'll be hard to track in all this rain."

Braziel sighed. "You're right about that, and I have no idea where those two Indians are at the moment."

A man in a flat-brimmed hat and wearing a city suit covered by a slicker pushed through the gathering crowd and appeared beside us. "What was this all about?" He pulled back his slicker to reveal a tin star and glanced down at the body.

The Ranger mimicked his actions. "Well, Marshal, your guess is as good as mine."

I picked up from there. "I was just walking down the street and this feller took a notion to put some holes in me."

"Looks like they failed, but you didn't. What's your name?"

Now that I had some company, I relaxed a little.

The marshal side-eyed me. "When'd you get to town? You don't live here."

"Just before all this rain started. Traveling through, on the way down south."

"You have a few miles on you, I suspect. You been on the owl hoot trail?"

"Nossir."

"You got any paper out on you?"

"If he did, he'd be my prisoner," Ranger Braziel said. "I'm Curtis Braziel, Texas Ranger."

"Good to meet you. I'm Marshal G.W. Middlebrooks. Having you here makes this easier if you're involved. How many others?"

"One." I waved a hand toward where he disappeared afoot. "Went that way behind the bricks."

"Why were they shooting at you? Is it because they didn't know your name?"

"Your guess is as good as mine." I knew what he meant, and why they were trying to kill me was none of his business, in my opinion. I didn't want any Springfield entanglements to hold me there in town any longer than was necessary. "Name's Cap Whitlatch. Ranger Braziel and I just got to town a little while ago and checked in the hotel. I'm escorting a prisoner down to Fredericksburg and he's been traveling with me. I went down to the telegraph office and the livery, and when I was coming back, they passed by. One of these two on horseback called my name, and then went to shooting."

The mention of the livery reminded me I needed to tell Braziel about the black stabled back there.

A smile touched the corner of Marshal Middlebrooks's mouth. "Oh, you're the ones who brought that Indian gal with you." He chuckled. "I got an earful a few minutes ago from the desk clerk over there in the Benjamin. Says you're traveling with that child and a woman who ain't your wife, along with a one-armed man."

"He had two when we started out."

Marshal Middlebrooks pulled at his bottom lip, thinking about what I'd just said. "All that true?"

"It is."

"Well, the clerk's also mad because there're two Indians standing in the hall outside of that woman's room since this shooting started. You know anything about that?"

A pleasant feeling came over me at the thought of those two taking the initiative to protect Esther and Gracie at the sound of gunfire. No matter how much Cornsilk complained about Gracie, he would stand between her and harm.

I remembered the shotgun and tucked it back under my slicker. "You know, I don't like standing here in the rain talking about this. We can go somewhere it's dry and I'll tell you everything that I know. Besides, we're standing here in the open and that feller who just tried to kill me's still running loose."

Ranger Braziel adjusted his collar. "I'd intended on taking supper with you tonight, Mr. Whitlatch, but people shooting at me makes me thirsty. How about we all go in that saloon over there and have us a drink?"

The marshal pointed at a well-dressed man coming down the boardwalk. "That's the undertaker. He'll clean this up, and I reckon it'll charge to the town, but now that he's here, I can go. I'd like to hear what y'all have to say about being here for a couple of hours and already shooting the place up, but not at a drinking establishment. Too many ears. What say we retire to one of your rooms to discuss this, *then* go get a drink?"

I almost grinned when I saw Cornsilk and Long Fox, who seemed to materialize out of thin air. "Marshal, do you have any objections to a couple of Indians joining us out of the weather?"

He followed my gaze and sighed. "I don't, 'cause I'm half Choctaw, but the owner of the Benjamin might have a word or two to say, though they've already been in there all this time."

"He can say it to me, then." Ranger Braziel smoothed his mustache and beard with the palm of his hand and led the way, waving at Cornsilk and Long Fox to follow.

CHAPTER 47

A shaken Ed Gentry made his way through the back alley to the livery stable. His horse was gone after he bailed off, but, surely, there were others there he could rent—and then not return. He needed to get out of town and settle his nerves.

That damned Whitlatch was cat quick and neither he nor Johns had expected him to shoot so fast. In his mind, Gentry had envisioned ambushing him on a trail somewhere and shooting before he knew what was happening. That was the best idea.

The second best was for one of them to find him on a street or alley, then keep his attention, while the other got the bulge and shot him from the side. Johns had suggested they find him in a town and wait until he was in a hotel room, where they would knock on his door in the early-morning hours, when a man was always sleeping the best, then push in and kill Whitlatch before he could respond.

But there he was, coming down the street, when they least expected it, and they were heading down to the livery to stable their horses. Above and beyond all that, who would have thought a rancher would be so ready for trouble that he'd yank up a shotgun hidden in his slicker and start shooting?

That dumb lawyer back in Springfield said he was just a cowboy with saddlebags full of gold. He didn't say anything about him ever being a gunhand, but that's what he was, out there in the street. It was their misfortune to suddenly meet him without being prepared. That's what had happened, and then Johns, damn him and his lack of maintenance on his pistol, had gone and gotten himself killed.

Well, he traveled well before he met Johns, and would be just fine alone again. In fact, he'd likely do better. Their ideas about going west were nothing but talk, even after they met Sparks and Dawes, who seemed to be pretty solid men, even though they were Indians.

If they'd been with him on the street, things might have turned out differently, but then again, the way that damned cowboy shot, and with the surprise appearance of that gray-bearded man who just waded in and started shooting, as if he knew what he was doing, they might have all wound up laid out on doors, like Johns in just a couple of hours.

Gentry stopped. Gray-bearded man. The rain was so heavy, it was hard to make out the details, but damned if he didn't look like that Ranger they'd killed.

He slipped in the back of the livery to find the owner sound asleep at his desk. Not even all that shooting just down the street had roused him, but the proprietor's boy was at the front doors, watching from the shelter of the shake roof as water poured from the sky at a tremendous rate.

Gentry walked down the long, dusty hall, looking left and right at the horses stabled there. His eyes locked on a black stud, with a drip of white between his eyes. He'd seen that animal before. Sparks was riding it that evening when they shot the Ranger.

He almost laughed. That was the horse the Indian wanted so bad, he'd risk a hanging. Gentry chuckled when everything outside of Margarite came clear. Of course, it would be stabled here, but he'd best move fast.

A lot was going on out in the street, and the kid seemed to be the only other person in the livery. Kids loved action, as Gentry did when he was young, and he figured the boy would stay right where he was until someone came to pick up a horse. Even if he did turn to discover Gentry there and saddling a mount that wasn't his, the kid was barely ten or eleven. What could he do but set up a holler, but he wouldn't holler twice with a knock on the head.

Saddle-trees made from pine planks lined both sides, some holding tack, others empty. A few rough-looking saddles were used so hard, they were nothing but slick pieces of weathered leather. The one in front of the black's stall had fine detailed work that spoke of money.

Keeping an eye on the boy's shape in the doorway, Gentry shifted toward the saddle and jumped when a low voice stopped him.

"I hope you're not thinking about throwing that over my horse."

Heart pounding, he turned to see Sparks and Dawes standing behind him with their hands on the butts of their pistols. Gentry held a finger to his lips. "The boy's right over there."

Shaking his head, Sparks kept his attention on Gentry. "Don't matter to me, but we're fixin' to saddle up and get out of here, on *our* horses."

Gentry whirled at a commotion at the barn doors, to find the boy holding up both hands to stop a riderless horse trotting into the barn. "Whoa! Whoa, boy. It's all right." The youngster took the horse's reins and patted his neck to calm him down. "Easy, big fella. Easy. It's all right now. Who owns you?"

Gentry's knees almost bucked in relief at the sight of his mount. "Hey, boy, he's mine. Thanks for catching him."

The youngster gave a start at the sound of his voice, while the buckskin pricked his ears forward. "Mister, you scared the pee-waddlin' out of me, especially with all that shooting going on out there. Where'd you come from?" He noticed the other two in the dim light. "Goshamighty. Y'all . . ." He trailed off, his eyes widened at the hard looks on their faces, as he put two and two together.

Sparks's voice snapped hard and sharp. "Be quiet and bring that horse over here to him."

Terrified, the boy led the wet buckskin deeper into the vast barn. "I didn't see anything."

"I know you didn't, but right now, you just be quiet." Sparks came forward and looked into the office. "What's your name, kid?"

"Rogier. What're you gonna do?"

Dawes said nothing, joining Sparks beside the office's open door.

Gentry kept an eye on them both. "We're gonna figure this out."

"I've already *figured* it out." Dawes finally spoke. "I'm putting as much distance between me and here as I can, as fast as I can. Did you see who was out there in that street? It was that Ranger who should be dead. I saw y'all shoot him, and now he's out there, big as life. He has medicine that I've never seen."

"Well, I'll be damned. I *thought* it looked like him, and now he knows everything." Gentry's eyes flicked to the boy. "Well, you just let the cat out of the bag right here in front of Mr. Big Ears."

"We have a plan for later," Sparks reminded him.

"Still?" Gentry grinned. "Right now, though, I intend to

finish what I started. Boys, you remember what I told you in the bar?"

Sparks rubbed his wide chin. "About the money in Whit-latch's saddlebags?"

Nodding, Gentry knew now there was no reason to try and hide what they were talking about. It wouldn't be him who killed the kid, but Dawes looked downright happy to do it.

"Well, now we know exactly where that money is, and I intend to get it before we leave."

Sparks took off his hat, revealing as much white scalp as thin black hair. He wiped the band and put it back on. "What's your plan?"

"There's that tack room over there." He jerked a thumb toward the back of the barn. "Us and this fine young man are gonna sit in there for a while, till it gets late and everybody calms down. Before long, a deputy or marshal'll be down here to check around after this rain lets off, and when they do, they're gonna shake this boy's daddy awake and he'll be wondering where his kid went off to. What's your pa's name?"

"Leon."

"Well, old Leon hasn't seen us, so he won't be any help. Then, when the law's gone and everyone's sound asleep, just before dawn, we tie pappy up alongside of Rogier here and then head for that hotel over there, and payday."

A cold look in his eyes, Gentry motioned for the boy to come close. "Over here, son, and hold out your hands. We're not gonna hurt you."

Rogier watched the hard-looking cowboy tie his wrists with a leather mending strip from a tangle of others hanging on the wall, while Sparks set about building a nest in the feed room, which would shield them until dark.

Finished, they stepped into the room and sat on feed sacks, which were as comfortable as a couch in a whore-house. It was silent for a while, except for the rain and thunder outside, until Dawes leaned in and spoke.

"You know, this'll work out perfect. We'll kill that Ranger, too, and he won't be on our trail anymore, so we'll be free and clear."

CHAPTER 48

Rain still drummed on the hotel's roof after we stepped inside the lobby. My room was out of the question, with Gil in there, and I wondered if he was still with the doctor. Ranger Braziel frowned at half-a-dozen men gathered at the door as we pushed through the crowd. Several onlookers asked questions of the marshal, but he ignored them.

"Talking down here is out of the question." Braziel pointed toward the staircase, which went up halfway and turned right at the landing, before terminating on the second floor. "My room, gentlemen." We passed the front desk and Braziel paused. "Clerk. Please send up a bottle of Dripping Springs whiskey and several glasses."

The irritating clerk's mouth fell open. "You don't intend to bring those damned savages in here, do you?"

"Are you talking about my deputies, sir?"

He swallowed at the fire in Braziel's dark eyes. "Why . . . well . . . I don't know."

I'd had enough of his guff. "They were in here earlier, protecting my ladies upstairs."

"They were not! I'd never allow savages to come through that door."

I almost grinned, that information I just heard told me they'd crept in somewhere through the back without him knowing. "Oh, they're coming up, all right. Where's Rogier? He'll fetch us that bottle, like this man asked."

"I have no idea. Probably still at the livery with his drunken father." The desk clerk fiddled with the register, then managed to touch everything else on the desk with nervous fingers. "It's the anniversary of his wife's death, and he drowns himself in whiskey. The boy is likely taking care of business down there." The clerk cattily shared this observation that Rogier had confided in me earlier.

Ranger Braziel adjusted his holstered pistol. "You just send that bottle up, like I said. Cornsilk, Long Fox, come with us."

"Yessir, I'll . . ."

Ignoring the man, Braziel led the way and we climbed to the second floor, with Cornsilk and Long Fox coming up last. We passed my room, which was closest to the head of the stairs. The door was open and I saw the doctor leaning over Gil, who was lying in bed, wrapping a dressing around his stump. Gil heard the commotion and turned his head to see us pass.

One eyebrow raised in question, he lifted his hand in greeting.

Esther and Gracie's room was directly across the hall from ours and was silent.

We passed two more closed doors on either side until we came to the Ranger's room on the right, at the far end of the wide hallway. A window at the end held open several inches by a stick told me where my "savages" had entered and left without the desk clerk knowing about it.

A puddle of water on the sanded and polished floor told us it should have been closed and likely forgotten in all the excitement of the sudden storm and shoot-out.

Braziel's door wasn't locked, and we went inside to find his room was twice the size of mine. Two rooms, actually, with a small living area divided from the bed by a folding screen. A plain wooden chiffonier took up the wall beside the door, and a washstand, with a white pitcher and bowl, occupied space beside one of two windows overlooking the street.

The bed was tucked away in the other side, bracketed by two tables holding lamps, alongside two cushioned chairs.

The Ranger hung his black hat on a freestanding rack beside the door and removed his coat as we all filed in gravely, like mourners at a funeral. I hung my hat there also. Marshal Middlebrooks plopped his on the bedpost, revealing a bald head, and slipped out of his wet coat.

The circular rug on the floor was soaking up water as I took off the slicker and leaned the useless Spencer in the corner. Clearly uncomfortable, Cornsilk and Long Fox stood in the middle of the room, holding their hats and looking as if they wished they were somewhere else.

"Have a seat, boys." Ranger Braziel hung his gun belt over the other bedpost and settled into a rocking chair beside the window, where he could see out. "Drag those two chairs in here so we can all sit down like civilized people. Now, Cap, tell me everything that happened outside."

Middlebrooks and I pulled the two chairs into the living area. I'd already taken a seat, when I realized there was no place for Cornsilk and Long Fox. I felt bad about not considering them, but before I could say anything, they pulled themselves up a piece of floor and settled down smooth and fluid to sit cross-legged with their backs against the door.

I related the events that led up to the Ranger coming outside with his pistol drawn, taking care not to mention the money in my saddlebags. When I finished, Marshal Middlebrooks fished a toothpick out of his vest pocket and worried at something caught between his teeth.

He drew a long breath. "Y'all were in town less than an

hour and got into a shoot-out. I could use a little less of that."

"We're leaving tomorrow." I watched rain run in rivulets down the closed window.

A knock on the door startled Cornsilk and Long Fox. They almost leaped to their feet, hands on their pistols, when the Ranger rose. "That'll be the whiskey."

He was right, the oily desk clerk stood there with a stack of shot glasses and the bottle. "Here you go, gentlemen."

Marshal Middlebrooks shifted on a straight-back chair. "Harry."

It was the first time I'd heard the desk clerk's name. "Yessir."

"Go find Deputy Reid and have him go down to the livery stable to see if any strangers're sleeping there, and if those men who were shooting out there had put their horses up while they were here. Ask him if he has the dead man's horse there."

"But it's raining out."

"You won't melt. Then have him come here when he knows something. Then I want you to bring the register up to me. You know that feller who was killed out in the street?"

"He wasn't staying here. I know that for a fact, because Bud Little came in and told me what he looked like."

"All right, then. Come back when you know something."

"You know, I don't work for you."

"No, you don't." Marshal Middlebrooks rubbed his bald head in thought. "But the next time you have some cowboy in here all drunk and tearing things up, I might have trouble showing up as fast as usual."

Harry's shoulders slumped in defeat. "I'll see what I can find out."

He left, and we heard him shut the open window before going down the hall.

Ranger Braziel poured everyone a glass from the bottle, including Cornsilk and Long Fox, who resumed their seats against the door. "That's a smart place to start looking."

"Well, it's all I can do in this rain. There won't be any tracks to follow, so there's no use going after them right now. I'll do a little digging around here in town to see if I can find out who they were, but I doubt I'll find out anything at all."

I sipped my whiskey and played the events out in the street over in my mind. Two men. One with a Henry rifle. "Those were the ones who ambushed us back at the ferry. They trailed us to the ferry, and failing to kill me there, they'd figured out where we were headed and waited for us here in Jeremiah."

Marshal Middlebrooks took a tiny sip. "Well, you've shot up a good piece of my town. I'll allow it this time, but I don't want any more killing going on here. What are your plans, Mr. Whitlatch?"

Cornsilk stuck his nose into the glass and inhaled the sharp scent of bourbon. He gave Long Fox a grin and received one in return. I watched them drink, and anger bloomed once again in my head.

This had all started because I wanted a drink of whiskey and a bed. Now I had both here in Jeremiah, and couldn't enjoy them. I tossed off the shot and answered the marshal.

"I'm going to end this as soon as I can, once the rain stops."

CHAPTER 49

I rose and shucked the wet shells out of my Spencer. They landed on the quilt covering my bed.

Ranger Braziel watched with interest as I checked them, one by one. "That's one downfall of shotguns. Them paper shells swell quick."

Every one of them was damp, and one was useless. "It's a problem, for sure."

Marshal Middlebrooks walked over to the window and stared down. "We sure don't need this trouble here in town. I'd prefer you let me handle it."

"I didn't intend to bring it." There were two dry shells in the pocket of my oiled slicker, but I didn't trust them not to have absorbed any moisture from the air or what had drizzled down into the pockets. "We're trying to get down to Fredericksburg and drop off Vanderburg."

"That the one-armed outlaw I heard about?"

"There's no proof he's an outlaw, but, yeah, that's the man I'm escorting to the marshal down there. The grapevine's fast here, too."

"Folks here know every time I trim my nose hair."

"Well, we'll be along tomorrow. I'd planned to take the train, until I found out this spur's not complete."

The marshal sighed. "They promised more business,

people, and wealth when it comes through. This place has boomed already, but most all it's brought is trouble, and it always lands square in my lap. Would you like to put him in my jail for the night?"

All four of us traveling with Vanderburg stifled grins. It was Ranger Braziel who spoke up ahead of me. "Well, sir, Mr. Whitlatch here vouches for Vanderburg, and they've traveled together for some time without incident, so I imagine there's no use for bars."

"I do need to check on him." I stood, waiting for Cornsilk and Long Fox to rise and move from their positions against the door. "I need dry shells for the Spencer, too. I have a box in my room."

"Then what?"

Marshal Middlebrooks's question stopped me for a second. "Why, then I reckon I'm gonna check on Esther and Gracie, then I'm gonna get that bath I've been wanting, some supper, and a drink. That should be no problem with Cornsilk and Long Fox watching the doors for me."

"I'd go over to Rosie's to eat. They have food in most of the saloons here, but hers is fresh and fine."

"That works for me, then. Mr. Braziel, would you meet us there in an hour?"

"I will."

Cornsilk and Long Fox exchanged looks. Cornsilk cleared his throat. "We will watch your back for you, if you'll allow us more of that fine whiskey."

Knowing they weren't allowed in a saloon, or any eating establishment, I didn't try to argue with them. They'd be just fine sleeping in the back of the livery, or somewhere they could find that was dry, once they finished their drinks.

"Fine, then."

Putting on my hat and slicker, I picked up the Spencer, and Cornsilk opened the door and followed Long Fox into the hall. I heard one word from Cornsilk: "Glucks!"

Glucks? What'n hell was that? Some Cherokee or Choctaw I didn't understand.

Then it dawned on me at the same time his exclamation was followed by the sound of a shot and Long Fox staggered backward, clawing for the revolver stuck in his belt. A second round followed, and then a ragged burst that dropped him to the ground as Cornsilk grunted, spun, and fell into the room at my feet.

CHAPTER 50

By God, Ed Gentry wanted Whitlatch's gold, and he'd earned it! He decided the hell with any plan. On the second-floor landing of the Hotel Benjamin's outside stairs, Gentry tried to decide whether to go in with his Henry rifle, or rely on the pistol still in his belt. Rain poured off his hat as he pondered the problem.

The big .44 would drop anything he hit, but then again, there was little room to maneuver in the hallway, though it looked as wide as a livery stable hall. The rain made his choice for him. Leaning the Henry against the window, he thanked the hotel's carpenters for thinking of the hotel's client's safety and providing a fine, stable stairway along the outside wall.

A tall wooden window was the only egress, but it would be enough if the hotel caught on fire. Guests could simply raise the window and step through onto the landing, then descend the rough wooden stairs with ease.

He peeked through the glass and saw a puddle of water on the inside. Someone had been tardy in closing the window against the storm. But three men were coming down the hall. He leaned back, hoping they hadn't seen him at the window.

His back against the wall, Gentry glanced back down at

the empty street, hoping no one passing by would look up. He knew which room he wanted, the one Whitlatch was in. Standing there in the storm, with rain pouring from the skies, he wondered if the gold that man carried was worth all this trouble.

Lawyer Penn said it was a lot, but until that moment, Gentry hadn't considered just how much it might be. He had visions of a grip packed full of gold coins, but could that be? How much had the fool paid for a herd of horses?

To top it all off, this whole job had cost in more ways than one: time, the death of Bill Johns, and almost all the cash that he had was now gone. His last five dollars went into the desk clerk's pocket for the room number.

But he'd gone this far, and Gentry never gave up on a job because it was too hard. He'd invested way too much. It was time to collect.

The door exactly on the opposite side of the wall opened and one word came through the closed window as clear as if the man was speaking into his ear: "Glucks!"

Wondering what Glucks were, he used one eye to peek inside and found himself looking down the barrels of three revolvers. They opened up with lances of fire and puffs of smoke. Slugs punched through the glass and the plank wall behind him.

"Dammit!"

CHAPTER 51

Glucks—that damned family of big-nosed, no-chin bastards had followed us all the way from Blackwater. I didn't have time to ponder the whys of their presence. The hallway was a killing zone for anyone coming out of the Ranger's room. The doorframe splintered from the impact of even more rounds as what sounded like a dozen guns opened up in a full volley of rolling gunfire.

Outside, the storm was directly on top of us, with lightning and thunder adding to the melee. The sounds of someone kicking at a door came next and then more bullets struck nearby. Window glass shattered, and I caught a glimpse of a pane falling into the hallway to land on Long Fox. He reacted slightly, and I knew the traveling Indian wasn't dead by a long shot.

A female scream filled the air, along with the sounds of running feet and shouts from down the hall.

Dropping to one knee, I stuck the twelve-gauge out the door and pulled the trigger, hoping like hell Esther and Gracie were still in their room. Immediately pumping the remaining shell into the chamber, I fired a second time, intending to sweep the hallway clean of murderous Glucks.

Two more pistol shots hammered the air, but these

sounded like they came from the room adjacent to where we stood. I didn't know if that one was occupied, but the next one down on our side was mine, and I figured Gil was in there, defending himself.

I shouted, hoping Esther or Gracie would understand I was addressing them. "Stay down!"

Another kick, and more gunshots. Two bullets smacked into the wall above Long Fox. He still had enough life in him to roll sideways and drag himself into the safety of the room.

There was no way any man worth his salt could stay huddled out of sight while all that was going on. Drawing the Russian and still on one knee, I risked a shoulder and leaned into the hallway as Long Fox wriggled and snaked his way farther into the room, leaving a smear of blood on the floor. Grabbing a handful of Long Fox's shirt, I drug him the rest of the way out of the hall.

Three men were there and I recognized the Glucks' features. Another volley of fire roared down the hallway. "Dammit!" I ducked back, almost tripping on Cornsilk.

Red-faced and eyes flashing in fury, Ranger Braziel took my place and leaned out. He fired twice, yelped, and stepped back.

"Damn them!" Blood flowed from his shoulder and the hole punched in the seam of his coat.

That familiar keening sound filled my head. I stepped over Cornsilk's legs as he pulled himself between Long Fox and the door in order to protect his friend. I braced my foot and kicked the wall between the room I was in and the unoccupied one next to it. I couldn't fight my way down the hall, but I could sure 'nough make new doors in the flimsy walls.

Wallpaper ripped as the boards gave a crack, which was covered by another roll of thunder. Stepping back, I braced my shoulder and threw my entire weight against the wall, which gave some more. Gathering myself, I charged again; at the same time, Marshal Middlebrooks joined me. The two of us hit the wall again and the soft pine boards gave, splintering inward against those forming the opposite wall. All our weight was against the nails that pulled out and we fell into the empty room as more gunfire filled the air.

Regaining my feet, I rushed to the door and yanked it open. The hallway was filled with gunsmoke, but those who were shooting had fallen back to the top of the stairs, preventing me from finding a good target.

The pistol in my room fired again, then again. Gil was giving as good as he got, I hoped, but at the same time, there was additional danger. Across the hall were Esther and Gracie. Any misses would penetrate the thin walls and endanger them both.

Even more danger developed when the door to Esther and Gracie's room splintered as one of them fired without opening it.

"Dammit!" One of the Glucks with his arm in a sling backed up and kicked Esther's door. It blew back and banged off the chair rail running the length of the wall. Pictures and paintings in the hallway leaped off their nails and crashed to the floor.

The man kicking the door barely steadied himself to rush inside when the interior of that room flashed, then flashed again in quick succession.

I surprised myself when I spoke aloud. "That's my girl."

Both Esther and Gracie fought back: The pistol I'd given Esther and the distinctive crack of Gil's cap and ball revolver told me neither of them was hiding under the bed. From that distance, it was hard to miss and the man already wearing a sling staggered sideways, presenting a face registering terrible pain.

Another shot followed those two, but they came from Gil's room and punched holes in the back of the attacker's shirt. Caught in a cross fire, he fell into the arms of those other two who were ready to get gone.

I stuck my head out as quick as the next flash of lighting came up the hallway and saw two muzzles flash. Bullets whizzed past my ear. The doorframe above my head splintered, but that slug came from behind and down the hall behind me, followed by half-a-dozen quick shots. I whirled, hoping it wasn't the Ranger or Cornsilk trying to shoot past me, and fired a shot at a shadow in the window.

The quick exchange told me something else was going on back there, but the shadow fell back and I had the sense I'd hit whoever was on the outside landing. My more immediate issue was only a couple of steps away and downstairs.

"Gil! Coming through! Esther! Don't shoot me!"

I hoped Marshal Middlebrooks understood what I meant as he leaned out and threw another shot down the hallway.

"Watch my back. The hall window!"

I ducked under his arm, firing the Russian as fast as I could and did what I do best. I charged the source of trouble.

The sheer audacity of my actions and the volume of gunfire pushed our assassins back down the stairs. I caught a flash of Gil from the corner of my eye as he pitched a shot at the three murderers stumbling down the stairs.

One yelped and fell and rolled as a gun down below covered their escape.

Footsteps descended the stairs and I went after them, thumbing fresh shells into my pistol.

Gil's voice followed me down. "Go get 'em!"

CHAPTER 52

Gentry grabbed the Henry, crouched, and dropped down the steps as the outside wall splintered from hot chunks of lead plowing through. Glass flew as rounds shattered the glass and sashes failed. Return fire rose in a crescendo and it sounded as if a war was going on in that hallway he'd just planned to enter.

With no reference as to how many people were shooting at each other, it sounded as if there were twenty people inside. Female screams rose out of the chaos and men shouted orders and questions. Cries of pain and curses increased in intensity. It sounded as if people were kicking walls down, and then the battle moved away and the sheer volume of bullets punching through the planks finally slowed.

It was risky business, but Gentry stayed low and peeked through one of the larger bullet holes. Men moved back and forth as they leaned out and then ducked back out of sight. More gunshots followed, but these weren't coming in his direction, as far as he could tell.

Then there he was—Whitlatch in the hall, with his back to him. Gentry shifted position and risked a look through the now-gaping window. The body of an Indian lay directly below, but he was long gone.

Caught up in the rush of battle, Gentry saw a target and, without considering the consequences, shouldered the rifle and sighted on Whitlatch's back. The man moved and Gentry followed, pulling the trigger when the barrel bumped the edge of the window frame. It was just enough to throw off his aim and the round missed.

Cat quick, Whitlatch spun and fired, driving Gentry back down the steps again. He took them, two at a time, until he reached the ground; then he ducked into the shadows to wait. He might get a chance at that gold, after all, because the fight was moving downstairs, leaving everything behind.

CHAPTER 53

The stairs went down halfway to a landing that turned at a forty-five-degree angle to the left and descended down to the lobby. Mad as hell, I walked down that hall to the stairs and clicked the Russian closed.

Halfway down the first staircase, someone opened up on me again from below. Bullets plucked at my coat, but I was already committed. I snapped two rounds at movement below and continued to descend, wishing like hell I had my Spencer.

I recognized a body lying beside the counter. It was the annoying desk clerk who would no longer raise anyone's ire. Two figures backing toward the door fired again, causing me to instinctively crouch, as if that few inches would make a difference in the size of their target.

Lightning flashed in the lobby, illuminating the pair helping a third out the door. Three targets instead of one gave me a better edge. I fired, thumbed the Russian and fired again. One man on my far left returned fire, but his burden caused the round to go wild, striking an oil lamp beside the register.

It exploded into liquid flame, which quickly spread across the surface and behind the counter. Still descending the stairs, I shot at the retreating figures that disappeared outside. They flashed past the window as fast as two men carrying a third can move and I emptied the Russian at them. The injured man fell, and after a moment's hesitation, the other two were gone.

By the time I reached the door, I was damned mad. Ears full of cotton from all the gunfire, I started out the door, when gunshots punched holes in the glass. I instinctively ducked back and was about to rush outside, until Marshal Middlebrooks's voice came from behind me.

"Wait! We need to get this fire out!"

I glanced past the desk clerk's body and the fire that was fast eating its way up one wall and across the floor. "You do it! I'm going after those three."

"Help!" His voice was high with fear. Fire is a town's worst enemy, but I wasn't worried because of the deluge still falling from the skies. There were others in the hotel who would help. I wanted those who tried to kill me.

Confident that Esther and Gracie could get Gil out of the burning hotel through the window at the far end of the hallway, I pushed through the front doors like a horse bolting from a stable and almost stumbled over a body lying on the boardwalk.

A river of blood ran across the floorboards and mixed with the rain. I toed him, just to make sure he wasn't playing possum, but you can tell when a man's dead from his weight and the limp way the body no longer responds.

He was the Gluck with one cloudy eye who'd been previously wounded, his left arm in a bloodstained sling. I knew Cloyce's name, and recollected the other two brothers were Itchy and Cheese, but wasn't sure which one was which, and didn't care.

He was one of three murderous brothers and that's all I needed to know.

This time, the rain worked in my favor. The other two angled off the boardwalk and into the street to the opposite side, leaving fresh tracks filling with water. They were heading toward the livery stable, which was almost full when I went to check on the horses, so I figured that's where those two would be found.

They were headed straight for the main entrance, which opened from the street, but I had no intention of running directly into their guns. Instead, I rounded a building and trotted around back, not running, for I didn't want to be out of breath when I got there.

Most of the buildings were dark, and those that had lights in the windows were yellow and dim in the storm. It was almost pitch-black between two buildings, and when I emerged around back, there wasn't much more than a sliver of weak light coming through the partially open rear doors made wide enough to accommodate a wagon.

Thumbing shells from my belt, I reloaded under the eaves of a nearby building, studying the corral and the milling horses that filled it. There was a chance one of the two might be in there, but I expected them to be inside, saddling their mounts for an escape.

But what if they'd already saddled them before they came in? I would have, in case someone like me was following and ready to kill everyone in sight. I was in that mood, for sure.

Voices came through cracks between the boards that were wide enough for me to sneak a peek inside. Three men stood in the wide hallway, arguing.

"Y'all ain't taking them horses unless you show me where you paid for board."

One man facing me was Cloyce Gluck. I remembered that horrendous scar across the bridge of his nose. He was wet and mad. Beside him, with his back to me, was another man, leaning on the outside of a stall, clutching the top horse-chewed board for support and bleeding badly from a stomach wound.

"Mister, we done paid your boy, now get out of the way before you get hurt. Itchy, we're getting out of here."

The one I took for Rogier's daddy had a pitchfork in his hands. The liveryman was white as a sheet and I wondered where the boy was. Barely sober, he leaned over and puked onto the dirt floor, and Cloyce doubled up his fist and hit him in the side of the head.

The man dropped in his own mess, groaning.

Cocking the hammer on the Russian, I stepped through the back entrance and advanced on Cloyce. "Don't you move a muscle!"

The shock on Gluck's face showed he hadn't expected me to follow. I guess back in Blackwater, when they got finished terrorizing the locals, those poor folks crawled off and licked their wounds.

Not me.

Itchy wasn't as bad off as I'd thought. He snatched a pistol from his holster and spun, firing too fast. The bullet disappeared through the open door behind me and I leveled the .44 and shot him in the chest. He fell against the stable, grabbed for it, and I fired again. All the strength went out of his hands and he dropped onto the dust and straw floor and didn't move again.

"Itchy!" Cloyce shot at me. That one missed and took a chunk out of a thick oak board that closed off what I figured was a feed storeroom.

A yelp from inside came at the same time I shot Cloyce. He staggered backward and thumb-cocked his pistol. I stepped forward and shot him again, but the man wouldn't go down.

"Don't raise that pistol again!"

He did, and I shot him a third time.

A fourth shot followed immediately, but it came from behind. Two more explosions came fast and I whirled to see Ranger Braziel in the middle of the hall, firing at one of two Indians who'd dropped down from the sky, as far as I knew.

One of them, with long, stringy hair, had a Colt revolver in his hand and he pulled the trigger. The round hit Braziel solid and he staggered back against a stall and triggered his own pistol, hitting the tall Indian in the chest. The man with stringy hair and a wide jaw twisted with the shock and pain.

I fired at another man, who looked to be half Black. He threw a shot at me, which stung my neck. Braziel shot the dark-complected gunman; then his knees went weak and he sat down hard.

Long Hair staggered, straightened, and dropped.

I thought it was all over, before the dark one raised his revolver again.

CHAPTER 54

Out of shells, I did the only thing I could think of. I dove toward the Ranger, who was still upright, with his back against the stall, and the Colt still resting on one thigh. Another gun roared, but the round went somewhere over my shoulder.

I snatched the pistol from the Ranger's hand and shot the dark one twice, and he fell sideways and stilled.

"I got you now."

Son of a bitch! There stood Cloyce Gluck, full of holes and bloody as a stuck hog, but he had a gun pointed at my head. Lying on the ground and in an awkward position, I gave it my best and twisted to bring Braziel's pistol to bear, but a shot rang out.

I expected to feel the impact of the bullet, but I was still alive.

Gluck's knees folded and the hot revolver dropped as he moaned. "This was all an accident." Only he knew what that meant, and it went with him as his last breath drifted out.

I looked to the left and there stood still *another* man I didn't know, with my Spencer in his hands and what looked like my saddlebags over one shoulder.

"Don't you move, Whitlatch, or I'll shoot you with your own shotgun."

"You're Gentry."

"I am."

Staring down that huge bore, I rested all my weight on my left elbow. "I'm not going anywhere."

"Good. Pitch that pistol away."

I flicked it toward the middle of the hall and saw young Rogier lying inside the storeroom, tied up and eyes wide as saucers. The boy was terrified, so I gave him a little wink.

It was all I could do for him right then.

"You know, Whitlatch, I think you're a hard man to kill."

"Up till now, at least."

"Well, you just stay right where you are and I'll let you see the sun tomorrow morning."

"Those are my saddlebags. And that's my shotgun."

"Were. I'm taking this money with me and getting the hell out of here."

"You kill Gil for them?"

"Naw, he was in with your girls and the door across the hall was wide open with these saddlebags and gun lying on the bed. It was easy to get in and out while they're trying to put out the fire, and thanks for this Spencer. Somebody shot the hammer off my Henry, but now I can afford a new one."

I would have shrugged, but it was a hard thing to do, lying the way I was on the floor. "How'd you know I had money in there?"

He grinned. "Lawyer Penn hired me and my partner to get this back after you cheated him."

"I didn't cheat anyone."

"I have paper says you did."

"Whatever you have ain't worth spit."

He withdrew an envelope from inside his vest. "Here it is." He flicked it toward me.

Now, I can't explain why I needed to open that paper

right then, but I did. The wax seal crumbled and I gave the pages a glance. It struck me funny, because they were a foreclosure notice on land outside of town.

I laughed and flicked the pages onto the floor. "Those are legal papers on land in Springfield. I imagine they're useless, too. Penn's using you to do his dirty work."

Gentry glanced down to see the forms. His face reddened. "Well, we did for him, anyway, and this gold's mine."

Keeping the shotgun on me, he opened the stall door and led that beautiful black stud out. It was already saddled, so I figured he had this pretty well planned out.

"You stay right there on the ground and don't move when I get on."

"Can I sit up?"

"Nope." For a tall man, he swung up on that horse in a smooth, almost unimaginable way, keeping the Spencer lined up on my middle. That's the thing about shotguns that I usually liked, but right at that moment intensely hated. Even if the barrel was off a little bit and he fired, at least some of that double-aught buck would get on me, and I didn't want that.

Mounted, he gave me a big grin. "Thanks for the gold. Now, you be still while I ride on out of here."

He heeled the stud toward the open back doors.

"Hold it!"

Damn, that was a busy livery. The voice that came from the front doors belonged to Gil, who had a pistol pointed at the middle of the tall man's back. "Drop that shotgun and those saddlebags."

The tall man stiffened and reined up. He turned the stud halfway around, his left side to Gil. "I'm riding on out of here."

"Nope."

Gil stood there, the stump of his left arm strapped to his

chest, but that revolver in his fist was steady as a rock. "Drop the shotgun and swing down off there."

"Fine, then." The tall man pitched the shotgun at a stack of loose hay, at the same time he drew the pistol on his right hip. He had Gil beat, but the Ranger still had enough spark to kick the stud's back leg. The black reacted, snorting and sunfishing to the side, and almost unseating Gentry.

Like a dueler of old, Gil angled his body, extended his arm, and shot the man smooth from the saddle.

He landed with a thud as Ranger Braziel withdrew a belly gun hidden under his coat and shot the tall man. "Damn, I'm shot to pieces again."

"You're too tough to die." So tired I could barely hold my head up, I rested my hand on the Sioux medicine bag once again outside my shirt, and thanked Naach for giving it to me.

CHAPTER 55

Five days later, me, Gil, Esther, and Gracie stepped down from the train in Fredericksburg, Texas. My old man was there, armed to the teeth, along with half-a-dozen cousins and uncles.

Dad stepped forward and gave me a bear hug. "Got your telegram."

I'd almost forgotten sending it. "Well, we don't need the guns now. It's all over."

He gave me a wide grin and took off his hat. "It sure is. Who're these ladies?"

"That there's Esther. She's gonna stay at the ranch with us awhile. She can cook up a storm, and she's a fair hand in a fight, too. This little lady is Gracie. She's staying with us, too."

"I ain't no lady." Gracie pulled at the dress I'd bought her in Dallas.

"I can see that." Dad smoothed his mustache. "Weren't there others supposed to be with you?"

"Well, there were. A Cherokee named Cornsilk, and Long Fox. They've both gone back to the territories. Cornsilk says it's safer there for them both, because he figures Gracie here's a witch and wanted no more truck with her."

He eyed Gracie. "Are you?"

"Naw, well, maybe. I gave Cornsilk a little amulet that might have saved his life, but, naw, I just liked to mess with him. Now, Long Fox is a different animal. He's Kiowa and a traveling son of a gun, and I figure as soon as he heals up, he's gone again."

I drew a deep breath. "There was a Ranger, too, Curtis Braziel, but he's still healing up, back in Jeremiah. I'll have to send him a telegram to untangle this mess down here. He'll probably be aggravated about the whole thing, because Judge Ivan's false accusations caused him to be shot in two instances."

"They take that risk when they pin on a badge, son." Dad considered Gil. "Been a long time."

He toed the ground. "Yessir."

"You left in a hurry."

"I did, that."

Dad nodded. "You still a deputy, son?"

"Never was, but like I said in the telegram, I had to bring Gil home." I explained all that had happened since I rode into Blackwater so long ago.

"Gil." Dad looked him in the eye.

"Sir?"

Dad pulled his coat back to reveal a badge. "I have a new job. I'm the marshal now, so I guess you'd be mine."

Gil wilted like a cut flower in the summer heat. "Aw, hell."

There was a glimmer in Dad's eyes, though, that spoke of something else. Folks say my eyes are a watered-down version of his, and when his went flint hard, they were dangerous. But right then, they twinkled. "Gil, about that little gal."

"I can explain."

"Don't say another word, if you know what's good for you. That's all over and in the past. Our former judge told me he'd issued that murder warrant after you skinned out of here. He was mad about you and his daughter, Alice, but she was also keeping company with that traveling salesman at the same time you were courting her."

Gil frowned. "I didn't know anything about that."

It had been a good long while since I'd seen Alice and this news wasn't interesting to me at all. I had Esther to think about.

"Well, you do now. Anyway, the town council caught Judge Ivan with his hand in the community fund a few days before he told me that, and when Marshal Daniels refused to arrest him, we kind of sent him packing, too."

I raised an eyebrow and Dad shrugged. "When you make a whole town mad, folks'll rise up. We did."

"Where's Alice now?"

"Still in Austin, I hear, but with that salesman, not her aunt." Dad pointed a finger at Gil. "The warrant was a lie. You're free and clear, though it looks like you're hobbled some."

"I can go?"

"You can, but it'll be hard to make a living with one arm. I need a deputy, if you know anybody who'll take the job."

Gil looked at me and I raised both hands. "Not me. He's offering it to you."

Confused and relieved, Gil turned to Esther. "Should I take it?"

Gracie groaned. "You're too dumb, if you have to ask somebody. I'll wear the damned badge."

Dad shook his head. "No you won't."

"All right, then. Sir, I'm your deputy."

I fished the tin badge Sheriff Kanoska gave me from my shirt pocket and pinned it on Gil's shirt. "That's about as much ceremony as *I* got."

I turned and Dad reached out. "Where you going?"

"I'm going to get a bath, for one thing, and a whiskey after that. It's been a rough road through hostile territory, and I intend to take it easy for a while. Hey, Gil."

He raised an eyebrow.

"Would you make sure the steeldust gets rubbed down and fed?"

He glanced down the track to see men walking horses off the train. "Just as soon as she comes off the car."

I turned to Esther. "We have a big ranch house. Plenty of rooms. Would you care for a job keeping house for a couple of bachelors?"

"For the time being." The corners of her eyes twinkled.

Gracie rolled her eyes. "If you two don't beat all."

I freed the Sioux medicine bag from inside my shirt. "Gracie, you ain't no witch, you're pretty close in spelling, but I know for a fact this works, so don't you try any of your love spells or curses on me. You hush and try to act right."

Esther took my arm and we walked into town, with Gracie following, frowning all the way and mumbling under her breath about white people and gosh darn fools in love.

Visit our website at
KensingtonBooks.com
to sign up for our newsletters, read
more from your favorite authors, see
books by series, view reading group
guides, and more!

Become a Part of Our
Between the Chapters Book Club
Community and Join the Conversation

Printed in the United States
by Baker & Taylor Publisher Services